THE QUEEN'S CORONATION

REBEKAH SINCLAIR

BEFORE YOU DIVE IN

Suggested Reading Order

Every story in the Forgotten Goddess multiverse can stand on its own. But if you wish to see how the pieces truly fit—how the gods fall, how the mortals rise, and how every love leaves a scar—this is the path you were meant to follow.

The Forgotten Goddess Series

1 The Forgotten Goddess

2 The Unforgotten Flame

3 Awakening the Forgotten Goddess

4 The Unforgotten Vow

5 Reclaiming the Forgotten Goddess

6 Vengeance of the Forgotten Goddess

Return to Avalon Series

1 Assassin of the Gods

2 The Queen's Coronation

3 [Title Forthcoming]

Read them in any order if you like.

But remember—fate rewards obedience, and punishes curiosity in equal measure.

CONTENT WARNING

The Queen's Coronation is a **dark fantasy romance** that contains mature themes, violence, and explicit content. While this story is crafted with care, readers should be aware of the following potential triggers before diving in:

Content Warnings:

⚠ **Violence & Gore** – Includes combat, battle scenes, assassinations, and graphic depictions of injury.

⚠ **Death & Murder** – Features on-page deaths, execution, war-related casualties, and past traumatic losses.

⚠ **Explicit Romance Scenes & Strong Language** – High-heat sexual content and frequent use of profanity.

This book is intended for **mature audiences (18+)** and

includes **dark, high-stakes themes** intertwined with romance, court intrigue, and supernatural forces.

Reader discretion is advised.

AVALON
FROSTHAVEN
ASTRALANA
CAIRNVALE
EVERSHADE
VALERA
ELDORIA
THORNSPIRE
CASTLE STARFALL
MOONSHADOW COVE
GLOAMREACH
UMBRANOR
SYLVADORA
MIREVALIS
WASTELANDS
UMBRAL TIDES

THE COURTS & RULERS OF AVALON

1. Eldoria (The Shimmering Court)

- **Ruler: Lady Liora**
- Eldoria represents the light Fae and stands in contrast to the dark Fae of Avalon. They are known for their radiant beauty and illusion magic.

2. Gloamreach (The Twilight Court)

- **Ruler: King Eryndor**
- This court exists in a perpetual state of dusk. They are the arbiters of balance, often mediating between the light and dark Fae realms.

3. Cairnvail (The Stone Court)

- **Ruler: Lord Granite**

- Located in a vast mountain range, Cairnvail is a kingdom of earth and stone, ruled by powerful Fae warriors. Their magic is tied to the earth, making them nearly indestructible.

4. Sylvadora (The Enchanted Forest)

- **Ruler: Lady Thalassa**
- A kingdom deeply connected to nature, where ancient trees and spirits dwell. The Fae of Sylvadora are protectors of the natural world and wield powerful elemental magic.

5. Umbranor (The Shadowed Court)

- **Ruler: Shade**
- A realm of darkness and shadows, Umbranor is even more mysterious and dangerous than Avalon. The Fae here are masters of shadow magic and deception, often acting as assassins or spies.

6. Astralana (The Celestial Court)

- **Ruler: High Seer Astrael**
- This court is tied to the stars and celestial bodies. The Fae of the floating islands of Astralana are scholars and seers, with the ability to predict future events and manipulate cosmic forces.

7. Mirevalis (The Swamp Court)

- **Ruler: Duchess Morwen**
- A kingdom of marshlands and mist, Mirevalis is home to Fae who are deeply connected to water and poison. They are often seen as outcasts, but their knowledge of the arcane is unparalleled.

8. Frosthaven (The Winter Court)

- **Ruler: Queen Eira**
- **Role**: A cold and harsh realm ruled by ice and snow. The Fae here are known for their stoicism and ability to endure extreme conditions.

9. Evershade (The Eternal Night Court)

- **Ruler: Lord Umbriel**
- It is unclear if Evershade is a close ally to Avalon but certainly harbors its own ambitions. The Fae here are deeply tied to death and the afterlife.

10. Thornspire (The Briar Court)

- **Ruler: King Thorne**
- A wild and dangerous realm where thorn-covered forests and treacherous landscapes dominate. The Fae of Thornspire are fierce and untamed, with a reputation for cruelty.

Times of Night:

- **Morning:** First Shade
- **Afternoon:** Mid-Shade
- **Night:** Evenfall

Salutations:

- **"Bright moon to you."** – A formal greeting, akin to "Good morning,".
- **"Steady stars."** – A well-wishing phrase, suggesting stability and clarity, much like "Have a good day."
- **"Darkness guide you."** – A respectful farewell, akin to "Safe travels,".

For those who look to the night sky,
searching for what they've lost.

May you find it again in the stars.

CHAPTER 1

tana

I will not break.

I will not make a sound.

He doesn't deserve it.

Not a gasp. Not a whimper. Not a single tremor that tells him what he already knows—that he's winning.

Orion's shadows coil around me, smooth and cold, binding my arms behind my back in an intricate weave that would almost be beautiful if it weren't his doing. The patterns slide over my skin like living silk, cinching at my wrists, my thighs, my calves. My body is pulled taut, chest arched, suspended by the night itself.

He's not touching me—not really. It's his magic that holds me, his power that keeps me floating there, trembling, high enough off the ground that we both know I'm not in control.

A bead of sweat slides down my spine. My lungs drag in a shaky breath I refuse to let turn into a moan. He's taken me to the edge again and again—testing, coaxing, punishing. Waiting for me to beg.

I won't.

He doesn't get that anymore.

Not since the day of the village attack, when he lied.

When he locked me away like I was something to control instead of the realm's chosen queen.

So no—he doesn't get to hear me.

Not even when his shadows tighten.

Not even when the pleasure burns hot enough to taste like fury on my tongue.

When I left the dining hall—another night of heartburn-inducing posturing and empty politics—I knew he was behind me.

I could feel him.

The swell of shadow that trails him like a second skin. The quiet weight of his presence, his hands tucked in his pockets like we're just two people heading back to our rooms.

Rooms that happen to be across the hall from each other.

I told myself I'd go straight to mine. Lock the door. End the night without giving in to the pull that's been undoing me for weeks.

But when I reached for the handle and felt his shadows curl around my wrist—when his voice spilled low and dark into my mind—

How much longer do you intend to punish me, Starling?

—the lie crumbled.

Chills race down my spine, heat blooming beneath them. Because we both know the truth.

He steps closer, the air shifting with him, his power brushing over my skin like smoke and silk.

"How can you keep pretending you don't want this," he murmurs, "when it's my door you came to tonight?"

My eyes snap up to his door, right in front of me. Then mine, across the hall. He's right.

I was at his door. Not my own. I hadn't even realized it.

And now I'm in his chambers, candlelight flickering along the walls, throwing molten shadows across my skin. The room smells like cedar and storm. He sits back in a chair, deceptively relaxed, watching me as his darkness winds around my body—binding wrists to spine, thighs to air, holding me on my knees in a cruel kind of worship.

Every time pleasure crests, his shadows pull away—a slow, deliberate torture that makes my pulse beat against the bindings.

"I told you before, my queen," he says, voice low and even, shadows tightening as he wills his darkness to bring me closer, "I am not opposed to keeping you tied up in my darkness until your ascension."

The word *ascension* thrums through me, sharp as a blade's edge.

His power shifts—I shift—gliding to him, suspended and helpless as he moves between my legs. His hands are hot against my thighs, sliding up, rough palms gripping my ass hard enough to ground me.

My knees bracket his head, my shins resting on his shoulders. And when his mouth finally finds me, the first touch is electricity—bright and merciless.

My breath catches. My resolve begs to splinter.

And still, I tell myself I won't break.

His power hums against my skin, the darkness rippling with every slow movement of his body. I feel the heat of him between my thighs, the brush of tongue on my pussy that makes my pulse falter—but I lock it down. I will not give him the satisfaction of hearing me.

Let go, Starling

His voice slips into my mind like smoke—smooth and

deep. He laps at me with his tongue, a tendril of shadow curling around my clit in a rhythmic, undulating dance until he closes his lips around me. He sucks on my cunt with an approving groan.

"You tremble like you want to scream."

Oh God. *Orion.*

I want to call out, but I don't answer.

Don't stop.

I want to let my head hang and moan out the pleasure of his tongue working my clit with relentless focus.

The bindings shift, tightening, forcing my head back until I can see nothing but the ceiling.

I could make you beg, he whispers—not with sound, but through the link that thrums between us. *One word, and I'll let you fall.*

My fingers curl uselessly against the invisible bonds. The heat builds until every breath feels like fire. He moves again —deliberate, knowing—as he slides three fingers into me. The slick sounds of my arousal join the static snap of his lightning as it gently bites along my peaked nipples.

I grit my teeth, forcing the sound in my throat back down where it belongs.

He chuckles, low and pleased. "So stubborn," he says. "Even now, when you're shaking apart, you'd rather burn than give me a single sound."

I squeeze my eyes shut, the world narrowing to the rush of blood in my ears—to the hum of his magic. Every nerve feels strung tight enough to snap, every heartbeat a dare.

He pushes a little deeper into my mind, voice rough now, strained. *Say it, Starling. Just once. Let me hear you moan my name and I'll let you come.*

No.

The word stays silent, sealed behind clenched teeth.

He brings me there again—rising, unraveling, pulse crashing in my throat—

And then he pauses.

But he's not teasing this time. Not punishing. He's listening.

His head turns just slightly, just so, toward the closed door.

The shadows ripple with sudden tension.

His grip tightens around my hips, rough fingers biting into skin as if he might ground himself there.

"Fuck," he mutters, under his breath this time, no longer speaking in my mind. "If I had more time, I'd fuck the stubborn right out of you."

Then his magic shifts.

It slides over my body with the precision of a weaver pulling thread, realigning the bindings until they wrap around me like a bodice of confinement. A second later, I'm upright—no longer floating—but pressed hard against the stone wall.

The cold bites at my overheated skin.

My arms are bound around his neck now, crossed behind him and held there by his shadows. My body is flush against his, bare skin to clothed form, trapped in the heat of him.

One arm locks me in place. The other slips between my thighs. His fingers move with an unholy rhythm—precise and devastating.

"Let me look into your eyes as I make you come, Starling."

The words curl through me like a command.

He finally pushes me over the edge, release crashing through my limbs like fire through frost—white-hot, blinding. But still—still—I keep my eyes closed.

He notices.

"You've hidden them from me for nearly half a moon cycle."

His shadows lace around my throat—not choking, but enough to pull. Enough to tilt my chin. His grip twists into my hair and jerks it back until I have nowhere else to look.

My eyes snap open.

And I drown in the silver storms that live in his gaze.

It's lightning and ruin and a promise I'm too afraid to name.

"There she is," he breathes, rough with possession. "Give me that fire, Tana."

His fingers don't stop. They move with purpose—expert and relentless.

"Keep ignoring me if it helps you sleep at night," he growls, voice thick with amusement and something darker. "You forget, Starling—I've had ages to perfect my patience."

His shadows flex, curling tighter around my body like a second skin.

"You think you can outlast me?" he muses. "Play mute until you win?"

A pause. A slow, dangerous smile that I feel rather than see.

"You'll crack long before I do."

Another wave crashes through me, and I'm helpless in it. My body spasms against him, heart pounding like it wants to break free of its cage.

"And when that happens, I'll drag every moan from your throat and devour every lie you tried to swallow."

My skin is too hot. My head too full. His mouth is so close I can taste him—cool and mint-laced—but he doesn't kiss me.

His power presses against the barrier I keep around my mind—the one I haven't let down since the day he betrayed me.

He presses against the edges, testing the barrier he knows I won't lower.

Not now.

Not for him.

Because if I let him in, he'll see the truth:

That I'm not playing some game of silent treatment.

I'm furious.

He locked me away when there was a battle to be fought —when people were dying.

He said I was the realm's chosen, but when it mattered, he treated me like something breakable. Like I needed to be protected instead of trusted.

And just before the first scream rang out from the village, I felt it—

The moment he pulled back from me.

He says I'm fate.

But he keeps stepping in front of me like I'm a fragile glass treasure to be guarded instead of a sword to be wielded.

I can't fight the realm, the court, the trials—and him.

Not if he's going to keep pretending I'm something less than what the realm already chose me to be.

So no.

I won't give him my thoughts or my words.

I stayed. I chose the realm. I chose the crown.

I chose this fight.

Now let him fight for me.

When he finally stills, I'm trembling. Panting.

We both are.

Pressed together like two sides of a war neither of us wants to win.

Our eyes lock—storm to storm, fire to fire.

Then—slowly—he draws his fingers from my body and slides them into his mouth.

Tastes me like a promise.

Eyes never leaving mine.

He steps back, and his warmth retreats as well, leaving me in a void of darkness. His gaze dances with mirth, and he cocks a tilted grin.

"It's time for you to wake up, Your Grace."

CHAPTER 2
tana

Three sharp knocks drag me out of the dream.

I jolt upright, chest tight, heart thudding like I'm still suspended in shadows. The cool air brushes damp skin. My wrists ache with remembered pressure, and my pussy throbs from the pleasure it wrung out of me.

The door creaks open and Aeris tilts her head in. "Bright moon, Your Grace."

"If you say so." I swing my legs off the bed and scrub a hand down my face.

She opens the door the rest of the way and strides in. Her mate—and my other attendant—Theren strolls in behind her, a tray balanced in one hand and a shit-eating grin on his face. His sandy curls are still a little damp, and his shirt's buttoned all wrong, like he got distracted halfway through dressing.

"What?" he asks casually, setting the tray down and handing me a steaming mug of moonbrew.

"You two stop for a fuck in the halls before you got here?" I ask, pulling teasingly at his misaligned collar.

"We wouldn't be the only two taking our pleasure in the morning, right, Your Highness?" he shoots back—then immediately moans in a high-pitched falsetto, "Ooh—Orion —don't stop—"

The pillow hits him dead in the face.

Aeris's mouth twitches in irritation as she gives him a firm swat to the arm. "Theren."

He lifts both hands, still holding the mug. "What? She was loud."

"I was not," I mutter, dropping back onto the bed. "And you don't know what you heard."

The look in his eyes tells me I'm full of shit.

He knows it.

And he loves that I know he knows it.

Asshole.

Aeris, ever the savior, changes the subject with a perfectly timed opening of the wardrobe. "What dress shall we choose today, Your Grace?"

I groan, sitting up and setting the moonbrew aside. "God, is it always dresses in this place?"

My mind flicks—annoyingly—back to a memory I didn't ask for.

Orion on the castle walls. The press of him behind me.

Wear a dress next time. His smug voice low in my ear, whispering how dresses were easier access.

Absolutely not.

"Pants," I say flatly.

Theren barks a laugh and drops into the armchair by the hearth. "Pants to your first meeting with the High Clave? They're going to love that."

I groan and fall backward onto the mattress again, arm flung over my face. "I forgot that was today."

"No, you didn't," Aeris and Theren say in unison.

I sit up and yank the pillow back into place with a sigh. "Fine. Pants and weapons. I may need to murder someone."

Aeris says nothing as she pulls out the black leather set—bless her.

Tight trousers. Fitted bodice. My thigh sheath already strapped, and the wrist cuffs—soft, sturdy, and snug. I tell myself it's style. Utility. A preventative measure in case someone tries to slit my wrists during council.

But really it's the pressure. The squeeze.

The memory of shadow coiled around me.

Of being held, restrained...seen.

As I tighten the leather cuffs around my wrists, I push out the last images of the dream.

"Fuck these assholes," I mumble, adjusting the straps tighter. "The queen-to-be is coming to council in pants."

Theren makes quick work of my hair. He always does.

I sit on the stool near the window, mug of moonbrew in hand, while his fingers move through my curls like he was born doing it. The fae have a knack for precision, for turning even the ordinary into art, and he uses it shamelessly.

"Keep most of it natural," I tell him. "Don't make me look like a court exhibit."

He snorts softly. "Wouldn't dream of it, Your Grace."

Thin braids wind back from my temples, disappearing into the sea of curls. By the time he's done, the weight sits comfortably off my face. I don't know how he does it so fast. When I try, it's a half-hour wrestling match with just one braid.

Aeris flits around the room, tightening bed linens, refreshing candles, folding the discarded nightshirt into nothingness. Always neat. Always quiet.

When Theren finishes, he fluffs out the ends of my

unruly hair. "There. Regal. Terrifying. Maybe even presentable."

"Perfect," I mutter, grabbing my jacket and sword belt. Realmbreaker, heavy in the scabbard.

I take breakfast where I usually do—in the kitchens with the Lesser Fae. Not because it's expected, but because I actually like them. They laugh. They swear. They don't weigh every word like it's a weapon. And, most importantly, the High Fae never comes down here.

The smell of baked root bread and spiced lunafruit hits me the moment I step in. The hearths are hot, steam fogging the narrow windows. Ylsa's already at the counter when I step into the kitchens, pounding something thick and fragrant in a stone mortar. The sound rings like a hammer on rock—I mean, it would—she is rock.

The Terra Fae from Cairnvail are built of the stuff they command, and Ylsa's no exception. Her tawny skin gleams like polished sandstone, shot through with faint amber veins that glow when she's worked up. Her eyes match—gold-brown, flecked with heat and humor in equal measure.

"Bright moon, queen-to-be," she rumbles without looking up.

"So I keep hearing," I say, sliding onto the stool across from her.

The moment I sit, pain clamps down behind my eyes—sharp, throbbing, a vise turning slow and mean. I press my fingers to my temples and hiss through my teeth.

Ylsa glances up, pounding never missing a beat. "Head again?"

"Like someone's tightening a belt around my skull."

She wipes her hands on a cloth and turns toward the

shelf where she keeps the tonic bottles Hestia made for me. All empty. She doesn't have to say anything—her expression does it for her.

"Figures," I mutter.

"I'll send one of the kitchen boys down to the village," she offers, already half reaching for her apron.

"No," I say before she can argue. "I'll go. Need the air anyway."

She grunts—half approval, half warning.

I eye the glowing amber lines across her forearms. "All the Fae of Cairnvail built like you?"

Her chest swells with pride. "Every one worth their salt. Finest soldiers Avalon's ever seen." She lifts the pestle again and slams it into the mortar; the sound echoes like a war drum. "We don't break easy."

I can't help but grin. "Remind me to keep on your good side."

I grab my cloak from the peg by the door, fastening it over my shoulders. The motion makes my ribs ache under the tight bodice. I ignore it.

Between the dream and the Clave meeting ahead, I can feel the castle closing in, the walls humming with politics and pressure. The village will be quieter.

Ylsa presses a hand to her hip. "Tell Hestia she's overdue to restock me, will you?"

"Will do."

Outside, the air bites cold—thin and metallic. The path to the village winds down through the glowing night fields, the eternal moon hanging like a watchful eye.

I've been prepared to the brink of death for the upcoming council meeting by Hypnos—the High Clave.

Fae nobles and advisers will gather, and I'm betting there will be exactly two topics:

Me.

And the whispers of war.

So yes, a walk will do. A visit to Hestia, a refill of the headache tonic, and a few minutes pretending I'm not about to be dissected by a council of immortals who still aren't sure if I belong here.

I tug my cloak tighter and start down the path, letting the chill steady my pulse.

The stone stairs cut deep into the cliffside, worn smooth by time and use. I take them slowly, my boots echoing a soft rhythm as I descend toward the village tucked at the base of Starfall's cliffs.

The wind shifts, carrying the scent of misty salt and hearth smoke, and just past the curve of cliffs, I catch a glimpse of the entrance to the Sanctum of Echoes.

I nod toward it out of habit—reverence, maybe—but I don't head that direction.

I've been in those caves twice. I have no intention of stepping into that place again anytime soon.

The village spreads out below like a tapestry of color and movement. The lesser Fae move through the market square with quiet purpose—selling goods, trading gossip, chasing wild sprites away from the fruit stalls. They greet me kindly as I pass, their bows shallow and warm, not worshipful.

No one stops me.

No one tries to crown me with their expectations.

It's why I like it here.

In this place, I'm not the mortal woman the realm

burdened with prophecy. I'm not the one the High Clave debates behind closed doors.

I'm just another body moving through the square.

Hestia's bakery is tucked along the rear row of shops, right next to Hephaestus's forge, where a pair of fire-born twins are arguing over whether steel should hum or sing when it's shaped.

The scent of the bakery hits first—warm, sweet, laced with citrus and something floral. Bread, I think. Or maybe a honeyed tart.

Two of Hestia's children dart across the square in a blur of bare feet and giggles, chasing a trio of flame sprites who are absolutely in possession of a (probably stolen) loaf of bread.

I smile before I can stop myself.

The door creaks open with a familiar chime, and the warmth inside greets me like an old friend.

Hestia stands behind the counter, flour dusting the edge of her soft pink skin, the delicate fin along her crown twitching as she glances up. Iridescent scales shimmer faintly across her cheeks and collarbone, catching the light like scattered moonlight.

Her eyes—deep, reflective, made for the ocean's dark—meet mine with quiet understanding.

I feel that soft pull of magic—warm and deliberate, like a weighted blanket settling over my skin. It brushes along the edges of my headache, smoothing the sharpest points, steadying the pressure behind my eyes.

I've come to recognize the way her power moves—slow and careful, never forceful, never loud.

And my breath eases with it.

"Rough morning?" she finally asks, her voice smooth as warm honey and twice as kind.

I nod, pressing my fingers to my temple. "Head like a war drum. Politics. Posturing. Leather pants."

She laughs, and the sound alone could probably cure a dozen ailments. She disappears behind the counter, returns with a small glass bottle of the drops and a bundle wrapped in cloth.

"This should help," she says, placing them gently in my hand. "Same as before—just a few drops on the tongue. And I infused some fruit leather with the tonic too, in case you're stuck somewhere with prying eyes and no time for subtlety."

I raise a brow at the bundle, sniffing to see if I can tell what flavor of fruit she used. "Ylsa's been asking about a restock."

Hestia sighs. "Of course she has. I'm running low on half my usuals—nightbark, frost fig, shimmerroot. The ingredients aren't hard to find, just scattered as the moon's moods. I'll need to go soon, before I run out of supplies to make your tonics."

Yeah, that would suck.

As I tuck the bundle into my coat, her expression shifts —curious, focused.

"When are the headaches worst?" she asks.

I blink. "Lately? The kitchens. And the caves... the Sanctum."

She hums low in her throat, thoughtful. "Interesting. Those places aren't just old. They sit over veins of magic— currents running just beneath the surface of the land. Like rivers." She pauses. "It would make sense. If the realm chose you, its power might be trying to reach you. But if you're not letting it in…"

"I'm not fighting it," I cut in, a little too fast. "At least not on purpose."

"Not on purpose still means not at all." Hestia steps closer, wiping flour from her hands on her apron. "You can't command what you won't receive."

I look away, jaw tight. "And how exactly do I receive something that feels like it's trying to break me open?"

She doesn't answer right away. She just studies me with those deep, depthless eyes. Then, soft as steam rising from fresh bread, she says,

"You're trying to master it like a sword. But the realm isn't a weapon to wield. It's a song to join."

I exhale—not quite a laugh. "You Fae and your metaphors."

She shrugs, unbothered. "You can't think your way into harmony, Tana. You have to feel it. Open yourself. Let it move through you. The realm doesn't want your obedience. It wants your trust."

Trust. Right.

Like that's ever been easy.

Still, her words settle somewhere deep in my chest, like a puzzle piece I'm trying to turn around and find its position.

"Thanks, Hestia," I say, already feeling the first stirrings of calm begin to unravel the knot between my brows.

She nods without words, already turning back to her kneading board, sleeves dusted in flour, peace wrapped around her like armor.

I step outside, tucking the tonic into my coat. The village

air is cooler now, the mist lifting slightly off the sea. I start toward the cliffs, toward the stairs that rise in brutal ascent back to Starfall.

Each step is a drumbeat behind my eyes.

Hestia's magic softened it, yes—and the drops should do the trick—but they aren't.

Halfway up the cliffside, I pause, bracing a hand against the stone railing. My breath is tight, my vision blurring slightly as the pounding shifts—no longer pain, but something else.

Something I recognize now, and I know what I'll see before I even look.

I turn my head, looking down toward the shoreline.

There—where the rocks jut out sharp and black against the waves—is the mouth of the Sanctum of Echoes.

And standing at its edge, veiled in mist, is the Lady of the Lake.

She doesn't move. She simply watches, face calm, unreadable as the lake on a still night. But I feel it—that subtle hum in the air, the pull beneath my skin.

Like gravity.

Like a heartbeat.

It pulses out from the Sanctum in slow, steady waves, and I feel it echo through my bones. A summoning. Or perhaps a warning.

Whispers swirl around me with a rush of wind and make me shiver.

Is she expecting me?

My mouth goes dry at the thought of being bombarded by the energy within that cave.

Before I can dwell on it, the Lady moves—just barely.

She turns, not toward the cliffs, but upward. Her gaze tilts in the direction of Starfall.

She cannot see it. Not from here.

But... maybe she can.

Maybe she sees through the stone. Through the sky. Through the kingdom itself.

And then—clear and unmistakable—one long, slow ring echoes out from above.

Then another.

And another.

The bells of Starfall are being rung.

The High Clave has arrived.

And I'm the guest of honor.

CHAPTER 3

The bells ring.

Low and deliberate—one for each seat at the High Clave's table. A ceremonial summoning meant to echo across the cliffs like some grand promise.

To me, it just sounds like the beginning of another day wasted on political pageantry.

The Clave is here—ready to talk in circles, to posture, to preen, and to pretend they haven't already chosen which side they'll stand on when the time comes.

My grandmother formed this council with hope. She envisioned balance—representation for every corner of Avalon.

But balance is a fragile thing.

When Demeter spilled royal blood to take the crown, she reshaped the Clave in her image—replaced seats with loyalists, stacked the court with power-hungry puppets and smiling snakes.

Every last one of them likely bartered something with the traitor queen before she betrayed the realm she claimed to rule.

I only hope it's one of the first foundations Tana chooses to burn and rebuild.

I sit in the tall arched windowsill of the council gallery, back against the cool stone, one booted foot braced against the opposite wall. The space is massive—vaulted and echoing, lined with polished obsidian columns and too much silver for anyone's good taste.

The seat I have occupied at the large round table—the one reserved for Starfall's appointed representative—remains empty.

That seat rightfully belongs to the queen who has yet to make her appearance in the gallery.

I keep my hands busy, a thin piece of wood resting against my thigh. My blade whispers as I drag it down the surface, carving off slender curls that drift to the floor beside me. I'm not even sure what it's becoming—only that the motion keeps me from pacing.

One by one, the council begins to arrive.

Each entrance more absurd than the last.

One arrives with an escort of floating flower petals that all drop to the polished floor at once. Another, an entourage of acrobats performing all sorts of tumbling and tricks. One with a full assembly of every stringed instrument in Avalon, it seems. By the stars.

They all put on a performance as they enter—eyes sweeping the room—and every single one of them crestfallen the moment they realize the mortal queen isn't here to witness their theatrics.

I smile faintly, watching another steep in disappointment.

When the representative from Eldoria enters, dripping in glass-beaded robes that chime with every step, I huff a quiet laugh through my nose. The male looks like a chandelier that came to life and never found his way home.

At least it isn't Liora.

I thank whatever gods are still listening that she's returned to the Shimmer Court—likely to lick her wounds and gossip about the mortal queen who dared to reject her courtship and live.

One of the council members clears his throat, voice slick with boredom barely disguised as civility.

"Something amusing, Your Highness?"

I don't bother to look up. My blade continues its slow, steady scrape along the length of wood resting against my thigh. Small curls peel away and drift to the floor like feathers.

"Many things," I reply mildly, not bothering to disguise the truth. "You'll have to be specific."

They're irritated, and it only helps to brighten my mood further than it already is.

Of course, there are other reasons for the lift in my step this nocturn—though none of them are ones I intend to share.

Before the conversation can stretch further, the Cairn-vail representative—sour-faced and perpetually unimpressed—lets out a low, disgruntled huff.

"How rude of the queen," he mutters, his words thick with condescension, "to not be here for the reception of her council."

My blade stills against the wood.

I glance up, slow and deliberate—the shift in my expression enough to draw silence across the table like a drawn curtain.

"I would remind the council," I say evenly, "that they are here to serve the queen and the realm. Not the other way around."

A hush falls—brittle and cold.

Beneath my boot, shadows begin to stir—soft at first, then curling forward with the lazy promise of something darker. They don't strike, but they make their presence known.

"She'll arrive," I add, letting my gaze flick from one stiff collar to another, "when she's ready."

And just as I say it, I feel her.

The pulse of her presence moves through the corridor outside—distant, but growing stronger with each deliberate step she takes. It's a quiet thing, but insistent, like the tug of a tide beneath the surface of calm water. Each thud of her boots resonates through the wards beneath the gallery floor, tethered to something in me I still haven't fully named.

I stand and lean a shoulder against the inset of the window, one foot crossed over the other and my hands in my pockets. I do my best to keep a neutral face, though I'm making a wager with myself and am quite eager to see if I'm correct.

The doors at the far end of the chamber open a heartbeat later, pushed wide by two lesser Fae dressed in deep indigo.

Her name is announced in full.

Her Royal Highness, Tana. Chosen of the Realm. Queen Ascending.

She enters without hesitation, her posture regal without pretense, her nod to the doormen one of simple gratitude, not show.

She pauses only briefly at the threshold, and her gaze finds mine in an instant—exactly as I knew it would. My wager, won.

For one heartbeat I let myself savor the win—a small, private cruelty. Then I clamp the feeling down. Nothing soft is allowed here. Not for me. Not anymore.

The glance is quick—barely more than a flicker—but it's there. Finally.

Those rich brown eyes she has hidden from me too many nocturns have finally set upon me.

It was my singular goal when she entered my consciousness last evenfall—like she has so many nights since the village was attacked.

In truth, it's the space between us—the bond we both ignore—pulling her toward me like a current. I shouldn't answer. I tell myself that every time. And every time, I do.

At first, I only reached back to prove I could—to test the thread between us. But restraint is a fragile thing. Now I tell myself one more night won't matter—that letting her in, just for a little while, is mercy.

She visualizes a door. *My* door. My chambers. And when she crosses the threshold, the realm itself bends to make it real.

These aren't dreams.

They're meetings of our consciousness—real in every way that matters, except the flesh.

I know it can't last. The moment she learns to open herself fully to Avalon's magic, she'll see it for what it is. She'll see *me*.

And then this small illusion I've built will shatter.

But until then... I'll let her keep pretending.

And I'll keep pretending I'm not the one who needs it.

It's easier that way—to convince myself these moments don't matter, that they're only fragments of a fading dream.

Except they never fade.

Not the way she looks at me when the pretense slips.

The way she finally looked at me last night—held my gaze every second she came undone on my fingers.

The way she looked at me as she entered the Clave just now.

But she's already looking away—her attention now on the Clave, who still haven't risen.

I straighten my posture and bow—low, precise, and without hesitation. A respectful gesture, just low enough to remind the others how it's done.

I know Hypnos would have explained the customs to her. She's not ignorant of what's expected here.

Which is why her voice, when it comes, is edged with ice far older than any mortal blood should carry.

"Have the legs of the council all stopped working at once?" she asks, head tilted ever so slightly. "Perhaps we should send for a healer."

A few of them shift uncomfortably, exchanging glances. But she doesn't press. She doesn't need to.

One by one, they rise—grudgingly, stiffly. Each motion pulled from them like a tooth. The representative from the Briar Court is the last to stand, his moss-wrapped hands curling into fists at his sides.

Which is exactly why I chose the windowsill instead of any other option for seating.

I am closer to him here. Closer than he realizes.

And if he so much as twitches toward the queen, I will tear the roots from his throat before he ever reaches her.

Mor and Hypnos slip in quietly and take their places along the wall.

Mor has an entire haunch of roasted boar—bone and all —steadily tearing away at the steaming meat. My expression must beg her to explain, because she only raises her shoulders once, as if she doesn't understand why this is odd.

Mor and Hypnos have always served as my seconds; now they stand as hers. As usual, Mor earns a side glance from one of the elders—her foreign blood still too strange for these halls—but no one dares to question her presence aloud. Even the arrogant learn quickly that crossing the Morrigan is unwise.

The High Clave always begins the same way: a recitation of custom that no one listens to.

Reports on the health of each court. Grain stores in the Briar. Trade routes through Umbranor. All the polite chatter that's supposed to prove the realm is flourishing.

I didn't think the civility would last long, and predictably, the rhythm of reports shatters.

The representative from Evershade leans forward, his voice cutting through the chamber.

"Are we going to ignore the matter that brought us here? We can trade niceties until first shade, but courtesy won't make any of this go away."

Tana's head tilts slightly. "And what would this be referring to?"

"The darkness that grows," he answers. "The whispers of uprising that swell with every nocturn. And the fact that your mortal blood is weak."

A murmur rolls through the chamber like wind through brittle leaves.

He presses on, emboldened. "We can all feel it. Let's not pretend we don't."

Arguments ignite instantly—each court talking over the other, voices rising in competing offers and thinly veiled insults. The Umbranor dignitary points out the short life-span our fragile mortal queen will have, then says nothing more.

One proposes that another Fae be *appointed* to take the crown as queen instead of Tana; another suggests they wait for the queen's trials to kill her before deciding whom to nominate.

I hold my shadows back from slicing the throat of that Fae on the spot.

A representative from Mirevalis recommends a coronation parade to reassure the people.

Tana and I both roll our eyes. At least we agree on something.

She waits until the noise begins to fold in on itself, then speaks—quiet, but every voice dies at the sound.

"Perhaps," she says, "instead of planning festivals, we focus on the source of this darkness. Find its root and end it."

Her gaze sweeps the table—sharp enough to draw blood.

"Or," she adds, "we could keep planning parties."

The representative from Frosthaven—icicle-pale and predictably smug—leans back in her chair. "And what makes the mortal so sure she can best the darkness when Queen Pandora herself could not?"

Her smile is slight, dangerous. "You're right," she says evenly. "Pandora couldn't. None of you could. Have any of you even tried?"

Silence again. Only the crackle of the sconces answers.

Then the Briar Court's envoy finally speaks—first words since the meeting began—and every muscle in my body tightens.

"The courts are unbalanced," he says. "Some believe the only way to even the scales is war."

Tana's tone turns deceptively calm. "When you say *some believe,* are you referring to the Fae of the Briar? Tell me, do these *some* also believe I am incapable?"

He meets her eyes without hesitation. "Of course they do."

Steel sings as Tana draws Realmbreaker from her scabbard, pushing her chair back and standing. The blade hits the table between them with a resounding clang that echoes through the chamber like thunder.

The entire Clave stills.

Even those who've seen the sword before can't help but stare.

That weapon isn't just steel—it's a miracle carved out of impossibility. For eons, Realmbreaker had been one with the stone beneath the dark sky of Avalon, fused by something no one could determine. Every generation, someone tried to free it—warriors, nobles, even would-be kings—believing Avalon would reward the one who succeeded. Some thought it would bestow higher magic. Others thought it would give them the crown itself.

I scoff internally, spitting a bit of splintered wood from the pick in my mouth.

Even Merlin came once, dragging his mad scrolls and alchemy with him. He left muttering nonsense, and the sword remained unmoved.

Until her.

And now the blade that had defied every hand before hers lies loose upon the Clave's table, glinting under the blaze of starlight from the gallery windows.

Tana leans forward, her voice low but clear.

"I was capable enough to draw the sword that had been fused in stone for eons," she says, every word a strike. "Were you capable of that?"

The Briar envoy swallows hard and says nothing.

"Were any of you?"

Still nothing. Only the weight of her stare.

"You think yourselves capable? Then by all means—take it now."

The Briar envoy moves, quick but not quick enough. Her smaller blade flashes from her thigh, pinning his sleeve to the table before he can stand. In the blink that follows, her main sword is back in her grasp, its point resting just under his chin.

"Exactly what I thought," she says, voice steady as still water. "You weren't capable before, and you're not capable now."

She sheaths her weapon. The envoy jerks free, ripping the fabric from his arm, leaving the blade quivering in the wood. I stand—not because she needs me, but because the sight of a weapon left within reach makes my instincts hum.

"The war against the darkness may have begun with Pandora." Tana straightens, her voice carrying again. "But this war will end with me."

Each member of the council shifts under the weight of her stare as her eyes move from one to the next.

"The darkness must be our priority. Your parades and dinner parties can wait."

CHAPTER 4
orion

She doesn't look at me again.

Not after that first fleeting glance when she arrived—chin lifted, eyes scanning the chamber. Our gazes locked for barely a second, and then... nothing.

For the rest of the Clave, I may as well have been a shadow on the wall.

She addresses the council. She listens. She debates. She holds her own with seasoned Fae who've ruled their courts for ages. And all the while, her knife remains exactly where she left it, buried unapologetically in the center of the round table.

A silent challenge.

And maybe a warning.

When she finally calls the council to a close, silence falls like a fog. Her fingers reach toward the knife.

But she doesn't touch it.

She doesn't have to.

A fraction of a breath before her skin meets the metal, the blade shifts—just enough. It lifts from the wood and moves into her hand, smooth as breath, seamless as thought.

She doesn't notice.

Not the motion. Not the hum in the air. Not the way the knife obeyed her like it had been waiting.

But I do.

I see it.

Avalon moved for her. The magic of this realm bent to her will, as if it's aching to settle into her bones, to pour through her veins and awaken what's already there.

And she doesn't even realize she wielded it.

Maybe because she's angry. At the Clave. At her fate. At me.

She's shutting it out—just like she's shutting me out.

But the realm won't tolerate her indifference forever.

And neither will I.

But I'll have to tolerate her silence a while longer.

The castle doesn't run itself.

Before she arrived, it fell to me to keep things in order, of course. The throne may have sat empty, but the realm doesn't sleep. It complains. It hungers. It hoards and needs and breaks.

And someone has to keep it all from falling apart.

I throw myself into the work because it keeps my hands full. Busy is easier than thinking about her silence—or the dreams I shouldn't be having.

So I sit on the stone dais below the throne Tana cannot yet claim, boots planted, arms folded, jaw locked so tight it aches.

One by one, the Fae file in with their grievances.

"Prince Orion," drawls a dryad from the western orchard of the Enchanted Forest, bark curling along her temple. "The Moonshade beetles have returned. They're eating through the root wards again. If we lose the trees—"

"Use ash oil," I interrupt, pinching the bridge of my

nose. "Soak the perimeter and charm the outer bark. If that fails, burn the nest and offer the flames a drop of blood."

She flinches. "Mine?"

I lift a brow. "Unless you'd prefer to take someone else's."

She bows and retreats without another word.

Next.

A pair of elven twins step forward, faces identical, complaints as sharp as their matching emerald tunics.

"Our neighbor," says the one on the left, "has been stealing our shade."

"He moved his moss-drapes two feet north," the right adds. "That's clearly against the binding agreement—"

"Then challenge him to a duel," I say flatly. "Or cut his drapes down. If he protests, tell him to take it up with your court's lord or lady."

They blink. "That's... it?"

"Unless you'd prefer to relocate the moon."

They bow. Hasty. Confused. Gone.

Next.

A kelpie stalks forward, soaked and scowling, water dripping onto the mosaic floor.

"There are whispers," he growls. "Some say the mortal is not truly chosen. That she'll abandon Avalon. That she can't command the magic. The waters have already turned darker—"

My fingers tighten around the arm of the chair.

"Those who whisper," I say, slow and deliberate, "are welcome to speak their doubts aloud. Preferably in front of me. So I can separate their tongues from their heads."

He bares his teeth. "Not my whisper."

"Then you have nothing to fear."

He dips his head and slinks back to whatever cursed river he calls home.

Another hour passes like that. Complaint after complaint. Petition after petty grievance. The food stores need fortifying. The treasury vault needs counting. A minor court wants permission to host a moon feast; another wants to cancel theirs in protest of the first.

By the time the last Fae bows and retreats from the hall, my patience is hanging by a frayed, splintering thread.

The castle is too loud, too crowded. The walls feel like they've crept in a few feet since this morning. Since she ignored me.

Again. It shouldn't bother me. Her silence is what I earned.

I stride through the kitchens, nodding once at Ylsa as I pass. She tosses me a piece of fruit without a word. I catch it midair, take a bite without slowing. Sweet. Overripe. It sticks to my teeth like syrup.

Outside, the night air cuts cleaner.

I exhale.

Another breath in. Out.

Then another.

The moon hangs full and swollen above the towers, its light bleeding across the courtyard stones. I tilt my face to it, letting the glow wash over me, letting it calm the clench in my jaw.

Every nocturn, the castle feels smaller.

Every day she stays silent, heavier.

I'm just starting to convince myself to stay out here longer, to not turn back and storm through whatever door she's hiding behind, when I hear the faint chime of bells.

Though not metal.

Wings.

I know that sound.

By the moon, what now?

A blur of color and light streaks toward me—a whirl of sprites racing through the air with flitting wings and flower petals formed to make their clothes, their hair tangled with vines and moss. They're breathless, panicked, tiny hands waving as they descend like a cloud of chaos around my shoulders.

All of them yap at once, their voices high-pitched and overlapping, the sound like a dozen silver bells dropped down a stairwell.

"Enough." I lift a hand. "One at a time. I can't tell a damn thing when you're all tinkling over each other."

They fall into a chaotic silence, hovering in tight little circles, eyes wide and gleaming.

They look behind them.

I follow their gaze just as more sprites emerge—slower, heavier in the air, wings trembling from the effort.

They're carrying something.

My chest tightens.

Tossing the fruit behind me, I stride forward in two long steps, hands already raised, palms open.

"Here," I say gently. "Give it to me."

They lower together, coordinated by instinct, and deposit the bundle into my hands.

It's another sprite.

But this one isn't flitting. Isn't panicked. He's barely breathing.

Just a whisper of movement remains in the small, fragile body curled in my palm. His skin—once the pale green of new spring leaves—is greying. His hands and feet are dark, blackened as if dipped in tar. His eyes are half-closed, too glassy, too still.

A cold dread slides through my ribs. It's against the laws of nature for such chaotic little devils of mischief to be so still and somber.

I look to the nearest sprite hovering near my shoulder.

"Retrieve Hestia," I say, low and firm. "From the village. She'll need her tonics."

The sprite nods and zips off in a blur of light.

But even as I say it, I know.

If this is what I think it is, it's already too late.

It's the same darkness that slithered into Avalon during Beltane.

When that rot slipped through the wards and took our people—twisting them into something unrecognizable.

Fae turned on their own. Fate-bonds snapped like threads yanked from a loom. Mates carved each other open with torn smiles on their faces and tar in their veins.

That blackness bled from their eyes, their mouths, their wounds.

Just like the thick sludge creeping up this sprite's limbs now.

His hands. His feet. His lips.

Covered in it.

A tremor works its way down my spine.

This isn't sickness.

It's not decay.

It's a warning.

The darkness didn't stay gone.

And if it's touching the sprites now—our messengers, our watchers, the ones most attuned to Avalon's pulse—then whatever door was opened may not have been fully shut.

I kneel in the cyan grass, the sprite cradled in my palms.

He's light as breath, but the air around him feels heavy—tainted.

The deep, rich void stirring at my back tells me Mor is here.

Her presence always folds the light away.

She moves without sound and kneels beside me. Her face is unreadable, head tilted as though studying an insect beneath glass.

"The sprite is dying," she says, her tone as plain as if announcing dinner. "But not dead yet."

I glance down. His chest still flutters. Barely.

"Suffering," she adds after a moment. Something flickers across her expression—an unfamiliar shape that almost looks like sympathy. "Macha would like to help the small creature."

Macha.

Mor's youngest sister.

The third soul sharing her body.

Badb, the eldest. Mor, the middle. And Macha—gentle, hidden, rarely seen.

I've met her only a handful of times in all the ages Mor and I have been friends.

I nod and carefully transfer the sprite into Mor's smaller hands.

The air shifts—an invisible pulse, like the world itself drawing a deeper breath. Shadows gather around her form, rippling as one soul yields to another.

Macha steps forward.

Where Mor's eyes burn red, Macha's cloud over—dark fog, the color of the mists that creep across Avalon's still lakes. Her posture softens; even her size seems to shrink. The tightly coiled violence constantly weaving around Mor leaves her frame.

She rises and walks toward the low stone wall that borders the courtyard, each step measured.

Hestia bursts through the archway, skirts gathered, a satchel of tonics clutched in her arms. Worry hollows her eyes.

I shake my head once. "There's nothing to be done."

She slows, understanding.

Macha kneels by the wall. Hestia and I join her, and so do the sprites—dozens of them now, their lights dimmed, their voices silent except for the soft hitch of sound that might be weeping.

Macha lifts her hands, bows her head until her lips hover near the dying sprite.

"Mercy," she whispers.

It should be quiet, but the single word ripples outward, echoing through the courtyard—not a prayer.

A summoning.

The familiar hands of my friend move so carefully to set the fading sprite upon the grass near the stone wall of the courtyard.

We watch, all of us frozen in the fate of the small creature.

A thread of black shadow uncoils from the ground, rising like smoke. It wraps around the small body, cloaking it completely, and I see it is a hand—some dark form called from the realm of Elysium. It reaches through the veil between realms, sweeping upward and shrouding the sprite in shadow.

The light within him fades. The trembling stops.

When the dark grip of obscurity sinks back into the earth, the sprite is gone.

Hestia presses a hand to her mouth, stifling a sob.

Where Fae return to ash, sprites return to starlight.

A shimmer of silver dust rises where he lay—soft, radiant, twinkling as it catches the moonlight. The breeze lifts it, carrying it toward the forest, upward into the dark velvet sky of Avalon's eternal night.

In its place by the stones of the wall, a single moonflower blooms—silver and luminous, petals unfurling toward the sky.

Macha looks to the gathered sprites. A small smile touches her lips, gentle and sincere.

"The purest of souls we've met in a very long time."

She bows her head to them.

Then the air stirs again. The gray light drains from her eyes. When she looks up, they're red once again.

Mor has taken back possession of her body—rigid, expressionless.

"We offer our sincerest condolences to your kin."

Death I understand. It follows rules. It ends cleanly.

It's the living—the waiting—that turns sharp edges inward.

Without another word, she rises and walks back toward the castle—no doubt to find the nearest buffet to conquer.

I watch her go, then turn to the weeping sprites.

"Take me," I say, nodding toward the moonflower glowing at our feet, "to wherever this happened."

CHAPTER 5
tana

The throne room is too quiet tonight.

I stand before the portrait of Queen Pandora, the first ruler chosen by the realm itself, not appointed by the Fae, and I try to imagine what it must've felt like.

Her gaze follows me from the canvas, eyes the same sapphire as starlight on water. She looks young, impossibly so. Barely more than a girl. But there's power in her posture, a calm assurance that speaks of someone who understood exactly what she was stepping into.

Crowned young.

Died old.

Her immortal reign ended not by age, but by betrayal, slain by her own daughter when the hunger for the crown grew stronger than love.

I wonder if she saw it coming.

Was she ever afraid? Or did she walk through those fears the way I walk through these halls, chin up, pretending I belong here, pretending the weight of this realm doesn't feel like it's pressing into my bones.

Because right now, I feel anything but prepared.

On any battlefield, I'd know what to do.

Assess. Adapt. Execute.

I was trained for chaos, bred for control. A soldier knows how to survive by understanding the terrain.

But Avalon isn't terrain. It's alive. It breathes, hums, reacts. And I don't have a map for it.

Every instinct I have is useless here.

Every weapon, except my will, is gone.

Still, I won't let this realm conquer me.

Not the throne.

Not the court.

Not the fear that I'll fail them all.

I look up at Pandora's portrait again, her youth immortalized while her centuries of rule have faded into dust.

If she could find her footing, so can I.

And if this realm thought it could choose me and break me in the same breath, it's in for a disappointment.

A soft shuffle sounds behind me. I don't turn.

"Thinking of redecorating?" Hypnos's voice is smooth, low, touched with wry amusement.

He joins me at my side, walking with slow, deliberate steps. The moonlight spills over his dark skin, gleaming faintly across the smooth curve of his bald head. His eyes, white and almost luminous, don't look at the portrait directly, but somehow I know he's seeing it.

Not the way I do. Not with sight.

He sees through something deeper.

"She was chosen," he says quietly, stopping beside me. "Pandora. The first queen Avalon claimed for itself. Before her, the throne was decided by bloodlines and politics. After her, everything changed."

"She looks young."

"She was," he murmurs. "Crowned in her second century. Still young, by Fae standards."

I glance at him. "You knew her?"

His head tilts slightly, the faintest trace of a smile ghosting his lips. "I did. For a time. I remember the sound of her laughter more than her face. I don't see faces the way you do."

He gestures vaguely toward the painting. "She burned bright—her emotions always gold, like a star. But near the end, the light around her dimmed. Her daughter's glow grew darker, heavier. The realm showed me that before it happened."

"So you saw it coming," I say softly.

"I felt it," he corrects. "The shift. The envy. The fracture before the fall. Most don't realize how loud emotion becomes when it's trying to warn us."

We both look at Pandora's portrait again.

"She ruled for ages," Hypnos continues. "And even then, she doubted herself in the beginning. You're not the first queen to feel unready. But you are the first to face a realm still healing from her fall."

His words settle like lead in my chest, but beneath the weight, something steadier takes root.

"Then I'll heal it," I say.

Hypnos turns his head toward me, the faint bioluminescent glow behind his white eyes pulsing softly. "You sound like her," he says, voice almost kind. "Where shall we begin, Your Grace?"

I draw in a slow breath, steadying myself.

There are a hundred answers to that question, every one

of them heavier than the last, but my mind goes back to something simpler. Smaller.

The headaches.

I rub a hand over the back of my neck. "There's something you should know," I say. "It's... about the realm. Or maybe me. I don't know anymore."

He inclines his head slightly, listening.

"There are places," I continue, "where the realm feels like it's pressing on me. Like it's trying to get in."

His expression doesn't change, but I can feel him focusing. Even blind, Hypnos sees more than most.

"Sometimes it's just a dull ache behind my eyes," I say quietly. "Manageable. Annoying. Like a constant reminder that I don't belong here. But other times..." I exhale, jaw tightening. "Other times it feels like my skull's being split open. Like something inside Avalon is pounding against me, trying to break through."

The memory makes me wince. Those moments when the pain is so sharp it cuts through thought, leaving only white noise and nausea.

"I can barely think when it happens," I admit. "And I need to think. There's darkness spreading again, there are trials ahead—if I can't focus, I can't lead."

Hypnos nods once, thoughtful. "Take me where the headaches are strongest."

My mouth flattens. "You sure about that?"

He turns his pale eyes toward me, the faintest trace of light shifting behind them like a current of starlight. "If the realm is speaking to you, I can listen in my own way. It does not whisper to me as it does to you, but I can feel its emotion. Its rhythm."

I hesitate. There's only one place where the pressure becomes unbearable.

"The Sanctum of Echoes," I say finally.

"Ah." A faint sound of understanding leaves him. "Then I suppose not."

I blink. "Not?"

"The Lady of the Lake does not welcome uninvited guests," he says mildly. "Even I wouldn't trespass in her domain without her summons. She guards the veil between Avalon and the realms beyond, and she doesn't take kindly to being disturbed."

"Hm." I think back to dropping in there with Orion after he scorched the Briar Warden into ash on my behalf. "Well, I did invite myself in once. She didn't kill me?"

"A fortunate outcome indeed," he says, straightening slightly. "Where else do the headaches plague you?"

I think for a moment.

There's one other place that comes to mind. Unexpected, but true.

"The kitchens," I admit.

A single brow lifts. "The kitchens?"

"Yeah." I rest one hand on the hilt of Realmbreaker. "It's worse there than anywhere else—aside from the Sanctum. I thought it was the heat, or the noise, but..." I shake my head. "It's something else. I can feel it crawling under my skin every time I step inside."

Hypnos smiles faintly, the corner of his mouth lifting. "Then to the kitchens, Your Grace."

I glance at him. "You sound amused."

"Perhaps I am. Few queens begin their reign with a pilgrimage to the pantry."

That almost earns him a smile from me.

Almost.

The kitchens are quiet at this hour. The hearths still glow, low embers breathing light across the stone floor. Copper pots hang in rows. Herbs dangle from rafters, perfuming the air with rosemary and sage.

Hypnos trails a hand along the wall, his head tilted as though listening to something I can't hear. "This is where the pain grows strongest?"

I nod. "Usually. It starts as a low hum, right at the base of my skull."

He steps closer, expression unreadable but somehow kind. "You're resisting it," he says simply. "The realm wants to move through you, and you're meeting it with walls. Pain is often the echo of denial."

"Denial?" I snort softly. "I'm not denying anything."

His pale eyes flick toward me, that faint light within them pulsing once. "Aren't you?"

I sigh, bracing a hand against the table. "I'm not used to —" I gesture vaguely. "Feeling everything all the time. I'm used to focus. Discipline. Command. This isn't command. It's chaos."

"Then stop commanding it," Hypnos murmurs. "Listen."

I close my eyes and try.

There's heat behind my eyelids, pressure building at the base of my skull. A heavy pulse that refuses to sync with my own heartbeat.

I breathe through it, but it doesn't ease.

Nothing changes. Just that dull ache, throbbing. Persistent.

"I can't—"

"Come," he says gently. "Not here. The walls hold too much noise. The stone remembers everything that's been said inside it. We need open air."

He leads me through the service archway and out into the courtyard.

The moment my boots touch the grass, pain hits.

It's like being struck between the eyes—white-hot and blinding. My knees buckle, and I drop, clutching my head with both hands.

"Tana." Hypnos's voice is steady. Calm. "Breathe."

"I—" The word breaks off into a gasp. "It's worse out here."

"Yes," he says. "Because you're closer to what's calling."

He kneels beside me, his hand a firm weight between my shoulder blades. "Do not fight it. You are not under attack. The realm is trying to speak."

"I can't—"

"You can."

His voice doesn't rise, doesn't waver. It's patient —anchoring.

"Find the rhythm beneath the pain," he murmurs. "There. Feel that? The pulse?"

I grit my teeth, forcing air through my lungs.

And then—

There it is.

A steady thrum, faint but deliberate. Not inside my head, but beneath it. Beneath the earth.

Hypnos's hand shifts slightly. "Good. Follow it."

I crawl forward once, still clutching my temples. Then again. The pain shifts—sharper, but focused now.

I lift my head, squinting through the haze. The world swims—stone, shadow, moonlight—and then I see it.

A flower, small and silver, newly bloomed by the wall.

"There," I manage, voice rough. I raise a trembling hand and point.

Hypnos follows the direction of my finger. His blind eyes glow faintly, as if reflecting light I can't see.

He studies the bloom in silence for a long moment, brow furrowing. "So much grief."

I stare at the flower, that faint pull still thrumming in my chest. But even as I focus on it, the sensation shifts —spreads.

A second pulse. Farther away.

Deep in the forest.

A low throb hums through the ground, steady and rhythmic, almost like a heartbeat.

It's not sharp this time. Not blaring. Just constant. Like a beacon that's been sounding for far too long, waiting for someone to notice.

The ache settles behind my eyes, and I press a palm to my temple, trying to breathe through it.

It isn't pain now—it's presence.

"I can feel it," I whisper.

Hypnos says nothing, but I can sense his attention sharpening beside me.

I don't know what it is—not really.

But my mind goes where it always does, where it has since the last attack.

The darkness.

It has to be.

The pulse is coming from beyond the castle walls, somewhere deeper in Avalon. In the direction of the Enchanted Forest.

Something's there.

Something suffocating.

And it's been there long enough to spread.

"I need Havoc."

The words slip out before I even think them.

A sudden wind stirs through the courtyard, rustling the trees like a breath drawn in answer. The air thickens, humming with quiet awareness.

My head still pounds, but the edge dulls—just enough for me to stand. My lungs burn, each breath shallow and uneven. Of course I wouldn't master it in one try; still, I'm a bit disappointed in myself that I didn't.

A thundercrack echoes from the stables. Then another.

I turn just as the great shapes burst into view—two Duskbanes, their hides black as obsidian, eyes glinting with molten light. Massive beasts with fanged tusks curling from their jaws and manes that shimmer like spilled ink.

Havoc leads, his riderless reins snapping in the wind. The second follows close behind, heavier, darker.

Hypnos smiles faintly, the expression small but knowing. "The realm can hear you. Speak to her when you can, and she will send what you need."

"Then I need the fucking darkness to go away."

His soft laugh carries no mockery—only understanding. "Then tell her that, too."

I grab Havoc's reins, the familiar weight grounding me. "We're not exactly on speaking terms yet."

"You will be," he murmurs.

I swing into the saddle, the leather creaking beneath me.

The second Duskbane paws at the ground until Hypnos steadies him with a touch to the neck before mounting him.

I let the throbbing guide me. It beats faintly behind my eyes, slow and sure, pulling like a tether through the night. I imagine a line between my heart and Havoc's—a single current, steady and shared. I don't steer so much as think, and it's working. He seems to understand.

The ground blurs beneath us. Wind tears at my hair. The trees stretch long shadows across the moonlit path, and still the pulse drags me onward.

By the time we break through the tree line, the pounding in my skull crescendos—strong, insistent. The air smells wrong.

Like iron and rot.

We've reached a small druid village tucked within the Enchanted Forest, right where open land starts to choke under a curtain of trees. Smoke drifts in thin ribbons above thatched roofs, the faint glow of lanterns trembling in the dark.

And he's here.

I feel Orion before I see him—his presence cutting through the noise like static. The same sharp gravity that always precedes him, a pull in my chest I can't seem to ignore no matter how hard I try.

When my eyes find him, standing among the druids and the guards from Starfall, my pulse spikes.

Of course he's already here.

The anger that rises is immediate. Sharp.

He should have sent for me.

Even if I wasn't speaking to him. Even if we're still caught in this silent war of stubborn pride. I'm the one

Avalon chose. He should have made sure I knew first. Not run over here like it's another thing he can shield me from.

Mor stands nearby, crouched low on a moss-covered stone, eating like she's at a festival. Sprites flit around her with offerings—fruit, dried meat, bits of cheese—and she accepts every one with casual indifference to the tension brewing in the air.

The moment I swing down from Havoc, boots sinking into the soft earth, Orion's attention snaps to me, his jaw tightening.

"What's going on?" I demand.

He moves toward me, his voice steady. "The sprites found—"

But I brush past him, ignoring the familiar jolt that rolls through me at the proximity. It's been weeks since I've let myself feel it.

Except in the dreams.

And those don't count.

I stop before one of the druids—a man with green-dusted skin and antlers polished to a faint sheen. "Tell me," I say, nodding for him to speak.

He bows his head slightly. "The sprites found a new spring, my lady. They were playing in it. One fell ill, but there is not much that can harm a sprite. We thought perhaps... an imbalance in the soil."

"I want to see it."

He leads us into the woods, the path narrowing as the trees close in. The air thickens—wet, heavy, humming faintly beneath my skin.

When we reach the small clearing, I see the source.

A spring, barely more than a trickle, glowing faintly under the moonlight.

The druid's voice is hushed. "A tar clung to the small thing. His hands and feet. It was not survivable."

I crouch beside the water, bracing a hand on my knee. From this close, I can see it—the shimmer of corruption threading through the current. Thin, inky ribbons winding like veins through otherwise clear water.

I reach out and feel it immediately.

The shift behind me.

Orion's instinct, his presence tensing like a storm about to break.

I don't look at him, but I tilt my head just enough—the barest acknowledgment. Enough for him to know I felt it. Enough for him to take a step back.

My fingers hover above the surface. The air there feels wrong—cool but heavy, like breathing through smoke. I pull back before touching it.

"Have you noticed anything else unusual?" I ask, rising.

One of the druids nods. "The flora, my lady. Some of the wild plants wither for no reason. Animals vanish or are found dead, untouched by predator or blade."

"Show me."

We move through the brush. The woods grow darker here, the canopy choking out the moonlight. I take in everything—every moving leaf, the easy sound of trickling water.

The druids exchange confused glances.

"There shouldn't be a stream here," one murmurs.

But there is.

We break through the undergrowth and stop.

It's a creek.

Only, it isn't water running through it.

It's black water.

Thick, flowing slow and deliberate through the channel, coating the roots and stones as it winds deeper into the forest.

The smell of it—burnt metal and decay—turns my stomach.

I stare at it, throat tight, the dull pulse behind my eyes syncing with the slow, dreadful current.

The darkness hasn't just returned.

It's spreading.

CHAPTER 6
orion

The forest is holding its breath.

A few druids huddle near the edge of the black creek, their voices a low murmur beneath the whispering trees. They speak in guesses—wards broken, spells miscast, something old waking beneath the roots.

None of them will say what they're all thinking.

The darkness is spreading.

Tana stands apart from them, arms wrapped around her waist, the silver light from the moon painting her in cold relief. She doesn't move. Doesn't speak. Just stares at the sluggish current as if daring it to speak first. Maybe she's listening for it. Maybe she's warning it.

The breeze shifts; her hair brushes her shoulders, and she looks like both curse and prayer.

My fist tightens at my side. Every instinct screams to go to her—to pull her back from that tainted edge. But I stay where I am. She doesn't want me beside her, and I've learned the cost of crossing that line.

She exhales—slow, deliberate—and when she turns back to us, the queen returns to her body. Her gaze sweeps over the druids before landing—briefly, pointedly—on me.

It's not a look; it's a knife's edge.

"How long," she says, "were you all planning to investigate this before informing me?"

The question cuts through the murmuring like a blade.

I shift, ready to answer—because the blame is mine—but one of the druids speaks first. His voice is careful, the sound of someone hoping to survive the exchange.

"The sprites came directly to Starfall for help, Your Grace, the moment they noticed the darkness in the water."

"I do not hold the village responsible." Her eyes flick toward me—sharp, assessing—before looking to the Starfall guards. "It seems Starfall sent that help, though the news never reached my ears."

Silence ripples through the group. The leaves above us rustle, uneasy.

She straightens, every inch the queen the realm chose. "Hear me clearly. From this moment forward, any matter that carries the faintest trace of uncertainty will come to me first. No filtering. No delay. Next time there's so much as a whisper of corruption in Avalon, I expect to hear it from my council—immediately."

The word *council* lands hard.

She's speaking to all of us, but we both know the rebuke is mine.

A response I earned, so I take it.

Another druid, younger, with silver moss threaded through her hair, speaks quietly. "If it can taint the water, it can move anywhere—through the roots, the rivers, even the wells."

A murmur of agreement follows.

Tana crosses her arms. "Then we don't leave it the opportunity."

She turns, addressing the Starfall guards. "You'll relocate the villagers to the castle grounds. Within the walls, they'll have protection and clean water. Until we find the source, I won't risk further exposure."

The elder druid bows. "And the fields, Your Grace? The harvest—"

She shakes her head once. "The harvest can wait. I want the high fae warding this area before the next moonrise."

Her gaze slides toward me, deliberate and cool. "See what can be done to halt the spread here. I won't have the water creeping closer to Starfall."

The words aren't sharp, but they hit their mark all the same.

A direct order.

And one she knows I'll take.

I incline my head, masking the irritation twisting under my ribs. "It'll be done."

Hypnos folds his hands behind his back. "And the source of the corruption, Your Grace? What course do you favor?"

Her eyes lift to the tar-black water winding away into the trees. "We follow it," she says. "Where it begins, that's where it can be ended."

I finally speak. "It's spreading faster than you think. We should—"

She cuts me off without looking at me. "Enough talk. Orders have been given. Let's get to work."

She turns sharply and strides past me, heading toward the village half hidden in the trees.

The druids scatter to follow, their hurried steps crunching through the undergrowth. Mor wipes her hands on her tunic and falls into step behind them, muttering something about things getting interesting. Hypnos only exhales softly, his pearly eyes glinting faintly under the moonlight when he looks at me and nods once.

I stay where I am for a breath too long, fists tightening at my sides.

Then I follow.

The valley beneath Starfall's cliffs glows with the light of hundreds of lanterns.

The forest here is alive with motion—druids, sprites, and lesser fae spilling from the trees in a slow exodus. Carts creak under bundles of belongings, children clutch carved charms, wings shimmering under moonlight. The cliffs rise above them like dark sentinels, the stone humming faintly with old magic.

It's a mess of movement, voices, and confusion. The evacuees from the Enchanted Forest are settling wherever there's open ground, while the villagers of Starfall scramble to make room.

Hephaestus stands in the middle of it all, a map spread across a worktable dragged outside his forge. His booming voice carries over the din.

"If we're keepin' this many souls for more than a few nights, we'll be needin' proper shelter. The caves'll do for storin' supplies, but the slopes'll take small dwellin's—stone first, timber after."

His massive hands pin the map's corners, calloused fingers smudged with soot. He's already sketching lines for foundations, muttering measurements under his breath.

Hestia moves through the crowd nearby, her expression tight as she surveys the incoming line of refugees. She keeps her ledger tucked close to her chest, thumb sliding over the worn edge of the parchment. I can see the worry behind her calm façade—the silent count of mouths to feed against dwindling stores of herbs, grains, and tonics.

She says nothing about the most urgent shortage: the ingredients for the tonic she's been preparing for Tana's headaches.

A queen can't be seen faltering—not in front of fae eager to interpret weakness as opportunity.

And Hestia knows better than anyone that secrets, once spoken aloud, have a way of echoing through these halls.

Much like my own failing heart—another truth best left buried.

Tana stands opposite Hephaestus, looking down at the map as he marks the ridges and waterlines. She listens quietly, one hand braced on the edge of the table.

"Here," she says, tapping the parchment near the northern grove. "That's where the black water was found. It's moving this direction, toward the swamps."

"Ah, bright starlight shines upon our needs." Hestia exhales, relief softening her features. "Most of the supplies I need restocked grow along that path."

Tana seems pleased to hear it.

Mor, however, releases a sharp groan.

"Problem here?" Tana looks to our small, dark enchantress.

"That route runs near the domain of the mad wizard—

the one who thinks explosions are a form of art and trousers are optional."

Despite my mood, the comment pulls a halfhearted chuckle from me as I glance over Hestia's grain counts.

"A mad wizard?" Tana asks. "Merlin?"

She's only heard the name before—and benefited from his alchemy when she needed healing.

The memory of her bleeding in my arms, stabbed and broken by greedy lesser fae, assaults my mind. My fingers tighten unconsciously, and I crumple the parchment before I even realize it.

At the name, Hephaestus lets out a booming laugh. "Och, Merlin! Haven't seen that daft bastard in an age. He'll talk your ear clean off about some right mad shite, but he means no harm."

Mor snorts. "No harm? He nearly turned half the Mirevalis swamp to glass after eating some odd berries that made him 'piss from his ass' for three nocturns."

"Mor." Hestia scalds her tone, eyes flashing with reprimand.

Tana—mid-sip from a water skein—chokes and sputters.

"Those were his words, not ours." Mor mutters, crossing her arms. Her mouth flattens into a deep frown. "He's a menace with a death wish."

"He's brilliant," Hestia counters evenly, still studying the map. "Half the salves and tonics I use came from his old notes."

I clear my throat, eager to shift the focus away from the talk of lunatic wizards and berries. "We should send a few fae ahead," I say, keeping my tone even. "Foragers, trackers.

They can bring back supplies and a report on how far the contamination's spread before we move the others closer."

Hephaestus nods, already reaching for the charcoal. "Aye, sensible enough. I'll have—"

Tana raises a hand, cutting him off. "No."

The single word stills the entire table.

Her gaze fixes on the map again, tracing the path of the black water like she's already walking it in her mind. "I'll go myself," she says. "And Mor will come with me."

Mor grins faintly, as if she's been waiting for this. Then I realize she is just spotting the platters of food Hypnos is arriving with. I know one is for her, the other for the rest of us to share.

Hestia's head jerks up. "Your Grace, that's—"

Tana lifts her chin. "Necessary. If I'm to rule Avalon, I need to see it. All of it. Especially the parts that would rather stay hidden. I won't lead a realm I don't understand."

She's right.

Of course she's right.

But every muscle in my body goes rigid at the thought of her stepping beyond Starfall's wards—into the dark, into that.

I force my voice to stay calm. "The wards are too new. The water's corrupted. If the darkness has rooted itself there—"

"Then I'll see it myself," she cuts in, sharp but not unkind. "Secondhand reports won't do."

It's the first time she's spoken directly to me in nearly half a moon-cycle. Even if it's to overrule me, the sound still lands like a blade I'm almost grateful for.

I force the words I want to say back down where they

belong and incline my head instead. "As you wish, Your Grace."

Tana rolls the map closed and hands it to Hephaestus. "Get started building," she says. "I'll return with answers."

Then she turns—already walking away, already gone.

I watch her disappear into the dark beyond the forge's light, her silhouette framed by the silver glow spilling down the cliffs. The rational part of me tells me she's capable. The rest of me wants to drag her back by the wrist and lock every gate in Avalon behind her.

I settle for neither. I just stand there, listening to the sound of her boots fading toward Starfall until all that's left is the pulse of the realm and the steady, unwelcome ache behind my ribs.

Mor takes her platter and saunters after Tana, the bone still clutched between her teeth like a trophy.

Hephaestus and Hestia linger long enough to wrangle a handful of their children who've taken to chasing a wayward moonkit—a small, glowing creature with fur like mist and eyes too big for its head. Their laughter rings through the courtyard as Hephaestus scoops one child under each arm and Hestia mutters about discipline and bedtimes.

Then it's quiet again. Just me and Hypnos at the workbench, the map rolled and left on the table between us. Unrolling it, the moonlight catches on the inked lines, turning the black water's path into a thin silver scar.

I lean forward, bracing my hands on the edge of the table. "She shouldn't be going into that forest alone."

"She isn't alone," Hypnos says, his voice calm as always. "She has Mor."

"You know what I mean."

He tilts his head, those pale, sightless eyes turning toward me. "You can't keep her safe forever, Orion. If you try, you'll only stunt what she's meant to become."

I clench my jaw. "She is mortal."

"She is chosen," he corrects softly. "The realm saw something in her that even you cannot see yet. Let her find it. Let her bloom into the queen she is meant to be."

I look away, out toward the cliffs where the torches burn low and the shadows stretch long. "And if the darkness finds her first?"

Hypnos exhales, folding his hands behind his back. "Then she will fight. And if she falls…" His voice trails off, then steadies again. "You will know soon enough whether she was meant to rise."

The words settle between us like smoke—heavy, unavoidable.

He turns toward the forge, lights flickering in the distance. "Now come. Hephaestus could use a steady hand. We've more mouths to shelter than stars overhead."

I stay still for a breath, staring at the ink on the map until it blurs. Then I push away from the table and follow.

Because Hypnos is right. If I can't shield her, I can at least keep the rest of her realm from collapsing around her.

CHAPTER 7
tana

The ride from Starfall shouldn't feel different. We rode this same path the night before, the moon hanging in the same place, the same pines bowing under its silver weight.

But it does.

The road looks like it's aged a decade overnight. Grass that brushed the duskbanes' knees yesterday lies flat and gray now, as if frost scorched it. The air smells metallic, like rain that never fell. Even the stones underhoof have changed color—veined with something dark that wasn't there before.

A broken milestone at the fork confirms we're on the right path: a half-erased sigil of Avalon's crown, chiseled deep into the rock. I brush my fingers across it as we pass, half expecting it to burn. It's cold instead—too cold.

Mor rides ahead, her tiny frame dwarfed by her dusk-black stallion. As always, she's eating.

I can't even tell what it is this time—some dried fruit or candied root, glinting amber in the moonlight. Her shadows move around her like helpful spirits: one clears brush from her path, another plucks a burr from the horse's mane, a third holds a husk of bread aloft like an extra hand. A tendril of shadow breaks off two pieces, offering them to our horses, who accept them with grateful snorts.

She glances back at me and holds out a bit of the same sweet. "Hungry?"

I chuckle, shaking my head. "We just ate only an hour ago."

"Then how are you not starving?"

"I don't know where you put all that food," I mutter. "You eat more than Hephaestus—and he's built like a wall."

Mor shrugs, eyes dancing. "You would not want to see us when we are hungry."

Before I can answer, her features flicker. The whites of her eyes vanish into molten gold, her skin paling until veins rise dark beneath it. For an instant she looks diseased—dead—but there's power in it, coiled and ancient. The Morrigan. The other thing that lives inside her. If that's what it is.

Then it's gone. She looks normal again. Small. Smug. Terribly pleased with herself.

I laugh under my breath and shake my head. "Point taken."

We ride in silence for a while. The forest thickens, trees pressing close like they're listening. The moonlight cuts strange through the canopy—thicker, bending at the edges. It doesn't spill the way it should; it sticks, like honey on glass.

Something moves in it. Not the comforting curl of shadow I know from Orion—his darkness always breathes, tethered to pulse and intention. This one slithers, weightless and wrong.

I rein in beside Mor. "You and Orion both command shadow," I say. "So why can't either of you drive this back?"

Mor reaches out lazily, pinching a thread of darkness off

a passing fern. It wraps around her finger, smooth as silk, luminous in its blackness. "Because the Obscura isn't shadow," she says softly. "Not anymore. Our kind of darkness has shape—lattice, rhythm. The abyss listens when called."

She lets the strand slip free as one of her shadows drifts ahead and plucks at a strip of bark peeling from a nearby tree. It brings the piece to her like an offering. Even before she holds it toward me, I can see the infection crawling across it—veins of obsidian slick, shimmering faintly as though alive. My dusk-bane stamps, ears pinned back.

"But the Obscura? It does not listen. It only devours."

Even from this distance, I can feel it. Not like cold, not like heat—something stranger. It pulls, a pressure in my chest that wants to match its rhythm.

So the blight was once part of the forest's shadow, maybe even born from the same depths Orion calls to—but it's turned on itself, folded inward until it became hunger.

Mor's voice lowers. "See the difference? Shadow absorbs. This consumes."

I nod slowly, unable to look away. The bark collapses in her hand, crumbling to dust. Her shadow scatters it into the wind.

Whatever this is, it isn't night. It's night after it's died and come back wrong.

A shiver ripples through me, colder than the air. I shake it off, forcing the weight of Mor's words away.

The path ahead is half-swallowed by brush, branches knotted tight like the forest doesn't want us passing through. I slide Realmbreaker free from its scabbard, the steel catching moonlight as it sings out. The sound feels too loud, too clean for this place. I use it to cut a way forward, slicing through vines that cling as if alive.

Next to me, Mor finishes gnawing the last of her fruit and flicks the stripped core into the shadows. The moment it lands, one of her shadows scoops it up and buries it out of sight.

She catches the blade in my hand, glimmering. "How did you pull it?" she asks. "From the stone. How did you pull it? We tried several times—only to see if we could."

I pause mid-swing, looking down the line of the blade. It reflects the moon back at me, pale and unblinking. My face looks strange in it—foreign, fierce, and maybe a little lost.

"I don't know," I admit. "I pulled until my palms split... and then it just came out."

I let out a humorless laugh. "Maybe it was when I told the moon to kiss my ass."

Mor's gaze drifts to her own palms—small, scarred things. She rubs her thumb over one as if something burns beneath the skin. A memory.

The duskbanes bristle before I can ask. Both rear their heads, ears flattening, a low sound rumbling in their throats.

"What is it?" I whisper.

Mor doesn't answer. She's already looking forward, her entire posture sharpening into readiness.

I follow her gaze—and my stomach drops.

The village sprawled below us is gone. Or rather, what's left of it doesn't deserve the same name.

The cottages that stood whole yesterday are nothing but husks, roofs caved in like crushed chests. Smoke—or something like it—seeps from the remains, drifting sideways in a wind I can't feel. The well in the center of the square glows faintly, the stones slick with something dark that isn't water. The air hums, low and constant, like the sound a wounded creature makes when it's too weak to die.

Every surface writhes. Shadows crawl over walls, through open doors, down collapsed chimneys. Not quick, not frantic—slow, patient, claiming everything.

I taste copper on my tongue and realize I've bitten it.

"This was thriving yesterday," I say, my voice thinner than I intend. "Children. Markets. Music."

Mor says nothing. Her hand moves to the hilt of one of her blades. Her eyes never stop moving—windows, rooftops, the broken well, the beaten path beyond. Always scanning. Always waiting.

Mor conjures something from the air—a long staff forming out of pure shadow. The darkness threads together like smoke spun into glass, solidifying as she closes her fingers around it. The top curls into a hooked shape, a crescent echo of the moon above us. She holds it loosely, but her stance says otherwise. Ready. Expecting.

"Can you send word to Starfall?" I ask quietly.

Mor doesn't answer with words. She raises one hand, palm open to the sky. Darkness pools there, thick as ink, then lifts—swirling upward until it takes the shape of a bird.

A crow.

For a heartbeat it's only smoke, but then feathers begin to form, layer by layer, until it looks real enough that I could reach out and touch it. Each plume catches the faintest shimmer of silver, and I can feel the magic in it—ancient and heavy, vibrating through the air like thunder muffled in cloth.

Mor's lips never move, but I can tell she's speaking to it all the same. The connection hums between them—soundless, telepathic. The crow's head twitches toward the ruins below, taking in the sight of the decimated village before it beats its wings once, twice, and shoots into the night—a streak of dark light heading toward Starfall.

"Let's check things out," I say, lowering my voice. "But be careful."

Mor hums a quiet acknowledgment. "Do not wander too far," she says. "We would rather not deal with a fussy Orion should something happen to the realm's chosen."

I roll my eyes, ignoring the small twist her words cause in my chest. "I can handle myself."

She doesn't answer—just smirks and starts forward.

We pick our way through the ruins. The silence is smothering—the kind that eats sound instead of holding it. The village feels abandoned but not empty. The air is thick with the residue of something unseen, like dust that clings to skin after a fire.

My gaze drifts toward the water. The dark stream cuts through the village's edge, running faster than it should. I could swear it's higher than yesterday—rising inch by inch, like the realm itself is swelling from within. The thought chills me, but not as much as the sight of the wards.

I step closer to the boundary where Orion's sigils glowed last night. My breath fogs in front of me. The wards still shimmer faintly, visible only in the corners of my eyes— flickers of silver and blue, fragile threads woven through the air.

It's the same feeling I used to get back home when I hunted vampires and werewolves—the shimmer of something unnatural, a second heartbeat under the world's skin.

I can see the magic here. And I can see what's killing it.

The Obscura have eaten holes straight through the lattice. Not large, not yet—but spreading, like rust consuming metal. The more I look, the more I realize the entire perimeter is riddled with them.

"We'll need High Fae here," I call to Mor. "Someone to replenish the wards before they collapse completely."

She nods, already a few strides away, her shadows circling like wolves. Another crow forms in her palm and takes flight—another silent messenger winging toward the castle.

The air feels heavier now. Still. Too still.

Movement catches at the corner of my eye.

I turn toward the dark water. Its surface ripples, faint and deliberate. Nothing else moves. The horses are silent. The trees stand dead still.

I draw Realmbreaker, the blade whispering against its scabbard. My pulse pounds in my ears as I watch, waiting for another disturbance. But there's nothing—no form, no shadow, just that faint current twisting like smoke through ink.

Is it the darkness itself flowing here? Or something living within it?

A pull hums low in my chest—compulsion, curiosity, something that doesn't feel entirely mine. My body moves before my mind can catch up.

I kneel beside the water, the ground damp beneath my

knees. My hand reaches out, slow as if caught in a spell. I know I should stop, that I should call to Mor, but I can't.

The surface ripples in invitation.

My fingertip breaks it.

And then—

A brilliant white light explodes behind my eyes, searing through my mind like fire through glass.

CHAPTER 8
tana

The moment my fingertip grazes the black water, the world detonates.

A white light sears through my mind—pure, blinding, absolute. It isn't light the way the moon shines or lightning flashes; this is light that hurts, light that rips through bone and thought alike.

I think I'm screaming. I can feel the shape of it in my throat, raw and endless, but I can't hear a thing. The world has gone silent—sound vacuumed out of it. Only the vibration remains, shaking me apart from the inside.

My hands convulse. My body jerks. Every muscle locks until I can't tell if I'm still kneeling or if the ground has dropped away from me. My fingers no longer obey me. My skin doesn't feel like mine.

It's as if something pries me open from within.

Then, suddenly—silence inside the silence.

The light dims, pulling itself inward until it becomes a thin, pulsing thread before collapsing entirely, leaving behind a black so deep it swallows my breath.

And within that dark... a shape begins to form.

At first it's just a smudge against the void, then a silhouette—shoulders, hair, the tilt of a head. A woman.

I should be alarmed. I should reach for *Realmbreaker*, should ready myself for a fight. But my limbs don't move.

I'm held still—frozen not by fear but by recognition I can't explain.

The figure steps closer. Light gathers around her like mist drawn to her skin.

She carries a sword. Long, slender, gleaming—the twin to mine. The same runes etched down its length, the same curved crossguard kissed with moonlight.

Realmbreaker.

Not a twin—it *is* Realmbreaker.

My breath shudders out of me, a whisper swallowed by the dark.

She's not just holding it. She's wielding it. And somehow, impossibly, I know—this woman isn't a stranger.

She's the reason the blade sings in my hand.

The gleam of silver takes shape first—faint at the edges, then burning bright until it blinds me. It shines like moonlight made solid, a beacon in the storm of night around her.

Her form sharpens from the ground up, beginning at the silver boots planted firm in the soil. Her stance is wide, unyielding—defiant. Around her, the world burns. Smoke rises from the ground in heavy plumes, dark and thick, as if the earth itself were venting its rage. The air hums with the sound of a dying battlefield.

I can still feel the scream tearing through my throat, my body trembling as if I'm the one standing in that ruin. The sound isn't mine anymore—it's hers.

Her arm lifts in slow motion, and my body mirrors it against my will. I can feel every muscle move as if strings pull from within me.

Shadows coil around her, spinning fast—an obsidian storm swirling at the edges of her light. Each rotation tightens the world, pressing inward until the pressure makes my lungs seize. The darkness feels alive, a thousand hands clawing at her silver light, trying to drag it down.

Her chest plate catches what little illumination there is, runes rippling faintly across its surface like light on water. Silver shoulders rise and fall with measured power—the calm before something cataclysmic.

She's holding something in one arm, but the shadows surge between us, thick and violent, blotting the sight away. The impact of it slams into me, making my vision fracture. I reel back, eyes squeezing shut against the pain.

When I force them open again, the storm has thinned.

The woman's face emerges from the smoke.

And I know it.

The hair—wild and glorious, a dark halo spilling past her shoulders like a living storm. The height—tall, strong, as if the ground itself bends to hold her weight. The mouth, the eyes, the proud line of her jaw.

My breath catches.

It's my mother.

Her face—my mother's face—is streaked with ash and sweat. A smear of blood glistens at the corner of her split lip. And her eyes—god, her eyes—burn like fire trapped in amber.

She's not screaming. Her lips are moving, forming words I can't hear but somehow feel. Each syllable rolls through me, vibrating in my bones like thunder beneath the skin.

The sword in her hand gleams silver-bright as she raises it overhead, the runes along its blade pulsing like a heartbeat. Then it comes down—not to strike, but to anchor.

The tip of *Realmbreaker* plunges toward the ground.

The moment before it hits, I feel it—the rip of magic, vast and raw, tearing through the fabric of the realm. It surges outward, a tidal wave of power that catches my breath, my blood, everything that's mine.

She's facing me still—my mother—her gaze locked to mine even as the world quakes around her. Those dark eyes, so much like my own, bore straight through me.

The sword meets the earth.

A shock of white light erupts—brighter, hotter, more violent than before. It sears through me, tearing me loose from the vision. My scream catches somewhere between body and soul, silent in the void.

The battlefield rips away. The smoke, the fire, the ash —gone.

Only moonlight remains.

It wraps around me, thick and fluid, like water made of light. I can feel it surging, dragging at me, pulling me upward—or maybe outward. The sensation is dizzying, like being caught in a rip current of pure luminescence.

I reach for something, anything to hold on to, but there's nothing solid left. I'm being wrenched from her—from the storm—from the sight of my mother standing alone on that broken field.

And behind her—something moves.

I can feel it there, vast and terrible, unseen but impossibly close. The air itself bends toward it, bending around it. Every instinct in me screams to turn, to look, because whatever it is—whatever she was facing—feels like the key to everything.

But I don't get the chance.

The light convulses.

A single word rips through the silence—clear and resounding, echoing through every part of me.

Morgause.

Then the moonlight collapses into itself, and the world goes black.

CHAPTER 9

orion

The hammering helps.

The noise, the rhythm, the strain in my shoulders as I lift each beam into place. It keeps my thoughts from drifting where they shouldn't.

Hephaestus works beside me, the last of the Flameborn. Eight feet of scarred bronze and molten patience. His people burned with their realm in the Titan War, and he's carried their fire alone ever since.

Around us, the lower ridge of the valley hums with motion. Refugees from the southern reaches spill into the clearing beneath Starfall, families fleeing from the edges of the Enchanted Forest before the blight can reach their doors. We build for them now: fresh dwellings, warm fires, safety.

I focus on the sound: the slam of the hammer, the hiss of the forge in the distance, the scrape of tools over stone. It's the closest thing to peace I can manage.

We build for the refugees.

We take in harvests meant for the castle.

We send envoys back for more.

Anything to keep from thinking about the queen I can't seem to stop thinking about.

A shift in the wind draws my attention to the lake beyond the trees. The water churns, gray and violent beneath a darkening sky. It's angry today, the way it gets when a storm is coming, or when something in Avalon is about to break.

Then I feel a pull.

Not the wind, not the water. The Lady.

Her call starts as a hum deep in my chest, threading through my ribs and tightening behind my sternum. My gaze drifts toward the rocky cliffs on the lake's edge, where the entrance to her sanctum lies half hidden in shadow.

I wipe the sweat from my brow and toss the hammer aside. "I'll return," I tell Hephaestus. He grunts but doesn't look up.

The path down to the shoreline is narrow, carved from centuries of waves battering the stone. The cliffs rise sharp to my left, jagged and unforgiving. To my right, the lake lashes itself against the rocks, froth and spray catching the wind.

It's restless. No, it's raging.

I've seen the lake calm, glassy as a mirror. But not today. Today it feels alive.

I pause at the water's edge and look toward the horizon, where the first flashes of distant lightning stain the clouds. The storm is building, rolling toward the very path Tana will be traveling.

She'll be in the middle of it.

For a heartbeat, I consider going after her, mounting Omen and flying on the Shadowmare's back, finding Tana before the storm does. But the pull grows stronger, sharp enough to make me grit my teeth.

The Lady's call isn't something one ignores.

By the time I reach the grotto, the light has dimmed to the soft glow of storm dusk. The cave breathes with its own rhythm, the air thick with enchantment and echoing whispers. The runes carved into the walls shimmer faintly as I step inside, casting reflections across the wet stone.

I can feel her presence before I see her.

Every part of me goes tense. The last time she summoned me, she showed me Avalon's death. Over and over. The same ruin, the same flames, the same shadows devouring everything I've sworn to protect.

But that wasn't all she showed me.

Eventually, she showed me her.

The mortal who would draw the sword.

The woman who would become our queen.

Tana.

And now that she is here, flesh and blood and fury, the Lady calls again.

I know better than to fight it.

I step deeper into the Sanctum of Echoes, into the mouth of the storm and the heart of whatever truth she means to show me next.

The air changes as soon as I step into the heart of the sanctum.

The water that pools here doesn't ripple; it breathes. Slow and steady, like the lung of a god. A low hum reverberates through the cavern, vibrating against my ribs.

Then her voice comes.

Not a sound exactly, more a thought made of water and light.

Orion of Starfall.

The ripples spread outward from the center of the lake,

glowing faintly as they go. The water rises, twisting upward until it takes the shape of a woman draped in moonlight. The weight of her gaze could turn the tides.

I drop to one knee out of instinct. Not reverence. Necessity. Her power crushes the air around me.

You would know the cost.

Her words aren't spoken; they bloom behind my eyes. The cave around us flickers, stone and water replaced by flashes of color and sound that don't belong to this realm.

I see her.

Tana.

She stands in a storm of silver light, hair whipping around her, her face drawn in determination and something else: fear. Her hand grips *Realmbreaker,* but the sword's glow falters, dimming with every beat of her mortal heart.

Then another sound. A second pulse. Mine.

The rhythm syncs with hers. One heartbeat. Two. Together.

The Lady's voice swells.

A life for a life. A heart for a heart.

The vision twists. The storm thickens, swallowing the ground beneath Tana's feet. I reach for her, but she's already fading, the color draining from her skin. My own chest tightens, breath turning ragged. I can feel her heartbeat faltering, and mine stumbling to match.

Pain lances through me. My knees hit the stone.

Mortality is a fragile thing, she whispers, though her mouth never moves. *She was not made for this realm. Its magic feeds her even as it devours her.*

Images flash: Tana falling to her knees, light bleeding from her like spilled moonfire. I see my own hand reaching for her, pressed over her heart. The instant my palm touches her chest, her pulse steadies.

Your flame is bound to hers. Your life to her breath.

The realization hits like a blade to the gut.

It's not just magic. It's a bond, old and irrevocable. Something primal that predates the fae themselves.

One will not beat without the other.

Her words echo, sinking deep.

The scene changes again: my reflection in water, eyes burning bright, veins threaded with silver light. Tana's image shimmers beside mine. Our chests rise in unison. One heart. One rhythm.

The Lady's presence surrounds me, cool and endless.

You have known this truth. Denied it. Fought it. But it was sealed the moment your shadows touched.

The pain recedes, replaced by something else: terror wrapped in awe.

"A soul bond," I whisper.

The Lady inclines her head.

A gift. A curse. A choice yet to come.

The water shudders, the vision beginning to unravel.

If she remains mortal, her heart will falter. If she becomes fae, she will live. But the bond will bind you both. Life for life. Death for death.

I try to speak, but my throat locks. The light consumes the grotto, washing everything in silver-white radiance.

Remember, the Lady murmurs, fading into mist. *A heart for a heart, Orion of Nightfall. The realm has chosen its balance.*

The vision collapses, and I fall to my hands, gasping.

When I finally lift my head, the sanctum is still again—

dark, quiet, the lake calm as glass. But my heart hasn't slowed. It beats too hard, too fast. Not from fear.

From her.

Somewhere far from here, I can feel her pulse answering mine.

And for the first time, I understand what the Lady's vision truly means.

If her heart stops, so will mine.

The echoes fade, but the silence that follows feels alive.

It crawls into my chest, sits heavy against my ribs.

My heart is still racing, refusing to calm, as if it remembers what the Lady showed me even when my mind tries to forget.

A life for a life. A heart for a heart.

Fate has tied us together.

If her pulse falters, mine will follow.

But if she rises... so will I.

The thought unsteadies me more than the vision itself.

For ages I've lived with the certainty of my own death. My heart has always been a ticking curse, each beat borrowed, each breath a warning. My mother died of it. My grandmother too.

At least, that's what I believed.

Until I learned the truth: that it wasn't weakness or blood that killed them, but Demeter's hand.

Still, I grew up believing I was made to die young.

And when you know the end is written, you learn to build walls.

You learn not to love—and worse, you make sure no one loves you.

It's easier that way.

Cleaner.

Because grief doesn't belong to the dying.

It belongs to the ones left behind.

I've spent my life making sure no one would have to grieve me.

But now—

I stare into the lake's mirrored surface. It stares back, silver and cruel, reflecting the tremor in my hands.

The vision showed me more than her fall. It showed me a chance I was never meant to have.

Not immortality. Not truly.

But something rarer.

A shared fate.

If she dies, I will follow.

But if she rises—if she claims what Avalon offers—then I will rise too, not because she grants it, but because fate decided we were the same story written in two hearts.

For the first time in an endless life of waiting to die, I feel something I shouldn't.

Hope.

It's a dangerous thing.

Because the vision didn't just show her ascension. It showed her falling.

Tana's body sinking into the black water, her light extinguished, her heart stilled.

If that future comes to pass, I won't outlive her.

Not by a single breath.

The Lady's whisper lingers in the air, soft and merciless.

The realm has chosen its balance.

I drag in a breath and look down at my reflection, at the faint ripple that cuts across it like a scar.

If she dies, I die.

But if she rises...

I will rise with her.

And for the first time in all my years, death no longer feels inevitable.

It feels negotiable.

CHAPTER 10
tana

The world slams back into me like a breaking wave. I hit the shoreline hard—stone and sand biting into my palms—as water gushes from my lungs. I'm gasping, choking, dragging in air that burns like fire. My stomach heaves, bile and water spilling between desperate breaths.

Everything hurts. My skull feels split open, my chest tight, my eyes still filled with light that isn't there anymore.

When I finally manage to lift my head, Mor is standing a few feet away, dripping from head to toe, soaked and—god help me—furious.

"Are you out of your damn mind?" she snaps, her voice sharp enough to slice through the fog in my head. "Diving into a river of darkness? What in the blighted moon possessed you?"

I can barely speak through the coughing, but I manage, "I didn't—dive. It—pulled me."

Her glare could melt iron. "It pulled you because you touched it. You're lucky it didn't drag your soul down with it."

I sit back on my heels, trembling, water dripping from my hair into my eyes. I barely hear her. My mind is still somewhere else—back in that storm of light and smoke and silver.

"My mother," I whisper.

Mor blinks. "What?"

"I saw her." I clutch my arms around myself, shivering though I can still feel the ghost of heat under my skin. "She was here, Mor. In armor. Silver like moonlight. She was—fighting. Bleeding." I swallow hard. "And she looked at me. She saw me."

Mor's expression shifts—irritation fading into something quieter, sharper. "You're sure it was not a trick of the darkness?"

"No." My voice breaks. "It wasn't darkness. Not Obscura. It was moonlight. The same as the realm's light, the same as..." I look toward the night sky, so calm and shining with brilliant stars. "I think the moon—or the realm—showed me something. A memory. A vision from the past."

Mor folds her arms, her dripping shadows slithering back around her feet. "Visions are not given lightly. What did you see?"

"A battlefield. Smoke. The sword..." I close my eyes and see it again—the flash of the blade sinking into the earth, the light consuming everything. "There was something else—"

I frown, trying to grasp the fading echo of the word. It lingers on my tongue like the taste of lightning.

"Morgause."

Mor tilts her head. "What is that?"

"I don't know." I look up at her, desperate. "A name, maybe. Or a place. Does it mean anything to you? Anything from your realm?"

She shakes her head slowly. "No. It's nothing of ours."

"But—'Mor.'" I gesture toward her. "The Morrigan."

Her mouth tightens. "Mor is a moniker of our people. The Morrigan. It isn't one of us," she says flatly. "After the fall of the Morrigan, we are all that remains. Morgause—whatever that name means—it's not from our line, nor our gods."

The answer leaves me hollow. I stare at the lake again, at the calm, glassy surface hiding something vast beneath. The air feels wrong here, still charged, as if the vision hasn't entirely released me.

My mother. Here. In Avalon. Wearing armor and wielding *Realmbreaker* before it was mine.

It doesn't make sense.

She wasn't fae. She was just—a human. A wife. A mother.

She never could have.

Right?

The thought lodges in my chest, heavy and cold as stone.

If the realm showed me her, then maybe everything I thought I knew about who I am—and what I come from—isn't true at all.

The air still smells of the dark water as we ride away, our duskbanes kicking up sprays of mud along the bank. Mor hasn't said a word since we left the ruined village, but I can feel her irritation radiating like heat. She's all sharp edges and clipped reins, jaw set tight. Every few minutes she mutters something under her breath that sounds suspiciously like a curse.

"Still angry?" I ask finally.

She doesn't look at me. "We would call it... concern, if you hadn't decided to swim in a river of corruption."

I snort. "I didn't decide to swim. It decided for me."

Her golden eyes flick my way, unimpressed. "You mortals and your excuses."

I let it go. She's still prickly—and honestly, I can't blame her.

We follow the dark river upstream, the steady thrum of hooves against wet soil filling the silence. The terrain grows rougher as we ride—slopes steepening, trees thinning. I pull a small map from my satchel, trying to match the bends of the river to the rough sketches Hypnos gave me before we left Starfall. I mark the places where the flow narrows, the spots where the soil changes color, the faint shimmer of corruption still seeping from beneath the moss.

I'll need to talk to Hypnos about this when we get back. He'll know if the ley lines near here have shifted.

As we climb higher, the river shrinks with every turn— first a deep, churning vein, then a narrow creek, then a thin thread of water twisting over stones. The sound of it softens until only a faint trickle remains.

And then... nothing.

I pull my duskbanes to a stop. The stream disappears into the ground, a small bubbling spring pushing up from beneath Avalon's soil.

"This can't be right," I murmur, sliding off the saddle. "This is the source?"

Mor dismounts as well, her boots squelching in the mud. She crouches beside the spring, dipping her hand in. Steam curls faintly around her fingers. "The druids said the river appeared overnight."

"Overnight rivers don't exist," I mutter, kneeling beside her. "There's no lake feeding it. No rainfall. Just this."

The water slips from my fingers, cold as starlight. I

frown, looking around. To the west, the swamps of Merivalis stretch in a dark haze, slick and endless. Behind us, the Enchanted Forest rises—alive and listening. And far beyond that, back the way we came, lies Starfall.

We're standing on the border of everything and nothing —where Avalon's pulse begins to slow.

It doesn't make sense. This trickle couldn't feed the river we saw. It couldn't carve through entire villages. Something else must be feeding it, hidden beneath the soil, deep enough even the realm's magic can't trace.

A headache starts behind my eyes, sharp and pulsing. I rub my temples, trying to shake it off.

Since crossing out of Starfall's wards, the headaches have come more often—each one worse than the last. Hestia said it's because I'm fighting it, keeping the realm's magic out. I don't mean to. I just... don't know how to let it in.

The magic knocks at the edges of me, patient and relentless, waiting for permission I don't know how to give.

Something flickers at the corner of my vision. I turn my head fast. Nothing there. Only the grass swaying.

Then—movement again. A ripple through the shadows. Always just out of sight.

Mor's head lifts sharply. "We are hunting."

Before I can ask what, she's already dismounted, stomping into the trees with all the grace of a thunderstorm. Her short legs have to lift high to clear the grass, and the image almost makes me smile. Almost.

I sigh and glance out across the wastelands. The horizon bleeds gold and violet; evenfall is coming fast. My limbs ache from the day's ride, and the cold bite of the river still clings to my bones.

While Mor hunts whatever has caught her attention, I swing down from Havoc and gather what dry wood I can find. The simple rhythm—stacking branches, striking flint—steadies me.

The first spark catches, licking upward into a small flame.

"If I know the dark enchantress," I mutter, feeding the fire until it glows bright, "she'll bring back enough for a feast."

The warmth reaches my fingers, and for the first time since I saw my mother's face in the moonlight, I let myself breathe.

The fire burns steady, a lone glow in a sea of shadow.

But the air has changed, and a chill races down my back.

We stopped to hunt.

But it feels like we're about to find out something is hunting us back.

It's first shade, the beginning of the next nocturn, and the sky is still heavy with the color of sleep.

I didn't get any.

Every time I close my eyes, I see her.

The battlefield. The silver armor. The blood.

The slow-motion reel of my mother's face over and over until the memory feels burned into me.

Only she didn't look like my mother.

In the vision, there was a scar, thin and pale, running from her cheek to her jaw. My mother never had a scar.

And the ears... god, the ears.

Pointed. Fae.

It shouldn't be possible. She was human. She raised me human.

Unless she wasn't.

Unless everything I thought I knew about her was a lie.

Could it have been a glamour? Like the one Orion used on me during Demeter's trial, softening my features, lengthening my ears so the court would see what they wanted? Could my mother have done the same? Hidden herself from the realm? From me?

None of it makes sense, no matter how I turn it over.

Mor hasn't said a word all morning, but she doesn't look like she slept either. Her shadows curl lazily at her heels while she finishes tying down the duskbanes' saddlebags. I swear I heard her roasting something in the dark hours, some small Avalonian hare or whatever creature is foolish enough to hop near her campfire.

I stretch, bones aching, and break the silence.

"Hope my tossing and turning didn't keep you awake."

Mor doesn't look up. "We do not sleep."

I blink. "You mean... you didn't last night?"

She swings herself onto her duskbane, movements efficient, practiced. "No. Ever. We do not require it."

I pause, halfway through tightening my saddle strap. "Wait. Like—ever, ever?"

"Ever," she confirms, matter-of-fact. "One of us always seems to be awake."

That sends a small shiver down my spine. "One of you?"

Her expression doesn't change, but I catch the faintest flicker of a smile. "It is easier not to explain before breakfast."

I let out a breath somewhere between a laugh and a sigh. "Right. Add that to the list of things I'll never understand about you."

Mor's shadows rise like smoke as she guides her mount forward. "We prefer it that way."

We ride in silence after that. The quiet feels heavy—not unfriendly, just the kind that belongs to two people used to keeping their thoughts to themselves. The longer route takes us along the old trade path, winding between low hills and twisted trees. It's slower, but it will bring us past all the places we need to forage for Hestia's supplies.

The misting realm of the fae lives up to its name tonight. Fog rolls thick as wool through the valleys, so dense I can hardly see the road in front of us. Our duskbanes' hooves splash through the puddles forming beneath us, their breath puffing out in quick, sharp clouds.

The weather turns worse with every mile. What begins as a fine mist becomes a steady drizzle, then a cold, needling rain that clings to our skin and armor.

Mor shifts in her saddle, irritation practically radiating from her. "We should turn back. The realm itself is telling us to."

"How far to the flowering fields?" I ask, squinting through the downpour.

"Too far in this storm," she says.

"Then we're close enough."

She makes a noise between a growl and a sigh. "You are stubborn, mortal queen."

"Not stubborn," I mutter, tugging my cloak tighter around me. "Desperate. This is the last thing Hestia needs for the tonic, and I'm not showing up empty-handed because I was afraid of a little weather."

Mor gives me a long, unimpressed look. The rain dripping from her lashes makes her seem even more otherworldly, like the storm itself is afraid to touch her.

But she says nothing more, and we push on.

The drizzle becomes a deluge. The wind howls, driving the rain sideways. My cloak clings to my legs, my hair plastered to my face. Every few seconds, thunder cracks so loud it shakes the ground beneath us. Lightning forks across the sky, white and violent, searing through the fog.

Mor's voice cuts through the roar of the storm. "This is madness! We should seek shelter before—"

"We're almost there!" I shout back, forcing my horse up the slick rise ahead.

The crest of the hill appears like a phantom through the haze, and beyond it, the field.

Or what should be the field.

We crest the ridge, and my stomach drops.

The rolling meadow that Hestia described, the one that should be alive with golden blossoms swaying in the night breeze, is barren. Just soaked earth and broken stems stretching as far as I can see.

The rain hammers down harder, drumming against the emptiness.

I slide off Havoc before Mor can stop me, boots sinking into the mud as I stumble toward where the flowers should be. I drop to my knees, pushing aside handfuls of wet grass. Nothing. Not even a single bud.

My heart pounds against my ribs. "They're gone," I whisper, rain running down my cheeks, indistinguishable from tears. "All of them."

Mor dismounts behind me, the storm flashing white around her as she surveys the devastation. Her voice is low, grim. "This field has stood for ages. Even fire could not wipe it clean."

I shake my head, unable to look away from the empty soil. "Someone did this."

Thunder cracks again, closer this time—too close—and for a moment, I swear the lightning answers me.

The wind tears through the field, whipping strands of my soaked hair into my face. The rain can't explain this. Neither can rot or disease or time.

These flowers weren't destroyed.

They were picked.

Every last stem cut clean, the roots left untouched. Whoever did it knew exactly what they were taking.

A cold fury slides through me.

The High Fae.

Scheming. Always scheming.

If even one of them learned about my headaches, about Hestia's tonic, this would be the simplest way to remind me what I am here: mortal, dependent, vulnerable. They couldn't strike me outright, not while the realm still whispers its favor. But this?

This is how they fight.

I dig my fingers into the mud, the rain running cold down my spine.

"They were taken," I say, voice rough. "Not burned. Not drowned. Taken."

Mor's gaze flicks toward me, sharp and knowing. "By whom?"

I look up at the dark horizon. "Who do you think?"

Thunder answers before she can. A brutal, cracking roar that splits the sky.

I flinch, instinctively looking up—and then freeze.

Lightning rips across the clouds in a jagged web, white and blinding. For a heartbeat, the whole world glows, washed in silver.

And something in me stirs.

It isn't fear.

It's recognition.

The air hums against my skin, the scent of ozone thick in the back of my throat. I can feel it—alive, aware—like it's looking back at me.

A pulse of light flashes again, brighter this time, and my heart kicks hard in my chest, answering it.

Orion.

His name moves through me like a current, sharp and electric, the pull of something tethered across distance and storm.

The lightning crashes again, closer, and I swear I can hear it whispering his voice.

Starling.

The ground trembles beneath my knees. Mor's shadows flare in warning, circling her like a shield.

"Stay close," she orders, eyes narrowing at the sky. "That's no ordinary storm."

I rise slowly, the rain stinging my face, my hand instinctively finding the hilt of *Realmbreaker.* "No," I breathe. "It's not."

Because whatever this storm is, it knows me.

And something inside me is answering back.

We can do nothing with a field stripped bare. The soil holds no answers, only the ghosts of what should have been here.

Mor reins her duskbane around, her expression unreadable under the curtain of rain. "We need to move. This storm isn't natural."

I glance back once more at the empty field and nod. "Let's go."

We angle south, trying to cut around the edge of the storm, but the rain only grows heavier. The wind shrieks through the trees, bending branches until they creak and groan. We ride until my muscles ache, until even the duskbanes' hooves splash through puddles we've already crossed.

It hits me after the third turn through the same thicket.

"We're going in circles."

Mor's shadows lash out, frustrated, tasting the air like snakes. "It's growing."

I wipe the rain from my eyes. "Or it's following us."

Lightning cracks so close the air burns white. The scent of ozone floods my lungs. One bolt hits the ground a few yards away with a deafening roar. The duskbanes rear in panic—Mor's steed kicking high on its hind legs before bolting, leaving a trail of fire where its hooves strike the ground.

"Mor!" I shout, but my voice is devoured by thunder.

Havoc dances beneath me, restless, half wild. Another flash tears the sky open, the boom hitting a breath later— and he rears hard, ripping the reins from my grip.

"Damn it—Havoc!"

He bolts after Mor's horse, a streak of motion swallowed by the storm.

I hit the ground hard, mud splattering up my side. For a moment, all I can hear is the rain—the relentless drumming of it, the thunder pounding through my chest.

I push to my knees, soaked through and shaking. My cloak clings like a weight, dragging me down. I yank it off and hurl it into the mud.

"Fine!" I shout into the wind, voice raw. "Have it your way!"

The storm answers with a growl that rattles the earth.

Lightning flashes again, so bright it paints the world in silver and shadow.

I spin, squinting through the downpour. We've walked

the storm's edges half the night, but it hasn't moved an inch. It's anchored, fixed above something.

Or someone.

My fingers tighten around *Realmbreaker's* hilt. "Is this you, Orion?" I whisper. "A test? Or the realm itself?"

Thunder rolls low, almost like a laugh.

I raise the blade, gripping it with both hands, the rain sliding down the steel like liquid light.

Another strike splits the sky—and from the crest of the hill, the storm finally shows me its heart.

Through the sheets of rain, beyond the trembling trees, a spire pierces the horizon—a tower, black stone and impossible height, stabbing straight into the heavens.

And above it, the storm churns in perfect circles, a vortex of light and fury coiled tight around its peak.

The wind tears at me, wild and alive, and for a moment I could swear it's whispering my name.

I lift my sword toward the tower, the lightning answering like a challenge accepted.

"Then let's see what you're hiding."

CHAPTER 12
tana

The storm pulls at me like a thread woven through my ribs, tugging me forward, deeper into the forest.

Each step sinks into the wet earth, my boots sliding through the mud and moss, the air alive with the taste of rain and something sharper: lightning. It doesn't just split the sky; it thrums under my skin, wrapping around my pulse like it recognizes me.

The feeling isn't unfamiliar.

I know this lightning—in the way Orion's shadows crackle when he's angry, in the way his gaze burns hotter than it should. The energy rolling through this storm carries him. The storm is him: brooding, relentless, impossibly proud.

He's following me.

He thinks I'm not capable.

The thought makes something hot spark beneath my ribs.

Branches whip against my arms as I push through the last stretch of trees, the wind screaming through the canopy above. The clearing opens suddenly, and there it is—the tower.

It rises from the forest floor like it's grown there, black stone slick with rain, climbing so high its crown disappears into the storm's gut. Lightning forks around it in circles, striking close but never touching the stone, like the tower itself commands the sky.

The power rolling through the air is almost physical—an ache against my bones, a pressure in my chest. I can feel the echo of him in it, pulsing steady as a heartbeat.

"Orion."

His name leaves my mouth on a breath, swept away by the wind.

I step closer, tilting my head back until the rain burns against my eyes. "If you're going to test me, then do it to my face!" I shout up into the storm. "You don't get to hide behind lightning and thunder and call it protection!"

The clouds churn above me, darker, angrier. The storm answers, but not with words. The next bolt slams into the ground yards away, close enough to send a rush of heat up my legs.

"Fine!" I yell, gripping *Realmbreaker's* hilt with both hands. "If you won't come down—then I'll come to you."

The tower hums in response, the stones trembling as another ripple of light rolls across the clouds.

I look up again. Lightning flashes once—brief, blinding—and through it I catch the outline of a figure pacing behind the single high window near the top.

A shape. A man.

My heart twists, traitorously hopeful.

But when the light fades, the window is dark again.

The storm growls above me, low and alive.

"All right then," I mutter, wiping the rain from my face. "We'll do it your way."

I sheath my sword, square my shoulders, and step to the

tower's base. Setting my hand to the first hold, I start to climb.

And it's brutal.

The rain hits like handfuls of gravel, each drop sharp against my skin. The stone is slick as glass, every handhold a prayer and a promise to regret later. My arms ache from the strain, my fingers slipping on the wet rock as the wind howls against me.

I've climbed worse—mountain faces, fortress walls— but never with the sky itself trying to throw me off.

Thunder rolls through the tower, a sound that feels alive, bone-deep. Lightning forks across the clouds, tracing crooked veins of white light that creep closer with every strike. Warning shots.

It's not trying to kill me.

It's trying to make me stop.

"Typical," I mutter, hauling myself another few feet up. "Of course you'd use theatrics, Orion. You're a damn prima donna—"

A crack of lightning slams into the tower just above me, sparks cascading down in a brilliant arc. I flinch, nearly losing my grip, and snarl up at the sky.

"—and a princess while we're at it!"

The wind howls louder, the storm's voice a mix of rage and laughter.

I grit my teeth, dragging myself higher until I find a narrow ledge barely wide enough for both feet. I press my back to the cold wall, chest heaving, the world spinning from the climb.

My heart beats too fast, painfully loud beneath my ribs.

The scabbard at my hip catches against the stone, jerking me sideways. "Damn it." I shift, trying to readjust, but the strap's twisted, the sword jabbing into my ribs.

For one reckless second, I consider throwing it down.

It would be lighter. Easier.

But the thought of being unarmed out here—with this storm snarling above me—snaps me back.

I reach for the hilt instead, pulling *Realmbreaker* free. The blade gleams, water streaming off it like mercury.

That's when I feel the shift in the air.

The hum—deep, resonant, alive.

I look up.

A streak of light flashes across the clouds, too direct, too deliberate. The hair on my arms stands straight, every nerve in my body screaming *incoming*.

The bolt doesn't strike the tower; it aims for me.

I can feel it choose me, the static building, guiding its path. There's no time to think.

Instinct takes over.

I raise the sword, both hands gripping tight, the blade angled just in front of me—the only shield I have.

The world goes white.

The sound isn't thunder; it's impact. Light slams into steel, into me. The force surges through my arms, through my chest, crackling under my skin. I expect pain, fire, death.

But instead...it settles.

The current races through me, a soldier awaiting orders, obedient, steady. Power hums in my blood, familiar as breath.

My hands shake—not from fear, but power.

This... I know.

This I can work with.

Another charge builds, different now that I can feel it coming. The static thickens, crawling across my skin like a thousand invisible fingers. The air tastes of iron and rain.

I know what to look for this time: the moment the sky goes white, the breath between thunder and strike.

When it comes, I lift *Realmbreaker*. The metal hums, alive and ready, as if it's bracing with me.

The lightning hits.

It detonates against the blade in a burst of white fire, the impact cracking through the air so violently it steals my breath. For an instant, the world dissolves into sound and light—then the energy ricochets off the sword, snapping back toward the clouds in a furious streak.

It slams into the heart of the storm, and the whole sky shudders.

The lightning disperses across the dark expanse, crackling like shattered glass. And for a heartbeat—just one—I swear I feel it recoil.

A yelp.

A jolt of surprise, almost wounded.

The storm didn't expect me to fight back.

I grin through the rain, wild and breathless. "Yeah, didn't see that coming, did you?"

Another strike builds. I can sense it gathering now, smell it, taste it. I shift my stance, sword raised high, waiting. When it descends, I meet it head-on, steel to sky.

Light crashes into me, sings through me, then tears away—another perfect reflection of its own fury.

Each strike I turn sends the storm folding inward, its edges tightening, retreating like it's being pressed back into its own chest.

And then—finally—light.

A single beam of moonlight splits the clouds, piercing through the chaos like a blade of its own. It lands across the tower, across me, silver and sharp.

I brace for another strike, but something changes.

The moonlight shivers against *Realmbreaker's* edge, a faint ripple of recognition, as though the blade can feel it too. The light bends toward the steel, dancing along its surface like it's being drawn in.

I angle the sword slightly, and the moonlight follows—moves—a silken thread waiting to be shaped.

Realmbreaker. The sword's very name makes me question if there is more to this sharpened point of steel than I know.

A laugh bubbles up from somewhere deep, half disbelief, half exhilaration.

"All right," I whisper to the storm, to the blade, to whatever power's listening. "Let's see what else you can do."

The next charge builds faster, closer, the air crackling around me like it can't wait to see what I'll do next. I raise *Realmbreaker* again, feeling the weight of the moonlight still clinging to its edge, a ribbon of silver twining with the faint electric blue running through the steel.

When the lightning drops, I don't brace this time. I move.

I push the blade forward and will the light to follow. Moonlight and lightning collide, twin currents roaring up the length of *Realmbreaker*, meeting in a blinding flash that tears across the sky.

It hits the storm dead center.

The impact is deafening, like the heavens themselves exhaling. For a long, suspended heartbeat, the world holds its breath. Then the sky folds in on itself, the fury breaking into a low, irritated grumble of thunder that echoes across the valley.

The rain softens to a mist. The clouds shrink back, curling into pale, silken ribbons that melt into the night.

Whatever that was, it wasn't like any storm I've ever seen.

I push my wet hair from my face and look at the tower. The window at the top remains dark. But I know someone's in there. I saw him—his shadow moving within the dark before the light vanished.

My jaw tightens. "You can hide all you want," I mutter, sheathing *Realmbreaker*. "You're getting an earful when I get up there."

The climb feels easier now, like the tower itself has stopped fighting me. Rain drips from the stone as I haul myself up, one slick handhold at a time, until I reach the window.

The ledge is narrow. I brace a boot against the sill, catch the window's edge, and yank it open hard enough for the hinges to shriek.

My breath fogs in the sudden stillness.

Then I swing myself up and through, boots scraping the stone, shoulders brushing the narrow frame.

Realmbreaker is in my hand before I even think about it.

I land inside, crouched, the blade leveled straight ahead,

its silver edge catching the faint glimmer of moonlight still breaking through the clouds.

And there, in the dark, it finds a face.

Not Orion's.

But the storm's.

CHAPTER 13
tana

"Where did I put the salamander spit?" a man's voice mutters somewhere in the shadows. "Ah! No, that's basilisk bile. Terrible substitute, terrible. Last time, the curtains tried to eat me."

The voice is old, but energetic. A little too energetic for someone who apparently survived a carnivorous home-décor incident.

I edge forward, sword raised, trying to make sense of what I'm looking at.

The tower looks like a wizard's fever dream. Shelves overflow with vials, jars, and a worrying number of things that still move. A cauldron bubbles in the middle of the chaos, glowing faintly green. Parchments float overhead like drunken birds, bumping into each other and then apologizing in tiny bursts of magic.

A brown owl sleeps on a perch near the window, its feathers puffed up in resignation.

The man himself, old, tall, with a beard that could double as a scarf, wears long blue robes tucked into what appear to be cut-off trousers. His pale legs stick out beneath them, bony and knobby, like he's part scarecrow. A pointed hat keeps trying to fall off his head.

"Don't look at me like that, Arthur," he says to the

sleeping owl, pointing an ink-stained finger. "You were the one who said we needed more sustainable reagents. This is sustainable. It's also possibly sentient, but really, that's a bonus!"

The owl doesn't move.

He frowns. "Oh, giving me the silent treatment, are you? Fine, be that way."

I clear my throat. "Uh...hello?"

He startles, blinking toward me as if I've materialized out of thin air. "Oh! Hello there. So lovely to see you again, old friend. You're letting in the damp, my dear. Do shut the window."

"The window..." I look behind me. "I climbed through the window."

And see me again? Who the fuck is this guy?

"Did you? How efficient of you!" His eyes widen suddenly, flicking toward the storm outside. "Ah! Finally. That dreadful tantrum in the sky has stopped throwing a hissy fit."

He waves a hand dismissively. "Good timing, then. You might as well make yourself useful."

Before I can reply, he thrusts a glass jar into my hands. The liquid inside glows faintly pink. "Stir this."

I blink down at it. "I—what?"

"Counterclockwise, of course!" he snaps, turning away to rummage through a pile of books. "It's alchemy, not a soup recipe. Honestly, what are they teaching you young people these days?"

I start stirring, mostly out of self-preservation.

He hums, digging under his desk. "At last, I can climb onto the roof and install my lightning rod. I knew the storm would come around eventually. Everything does, once they've had their tantrum. Now—where did I put my pants?"

"Your—what?"

"Ah! Never mind. I've got shorts on, that's close enough."

I open my mouth to speak, but he's already muttering again, grabbing a long metal rod, tucking it under his arm like a walking stick, and spinning toward a ladder.

"Wait," I call, raising my voice over his rambling.

He freezes mid-step, eyes widening. "Oh, stars above—don't stop stirring!"

"What? Why?"

"Because if you stop, we'll explode!"

He darts back toward me, grabs my wrist, and starts moving my hand again in frantic little circles.

I stare down at the swirling pink mixture. "You're kidding me."

He looks up with absolute seriousness. "Do I look like I'm kidding?"

I glance at the hat. The beard. The bare legs. The shorts.

"Yes."

My arm is starting to ache. I've been stirring this pink-glowing disaster in circles for what feels like hours while Dumbledore's twin flutters around like a manic crow.

"Right, right, that should do—no, no, don't stop, keep stirring!" he calls over his shoulder, rummaging through a pile of parchment taller than me. "Where is my hat?"

He pats around his robes, checking random pockets and sleeves like it's hiding somewhere on his person. "Must have put it with my spectacles," he wonders as he taps said spectacles on the tip of his nose.

"They're in your hand," I point out.

He freezes mid-pat, peers down at his fist—and sure enough, there they are.

"Ah! So they are!" He slides the spectacles onto his nose, blinking owlishly. "Excellent deduction. Sharp eyes, you."

He squints around, then drags his forearm over his head, jostling the pointed hat that's already there.

"Your hat is also on your head," I announce blandly. I don't know how much more of this I can take without killing something.

"Ha!" He bursts out laughing, half cackle, half hiccup. "Crazy owl is always misplacing things."

The owl doesn't even bother opening an eye.

I grit my teeth, stirring faster. "Could you maybe tell me what's happening?"

"Hmm?" he hums, half listening.

"Where are we?" I demand, still stirring the weird pink sludge that smells faintly like burnt marshmallow and regret.

"My home," he says, as if that should be self-evident. "I thought that was obvious. Keep stirring now —clockwise."

"Clockwise? You said counterclockwise."

"Did I?" He glances toward the sleeping owl. "Are you sure the owl didn't give you the wrong directions?"

"The owl doesn't speak."

He gasps like I've just suggested something blasphemous. "Thank the stars he's sleeping and didn't hear you say that."

I stare at him, waiting for sense to return to the conversation. It doesn't.

He claps his hands once, turning in a slow circle. "Now, where was I? Ah, yes. Must prepare for the queen's arrival!"

"I'm sorry—who?"

"The queen!" he declares, as if this is the most obvious thing in the world. "The bog sprites are spreading rumors faster than starfire that the new queen is tromping through the forest like an Afanc."

"I don't tromp," I mutter under my breath. "And what's an Afanc?"

"Quite clumsy creature," he says, waving a distracted hand. "It's the short legs. Terrible balance. Now hush—can't have soot about. The queen will need to rest after all her...tromping."

I blink, halfway between disbelief and fury. "You do realize I'm the queen?"

He pauses mid-step, peers over his spectacles, and studies me as if I've just announced I'm a talking chair.

"Well," he says finally, crossing one arm over his chest and stroking his beard with the other. "How convenient." His eyes narrow, mischievous. "Although I did think you'd be much smaller by all accounts."

He barks out a laugh. "Can never trust a pixie!"

That's it. My patience snaps.

I slam the jar down on the table. The liquid bubbles once, then turns from pastel pink to a deep, ominous violet.

He leans in, eyes bright. "Huh. It seems it didn't explode."

"Shame," I mutter.

He doesn't hear me; he's already scrambling for a nearby

journal, flipping through pages, muttering to himself. "Counterclockwise, clockwise...fascinating. Fascinating."

"May I?" he says, though he clearly doesn't need or want an answer.

Before I can react, he reaches out, plucks a single hair from my head, and tucks it neatly onto the open page. The book snaps shut and disappears into the folds of his robe like a magician's trick.

I gape at him. "Did you just—"

"Where were we now?" he interrupts cheerfully, taking off his spectacles and polishing them on the hem of his robe. "Ah yes—you're the queen."

"And you are—?"

He beams, sliding his glasses back into place. "Why, I'm Merlin, of course."

He pauses then, eyes narrowing, like a thought just collided with another inside his head. His fingers twitch, lips moving silently as he seems to listen to something I can't hear.

Then he gasps. "Ah—right. Nearly forgot about that."

Before I can ask what that is, he whirls around, grabs the long lightning rod leaning by the wall, and brandishes it like a sword—one arm flung protectively behind him like he's about to block something from getting to me.

"What are you—"

The tower groans. The air thickens. A low, rolling growl of thunder rumbles directly overhead. The same storm I tamed—or thought I did—answers back, angry and restless.

The hair on my arms lifts.

Then the blank stone wall in front of us flickers, like the air itself is being peeled back. Runes flare in pale blue light, and a door I swear wasn't there a second ago snaps into existence.

Merlin lifts the lightning rod higher, shoulders squaring. "Back, foul spirit, back! I've already bathed today!"

The door bursts open.

Mor stands there—mud caked to her boots, soaked to the bone, shadows snapping around her like irritated cats. Her hair is a mess of leaves and twigs, her expression even worse.

Her chest rises and falls with each heavy breath. "We," she huffs, stabbing a finger toward me, "have been looking everywhere for you."

CHAPTER 14

The wind bites colder tonight. It carries the scent of wet ash and smoke from the fires below, where the newly arrived refugees huddle together at the base of Starfall's cliffs. From this height, the village looks like a constellation, pale tents and flickering flames scattered across the dark hillside.

Hephaestus moves among them like a walking furnace, the glow of his power warming the air around him. Beside him, Hestia trails in his wake, her soft hand calming the tensions every place his shadow falls. The lesser fae look up to them as though they're gods descended to guide them through ruin. Maybe they are.

Hephaestus raises one enormous hand, fingers flicking like a spark striking flint. Fire leaps to life in the freshly built pits around the encampment. A low cheer hums through the refugees, weary but grateful.

"They're good for them," I say quietly. "The people need someone to look to."

Hypnos stands beside me, leaning lazily against the balustrade, his silver eyes reflecting the lights below. The shadow messenger Mor sent earlier is perched on his shoulder. "Mmh. Someone steady. Someone kind." He tilts his head toward me, a faint smile tugging at his mouth. "Neither of which are you, Your Grace."

"Charming as ever. And drop the titles, old friend. It is just us."

He only hums, gaze sliding toward the horizon. Lightning flares far off above the Enchanted Forest, bright enough to illuminate the clouds in silver. The air shifts with it. I can taste the current in my mouth, metallic and sharp, familiar.

It's her.

I know it the way a blade knows its edge. That pulse of wild energy, reckless and raw, is unmistakable.

"She's learning to command what she shouldn't yet be able to touch," I murmur.

"Agreed. The Trial of the Elements," Hypnos says softly. "It's presenting itself to her." He watches the distant storm, eyes glowing faintly, as though he can see her through it. "I have every faith she'll conquer it."

"After all..." A pause. Then a sly grin, rare from him. "She has already tamed our prince."

I shoot him a warning look, but he only laughs, clapping me twice on the shoulder before turning away. "A typhoon should be a breeze, then."

"Don't you have some High Fae to send to the forest? I seem to recall a dark river that needs warding."

I stay where I am, watching the horizon as the storm flashes once more. The sky calls to me, low and alive, each crack of lightning whispering my name through the clouds.

I want to answer.

Gods, I ache to answer.

But I can't. Not yet.

Duty anchors me here: the refugees, the wards, the politics. While she battles the storm, I'm trapped in one of my own making.

All the excuses I use to avoid confronting the vision the Lady showed me.

I exhale and turn away from the horizon, forcing my attention back to the fires below. The hum between us lingers, alive beneath my skin, a promise and a warning all at once.

A ripple moves across the clouds above me, an echo of something darker than the storm.

I don't need to look up to know who it is.

Omen's shadow cuts over the terrace like a living eclipse, silent and sleek. My Shadowmare. The only creature in Avalon who really knows me.

She lands in a sweep of obsidian wings, the wind of her descent scattering leaves and ash across the stone. Her eyes, twin galaxies of starlight and shadow, fix on me, seeing everything, judging nothing.

"You always know," I murmur, reaching up to rest a hand against her snout. Her skin hums faintly, like she's made of the night sky itself. "You came because you felt it, didn't you?"

A low rumble vibrates through her chest—agreement, soft but sure.

I rest my forehead against her muzzle, breathing in the scent of crackling atmosphere and midnight. "Are you worried for them?"

Her starlit eyes flicker, a constellation shifting. The question doesn't need an answer, but I give one anyway, my voice rougher than I mean it to be.

"I know Havoc will take care of her," I say quietly. "You need not remind me."

Another rumble, lower this time, like she knows I don't entirely believe myself.

I draw back and manage a faint smirk. "You've gotten nosy in your old age."

Omen exhales, and a pulse of night air rolls over me, the kind that smells like rain before it falls. Then she crouches low, massive wings flexing in anticipation.

"All right," I whisper, gripping the edge of her saddle and hauling myself up onto her back. "Let's see what waits for us below."

With a single powerful beat, she launches into the air, darkness given form, and we climb into the storm. The wind slams against my face, sharp and clean, the scent of storm and pine washing the world below into something small and distant.

Up here, I can breathe.

Few fae take to the skies anymore. The winged races keep mostly to Astralana, the floating isles of the Celestial Court, too far above to care about the ruin below. But Omen and I were born to the storm. She carries me through it like she was forged in the same strike of lightning that shaped me.

I push my shadows outward as we fly, testing the wards woven around Starfall. Each line hums steady, solid, our work holding strong. No breaches. No weak points.

And yet, something pricks the back of my neck. Movement below.

Through the mist and the faint shimmer of wards: two carriages, their banners snapping wet in the wind.

The first, unmistakable: the Briar Court. Roses and thorns twined into a sigil of poisoned beauty. Their envoy, Lord Cassian Virethorn, steps from the carriage in dark crimson armor etched with vines that move faintly under his skin. Every inch of him looks like he was grown, not born.

Beside him, the shadow spilling from the second carriage is colder. Deeper. Umbranor, the Shadowed Court. A single figure descends: Lirael Shadeborne, the assassin emissary of her father's house. Her black hood gleams faintly like wet ink, and even from here, I can't see her face.

Omen circles lower, silent. My irritation builds.

Cassian's gait is all arrogance, scroll clutched in his hand, purpose in his stride.

An official summons, no doubt. An attempt to remind us who thinks they hold the power here.

And he's marching directly toward my doors without invitation.

"Unannounced," I grit out. "Unwise."

Omen dips her head slightly, reading me as she always does. The air thickens around us, electric. A low growl of thunder rolls behind us.

As Cassian Virethorn places one vine-wrapped boot on the first step of Starfall's stairs, I let the storm answer for me.

A single bolt of lightning splits the sky.

It strikes the ground at his feet with a crack that shakes the stones, sending arcs of blue-white energy dancing across the terrace. The Briar envoy stumbles back, roses withering black on his armor where the heat touches.

Omen lands with a soundless sweep, wings flaring wide. The dignitaries stagger against the wind of her descent.

I dismount slowly, deliberately, my boots meeting stone as thunder rolls in the distance. My cloak snaps in the wind. The scent of my magic burns in the air.

"Welcome to Starfall," I say, my voice even, deadly calm. "I wasn't expecting company."

Cassian's jaw tightens. His companion from Umbranor merely inclines her head, shadows rippling faintly around her like smoke.

"Lord Virethorn," I continue, giving the Briar envoy a cold smile. "And Lady Shadeborne. To what do I owe the pleasure of uninvited guests?"

The tension between us crackles, alive as the storm still coiled behind my teeth.

Shadeborne moves first. The shadow around her deepens, and when she steps forward, her form wavers like smoke in moonlight. She bows low, her hood dipping, voice a silken thread.

"Umbranor begs an audience with the Queen," she says. "There are whispers, rumors of the Obscura creeping through the lowlands. Villages already lost, their lights snuffed out. The corruption moves toward the swamps of Merivalis. My father grows...uneasy. The Shadow Court's borders lie just beyond."

A prudent messenger. Careful. Calculated. Umbranor never reveals a hand it hasn't already played twice.

Before I can answer, Virethorn cuts in, his tone sharp and impatient. "Enough of this gloom. King Thorne demands the mortal pay him respects. If she intends to rule, she'll do so properly. He also wishes to renegotiate the trade agreements between the Briar Court and Starfall."

My jaw tightens at that word: mortal.

I step forward once, slow and deliberate. The sound of my boot against the stone echoes like a strike of thunder.

"Watch your tongue, Virethorn."

His shoulders twitch, but he doesn't bow.

"The Queen Rising," I say, the title rolling off my tongue like a blade, "is not to be addressed as the mortal. She was chosen by Avalon itself, a power far older and far less forgiving than your vine-choked king. You'd do well to remember that before you speak her name again."

I let my shadows bleed across the stones, tendrils rising like mist. "As for your lord who sits on a chair he calls a throne, waves a title he declares makes him a king: he holds no power here. Certainly none to demand anything of her. But I'll offer you this kindness, Lord Virethorn: it would be difficult to demand an audience with anyone should I cut out your tongue and burn the stump with lightning to make sure it never grows back."

Virethorn pales beneath the glow of the terrace lamps. Thorns bloom defensively across his armor, sharp and glistening with crimson sap.

"You wouldn't dare—"

I smile. Just enough teeth. "The fuck I won't." Each word slowly delivered, the weight of them landing on him as I intend.

The shadows twist tighter. Thunder rolls low and hungry overhead. Even Omen shifts her wings behind me, her gaze fixed on him like she'd rather be the one to finish the threat.

Shadeborne says nothing. But her head inclines slightly, like she approves.

I take a slow breath and rein it all back in. "I've no patience for politics and posturing. Not when greater concerns plague our realm. Tell your king the trade agreements stand as they have for ages. The arrival of Avalon's chosen queen doesn't suddenly demand renegotiation."

Virethorn's lips curl into a snarl. "If Starfall refuses to trade with the Briar, then trade will cease—not only here but across all of Avalon. We'll see how long the courts praise their new queen when their stores of elixirs and harvest wine run dry."

So that's the game. The Briar's exports: nectar, medicine, and the rare crystal sap that powers most of Avalon's healing wards. He thinks to choke us out.

I take a measured step toward him, letting the full weight of my power press against the air. The next roll of thunder is closer now, almost personal.

"Listen well, Lord of Thorns," I say quietly. "You'll leave Starfall now. Tell your king that his greed will starve his own before it touches mine. The realm is sick enough without his rot spreading further."

Lightning flashes behind me, bathing the terrace in white. The air hums with static, tiny bolts crackling along the edges of my cloak like restless serpents of light. Virethorn flinches, then bows stiffly, the gesture more self-preservation than respect.

Shadeborne dips her hood again, murmuring, "We'll await the Queen's message, my lord."

"Do," I say. "And tell Shade that if the darkness reaches

his borders, he need not wait for the Queen's command. He'll have my blade beside him."

Virethorn bristles, wanting the last word—but my shadows coil tighter, warning him off.

"Go," I growl.

They do.

Omen's wings stretch wide again behind me as the envoys retreat to their carriages. The scent of burned roses lingers in the air.

I exhale, watching them disappear down the mountain road, then glance toward the horizon—toward the faint silver flash of lightning still threading the clouds over the Enchanted Forest.

Hold steady, Starling, I think. Because when you return, the courts will demand a queen—and they aren't prepared for the storm you'll bring with you.

CHAPTER 15
tana

"We have been looking everywhere for you."

"Morrígan, you wicked thing—get over here." The old wizard lifts his arms like a man greeting a lifelong friend.

My mouth falls open. *Wicked thing?* He says it with affection, like she's a wayward niece instead of a dark enchantress.

Before I can blink, he's got his arms around her. Hugging her.

I nearly choke on air. No one touches Mor. Not once since I've met her has anyone dared. Most fae give her a wider clearing than necessary.

For a heartbeat, I think she might return it... until I catch the subtle signs of her power shifting. That flicker from her small, dark melancholy self to *The Morrígan* threatening to take over—then fading back, as if she's fighting against it.

He pulls back with a grin that creases his entire face. "You look positively dreadful, my dear."

Mor's red eyes flare. "Get your hands off us before we peel your flesh from your bones."

Ah. There she is.

Merlin chuckles. "Excellent. I've been meaning to see if that new regeneration charm actually works."

A low rumble shakes the tower, deep enough to vibrate

the floor under my boots. The air turns sharp, metallic—smelling of charged rain.

At first, I think it's thunder rolling through the cliffs, but the sound keeps deepening—low, steady, like the world itself is growling. The air tastes sharp and electric, every breath pricking my tongue like ozone before a strike.

There's a storm outside. I can feel it.

Not just hear it—*feel* it.

The weight of it presses against my chest, heavy and alive.

I walk back to the window I crawled through and look at the slow swirl of clouds. Still overhead. Still watching. "What is that?"

"Ah," Merlin says brightly, as if we've asked about a pet. "That would be Sir Rumbleton Tempestus Maximus."

I blink. "I'm sorry—what?"

"The storm," he explains. "He's been rather moody today."

Another crack of thunder rattles the glass panes. I swear the sound almost resembles a growl.

Mor narrows her eyes. "You named the storm?"

"Of course," he says, as though it's obvious. "All living things deserve names. Otherwise, they risk being forgotten altogether."

I glance toward the window, where lightning flashes white against the clouds. "So it's alive?"

"Seems so," Merlin says cheerfully, stepping closer. "Not terribly bright, though—"

A thin bolt zaps the stone, and he yelps, jerking his hand back to suck on a singed fingertip. "Touchy!"

I stare at him. "How in the name of everything holy does a storm grow a conscience?"

"Well," he says, sheepish now, "I may have borrowed a bit of lightning from your princely friend. Needed something for an experiment—portal work, you see. But the bolt got a little too sassy with its thunder, and—bam—" He gestures toward the window. "Sir Rumbleton was born."

Thunder booms in reply, louder this time.

Merlin frowns toward the storm. "Well, if you're only going to insult my mother, I'm leaving. You stay out there and get yourself together."

Another roll of thunder sounds suspiciously like laughter.

I exchange a look with Mor. Her expression says exactly what I'm thinking—this man is insane.

But beneath the absurdity, something tugs at me. The air feels heavy, charged in a way I can't quite name. Every breath hums like the storm's inside me, not outside.

The Trial of the Elements.

The third trial.

Could it be?

I can feel it now in a way I never could before—as if the tempest is aware of me too, pressing against my ribs, whispering through my veins. It's impossible to explain, but I know it. I *know* it.

A memory surfaces, unbidden—Hypnos's voice during one of our lessons: *Pandora tamed a wildfire that threatened all of Thornspire. She didn't smother it—she taught it restraint. Control through understanding, not fear.*

And now here I am, sitting under a roof with a storm that feels like it knows my name.

Pandora tamed fire.

And somehow, I've tamed a storm.

Merlin waves a hand and a door appears in the wall—rough-hewn oak, iron hinges gleaming. "Come along then."

When the door swings open, my heart sinks.

A staircase. A *motherfucking* staircase.

A long, spiraling stretch of stone winding down into darkness.

"There are stairs here?" I ask, like it's a personal insult. My fingers graze the cool wall as I follow him, the scent of damp stone thick in the air.

"How do you think you got up here?" Merlin tosses the words over his shoulder, voice light with mockery. "Through the window?"

I stop dead. My eyes snap to his back.

"I did come through the window," I say, incredulous.

He doesn't look at me. Doesn't slow. Just keeps walking like he didn't hear a word.

But he did. He had to have seen me.

I press my hand to the wall again, meaning to steady myself. My fingers brush over a crack in the stone—a vein of mineral threaded through rock, faintly pulsing with light.

And then there is nothing but pain.

It detonates behind my eyes, white-hot and blinding.

Sound vanishes. The air stills.

I'm falling, tumbling through nothing as the world collapses inward.

The last thing I see is Mor's red eyes glowing in the dark, a rush of shadow blooming around her like wings—

—and then, nothing.

Pain tears through my chest like I've been struck.

I hit the ground hard—stone, dirt, ash—I can't tell. My palms scrape against it as I push up onto my hands and knees, gasping, choking, like all the air has been ripped out of my lungs.

When I finally manage to breathe, the air burns—thick with smoke, magic, blood.

Around me—chaos.

The world is aflame. The sky churns with red lightning, the ground split open like it's trying to swallow itself whole. Magic crashes against magic in waves, rippling through the battlefield with the sound of breaking worlds.

Mor's shadow lashes through the chaos like a living storm, wings of darkness cutting down soldiers I can't see clearly. Hephaestus's forge fire burns in the distance—metal screaming as it's shaped into weapons mid-battle. Hypnos moves through the haze like smoke itself, every step leaving trails of spectral light.

And Orion—

God, Orion.

He stands at the center of it all, lightning crawling over his armor, the rage in his eyes enough to set the sky aflame.

The world shakes with the force of his roar.

Something explodes nearby. The shock wave knocks the breath from my chest, sends debris raining down in molten fragments. I try to crawl, to push up, but the air thickens—

gravity itself pressing me down. My vision doubles, blurs, like I'm seeing two versions of the same moment bleeding together.

My body won't obey, but my mind screams one thing—

Don't stay still.

Battlefields don't forgive stillness. A still target is about to be a dead one.

I drag myself forward, elbows digging into the ground, vision blurring until I can't tell friend from foe. The noise starts to fade, swallowed by a low, rushing hum in my ears. My arms give out, cheek pressed to the earth.

Everything tilts.

The edges of my vision darken, creeping inward like ink in water.

And then—above me—

Wings.

Massive, endless shadows unfurl across the battlefield, blotting out fire and light alike.

The last thing I see before the darkness swallows me whole.

I wake on something soft. Not a bed exactly—more like a mound of furs and old fabric that smells faintly of cedar and dust.

It's dark. The air hums with faint magic, the kind that feels alive when I breathe it in.

"And the queen wakes," comes Merlin's voice, lilting and amused.

Before I can move, something cool dribbles past my lips. I swallow on instinct, and the effect is immediate—like being struck with a bolt of lightning straight to the lungs. My eyes snap open.

I suck in a sharp breath and push upright, the pounding in my skull making the room sway. "God," I groan, pressing my palms to my temples. "Feels like I got kicked in the head."

Merlin's silhouette looms over me, a small vial in his hand. "Drink this."

The smell hits me before I even take it—the faint sweetness of moonpetal blossoms. My head jerks up. "That's Hestia's tonic," I say. "Where did you get the flowers for it? The field was completely bare."

"He picked them," Mor answers before he can. Her voice drips boredom, mouth full of food. "All of them."

I turn and find her sitting at a low table piled with roasted meats, potatoes, and roots. She's already halfway through demolishing it, tearing a leg of something unidentifiable in half with her teeth.

"How long have I been sleeping?"

"Only a few moments." Merlin shrugs, utterly unbothered. "A goat told me I'd have visitors."

I stare. "A goat."

He nods solemnly, as if this explains everything. "So I prepared. A meal for my hungry friend—"

"Not friends," Mor cuts in, mouth full.

"—and flowers for the queen's…" He lowers his voice dramatically, leaning close as if the shadows might eavesdrop. "*Special tonic.*"

Then he winks, clearly pleased with himself.

I sigh, but the corner of my mouth betrays me, twitching upward.

He presses a small bowl into my hands—broth, steaming and golden, with threads of something luminous swirling through it. I drink without question. Warmth rushes through me in a single sweep, chasing away the ache in my skull and the last dizziness in my veins.

When I exhale, it's easier—like breathing air that finally belongs to me again.

Merlin lowers himself to the floor beside me, legs crossed like a child sitting down for story time. His robes pool around him in messy folds, one sleeve still stained with something that looks suspiciously like soup.

"Do you often fall asleep while walking down stairs?" he asks lightly, as though I didn't just wake up from a collapse that nearly stopped my heart.

I shoot him a look. "I didn't fall asleep." My voice comes out rough. "I saw something."

He hums, tilting his head. "A vision, then."

"I don't know. Maybe."

But from the way he watches me—eyes sharp and old and too knowing—it's clear he knows.

"The stone you touched," he says after a beat, "it's rich with Avalon's magic. Very few veins of it left so pure. It recognized you. Or rather..." He taps his temple with one long finger. "It wanted you to recognize it."

Before I can ask what that means, he's already moving— pulling a shallow bowl from a nearby shelf and scattering bits of bone and stone into it. A feather. Something that glitters like quartz. He shakes the bowl once, twice, and lets the pieces fall into place.

He stares at them as if they've written a sentence only he can read.

"Ah." His tone shifts, all humor gone. "The headaches. The dizziness."

"Yeah?" I murmur. "You've got a cure for that too?"

"In a manner of speaking." He gestures to the stones. "They're tied to the ley lines of Avalon—the veins through which the realm breathes. The courts have drawn on that power for eons, but now…" His gaze flicks up to mine. "Now they're angry. And the realm reflects their discord."

"The realm's angry?" I exhale slowly. "So what, I'm supposed to… fix it?"

"Not fix," Merlin says, tracing a lazy circle around the bowl's rim. The bones shift and clatter as if alive. "The bond between you and Avalon must settle. The courts are its pulse. When they rage, the realm convulses. You feel it because you're part of it now."

His words settle in my chest like stones. "You're saying the headaches—"

"—are Avalon screaming through you," he finishes. "Until you make peace with the courts, you'll keep tearing against it—two forces pulling at opposite ends of the same tether."

I stare at the faintly glowing wall until my vision steadies.

A living realm. Angry courts. Magic that won't stop clawing under my skin until I make peace with it.

It shouldn't make sense—but it does.

Every headache. Every dream. Every time the air hums like it knows my name.

Maybe the Clave's parade wasn't about politics after all. Maybe it was survival.

The thought leaves a hollow ache in my chest. I rub the heel of my hand there, as if I could press it back into place.

"Calm the courts," I whisper, more to myself than anyone else. "Right. How hard could that be?"

No one answers. Not Mor. Not Merlin. Not the realm.

Only the pulse beneath the stone—steady, waiting.

CHAPTER 16

The road to Cairnvail cuts through the bones of the world.

Stone ridges rise like jagged ribs on either side of the path, the peaks high enough to scrape the silver haze of Avalon's moonlight. The Duskbane convoy moves in a disciplined line—black carriages drawn by Shadowmares whose hooves make no sound against the rock. Their breath fogs into ribbons of shadow that trail behind us like ghosts.

The air here hums differently. Thicker. Older. It carries the scent of earth and iron—of something buried too long and remembering its name.

Ahead, the queen rides without me.

Tana's Duskbane moves steadily beside the lead carriage, her back straight, her hair a wild tangle from the mountain wind. She refuses to ride inside the carriage, of course—says it makes her feel like a prize being paraded. I didn't argue. There are some fights I know better than to pick.

She and Hypnos have ridden in silence this second half of the journey, the first filled with strategy and readiness for what she should expect.

Behind us, Merlin hums off-key on his sled, drawn by a single Moonhorn whose antlers gleam wide enough to eclipse the light. The creature glides just above the ground, hooves never touching stone, every step scattering faint sparks like fireflies. Such a massive beast to pull the old wizard and his satchel of novelties—it's almost ridiculous. Overkill, even by Merlin's standards. But then again, subtlety has never been one of his virtues.

He feeds the Moonhorn something that looks like glowing moss and waves his wooden staff, knobbed and twisted, as he hums.

Mor rides beside the second carriage, bored out of her mind. Hephaestus and his brood bring up the rear with their supplies, the soft clatter of metal faint beneath the rumble of the wind.

The storm still follows us—a dark smear across the horizon.

Merlin insists it's tame. I'm not convinced. Though I have never met a storm, I cannot imagine it would be in their nature.

A low growl of thunder rolls over the mountains, and Tana's horse flicks an ear. She feels it too—I can tell by the way her shoulders stiffen, the way she looks back over her shoulder at it.

She hasn't spoken to me since Starfall, but I can read her silence like scripture.

She's angry.

She has every right to be—but she's also acting childish in her refusal to voice her sentiments.

But I'll wait her out.

I've waited out gods, wars, and ages of silence. I can wait for her temper to thaw.

At least, that's what I tell myself.

The Lady's vision still coils in the back of my mind—the

one she offered me in the lake, when her voice sounded like the end of the world and mercy in the same breath. *If she remains mortal, her heart will falter. If she becomes fae, she will live. Immortal. Fae. And her heart will heal.*

Ours will heal.

Life for life. Death for death.

The words have been gnawing at me ever since.

It should have been a comfort—proof that she could survive what's coming, that she could outlive every danger waiting in these mountains. But all I can think about is the price—what the realm takes when it gives.

Should I tell her?

Would she even listen?

She barely looks at me, and I can't decide if keeping silent is wisdom or cowardice.

Maybe it's both.

I grip the reins tighter, the leather creaking under my palm. The storm rolls above us like a held breath, and I wonder if it can smell fear the way I can—because mine has her name all over it.

Some courts will bend easily when we reach them. Some won't. Cairnvail, though—Cairnvail is a mystery. The Stone Court bows to no one. Their ruler, Lord Granite, has skin like carved rock and a heart rumored to be the same. I'd rather fight him on the battlefield than negotiate across a table.

Still, the queen insists on meeting every court herself.

Diplomacy before war.

Hope before surrender.

I glance up at the storm again. A thin vein of lightning forks across the clouds like a warning.

Merlin lifts his staff and waves it at the sky. "Don't start, Rumbleton! We talked about this!"

The thunder answers in a sharp crack that even makes Omen shudder.

Mor scowls at the disturbance. "Your creation's still angry."

Merlin shrugs. "He's in a rebellious phase. Adolescent weather is notoriously unstable."

Lightning forks across the sky.

Merlin points upward. "See? That's acting out, that is!"

I rub a hand over my face. Gods help me—this is my entourage.

And the woman meant to rule them won't even look at me.

The gates of Cairnvail rise ahead like a wound in the mountains—twin slabs of black stone veined with blue light, tall enough to swallow a fortress whole.

When the first of the Duskbane carriages crosses the threshold, I feel it—their wards.

The magic moves through us like a ripple in the marrow, pressing and searching, heavy as the weight of the mountain itself. The Shadowmares falter for half a stride, their ears flattening before steadying again.

Every court layers its defenses differently.

Eldoria's wards shimmer like spun glass—truth wrapped in beauty, bright enough to blind the dishonest.

Gloamreach weaves its protection in soft shadow and balance, its magic a quiet negotiation between light and dark.

But Cairnvail's wards are neither.

Theirs grind deep—slow and relentless—testing strength the way the earth tests roots.

The pulse fades, but the tension doesn't.

As we pass through the gate, the convoy tightens into its proper formation—security to the flanks, the queen in the center, and me beside her. It's ceremonial, yes, but necessary. There are still those who believe the mortal crown is a joke, and Cairnvail is not a place that tolerates weakness.

Tana was also quite displeased to have to wear the ceremonial queen's armor. She muttered many curses as the metal pieces were fixed around her—something about having trouble should she need to remove the head of any stubborn males.

I do not believe she had any particular male in mind when making that comment, seeing how my head is firmly on my shoulders.

Tana shifts her reins, straightening in the saddle as the wind whips strands of hair across her face. She doesn't look at me, but her jaw is set hard enough to cut stone.

The escort appears a moment later—six fae carved from the mountains themselves. Basalt skin, armor forged from the same dark mineral, eyes gleaming like cracked sapphires. Their steps land with the dull rhythm of war drums.

Their leader inclines his head. "Queen of Avalon. Lord Granite awaits your arrival."

Tana nods once, voice steady. "Lead on."

The escort pivots sharply, and we follow.

The path winds deeper into the pass, and slowly the austerity gives way to wonder. The cliffs rise and fold into spires that glow faintly from within, streaked with veins of mineral light—gold, silver, and deep blue. Waterfalls cascade from unseen heights, their spray catching the moonlight and scattering it in prisms across the rock.

Even Mor stops to stare.

Tana draws a quiet breath—the smallest sound—but I hear it.

Lovely, I think. Terrible, and lovely.

Cairnvail isn't cold like the Frost Courts or decadent like Eldoria. It's breathtaking in its simplicity—a beauty born of permanence.

The main passage widens into a cavernous valley carved into the mountain's heart. Here the Stone Court waits. Great pillars rise from the ground like ribs holding up the sky, their surfaces etched in runes that hum softly as the queen approaches.

At the far end stands Lord Granite.

He's a figure of the earth itself—broad-shouldered, his skin a tapestry of stone layers and silver veins that shift faintly as he moves. His armor is carved directly from the mountain, every plate grown rather than forged. His eyes burn an impossible pale blue, sharp enough to catch and hold the light.

He waits at the grand entrance of the inner stronghold, flanked by his guard, still as the cliffs that birthed him. When he speaks, his voice rumbles through the valley.

He stops beside her mare and inclines his head. "Queen of Avalon," he says, voice like gravel over steel. "Cairnvail welcomes you."

The words roll through the space, deep enough to stir dust from the stone.

Tana opens her mouth to respond, but he extends a hand first.

"To step on Cairnvail soil," he adds, tone grave but not unkind, "is to be honored as its guest."

I stiffen before I can stop myself.

He's offering to help her down.

Every muscle in my body coils.

I've seen that gesture before—lords offering their hand to queens, generals to rulers, equals to equals. It's symbolic. A claim of protection.

And she takes it.

Her fingers slide into his stone-rough palm, and she lets him guide her down from the saddle. The escorts kneel as her boots touch the ground, the wards thrumming faintly around them in what sounds dangerously like approval.

My jaw tightens as he falls into step beside her, leading her toward the stronghold's entrance.

I keep my place a pace behind, where I belong—but the sight grates.

The mortal queen and the Lord of Stone walking shoulder to shoulder—two figures carved in contrast: her soft and golden, him hard and unyielding.

The show of it is perfect. Regal. Measured.

A performance shaped from politics and duty.

But beneath the hum of the wards, I feel something shift —like the mountain itself is holding its breath.

I can't tell if it's the anticipation of an alliance forming...

or the quiet patience of a trap waiting to be sprung.

CHAPTER 17
tana

The heart of the Stone Court is carved from the mountain itself—but it isn't cold the way I expected.

The stone breathes. It glows faintly beneath my boots, alive with veins of light that pulse like trapped starlight. The air hums low and constant, a vibration that slides under my skin until I can't tell where the mountain ends and my heartbeat begins.

Lord Granite leads me through a corridor of pillars carved from living rock, each one etched with runes that shift and shimmer as we pass. The light they cast is soft—not the harsh burn of mortal torches, but something more alive, more intimate. Like moonlight caught in water.

The fae here move as if carved from the same stone as their court—tall, regal, eyes the color of cut crystal. All high fae. Not a single lesser among them. At Starfall, it's common to see both mingling as they please. Here, the absence feels deliberate—the divide palpable.

It's beautiful, yes—breathtaking even—but it's a beauty that keeps its distance.

A beauty meant to remind you that you don't belong to it.

The council chamber is circular, vast, and hollow. Runes crawl across the walls like veins, their light flickering with faint rhythmic pulses. A long slab of obsidian serves as the table, and chairs—more like thrones—have been carved from the mountain around it. No two look the same.

He gestures for me to sit.

I take the central seat at the table's end.

Orion stands behind me, to my right, close enough that the heat of his temper ripples against my back. He hasn't said a word, but the air already hums faintly with static—a warning I doubt any of the stone-skinned fools here are clever enough to heed.

Mor leans against a column, eyes sharp and amused. Hypnos claims the chair beside mine, graceful as shadow.

Lord Granite sits opposite me, surrounded by a half circle of his own—stone-skinned fae whose expressions are carved in permanent disapproval. His advisers, no doubt.

My guards and his wait outside. The door shuts with the sound of a cliff collapsing.

For a breath, no one speaks.

Then Granite breaks the silence. "So," he says, voice deep enough to rattle dust from the ceiling, "the mortal queen walks the courts."

His words aren't cruel—not yet—but they hang heavy, weighted with curiosity that feels too much like judgment.

I fold my hands on the table. "The realm asked it of me."

He hums low in his chest, like distant thunder. "The realm asks much. Few have survived the asking."

"I'm not few," I say.

A murmur ripples among his advisers.

Granite's gaze sharpens—not angry, interested.

He studies me for a long moment before speaking again. "Your kind burn bright and brief. What claim does a mortal have to a crown that was forged before her bloodline learned fire?"

The insult is gentle, wrapped in courtesy, but it cuts all the same.

I meet his stare. "The same claim anyone has when a realm chooses them."

His lips twitch—not quite a smile, but close. "Spoken like someone who's been told she's special."

Mor snorts softly from her corner.

Behind me, the scrape of leather—Orion's gloves flexing as his fists tighten. The faint crackle of restrained power licks through the air. He doesn't speak, but every muscle in my spine feels the words he wants to unleash.

"I've heard of your trials," Granite says, drumming a single stone finger against the table. "The sword. The storm. The shadow that follows." His gaze flicks briefly to Mor, then slides—deliberately—to Orion. "And now you come to my court to seek what, exactly? Approval? Allegiance? Or forgiveness for the realm's choice?"

Granite shifts suddenly, the motion sharp enough that for a split second it looks like he's about to rise—step toward me, maybe.

Before I can blink, Orion's shadows surge, curling around me like a living storm—protective, possessive, dangerous. The runes along the wall flicker in answer, reacting to the sudden spike of magic.

Granite freezes mid-motion and then—goddamn him— smiles. A slow, amused curve of his mouth as he eases back into his chair, pretending it was nothing. "Forgive me," he says lightly, brushing invisible dust from his sleeve. "The chair creaks."

Liar.

He was testing a theory—measuring how close he could lean before the storm at my back struck.

He's searching for weak spots—where to throw the next hook, who will bite first.

And I need to make sure neither of them does.

I can feel every pair of eyes in the room pressing against my skin, waiting to see if I'll bend or break.

I inhale slowly, steady. "We can sit here and measure our dicks to see whose is bigger," I say, voice calm but sharp, "but I'd much rather cut to the chase of how we work together to keep Avalon from breaking. And you're one of the few who can help hold it together."

The room stills. Even the faint hum of the runes seems to fade.

Granite's expression doesn't change—stone doesn't crack easily—but his eyes narrow in appraisal. For a heart-beat, no one breathes. The chamber hangs suspended between insult and respect.

Then he laughs.

It's a sound like thunder breaking through the mountain —loud, deep, and unexpected. The advisers startle; one of them drops his quill.

Granite grins, teeth like polished stone. "Direct," he rumbles. "Good. The realm doesn't need poets."

The tension snaps, leaving the faintest trace of something warmer behind it.

He gestures to one of his advisers. "Bring wine. The mountain will listen while we talk."

The wine is dark and heavy, tasting faintly of iron and

smoke. I set it down but don't drink it yet. I want a clear head, and fae wine can be potent.

"I'll be direct, Lord Granite," I say. "I came to secure your alliance—and Frosthaven's. The realm won't survive without its strongest pillars standing together."

He regards me over the rim of his goblet, pale eyes catching the dim runelight. "Flattery."

"Fact," I counter. "No army can match Cairnvail's strength. Avalon needs indestructibility—and that's you." I keep going. "Cairnvail has never fallen, not once—not to war, famine, or the realm's shifting tides. When every other court fractured under pride or greed, the mountain always holds."

A quiet scoff behind me, almost a growl. Orion hates flattery, hates diplomacy that tastes like begging. Granite's smirk widens at the sound.

Fucking Christ, the male egos in this room aren't going to need to wait for a war of the courts. They're about to start it right now.

I have to keep this moving the way I want it to.

"What Cairnvail's warriors have in indestructibility, Frosthaven's have in perseverance. They've survived the coldest peaks and the longest sieges. They don't fall—they endure."

I rest my hands on the table. "If I can secure both, Avalon won't just have strength. It'll have stamina. Staying power. The kind of force that doesn't break when the realm starts to crack."

Granite hums, a sound like he's considering what I'm saying. "And how, exactly, do you plan to reach Frosthaven? The southern slopes are impassable this season."

A faint exhale behind me—Orion. Not impressed with the game.

"You know the eastern pass is clear," he says flatly.

Granite's grin is slow, deliberate. "And the only way there is through my court."

The glance he cuts toward Orion is sharp, teasing—as though daring him to intervene again.

The Lord of Stone is a self-centered bastard.

Saving his realm isn't enough; saving his people isn't enough. He wants something. Fucking fae. I swear.

"You need some very big things, Queen Rising," he says. "An army. Safe passage. Allies who will bleed for you." His hand curls loosely around his cup. "What do you have to bargain for them?"

I meet his gaze evenly. "I would wager you already have something in mind?"

He smiles—broad, unyielding, knowing. "Indeed, I do."

He leans back, eyes gleaming faintly with reflected light. "Cairnvail needs an heir. I need a mate."

The words drop like a hammer between us.

For a heartbeat, no one breathes. Then the air itself changes—pressure building, faint static in the air.

Orion bristles behind me. I can feel the anger radiating from him, thick and electric. Above us, thunder growls through the mountain's hollow heart, too deep to be coincidence. Granite's eyes flick upward, amused.

I reach for calm—for control—my hand still on the arm of my chair. Slowly, deliberately, I let my fingers drift until they brush against Orion's.

It's the smallest contact. Barely there.

But the jolt that follows feels like lightning straight through my veins.

For weeks, I've denied myself of him—of looking, speaking, touching. And now, one brush of skin and I remember exactly what I've been starving for.

I hope he understands my message. *Stay calm.*

Swallowing hard, I pull my focus back to Granite. "A marriage bargain for an alliance and passage to Frosthaven seems steep."

"Yet a fair trade," he says, tone smooth as stone. "My loyalty is not a trinket, Your Majesty. I do not give it lightly."

He's not bluffing. I can see it in the stillness of his jaw, the unbending certainty in his posture.

Every lesson Hypnos ever taught me about fae bargains runs through my head—the precision of words, the price of pride, the traps hidden in civility.

I glance to my side. Hypnos's expression doesn't change, but the faint flick of his eyes tells me everything: he doesn't like this.

Neither do I.

Behind me, Orion shifts again—the restrained kind of movement that means if I don't end this soon, he will.

Granite drains the last of his wine and sets the goblet down with a thud that echoes through the chamber. I follow his cup all the way down to the table.

"My price is a union," he says. "You and I joined—our courts, our rule. That is what I offer."

"So let me get this straight."

I rise, bringing the cup I haven't touched. The dark liquid catches the runelight as I make my way around the table.

"An alliance," I say slowly. "We get safe passage through Cairnvail to Frosthaven and back. And when Avalon calls, Cairnvail answers—as the crown's first and closest ally."

He inclines his head. "That's the shape of it."

"Good."

I offer him my untouched goblet. At the same time, I reach for the bottle of wine.

He takes my cup, his eyes never leaving mine—though I can feel Orion's stare burning through Granite like a blade. The lord's grin deepens, savoring every heartbeat of it.

I pour a fresh measure into his empty goblet, taking it for myself, and lift it in salute.

"Then let's get ready for a trip to Frosthaven."

The stone thuds as our cups meet. I drink. So does he.

The runes along the walls flare once—bright, brief, approving—and fade. The bargain is set.

Granite's grin says he thinks he's won. "Your escort will be ready by first shade," he says, rising. A cold, hard hand takes mine as he raises it to his mouth. "You'll have safe passage through the eastern ridge." He places a peck on my knuckles and lets me go just as slowly.

I nod once, turn, and lead the way out. Hypnos falls in beside me. Mor and Orion follow.

Even without looking, I can feel the storm trailing behind me—silent, waiting, and furious.

The moment the doors close behind us, the air changes —sharp, like the split second before lightning strikes.

Hypnos doesn't say a word aloud, but Orion's reaction says enough. His head jerks toward him, eyes flashing silver, jaw locking tight. I don't hear what Hypnos said in his mind, but it was meant to keep him from exploding.

For a second, I think it might not work. There's a crackle in the air—real, visible. Lightning dances across Orion's knuckles before fading. When his eyes find mine, it's not subtle.

The storm behind them isn't, either.

I clench my jaw and glance away, focusing on the tunnel ahead.

I'm not explaining myself to him. Not now. Not when he'd rather cage me than trust me. He can sit with that silence for a while. See how it feels.

He stalks off without a word, boots striking hard against the stone.

"Well, thank the shadows it was not dramatic." Mor follows, the barest of smirks at the corners of her mouth.

"That bargain was binding, Your Grace." Hypnos's voice is deep and even, as always.

"That was the point."

"By the laws of Avalon." He stops now, turning toward me, and I know he can see every emotion pouring off me. "To break it would mean blood, debt, or death. Possibly all three."

I square my shoulders. "Then let's hope it doesn't break."

Hypnos releases a deep sigh and gestures toward the outer gates. "After you, Queen Rising. Nine courts left. Let's see what the next one wants."

CHAPTER 18
orion

The walls here hum with smug silence.

Stone, carved and polished smooth—Cairnvail's idea of hospitality. A guest chamber fit for a prince, if the prince weren't ready to tear the mountain down brick by brick. The runes carved into the lintel pulse faintly with containment magic, meant to steady the air. It's working on everything except me.

Lightning snaps from my fingers before I can stop it, tracing a sharp crack through the air. It leaves a black scorch across the edge of the table, the scent of burnt stone curling upward like smoke from my restraint.

She promised herself to another.

A binding fae bargain.

My hands curl into fists, knuckles aching. She has no idea what she's done. No idea what those words mean when they echo against the laws of Avalon. A mortal might think a bargain is just a promise—a gesture of diplomacy. But this isn't mortal politics. Here, words are chains. Blood remembers.

And now she's shackled herself to him.

My pulse beats like thunder, heavy and uneven. The room feels too small. The walls too close.

I blame myself. Gods, I should blame myself.

When Granite feinted toward her—just a shift, a movement of his arm—I reacted. Instinct, not thought. Shadows surged around her before I could leash them, and that bastard saw it. Saw me.

That's when he knew exactly where to strike.

The offer of marriage wasn't just a ploy for power—it was a test. A performance before the entire court. Granite wanted to see how far he could push before I broke, how quickly he could drag my temper into the open. And I gave him the answer.

He saw the storm unravel.

He saw the prince of Avalon lose control.

He saw everything he needed to know.

The look in his eyes when she accepted... gods, I'll never forget it. Not satisfaction—certainty.

As if he were already picturing himself standing where I do. At her side. At her back. In her bed.

A low growl rumbles in my chest. Lightning flares again —brighter this time. The stone floor vibrates beneath my boots. I press a hand against the wall, forcing the power down before I turn the whole chamber to ash.

He wants her crown. Her alliance. Her hand.

She's a conquest for him and nothing more. All he wants is to stand in my place at her side.

He'll not have it.

Not while I still draw breath.

I pace the length of the room, the echo of my boots bouncing off the walls. The shadows twist and coil at my feet, restless extensions of my mood. I can't go to her—not with Granite's spies stationed at every door and his guards prowling the halls like stone statues that see too much.

It would be too dangerous to try to reach her room.

Her chambers are not beside him. She is between us.

Granite's chambers on one side, mine on the other—a deliberate placement, if ever there was one. A message carved in stone and smugness. The queen in the middle, the mountain lord at her right: an equal. And me, the storm at her left: an adviser's station.

Not the Prince of Avalon.

A reminder that another stands close to her now.

The image of her hand in his won't leave me. The way she looked up at him—steady, regal, unafraid. She doesn't even realize what she's done. She doesn't know the weight of the vow. To break a binding bargain forged before witnesses and runes would mean pain beyond death. It would tear at her soul.

My jaw tightens.

She would never survive it.

I will never let her try.

But I cannot reach her like this—not in the waking realm. Not with eyes everywhere.

There is only one place she's truly unguarded.

Only one place Granite can't follow.

The dreamscape.

A dangerous idea. Fae magic woven through sleep and shadow is delicate, and crossing that boundary without invitation is forbidden. But I've walked those roads before. I know how to find her in the quiet between breaths, where thought turns to memory and the heart speaks louder than reason.

If she will not listen to me awake, she may listen to me there.

In her dreams, there are no guards. No bargains. No lies.

Only truth.

I glance once toward the wall separating her chambers from mine, the torches' fire faintly pulsing with the same rhythm as her heartbeat. The air tastes of rain and coming storms.

"Sleep well, my queen," I murmur. "I'll see you soon."

The lightning fades, but the shadows do not.

They rise at my command, curling around me like wings.

The dream doesn't come all at once.

It pulls.

In waking, she won't speak to me. Won't look at me. But here...

In the place between thought and memory, I can feel the bond stirring. A faint pulse. A tug beneath my skin.

I close my eyes and reach for it.

Testing.

Calling.

In the dreams, she used to come to me.

Now I call her.

I rise from the chair by the fire—an echo of the room I just left—and move to the door. My hand wraps around the knob, and when I turn it, the sound is thunder-soft, the kind of hush that only exists in dreams. Still, it rolls outward like a ripple through the illusion.

Across the short hall, another door opens.

Hers.

She stands in the doorway, one hand still on the latch, chest rising and falling as if she's just woken from something she hasn't yet escaped.

Her curls spill around her face in waves—a wild, untamed halo. Her nightdress clings to her skin, black satin catching the runelight in soft flickers.

Gods.

She's barefoot.

She's beautiful.

And she's breathing like I've stolen the air from her lungs.

We don't speak.

Not yet.

I look at her—and for the first time in what feels like forever, she looks at me.

Her gaze is sharp, unreadable. There's no warmth in it. No invitation.

But she came.

That has to mean something.

I want to pull her into my arms, bury my face in her neck, and beg her to let me hold her until the ache dulls.

But if I reach for her too quickly, she'll likely stab me through the heart and call it even.

So I don't touch.

Not right away.

Instead, I let one hand lift—slow, reverent. My fingertips brush the curve of her cheek. She doesn't flinch. Doesn't lean in, either.

But gods, she's soft. Still warm from whatever dreams I interrupted.

I step past her—close behind. The scent of her, wild jasmine and shadowed air, wraps around me and stirs something deep in my chest.

My mouth finds the space just behind her ear. I don't kiss her. I only breathe.

"I've missed you," I whisper.

Three words. Barely a confession. But they burn in my throat.

Her breath catches. She doesn't speak.

I let my hands find her waist—fingertips grazing the swell of her hips beneath the silk. She's solid beneath my palms, muscle and moonlight, every inch of her a woman built from war and wonder.

She doesn't move. Doesn't resist.

Then slowly . . .

she exhales.

And I feel it—

The tension in her shoulders melts.

The stiffness in her spine loosens.

She leans.

Just enough to tell me she isn't ready to forgive . . .

But she's tired of fighting.

I hold her like a storm learning how to be still.

And for one fragile breath, she lets me.

Her silence is permission enough.

So I take more.

My lips brush the soft skin of her neck—once, then again, slower. The third time I linger, inhaling her. Jasmine and heat. Thunder and woman.

My hands curve around her breasts, firm beneath my palms. I squeeze, just enough to draw a quiet gasp from her lips, and press another kiss to her shoulder.

"You cannot do this, Starling," I whisper, my mouth at her throat now. "The bargain."

"It's done."

"It's not."

She stiffens slightly, like the words are an insult instead of a plea. But she doesn't pull away when my fingers slide beneath the thin straps of her nightdress. I take my time, easing them down over her shoulders, baring inch after inch of her warm brown skin to the moonlight leaking through the illusion.

The silk slips past her hips, puddling at her feet.

She's bare.

My shadows pulse in response, reaching for her like they've missed her too. One brushes her back, and she sucks in a breath, spine arching. The chill of it dances down her spine.

"Let me end it for you," I murmur, my lips ghosting just behind her ear again.

My hand slides between her thighs—slow, deliberate.

She's wet.

Hot, slick arousal coats my fingers as I find the proof of what she hasn't said aloud. The scent of her hits me like a drug, her need saturating the dream around us. She trembles under my touch, and I know—gods, I know—she wants to give this game up. This defiant wall between us.

She wants me.

My fingers circle her clit, and she gasps, her mouth parting in an unspoken plea. I groan softly against her neck, struggling to keep my restraint.

I want to kiss her.

Take her mouth with mine.

Slide my tongue between her lips and taste every broken apology she hasn't spoken.

But I can't. Not yet.

She has to hear me.

"You don't need him," I say, voice hoarse.

"I know I don't," she breathes.

I close my eyes at the sound of her voice—softer now. Open. Bare.

My shadows slither down her hips, dark silk against glowing skin. One coils between her legs.

With two fingers, I part her gently—pulling back the slick folds to expose her clit, flushed and throbbing.

My shadows strike.

A flick—sharp, precise, like a tiny whip—and she moans.

The sound tears through me.

Her body arches back into mine, her hands reaching behind for balance—for me—as she gives herself over to the pleasure.

She trusts me. Even here. Even now.

And I will not let her be bound to another.

Not while she still trembles under my hand.

Not while she fights to hold back gasping my name.

My shadows swirl tighter around her clit—an undulating, pulsing motion that draws a loud, guttural moan from her lips. The sound shoots straight through me, thick and raw, and I feel it everywhere.

Gods, I'm hard.

Painfully so.

The weight of my cock presses against her ass with every small roll of her hips. She grinds back against me—maybe without meaning to, maybe entirely on purpose—and I can't help it. My hips flex forward in return, rutting against the soft curve of her, chasing friction like I'm losing my mind.

I can feel the heat building inside her—coiling, tightening. Her climax gathering like a storm behind her ribs.

"Starling," I breathe against her neck, voice low and hoarse. "You must trust me. Granite will hold back no mercy should you break your bargain."

My tongue licks a bead of sweat from her skin, slow and deliberate. She shudders in my arms, and the sound she makes nearly undoes me.

"You should trust me," she pants, voice cracking under the weight of pleasure.

She's panting now. And still my shadows work—sharp, fast flicks, one after the other, teasing her higher. My cock throbs against her, aching from the tension. I grind against the swell of her ass, not even trying to hide the need anymore.

"I fear for you, my queen," I murmur, barely able to speak around the need swelling in my chest—and lower.

She reaches back suddenly, fingers wrapping around the back of my neck, and a rush of heat barrels through me. Touch. Her touch. The one I've been starving for. My whole body goes taut, locked in that contact.

She rises to her toes, her back arching, and I swear I feel her entire being open to me—her need, her heat, her fucking soul.

"Let this go, Starling," I whisper. "Let me end it."

"No."

And then she breaks.

"Orion—"

The way she says my name—like a prayer and a sin— makes me growl.

I slide two fingers inside her, thick and slick with her arousal. She's clenching around me, soaked for me. My shadows do not slow. They tease and flick her clit even as I fuck her with my hand, matching the rhythm of her convulsions.

"I could take you right here," I murmur, hips pressing harder against her. "Bend you over and bury myself inside this dripping cunt."

She moans louder, and I can feel my cock pulse, leaking into the dream, so hard it hurts. I grind against her again, pushing my length between the cheeks of her ass, desperate for friction—desperate for her.

"You'll give me this cunt," I groan. "But nothing else?"

My other hand rises to her chest, fingers pinching and twisting one nipple as my shadow tongues work the other —licking and flicking in sync with every pulse of my fingers inside her.

And then she shatters again.

A powerful, violent orgasm that has her curling forward, hands flying to the stone wall for balance. Her body trembles, hips jerking, thighs slick with arousal.

I fuck her through it—deep, slow thrusts of my fingers as she cries out and shakes.

Her slick coats my palm. Runs down her legs. Drips to the floor beneath us.

"I can have this cunt," I grit out, barely breathing, "but nothing more."

It's not fury that grips me—it's frustration. The kind

that wraps around your ribs and squeezes until it becomes grief.

"I can fuck you. Lick you. But I cannot—"

"You can end it," she pants, her body still shaking with aftershocks.

She turns, and gods, I lose the breath in my lungs.

Cheeks flushed. Lips parted. Chest rising and falling. Her curls wild, her skin glowing—wet and marked by me.

Her eyes hold mine.

"Tell me," she says. "Say the words, Orion."

I want to. I ache to.

Everything in me—my body, my soul, my fucking cock—screams to give in.

But I can't.

Not here. Not in a dream she'll write off as longing. Not when I need her awake and sure.

"I cannot."

Her gaze shutters. Hardens. And the wall slams back into place.

"Then leave."

And I do—

Cock still hard.

Hands still wet.

Heart, a wild cannon in my chest.

CHAPTER 19

It's First Shade, and the path to Frosthaven looks anything but welcoming.

Fine-powder snow curls off the ridge, spinning into the air like ghost breath. Too early for this kind of weather. Too heavy for coincidence.

A storm.

Odd for this season.

I was summoned by one of the lesser fae before dawn—a stablehand, trembling from more than cold. He has bruising along his cheekbone, discolored stripes along his back.

Punishment marks.

Granite's kind don't bother hiding the evidence of their discipline, and it explains why we have not seen many lesser fae around.

It is barbaric.

Not illegal—not here. But at Starfall, it's forbidden. Not by decree—by me.

Any High Fae who strikes a lesser will earn the same from my hand.

And my belt is not forgiving.

The shadow coiled around my waist stirs at the thought, slithering against the leather with a faint hiss, as if it's already tasted blood and wants more.

The stable smells of smoke and iron and damp hay. The air hangs thick with the quiet tension of creatures who feel too much—shadowmares pawing the ground, their wings twitching against the early moonlight. The lesser who summoned me keeps his head low, pointing toward the far stalls without speaking.

The disturbance becomes obvious once I step inside.

A rumble, low and steady, vibrates through the ground like a heartbeat. Then another. Followed by a sharp crack of miniature lightning.

In the corner, the small storm cloud—no larger than a pillow—rolls lazily in place, thundering softly. It growls once, then resumes what I can only describe as snoring.

The moonhorn—Merlin's overgrown beast—sleeps soundly, its great silver head resting on two crossed hooves, breath glowing faintly in the dark. And nestled between its antlers—lounging as if he's found the most comfortable hammock in all of Avalon—is Merlin himself.

His heavy blue alchemy robes drape over him like a blanket, his white beard rising and falling with each exaggerated snore.

I study him for a moment—thin, frail, that ridiculous beard curling down to his navel.

It's hard to reconcile the image with the stories. The Merlin—fierce wizard, alchemist of legend, a storm in his own right during Pandora's reign. Her most trusted adviser.

Curious to see him now—nothing but the shadow of the past he once was.

As if to emphasize the thought, he shifts, grunts, and lets out a startlingly loud burst of gas.

Omen snorts, stamping her hoof in protest, wings twitching with indignation.

I pinch the bridge of my nose. "Merlin."

No response.

"Merlin."

A snore is the only sign of life from the old wizard.

I glance around the stable for something loud—or edible. A basket of golden apples sits near the feed trough, faintly shimmering with a dusting of frost. The scent of honey hangs in the air.

Perfect.

A tendril of shadow splits from the basket, curling toward one of the apples. It wraps around the fruit, squeezes, and splits it neatly in two. With a sharp whistle through my teeth, the sound—or maybe the scent—does the trick.

The moonhorn snorts awake, massive nostrils flaring, that ridiculous storm cloud above him flickering once in alarm. The beast's eyes blink open, pale and glowing, tracking the scent immediately.

My shadow tosses one half of the apple toward him. The moonhorn snaps it out of the air with a pleased rumble, crunching loud enough to shake the rafters.

Merlin, unfortunately, goes with it.

The sudden movement jolts him out of sleep—he shoots upright, arms flailing, both hands gripping the moonhorn's antlers for dear life. "By Pandora's left shoe!" he yelps, blinking wildly. "We're under attack! Quickly, someone fetch the dragon!"

I sigh. "You are safe, old man."

He blinks down at me, disoriented, beard askew. "Oh. Bright moon to you, then, lad."

"Why are you sleeping in the stables, Merlin?"

His face twists into a scandalized frown. "Can you believe they wouldn't let Aurelian sleep in one of the bedchambers?" He gestures to the moonhorn. "What's he supposed to do—sleep in a barn like an animal?"

I glance around us pointedly. "This is a barn. And he is an animal."

He ignores me, sliding down from the moonhorn's antlers with surprising grace for someone who looks older than dirt and whom a strong breeze could take out.

I can't help but grin as he stands—beard extra wiry, hair sticking out in all directions, barefoot and wearing trousers cut awkwardly above the knee. His patched tunic hangs open, exposing a spindly chest that should not be exposed to moonlight.

He raises his arms high and stretches with a loud groan of satisfaction. "Ahh, that's better. Blood's flowing again. Lovely nocturn for a stroll to the Frost, don't you think?"

And then his trousers slip straight down.

"Whoops."

I mutter a curse under my breath and turn away. "For the love of the gods, Merlin, get dressed."

He chuckles, bending—too leisurely—to retrieve them. "You're such a prude, Orion. I've seen less shame in a changeling orgy."

"Remind me not to ask how you know that." I rub at my jaw. "Tell me you've got some lunabloom on you."

"None left, I'm afraid," he says cheerfully, tying his

drawstring. "Took everything I had to calm that blasted storm last night. I would've gone mad otherwise."

I exhale through my nose. "Well, wouldn't want that."

Merlin slides his arms into his robes and rummages around inside a pocket. A second later, he produces a long pipe and strikes a match against his thumb. The faint scent of sweet smoke curls through the air.

He's lighting the very bloom I just asked about.

"You just said you had no lunabloom."

"In the name of the realm, why would I say that?" he asks, utterly serious. "I always have lunabloom."

I stare at him. He takes a long drag, exhales a cloud of shimmering smoke shaped suspiciously like a middle-finger gesture Tana gives me, then offers me the pipe.

I mutter another curse under my breath, brushing a hand along Omen's neck as she paws the ground impatiently.

This nocturn is going to be a long one.

Merlin talks the entire way back to the castle.

Gods only know what about.

Half of what he says trails off mid-thought, his mind leaping from one subject to the next like a hare through brush. One moment he's rambling about lunar ley lines, the next about the sociological impact of enchanted poultry, and then—just as suddenly—he stops dead in his tracks, squinting at the sky with furrowed brows. "Interesting . . ."

From somewhere in his robes, he fishes out a weathered journal and a quill that looks like it's been gnawed on by a sprite. "Hold that thought," he mutters—though I'm fairly certain he was the one talking—and starts scribbling. "Note to self: possible connection between storm density and gravitational humor. Further study required."

I roll a lunabloom smoke and light it, taking short, slow drags while he mutters about humor density and star alignment. The bloom softens the sharp edges of my mood, though not enough to dull them completely.

By the time we reach the lower corridor of the castle, he's wandered off again—still talking to no one in particular, still gesturing wildly.

I step through the main archway, the scent of stone and charred meat in the air. My shadows peel away from me, spreading like mist over the floor, searching.

Where is she?

Mor's voice threads into my mind, smooth as always. *Breakfast hall.*

Of course. Eating.

But I'm not looking for her.

I send the shadows farther—down the corridor, through an open arch, curling around the faint shimmer of energy that always clings to her.

Tana.

She feels me the moment they touch her.

I feel it too—the faint shiver that runs down her spine, the hitch of her breath as she rounds the corner.

Hypnos walks beside her, their pace slow, measured. She's dressed for Frosthaven: fleece-lined leather trousers with boots laced mid-shin to traverse the deep snow.

Realmbreaker hangs at her side. Her wild curls are braided back, away from her face.

Her eyes find mine immediately.

For a heartbeat, neither of us says anything.

Her gaze drifts down—slowly—to the rolled bloom between my fingers, then back up to my face.

I extend it toward her and raise a brow.

A silent question.

She studies it. Then me. I wonder if she's thinking of Bloomrise—the two of us lounging on the rooftop. I stop the memory there.

Her expression doesn't move an inch as she says, flatly, "No, thank you."

Still a wall. Solid and high.

She walks past, her perfume brushing my chest like a memory. I catch the deep inhale she takes as she passes. She was always burying her nose in my neck, taking in my scent. I happen to know she rather enjoys the fragrance of lunabloom clinging to me.

The stubborn queen is not as indifferent to me as she pretends.

Hypnos follows, but not before patting my shoulder once as he passes. "Congratulations, Your Grace," he says dryly. "Progress."

I take another drag, exhaling smoke through a thin-lipped, emotionless smile.

Three words after nearly a moon cycle of silence.

I'll take it.

The breakfast hall smells of butter and boar and too much warmth for the season. Moonlight fractures through high windows, catching on sweating platters and silver cutlery. Cairnvail's provisions are obscene—mountains of meat, loaves the size of shields, jellies in colors I don't trust. Granite loves abundance like a man who thinks feeding the room will feed loyalty into their hearts.

Mor is already on her second platter, picking at something with a look that says she eats out of spite more than anything else. Around her, several High Fae trade glances and quiet murmurs—thinly veiled appraisals of our dark enchantress.

Little do they know, she would likely rather eat them than the food before her.

I lean against the wall, one boot propped, a small wooden artifact in my palm. The short knife I keep in my pocket slides across it, scraping away thin slivers of wood. The motion steadies me more than the smoke in my lungs ever could.

Across the hall, Granite is in full showman mode, boasting about cellars and bannermen, casters and keepers —each sentence a small pebble tossed into the pond to watch the ripples. He says things about provisions and hospitality as if abundance equals magnanimity.

Tana sits at the head, taking in the display with that calculating calm that has always made me both proud and irritated. Her eyes move like a litany—plate to plate, servant to guard, face to face. She catalogs like a scholar.

"Why are there no Lesser Fae?" she asks, quiet but loud enough for the room to fall a notch in temperature.

Granite chuckles, snapping two thick fingers. A dozen Lesser Fae step out as if from the stone itself—clothes the color of the hall, skin the color of the wall. They shift, stiff and obedient, like statues finally permitted to breathe.

Tana gasps. It's small, genuine. The sight of them—made to blend—does something ugly to her. Thunder rolls low outside, and I don't even try to tamp it down.

"That's terrible," she says.

"That is Fae social status," Granite answers, with the arrogance of a man teaching the room how to bow.

Anger pools hot and immediate under my skin. It mirrors hers. I can feel the shadow around my waist stiffen, tasting the injustice like blood. Granite doesn't deserve a lordship; he deserves a lesson. Beating them—making them part of his décor—is barbaric. Lesser or not, they are not ornaments.

He shifts his subject like a man changing coats. His cold eyes flick over to me. A small, poisonous smile curls his mouth. He pauses his own wine-cradling and cocks his head, as if measuring the next insult for weight.

"Queen," he says smoothly, "are you looking forward to our union?"

Tana's hand stays on the rim of her goblet. "I have more important matters—alliances to secure," she says. "But if you are excited for your... celebration, then I am glad for you."

The hall tenses a fraction—Granite thinks he's goaded her. Then, like a blade slipping free, he says, "You sounded very excited last night in your chambers—" and the rest of it never comes.

Lightning rips behind me and strikes every window of the hall. Glass shatters in a chorus that sounds like a thousand small betrayals. Shadows explode out of me—black, living ropes that lash and coil—sentences of force become law across the floor.

Hypnos stands, his calm composure now a mask of pure fury, hand slamming on the wood. The room tightens like a fist about to close.

But Mor—small, pale, and chewing through her second platter—moves first.

One blink, and she's gone from her chair.

The next, she's there—crouched on the table before Granite, shadow-jumped through the air so fast the torches gutter. The moment her boots hit the wood, the power hits us.

The air splits.

Her black hair whips as if caught in a storm that isn't here. Her skin yellows sickly beneath the candlelight, veins darkening to ink. Golden light flares behind her eyes—too bright, too wrong—and thick black tar begins to spill from her scalp, dripping down her cheeks, over her teeth, staining her lips with rot.

The Morrigan has taken her.

Three voices fight through one throat—screams tangled with whispers, every word pressed through broken glass. It's not sound so much as plague given breath.

Darkness rolls off her in waves. The stench of decay, iron, and something ancient fills the hall.

She leans forward, one foot braced on a platter, the other on the table's edge. Her head cocks sharply from one side to the other, birdlike, each movement punctuated by that dreadful clicking—like wet bones snapping underwater, echoing off stone.

Granite freezes. The color drains from his marble skin.

The tar dripping from her hair hisses where it lands, eating pits into the table. The air hums with sickness.

He tries to move but can't. It takes me a breath to realize it's my shadows holding him—binding his legs to the floor, wrists to the chair. I didn't summon them. They simply obeyed the fury that burned through me at his attempt to embarrass my queen.

The room narrows to the sound of her many voices trying to become one. The Morrigan leans closer until her breath fans Granite's face, and the scent of rot makes the lord of stone flinch.

"Apologize," she says—three voices, three tones, all layered together. The word crawls across the walls, vibrating through the marrow of everyone in the room.

Granite swallows. His jaw works. He nods like a man trying to remember how to nod. "I—" he stammers, then, to my surprise, finds his words, trembling. "I apologize, Your Grace."

The Morrigan retreats only a beat, still inches from him, eyes fixed, waiting. The tar drips and smokes; the lesser fae avert their faces. The High Fae stare at the ceiling.

He tries to save face. "I was merely—caught up in the festivities to come—"

The scrape of Tana's chair on stone is the only sound that slices through it. She stands slowly, the blade sliding free from its sheath with a metallic whisper that makes men who have screamed in battle pause mid-breath.

She could kill him for what he said. I hope she does.

She steps forward until the point rests against the soft hollow at Granite's throat. Her face is a cold jewel. Her voice, when she speaks, is a blade wrapped in silk. "Insult me again, and bargain or none, you will swallow the steel of my sword."

The hall holds its breath. Granite's face shifts from carved stone to very human—very small, very terrified. The Lesser Fae look down at their stone hands as if ashamed.

The Morrigan eases back from the table, but her presence lingers like a storm cloud. My shadows uncoil just enough to let Granite breathe—but not enough to let him move. I step off the wall, leave my wood shavings in a pale trail, and for the first time since the dream, something inside me feels steadier. Not forgiven—never that—but steadier.

Tana slides back into her chair. The sword remains pointed at Granite's throat, the threat calm and absolute. The room resumes its measured murmurs—this time a little more respectful, a great deal more cautious.

CHAPTER 20
tana

Lord Granite grates on my nerves like steel against bone.

Diplomacy has never been my favorite art, but I've practiced it well enough to survive courts more dangerous than this one. I was a soldier before a queen. A soldier learns restraint: rules of engagement, command, confirmation before a kill.

Granite is lucky that training still holds.

After the spectacle in the hall, I walked out before I said or did something that would start a war. Mor followed, plate of food in hand, her teeth still bared faintly. A growl vibrated low in her throat as she passed Granite's chair, tar still drying in her hair. I didn't look back.

Hypnos stayed behind a moment longer.

Orion didn't move at first.

I could feel the storm gathering behind me even as I crossed the threshold, the charge of it raising the hair on my arms.

Glass cracked under his boots where the windows had shattered, every step a threat written in thunder. His shadows hadn't yet settled. They were still alive, restless, dark ribbons swirling through the air like smoke seeking an outlet.

I didn't turn around, but I heard the sound: the deep scrape of Granite's chair dragging across the stone floor.

Then Orion's voice, low and even: "Look at me."

The room went so still it hurt.

When I glanced back just once through the open arch, I saw the full weight of his fury contained in perfect, quiet control. Granite sat bound in place, thick cords of shadow coiling around his limbs, the darkness pulsing faintly as if alive.

Then those same shadows lifted him, slowly, effortlessly, until the Lord of Stone hung suspended in the air, face-to-face with Orion. Granite's boots scraped uselessly at the floor before dangling above it, the muscles in his jaw twitching as he realized there was nothing he could do.

Granite is tall, broad, carved from his namesake. But next to Orion, he looks . . . small.

Because Orion is no man.

He stands in the ruin of shattered glass, the moonlight making his skin glow with an otherworldly sheen. His long white hair shimmers faintly, pulled back into a tie at the crown of his head. A few errant strands hang before eyes burning cold silver. The three scars that cut from brow to scalp only make him look more divine, not less. The tattoos that mark his skin coil and shift like ink remembering the shape of storms.

And when he speaks, even the wind holds its breath.

"The Queen has spared you," he says, voice deep enough to quake the foundations. "Because Avalon is greater than your greed. Because her mercy still believes this realm can be saved from the rot of arrogance that eats its core."

He steps closer. The shadows tighten.

"But I am not so merciful."

The whispered words slide through the air like blades dipped in frost.

"If you ever, ever speak to my Queen with anything less than reverence, I will carve your heart from your chest and feed it to the mountain that made you. Your title will crumble with your teeth, and your name will be dust before moonrise."

A long pause. The sound of power curling back on itself. Then the dull thud of Granite being dropped roughly into his chair.

The air goes still. The storm dissipates.

Two sets of footsteps follow, measured, deliberate: Orion and Hypnos leaving the hall, their silence saying more than any words.

And though I don't turn to see him, I can feel Orion's darkness behind me, quiet as smoke, loyal as a shadow that would burn the world for me if I only asked.

The Duskbanes stand ready in the courtyard, their hooves sinking slightly into the frostbitten earth. Their sleek, shadow-dark coats glimmer faintly beneath the muted morning light. They can handle the cold, bred for endurance and the climb, but the Shadowmares remain behind. Their wings wouldn't survive the freezing wind this high in the mountains.

The air is sharp and quiet, each breath a ribbon of fog. A small escort of Stone Fae waits near the gates, astride their beasts, creatures with hides like weathered granite and eyes that glow faintly blue. Their steps leave shallow cracks in the icy ground, as if the mountain itself bends to make way for them.

Havoc stands at the front of the line, proud and restless, breath steaming in the morning air. When he sees me, he lowers his massive head and snorts softly.

I cross to him, gloved hand finding his muzzle. "Good boy," I murmur, rubbing the bridge of his nose. His skin is cool, almost smooth like slate, and he exhales through my fingers, warm and steady.

"Ready?" I whisper.

He nudges me once in answer.

Across the courtyard, Merlin lounges on his moonhorn as if the world were made for his comfort alone. One leg crossed, one arm tucked behind his head, pipe clamped between his teeth, he's pointing lazily toward the sky.

"Do you see that patch there?" he calls out, pipe stem lifting toward a cluster of empty space above the ridge. "That void used to hold the Three Fates. The Sisters of Thread and Cut." His voice softens, unusually solemn. "They've been gone for ages now. Three dark holes where their stars once burned. Beautiful, isn't it? And rather sad."

Mor looks up, squinting at the emptiness. "Very sad," she mutters, tugging her cloak tighter around her shoulders.

Orion doesn't respond. He adjusts his saddle straps, movements precise, deliberate. The black cloak around his shoulders stirs with the wind, the silver thread along its hem catching faint light. The same crest, Avalon's sigil, is stitched over his heart, mirroring mine.

The cloak is heavy and warm, the fur-lined hood pulled close around my neck. Even through the thick material, the chill seeps in. The wind here bites like it resents intruders.

The four of us mount our Duskbanes, Orion, Mor, Hypnos, and I, and turn toward the eastern pass.

"Why can't you just shadow-walk us to the ridge?" I ask, my eyes remaining on the giant mountains we need to face.

"The wards make it very difficult," Mor answers plainly, already bored. "We would not make it far, and it would take considerable energy."

Behind us, the Shadowmares flick their wings once before retreating toward the stables. Merlin waves goodbye, a plume of white smoke from his pipe disappearing into the dark sky.

Then we ride into the cold.

Hours pass.

The mountain wind howls against us, whipping our cloaks, biting at our faces. The Duskbanes climb without complaint, their hooves sure and steady even on the narrow, ice-glazed trail. The higher we go, the quieter it becomes: no birds, no rustle of trees. Only the sound of hooves and breath and the occasional jingle of reins.

By the time Orion signals a stop, my fingers are numb inside my gloves. We have reached a small ridge, high enough to overlook the valley below. The snow here glows faintly with its own light, a pale silver reflection of the moon above.

"Here," Orion says, his voice carrying easily over the wind.

We dismount, letting the Duskbanes rest. They lower their heads to drink from a small pool where moonwater trickles down slick stone, faintly luminous against the dark. But they need more than water. They need shadow, substance to feed their strength.

Mor closes her eyes and raises a hand. The shadows bend to her like loyal things, spreading across the snow in rippling waves. Orion adds his own, deeper and smoother, until the hollow fills with darkness thick enough to breathe.

The air feels warmer almost immediately.

Havoc lets out a low sound of satisfaction, shaking his mane before nudging Orion in approval.

Orion smiles faintly, barely there but real, and lifts a hand to rub the Duskbane's jaw. For a heartbeat, he looks . . . human. Almost at peace.

When he glances up, he catches me watching.

The moment hangs between us, weightless and heavy all at once.

I look away first, pretending to check the saddle straps, though my pulse betrays me. The heat under my skin has nothing to do with the climb.

The Duskbanes feed quietly in the darkened hollow. Snow drifts lazily from the cliffs above, whispering against stone.

And for the first time since leaving Cairnvail, I let myself breathe.

The air stills for a moment, heavy and sharp, and I let my breath slip free.

It catches before I can take another.

Across the valley, the horizon is moving.

At first, I think it's a trick of the light, mist rolling off the mountain peaks, shadows shifting with the wind, but then the shape of it comes into focus. Enormous silhouettes, slow and deliberate, wading through the frozen ridges like the earth itself has decided to walk.

Giants.

There are several of them, their forms massive and ancient, draped in stone and snow. Each step lands with a deep, resonant thud that vibrates through the mountain beneath my boots.

I can't look away.

They move with impossible grace, like they've been doing this since the dawn of the realm, carving paths into the mountains just by existing. And they're walking away, vanishing into the fog one by one.

"Beautiful, aren't they?"

Hypnos steps up beside me, his voice soft, almost reverent. His eyes stay on my face rather than the valley. "You look like you've never seen them before."

"I haven't," I admit. "We don't have giants back home."

"Most realms don't anymore," he says. "They go where they please. And only when they're needed."

Needed. For what, I wonder—but I don't ask. Some questions aren't meant for words.

Mor's voice cuts through the wind. "Let's move. The cold won't wait for you to finish staring."

I linger for one last heartbeat, watching until the last giant disappears into the clouds. Then I turn.

And find Orion watching me.

He's standing near Havoc, one hand resting on the Duskbane's neck, cloak snapping in the wind. His gaze is steady, unreadable, but there's something in it. Something that warms and unsettles all at once.

Before I can look away, the wind rises again, howling through the pass, and for a breathless instant, it speaks.

A single word, soft as breath, carried on the gust.

"Morgause."

The name hits like a heartbeat under my ribs.

It's the same word I heard in the vision, when I saw my mother before the realm tore me back. Then, it had been shouted. This time, it's a whisper.

The air hums against my skin. My chest burns. I listen harder, every muscle tight with focus.

But there's nothing. Only wind.

I don't realize Orion has moved until he's beside me, his voice low enough to sink straight through my bones.

"What is it, Starling?"

That name rolls through me, dangerous and intimate. I swallow hard, forcing the warmth in my chest back down where it belongs.

"Nothing."

I swing back into Havoc's saddle, fingers tightening around the reins.

He studies me for a moment longer but doesn't push.

The wind howls again, just wind this time, and I flick Havoc's reins once. The Duskbane snorts, hooves crunching through the frost as we press on toward the next climb.

But even as the sound of the giants fades behind us, the name won't leave me.

Morgause.

CHAPTER 21
tana

The world narrows to white.

It's endless, an ocean of ice and jagged stone, frozen waves cresting into sharp ridges that catch the wind and fling it back in our faces. The snow drives harder every minute, biting through our cloaks, needling exposed skin until even breathing hurts.

The Duskbanes trudge forward, heads bowed, hooves sinking deep into drifts that swallow sound. Their steady pace is the only rhythm left in the storm.

The Stone Fae escort turned back hours ago. They argued with Mor when they complained about the blizzard, and she said it was nothing more than a breeze. "We have seen worse." She had this far-off look in her red eyes. "Far worse." She whispered it, almost like she forgot she was speaking at all.

Orion rides beside me, his cloak drawn tight, black fabric whipped by the wind. The silver crest of Avalon gleams faintly beneath a layer of frost. Every few minutes, I catch his eyes flick toward me, watching the way I pull my own cloak tighter around my shoulders.

He doesn't like this. I can feel it in the way his jaw sets, the tension radiating from him like heat from a forge. Whether it's the cold, the danger, or the simple fact that I'm out here in it, I don't know. But his mood darkens with every gust that howls down from the ridge.

Hypnos rides a few paces behind, his hood drawn up, expression unreadable. "Maybe we should turn back," he calls, voice half-swallowed by the wind. "The storm's worsening. The pass could be closed before we reach the top."

"We're close," I answer, raising my voice against the howl. "Once we crest the ridge, we'll see Frosthaven. I can feel it."

"We should go back to Cairnvail." Mor's cloak flaps violently behind her, but she doesn't seem to notice or care. The cold barely touches her. "The horses are struggling in the drift."

Orion doesn't respond. He's studying me instead, silent and steady, the faintest flicker of something, conflict maybe, crossing his face. His Duskbane stamps impatiently in the snow, sensing his uncertainty.

I can see him thinking it through. Weighing risk and reason. Duty and instinct. The protector in him wants to listen to Hypnos. But something else in him . . . doesn't.

His shoulders drop, and the decision's made. I clench my jaw and stare at the snow, knowing what he's going to say. That we need to leave.

He turns in the saddle toward the others. "Hypnos. Mor. Go back. Tana and I will press on."

Hypnos' expression is all tension and warning, but he nods once. "Don't linger. If the storm grows worse, you won't find the path back."

A tightness in my chest eases, my jaw relaxing as I realize he's staying. With me.

I don't have time to say anything before the mountain itself answers with a sound that shakes the world.

A deep, bellowing roar rolls through the storm, low and guttural, vibrating through the ground and up my bones.

Havoc rears, hooves slamming into the snow, and the Duskbanes cry out in panic.

I twist in my saddle toward the sound, my heart hammering in my throat.

The storm parts just enough for me to see a shape moving through the white, massive, dark, and all too alive.

It's a giant.

A massive one, close enough that I can see the shape of its ribs beneath the stone-slick skin, the slow roll of muscle beneath the frost. It towers at the top of the ridge, half shrouded in mist, one arm braced against the mountain's spine.

It stumbles.

The sound that follows isn't just noise; it's the mountain groaning. The giant's weight shifts, and a deep crack ripples through the peaks, leaping from ridge to ridge like thunder with bones.

The snow trembles beneath us. The wind howls louder.

Then the rumbling starts.

At first, I think it's the storm again, wind echoing through stone, but then I see the shadows moving through the fog, growing larger, faster.

Not shadows. Boulders.

They're tumbling toward us, tearing down the slope, the ground shaking with every impact.

"Orion!" I shout, but he's already moving.

His shadows lash out, fast and alive, snapping around

the reins of my Duskbane and his own. One sharp whistle and a low command, and the mounts obey instantly, surging sideways through the snow.

The first boulder slams into the ground where we'd been seconds before, exploding into shards of ice and rock. The shock wave hits my chest like a hammer, stealing my breath.

Mor and Hypnos aren't as lucky.

They're farther down the trail, and the avalanche's edge cuts straight toward them. The Duskbanes scream in panic, rearing against the chaos.

Mor's mount throws her. She hits the snow hard, rolls, curls in on herself as her horse bolts down the slope, vanishing into the white. She can't shadow-jump them out of harm's way. The wards.

"Mor!" Hypnos yells. He dives from his saddle, sprinting toward her just as a cluster of boulders tears loose from above.

The sound is deafening, stone colliding with stone, the mountain protesting the assault.

I scream their names, but my voice vanishes into the wind.

Hypnos doesn't hesitate. He throws himself over Mor, body shielding hers as the barrage slams into the snow around them. Shards of ice spray through the air like razors.

Then, as suddenly as it began, it ends.

The last echo fades into silence, the only sound the slow settling of snow.

Orion's shadow still grips my reins, anchoring both mounts in place. My heart hammers against my ribs as I twist in the saddle, scanning the white blur for movement.

"Hypnos! Mor!" I shout again, louder this time.

A shape moves near the base of a shattered ridge.

Hypnos pushes himself up, brushing frost and dust from his shoulders. He turns to Mor, crouched beside him, her black hair spotted with clumps of snow.

"You alive?" he asks, voice low but steady.

Mor exhales sharply, nodding once. "Unfortunately."

"You're both okay?" Orion calls, his voice cutting through the wind.

Hypnos looks up from where he's steadying her. "We're fine. The horses, however, have fled."

I lift my gaze toward the ridge, and my heart sinks.

The way ahead is gone.

Where the path once curved toward the upper pass, there's nothing but ruin. Massive boulders lie strewn across the slope, jagged fragments of mountain piled atop one another like broken teeth. The giant's clumsy stumble has sealed the way forward completely.

And now, the storm is closing in again. Snow whirls thick and fast, swallowing what little distance we can still see.

I don't need to say it.

Orion already knows.

"We'll wait for the storm to pass," he says, his voice measured, calm. "When it clears, we'll return with Granite's fae to remove the stone."

I nod once, not angry, just disappointed.

If only I could tame this blizzard like I tamed the thunderstorm in the Enchanted Forest. Feel the atmosphere like I did then and push this gale back.

I'd hoped to secure both alliances before word spread. To win two courts in quick succession and let the rest of Avalon feel the weight of it before I even arrived. To turn the threat of war to ash before it could take shape.

Now, all of it will have to wait.

Orion dismounts. The snow is nearly to his thighs, made loose and heavy by the avalanche. Every step sinks deep.

He offers his Duskbane to Mor. She takes him without argument, small and pale against the storm, the snow almost swallowing her whole.

Hypnos and Orion start leading our mounts through the drifts.

"This is ridiculous," I call, voice half-lost to the wind. "You'll freeze before we reach the base. Just . . . get up here."

Orion glances back at me, and the look he gives could melt half this mountain.

"It would be my pleasure, Starling."

I roll my eyes, but there's no point arguing. They can't walk in this.

He climbs up behind me, his weight settling solid and warm against my back. The heat of him hits instantly, radiating through my cloak, through the layers beneath. I nearly groan at the relief but bite it back. Orion doesn't.

A low growl rumbles in his throat as Havoc starts forward again, the movement rocking us together with each step.

"This is going to be a long fucking walk down," he mutters near my ear.

Mor also shares her horse with Hypnos. She elects to sit sidesaddle on the back while Hypnos guides their horse forward.

Orion's hands hold the reins steady until Havoc slips on

a patch of loose ice. My breath catches, and my hands tighten on the saddle horn as I lurch forward.

Orion reacts instantly—one arm wraps around my waist, the other gripping the horn beside mine. His voice drops into command. "Easy, Havoc. Easy."

I feel his erection against me. The roll of his deep voice—so low and close to my ear—makes my stomach flip, my hips instinctively wanting to push back into him. But I don't.

The Duskbane steadies. The world rights itself. But Orion's arm doesn't move. His palm stays firm against my stomach, the weight of it anchoring me in the storm.

And I don't ask him to let go.

We keep descending, slow and cautious. The snow deepens, the wind sharper now as evenfall creeps in, bleeding the last of the light from the sky. The cold grows crueler—biting, merciless. I start to shiver, my teeth clattering against one another no matter how tightly I pull my cloak.

Orion feels it—his fingers tightening just so against my waist.

"I know you're still angry with me, Starling," he says softly, voice roughened by wind and something else. "But you don't need to freeze to death to prove your point."

I half turn toward him, the motion stiff and small. My body's too cold to hold on to pride. Even stubbornness has limits.

"Let me shield you from the storm."

It's awkward, but I shift my leg over the saddle, turning sideways until I'm curled into his chest. The movement earns a deep exhale from him, one that warms my hair where it brushes his jaw.

He pulls both our cloaks tighter around us, tucking them close so the wind can't find a way in.

The relief is instant.

The warmth of his body seeps into mine, steady and consuming. The scent of him—smoke, leather, that faint trace of electricity that always follows him—wraps around me like something familiar I've been trying to forget.

I exhale and lean into him, the tension in my shoulders unraveling. His arm tightens instinctively, pulling me closer still, until there's no space left between us.

And as Havoc carries us down the frozen slope, the world narrows again—not to white this time, but to warmth.

And the slow rhythm of Orion's heart beneath my ear.

W e returned to the castle only a few hours ago. I fell asleep halfway down, held within Orion's warm shelter and strong arms—missing it more than I want to admit.

The halls of Cairnvail feel colder than the mountain pass we just left behind. The stone hums faintly underfoot— alive, unyielding, as if it can taste my failure in the air.

Orion took the Duskbanes to the stables, and I'm staring intently at the mural on the wall to keep from looking for him every few seconds.

I stand near the massive hearth, a goblet of wine in my hand. The fire snaps and spits, its glow dancing across the mural that dominates the wall above it. Hephaestus went to fetch more wood; the rest of the room is swallowed in dim gold light and long shadows.

Weariness clings to my bones. Defeat, heavier still.

Frosthaven feels a lifetime away.

My gaze drifts back to the fresco, delicate and sprawling across the wall like memory made color.

Valkyries.

Dozens of them—wings spread, armor gleaming like burnished moonlight. A host of winged women marching in perfect formation, their faces fierce and resolute. Above them, more fly in sweeping arcs, spears raised in salute. Leading them all is Pandora—her expression serene, her eyes forward, astride a Shadowmare whose mane looks painted from the night sky itself.

It must have been from her coronation. Maybe she, too, traveled the courts in triumph. Maybe she stood right where I'm standing now, proud and certain of her reign.

My gaze traces the lines, following the parade of warriors—until something catches.

A gap.

An absence where another Valkyrie should be.

Someone has been removed. The figure is gone, erased with care and precision. All that remains are faint traces of a horse's hooves, the smudge of where a spear once rose high.

I move closer, squinting at the edges of the damage.

There—fine strands of dark, wiry hair curling out from what's left of the paint.

Hair like mine.

Like my mother's.

My throat tightens.

Could it be her? The woman from the vision—the one who screamed as she drove the sword into the stone, sealing it there for centuries?

Sealing it for me.

The thought roots deep, heavy and unsteady.

"Beautiful, isn't it?"

I don't need to turn to know who's joined me. The air shifts before he speaks—the faint tremor of the earth giving him away.

Lord Granite steps up beside me, holding two goblets of wine. He offers one.

I glance over his shoulder. Beyond him, I see Hypnos seated near the far table. His eyes flick briefly to mine, a faint smirk tugging at his lips before he returns his focus to the game he's playing with Mor. She's losing, if the scowl twisting her pale face is any indication.

"No, thank you," I tell Granite, lifting my own goblet, still half full.

He nods, the faint smile that says he knows a joke I don't never leaving his lips.

My attention returns to the fresco. I point to the missing figure. "Who was that—the one that's been removed? It was deliberate, wasn't it?"

Granite hums low, like a rumble from deep inside a cavern. "Indeed, it was. She was the traitor—the Valkyrie who let the darkness in. Betrayed her sisters. Betrayed her kin. So we erased her. Pandora ordered it everywhere. It is one of the greatest dishonors we can give: to remove the memory of an immortal after they've returned to the stars."

He turns his pale gaze toward the mural, his stone face solemn. "They will look down upon our eternal night and know we've chosen to forget them."

I sip my wine, thinking.

If she truly was the one who drove the sword into the

stone . . . what would drive her to it? What could make a warrior turn on her sisters?

I'm about to ask when Granite's voice cuts through the silence again.

"I heard about your unfortunate encounter on the mountain," he says, tone carefully polite.

"We'll go back once the storm clears," I answer evenly. "Try again."

He chuckles.

The sound grates instantly against my skin. I turn toward him, every instinct sharpening.

"What's funny?"

He waves a finger lazily. "You see, that's the thing with Fae bargains . . ."

His tone turns almost teasing as he shakes his head. "You must be specific."

I narrow my eyes. "What are you getting at?"

Across the room, Hypnos and Mor both look up from their game. The air thickens, the firelight snapping louder as though it, too, waits for his answer.

Granite smiles—a slow, terrible curl of his lips.

"You asked for safe passage through Cairnvail to Frosthaven and back," he says, savoring the words. "As in one trip. Not—as many as you wish until you succeed."

A wave of heat floods through me, molten fury that starts in my chest and rolls outward.

Granite steps closer, snapping his thick fingers once. The sound echoes through the chamber.

"I have fulfilled my part of the bargain," he says smoothly. "You were given safe passage. You went—and you are back."

At his signal, a line of Lesser Fae enters the room, each one carrying an elegant gown draped over their arms. Silks, lace, jewels—each dress more extravagant than the last. They hold them with reverence, displaying them like offerings.

Granite's grin deepens. "Now it is time for you to fulfill yours."

He circles behind me, slow, deliberate, the faint scrape of his boots over the stone setting my nerves on edge. I track his movement without turning my back, my hand sliding near the hilt of the dagger strapped against my thigh.

"Be sure to pick a fine one, Your Majesty," he says softly, the words twisting with satisfaction. "Tomorrow..."

He pauses just long enough to meet my eyes, his smile sharp as a blade.

"...we shall marry."

CHAPTER 22

I didn't return to the castle all night.

It's nearly First Shade when I finally take the steps of Cairnvail's stronghold, one hand buried in my pocket, the other tracing the railing slick with dew. The air is heavy with storm residue and woodsmoke, the kind of silence that hums through stone after too much shouting. My mind is heavier still.

She rode with me for hours.

Her hands gripping my coat.

Her breath on the side of my neck.

Tana's scent still clings to me—wildflowers and storm-fire. The memory of her weight against me has burned itself into my skin, and no amount of cold wind could strip it away.

On the ride back last nocturn, I almost told her what the Lady whispered.

What it would mean for her if I was right.

But she had fallen asleep against my shoulder, and some things should never be spoken beneath the same sky as a broken mountain.

The castle greets me with a strange stillness. The wards hum thicker than usual—too tight, too muffled. It could be my nerves, or the exhaustion, or the lingering edge of the storm still crawling through my blood.

I make my way to my chambers, light the hearth, and fill the copper tub. The pipes groan to life, bringing steaming water that fogs the air. I sink down until only my mouth and nose are above the surface, letting the heat swallow me whole.

My bottle of wine is nearly empty, and the last of the lunabloom smoke—a joint, as Tana insists on calling it— burns low between my fingers. I take a slow drag, exhale toward the ceiling, and flick the spent roll into the fire.

For a moment, I let myself drift.

The water laps at my collarbones.

My body hums with her ghost.

Then something sharp and wrong cuts through the quiet.

Unease coils low in my chest, instinct clawing at the back of my skull. It isn't just the storm inside me; it's something else. Something foreign.

I sit up fast, water sloshing over the sides. The chill hits as I rise, drying myself only enough to pull on trousers and a loose tunic. My sword rests by the door; I grab it before I even think to.

When I wrench open the door, Hypnos stands there.

Eyes bright white.

Sweat streaking his temples.

"Hypnos?" My voice cracks like a whip. Shadows flood the corridor before I can stop them, curling up the walls and choking the light. "What is it?"

"The wards," he grits out, voice strained. "The ones Granite raised while you were away. Silencing wards. Suppression runes. I've been trying to reach you for hours."

My pulse spikes. The thunder outside answers it,

rattling the glass panes, but it sounds far off, like I'm hearing it from underwater.

"Why would he—" I start, but my words die in my throat. "I've been in my chambers only an hour."

Hypnos shakes his head, the glow of his eyes flickering. "No, Your Grace. It's been hours. Nearly a full cycle since you returned."

The blood drains from my face. The shadows around us shift, restless, whispering in warning.

"Where is she?" I demand.

Hypnos' throat bobs, and for the first time since I've known him, he hesitates. "She's in the room near the great hall. Chambermaids preparing Her Majesty," he says quietly. "About to walk down the aisle... to marry Lord Granite."

The sword trembles in my hand.

And the thunder outside finally finds me.

I move before I can think.

Hypnos is already laying out my regalia: formal armor and cloak, the silver threading catching faint blue light from the windows. But I can't stand still long enough to let him finish. The air itself vibrates with my pulse. Every second I waste feels like a blade against my ribs.

"Hold still," Hypnos says tightly. He fastens the clasp of my cloak across one shoulder while I tie my hair back with a strip of leather at the crown of my skull. His hands tremble only slightly, but I feel it—the tremor of a sensor elemental bracing against an oncoming storm.

I have only minutes before my patience fractures this mountain in two, and Hypnos knows it.

"Tell me what happened."

His eyes flash pearly white, a flicker of guilt and dread.

"Granite cornered her in the study. Demanded the union of their bargain. The wards were already in place before he stepped into the room."

My grip tightens on the hilt of my sword. "Where is Mor?"

"She's outside the castle," he answers. "She shadow-walked beyond the wards to bring them down. It took considerable energy—she nearly collapsed doing it."

I nod once, jaw set. "I bet that pissed her off."

"Indeed. Very unfortunate for the Lord of Stone." Hypnos speaks as he helps pull tight the laces of my vest's corset.

Mor is not of the fae, so the ward laws do not bind her. She can tear them down without invoking death. And aside from the Lady of the Lake herself, she's the only being in this realm powerful enough to do it so quickly.

I could, perhaps—if my cursed heart were not already at war with the immortal life I am fated to lose early.

I fix the sword to the scabbard at my hip. My long black cloak drags behind me as I cross the room. The moment my boots strike the corridor stone, the castle feels it—shadows recoil, the light guttering out as I move.

"Your Grace," Hypnos calls after me, following in a near run, "you cannot simply—"

"What law has he broken that I can use to stop this?" I cut in.

Hypnos hesitates at my side. The silence between us is answer enough.

"None, I'm afraid," he says finally. "We must see this through and trust the queen."

Trust her.

The words do not cut because I doubt her—I never could. I've seen her stand before the very forces in this realm that would see her broken.

It's him I don't trust. Granite. The Stone Lord with his cold ambition and buried motives.

I tighten my cloak and move, each stride heavier than the last, thunder pressing against my ribs.

He would see her bound before she ever wears the crown. Would twist her power to serve his own. But I will not stand by and let him.

Not while she's still fighting to claim what's rightfully hers.

The corridors twist and narrow before spilling into the grand entry of Cairnvail. A sea of polished stone and silks fills the space—Granite's court assembled in all their finery, eager to witness their lord's union with Avalon's chosen queen.

My queen.

The title echoes like thunder behind my ribs.

A lesser fae spots me near the archway—the same one who fetched me to the stables yesterday. His eyes go wide, and without a word he slips away into the crowd. Likely ordered to report the moment I was seen. I don't blame him; Granite's punishments are the kind that leave scars in the marrow. But it doesn't stop the anger that rises in me like a storm tide.

My shadows reach ahead, searching for her, yet the wards still warp and scatter their sense. I can't see her, can't feel her—

Not until I stop fighting it and follow the pull instead.

The bond hums beneath my skin, a thrumming heat that answers to her even when she doesn't call for me.

Because that's what it is.

Not a tether of duty or protection.

A bond. Soul-deep. Unmistakable.

I admit it now, even as it claws at me.

My magic knocks against hers, seeking entry—but she doesn't yield. Perhaps she doesn't know how. Perhaps she doesn't know what it is that she's feeling.

Hypnos moves ahead of me, power coiling around him in soft white tendrils as he faces the guards at the chapel doors—two Stone Fae who dare to block our way. "Move," he commands, voice low but thrumming with compulsion.

They step aside instantly.

I push the doors open so hard they slam against the walls. The echo ricochets through the chamber, and my voice follows it like lightning.

"Leave."

The gathered Terra Fae freeze. My shadows flood the floor, curling at their ankles. It takes only a heartbeat before the room empties—those loyal to Granite scattering like dust as I set my eyes on her.

And for a moment, I forget to breathe.

She stands at the center of it all, bathed in the pearlescent glow of moonlight spilling through the windows. Her gown plunges deep, clinging to her curves, the pale sheen turning her dark skin into something holy. Beautiful—so achingly beautiful it nearly undoes me.

But it's wrong.

That dress.

That altar.

That lord waiting for her on the other side of the doors.

I cross the distance in a handful of furious strides and seize her by the arms. "What the fuck do you think you're doing?" My voice is low, dangerous, my rage barely leashed.

She jerks away from my hold, fire blazing in her eyes. "Get your hands off me."

"This is madness," I snarl. "A trick—"

"I know what I'm doing." She cuts me off sharply, gathering the ends of her dress and brushing past me.

The glamour around her flickers. My magic brushes against it and catches the glint of Realmbreaker at her hip. The sight offers only a small measure of comfort—she's armed, at least—but it does little to cool the fury pounding through me.

I tighten her glamour with a thread of my own power, shielding her further from the eyes that would pry, and follow her into the vestibule beyond.

The chamber ahead hums with ceremony. Music drifts through the open doors to the great hall, where I can already imagine Granite standing tall before the crowd, chest puffed, ready to claim a prize that was never his to touch.

Tana stands before the double doors, facing them in stillness, her hands clasped in front of her. Waiting.

I reach her again, grip her arm, and turn her to face me. "Tana."

The name—her name—lands between us like a weapon. I rarely speak it aloud. It's too intimate. Too raw.

She stiffens, the faintest tremor passing through her before she schools her expression.

"You cannot do this," I say. My voice is a low growl, all steel and warning.

She meets my stare head-on, chin high. "Why shouldn't I?"

My jaw clenches so tight I feel the crack in my teeth. I look away, drag in a slow breath through my nose, and exhale through the anger burning in my chest—anger that isn't entirely for her.

I could tell her everything—the Lady's warning, the prophecy whispered in shadowed waters. But not like this. Not when every word would sound like another chain. Another man trying to control her destiny.

The silence stretches, thick and unbearable.

For all my power, for all the storms that answer when I call, I've never felt so helpless. The weight of it presses against my ribs, suffocating. I could tear this castle apart stone by stone, and it wouldn't change the truth of it—she doesn't need my protection. And I... don't know how to stand by without giving it.

Her gaze stays fixed on me, sharp and searching, the fight still simmering beneath her calm. But when I don't speak—when I can't—something in her hardens.

Her shoulders square. Her chin lifts just slightly. And then her expression shifts, that flicker of hope or patience extinguishing behind her eyes.

"That's what I thought."

The words slice through the quiet, colder than any blade ever forged.

The doors open.

She steps back to the center of the threshold, hands folding once more in front of her. And without a glance behind her, Tana takes her first step toward the Stone Lord waiting to claim what he does not deserve.

I pace.

The floor beneath me has memorized the rhythm of my fury by now—each step a drumbeat, each turn a storm. My hands drag through my hair, smoothing what doesn't need smoothing. I release a sharp breath that does nothing to steady me.

The great doors close, cutting me off from the hall beyond. But I can feel it—through the thin threads of shadow I've left behind.

She's there.

Standing at the altar like a lamb to sacrifice.

But gods, she doesn't look like one.

She looks like a queen.

Regal. Composed. Defiant even in stillness.

And it's that defiance that guts me most—because it isn't me she's defying. It's the world that would cage her. The bargain that binds her. The fae who dares to think he's worthy of her crown.

The storm building inside me has nothing to do with magic. It's older, rawer. It's jealousy and terror and love all tangled in one unbearable knot. The thought of Granite standing beside her—touching her, claiming her—makes my vision go white at the edges.

He thinks he has the right to call her mate.

To speak vows over her like she's something to be taken.

He doesn't.

This will start a war. I know it.

To step between a sealed bargain, a mate claim, to break a union before it's formed—it's against every law of the fae.

But I don't fucking care.

I will break it.

I will break all of it—the law, the realm, the sky itself—if destiny requires it.

Granite will not live to see another nocturn if he forces her hand.

The decision settles in me like steel.

I draw my sword. The sound sings through the corridor, sharp and final. My shadows shudder in anticipation. I turn toward the double doors—the ones she just disappeared behind—and the fury in me finds its focus.

Inside, Granite's voice carries across the hall, low and self-satisfied as he delivers his union promise. The crowd falls silent, waiting for the Queen Rising to respond.

My boot meets the seam between the doors with the force of a lightning strike.

The doors explode inward with a crash that shakes the rafters, splintering on the stone floor at my feet. Gasps ripple through the assembly as I step into the great hall, the storm following me like a living thing. Every pair of eyes turns to me—but I see only one.

Her.

Her rich brown eyes meet mine, and something unstoppable ignites between us.

I raise my sword, its tip leveled at Granite's heart. My stance is steady, my voice steady too—clear enough to drown the hush that falls over the room.

"I object."

CHAPTER 23
tana

I can feel it—the storm about to break.

Granite is speaking. I only know because I can see his mouth moving, the faint curl of triumph at the corners of his lips. But I can't hear him over the ringing in my ears, the pounding of my own heart. Every breath I take is deliberate—slow, steady, measured—because if I let it falter, everyone in this hall will see the truth trembling beneath my skin.

On the other side of the doors, I can feel him.

Orion.

His pulse beats through the stone like a war drum, matching the rhythm of mine until I can't tell where one ends and the other begins.

Then movement catches my eye. A side door, cracked open just enough for a sliver of light—and a familiar face. The stablehand. The one Granite struck for daring to be seen during a dinner service. The bruise still shadows his cheek like a mark of defiance.

He finds me through the narrow space.

Nods once.

And before he can even ease the door shut again—before he's caught—

The world explodes.

The great doors at the end of the hall shatter inward, a

thunderclap that sends splinters skittering across the marble floor. A surge of wind tears through the chamber, snuffing out half the torches in a single breath.

A typhoon.

A storm made flesh.

Orion stands in the doorway, sword drawn, cloak sweeping around him like a wing of darkness. Power rolls off him in waves, bending the air itself. He doesn't look at the crowd, or the altar, or the guards rushing to intercept.

He looks only at me.

And the wall I've held up so carefully these past weeks—my calm, my restraint, my control—shatters in an instant.

"I object."

His words strike through the air like lightning. There's claim in them. Challenge. And something far more dangerous pulsing beneath both—something that calls to the part of me I've tried to ignore.

I move.

Spin away from Granite, skirts whipping around my legs as my hand finds Realmbreaker beneath the fold of my gown—the hidden scabbard that Orion spotted through Hypnos's glamour, the one he fortified before we entered this godforsaken hall.

The blade shrieks as I draw it, the sound pure and sharp. I turn back toward Granite, widening the space between us until the tip of my sword hovers at the hollow of his throat.

"I also object," I say, my voice steady against the fury rippling through the hall.

Granite's skin flushes a deep, mottled gray. His jaw tightens, veins rising along his neck. The wards shimmer faintly at his back, reacting to his temper. He's losing control of them—no, he's trying to tighten them.

I can see it. The faint shimmer of power choking through the air, tightening like chains.

Hypnos was right. Wards to keep the lesser fae silent. And new ones—crafted for us. Woven in secrecy before we even arrived. Granite's plan was never unity. It was domination. To bargain for power and bind us beneath his control.

To force our agreement—or die trying.

But he doesn't get the chance.

The mountain groans with a deep, ancient sound—a thunderous boom that rattles the walls and sends dust cascading from the vaulted ceiling. The floor quakes beneath us, so violently I stumble, catching myself only by the blade I've driven into the stone.

Screams echo from the assembly as Stone Fae brace against the trembling earth. Granite staggers, eyes wide, his composure cracking for the first time. He's looking around wildly—not at me, not at Orion—but at the air itself.

At his crumbling wards.

A surge of power rushes through the hall like a tidal wave—first pulling all the breath from the room, then slamming through it in a roar of wind and magic that knocks several fae from their feet.

The sound is deafening. I drop to one knee, hands covering my ears, Realmbreaker clutched in white-knuckled grip.

And when I look up—Granite stands frozen.

Color drained from his face.

Eyes wild.

The look of a desperate man who knows his game is over.

He just has no idea how fucked he really is.

I push to my feet, balance returning as the rush of power begins to ebb. The air is still electric, humming with whatever force just cracked this mountain's spine. Dust drifts in lazy clouds, and I can taste stone on my tongue.

Granite's face is a storm of fury and disbelief, but I know better than to think this is over. He'll fight. His pride won't let him do anything else. The Lord of Stone would sooner shatter himself than bend a knee to the mortal queen the realm chose over him.

"Guards!" he bellows, voice booming through the hall.

I lift Realmbreaker again before he can move. The tip kisses the soft flesh beneath his jaw, a bead of blood blooming where steel meets skin.

Stone guards surge forward at his call—but they never reach me.

Orion is already there.

I can feel him behind me—solid, unshakable. His belt unfurls into a whip of shadow in his hand, black smoke bleeding from it like ink in water. He cracks it once, the sound a snarl of thunder, and keeps his sword angled forward, the storm around him barely restrained.

"Take one more step toward her," he warns, his voice a blade in the dark, "and I will let loose my darkness and let it have you."

The shadows hiss in response, curling like serpents around his boots.

A rush of pride floods through me, hot and sharp.

Finally.

He's not shielding me. Not controlling me. Not questioning me.

He's standing with me.

Granite's fury deepens, veins bulging at his temples. His mouth twists as he spits an insult, something vile and dripping with the poison of his ego. "You fucking—"

But he never finishes.

The tremor hits first—just a faint vibration underfoot. Then another, stronger. The chandeliers sway. And before anyone can move, the far wall of the great hall explodes.

Stone and dust and shards of marble rain down as a beast the size of a fortress bursts through, its roar shaking the air itself. The force of it knocks me backward, my arm thrown up to shield my face as rubble flies.

Moonlight floods the hall through the gaping wound in the southern wall. I can feel it—the way it reaches for me, answers me. I don't even have to call to it; it comes as naturally as breath.

At my side, Orion moves with the same instinct. His shadows surge outward, coalescing into a solid wall before us. But something else races with it—through it.

Light. My light.

A burst of silver-white moonlight streams from my hands, merging with his darkness until the two fuse— shadows veined with light, light stitched with shadow. The effect steals my breath. Beautiful. Terrible.

I glance at him.

Orion's eyes are wide, his expression one of pure shock and awe.

From the swirling dust and moonbeam haze, something massive moves. Two curved tusks appear first—ivory white and ancient, like the bones of a god's forgotten beast. Then the rest follows.

A mammoth.

But wrong.

All wrong.

The creature is made entirely of bone, each rib and joint gleaming under the moonlight. Its skull is enormous, hollow eyes like bottomless wells, its trunk nothing but a twisting chain of vertebrae snapping through the air. When it steps, the floor groans beneath the weight.

The sight freezes the entire hall.

The beast draws a breath—a deep, hollow, rasping inhale—and the growl that follows shakes through the marrow of every living being present.

And then, standing atop one of the tusks, balanced like a rider on a wave, is the Morrigan.

Tar drips from her bare feet, sizzling as it hits the floor. Her golden eyes gleam like molten metal as she grips a shard of bone near the beast's face, utterly unbothered by the chaos around her.

Her gaze fixes on Granite. The air vibrates with the sound of her presence, that chorus of voices braided into one divine, terrible tone.

"It is best you do not finish that sentence."

The words crawl through the hall like a curse, echoing in every corner of my bones.

The Morrigan's voice fades into the charged silence, and slowly, the walls of light and shadow Orion and I cast begin to fold back toward us. My moonlight withdraws like a tide, his darkness slipping back into him like smoke curling home to flame. The two magics separate, leaving the hall still humming in their wake.

Granite's face has gone pale as limestone, eyes wide and locked on the bone beast and the goddess who stands upon its tusk like judgment incarnate.

"So, Granite," I say, my voice steady, cutting through the quiet. "About that bargain."

His throat bobs. "It is binding," he insists, voice breaking halfway through. "It is law. You must marry me."

I blink at him, honestly stunned. Of all the ways I thought this might go, hearing him sound like a sulking child wasn't one of them. With a sigh, I slide Realmbreaker back into its scabbard.

"You see, that's the thing with Fae bargains . . ."

The words taste sweet in my mouth—his own, thrown back at him.

Across the hall, Hypnos has moved closer to the beast, the crunch of gravel beneath his boots echoing softly. He joins the Morrigan, who doesn't move, her golden eyes still fixed unblinking on Granite as if daring him to test his luck further.

"You must be specific," I say.

"I was specific!" Granite snaps, desperation cracking his voice.

"Were you?" I tilt my head. "Let's review, shall we?"

I take a slow step forward, the click of my heels deliberate against the stone. "You see, I learned something early on about Fae bargains—from Hypnos, actually. My first Beltane in Avalon." I glance toward the god of sleep, who offers a small, knowing smile. "He told me: 'Don't take an offered drink unless you're ready to bind yourself.'"

I let that sink in, watching as Granite's expression falters. I can see the moment he starts to replay it all—our first meeting, the negotiation, the pride that had lit his eyes when he thought he'd trapped me neatly within his deal.

Orion gets it first. I hear his breath catch—a sharp inhale as his head snaps toward Hypnos, who only grins wider.

"See," I continue, "I gave you my terms. And then I offered you my drink. You accepted. You drank. And in doing so, you bound yourself to me. As my ally."

Granite shakes his head, sputtering. "You did—you agreed to a union!"

"An alliance," I correct softly, clicking my tongue in mock disappointment. "Not a union."

Then, for the entire hall to hear, I recite it—every word of the bargain.

"We gain safe passage through Cairnvail to Frosthaven and back. And when Avalon calls, Cairnvail answers—as the crown's first and closest ally."

The hall is silent but for the faint groaning of the mammoth's bones as it shifts behind the Morrigan. Granite stares at me, working his jaw, searching for a loophole that isn't there.

Behind me, Orion slides his sword back into its sheath. He knows it too—knows Granite can do nothing against me now. The moment he'd said, "That's the shape of it," and lifted my cup, drinking what I offered him, the bargain sealed. The runes of the mountain had burned to life to mark it.

He wasn't binding me.

He was binding himself to me.

To the crown.

The realization settles over the room like dawn breaking after a long night. Granite's expression twists—shock, then rage, then the hollow defeat of a man who's just realized the game he thought he was winning is already over.

He was undone by a mortal.

And I—

I feel it. The shift in the air, the pulse of the realm's approval. Moonlight streams through the broken wall, warm and cool all at once as it spills across my hands.

The Trial of Sword and Chalice.

A test not of might, but of wit. To see if I could wield something other than steel. To rule with both edge and mercy.

I offered a chalice—and won the allegiance of the realm's most unbreakable warriors. And by all accounts . . . one of its most impossible lords.

CHAPTER 24
tana

Orion's gait—steady and unrelenting—is like a silent promise behind me as I leave the great hall.

He doesn't speak. Doesn't ask me to wait.

He doesn't need to.

His presence crackles against my spine like lightning warming the air before it strikes.

I barely clear the threshold—just one turn into the corridor—

and a hand grabs my upper arm and spins me.

Orion wraps his other hand around my throat, not too tight but firm enough to steal the breath from my lungs in a single gasp. My back slams into the wall, and his mouth is on mine.

Fuck, yes.

It's not soft. Not gentle.

This is a kiss made of war.

Tongue and teeth and heat—mouths crashing with all the fury we've buried for weeks. His other hand fists in my skirts, pulling me closer, pressing the full weight of him against me like he means to pin me through the stone.

I moan into him, and he swallows it down like water after a drought—with a snarl.

"You stubborn, impossible woman," he breathes against my lips before diving back in.

My hands claw into his shoulders, gripping hard. "You arrogant, insufferable asshole—"

He growls, deep and rough, breaking the kiss just long enough to nip at my jaw, my throat. "Keep talking, Queen. I'll make you scream your defiance into the fucking mattress."

A whimper escapes me—need and fury tangled together. My legs start to shake, and he grips my thighs, lifting me like I weigh nothing. "This ends now."

Then—suddenly—I'm up and over his shoulder.

"Orion!" I shout, breathless as he storms down the hall with me slung like a conquest, one hand gripping my ass.

"You want a storm, Starling?" His voice is dark silk and thunder. "Then brace for it."

"Put me down!" I smack his ass hard. He doesn't flinch —just chuckles low in his chest and smacks me back, the sound echoing through the corridor like a promise.

"Time to punish you," he growls, palm landing again. "For being such a damn stubborn queen."

He pushes open the door to his bedchamber and storms through it like a man possessed—because he is. Possessed by fury. By lust. By me.

The door is kicked shut behind us with a violent crack, and he drops me with such urgency that I stumble, my cheeks flushing hot as blood rushes back to my limbs.

But he's waiting for nothing.

Whatever chasm existed between us—weeks of silence, anger, longing—it snaps shut in an instant, not by fate or apology, but by force.

His hands fist the front of my dress, and he rips.

The sound is vicious, satisfying. The fabric tears down the center, and I gasp as cool air licks across suddenly exposed skin.

"The next time I see you wear a dress for another male..." Orion's voice is low—gravel and smoke.

He lifts my thigh with one hand, the gesture rough and reverent all at once, fingers finding the strap of the blade he gifted me—my blade, the one that never leaves my side.

He unsheathes it smoothly. The cool metal glints once, and then he cuts the rest of the dress away, eyes never leaving mine.

"I cut it off you," he says darkly, tossing the knife to the nearest tabletop, "the second my eyes find you."

Then he's kissing me again—no, consuming me. Desperation poured into every touch, every breath, every press of his body to mine.

I'm just as wild. I grab the front of his vest and yank—so hard the buttons pop free and scatter across the stone like fallen beads.

His tunic is next—he tears it over his head, breaking contact with my mouth just long enough to throw it aside. Then he's back, hands cupping my cheeks, lips crashing into mine as he backs me toward the bed.

It hits the back of my knees, and I fall with a soft *oof*, catching myself on my elbows.

He follows—

crawling toward me like a predator, all shadows and hunger. His long hair slips over one shoulder, wild and beautiful. His eyes are fixed on me like I'm prey and salvation both.

His shadows do the work of untying his trousers, freeing that massive cock.

I spread my legs slowly, deliberately—an offering and a challenge—and pull my panties to the side. His gaze flickers lower, and then—

"Starling."

God.

His tongue drags along my center in one long, devastating sweep. My hips jolt, a low moan escaping me before I can stop it.

"Fuck—Orion—"

He hums against me, and I swear I feel it in my spine.

I've missed this.

His mouth—his mouth that never stops running unless it's here, buried between my thighs like he belongs there. Like he knows it's the only place he ever truly shuts up.

I've missed the way he makes me feel—settled. Whole. Like the part of me that's always on edge can finally breathe.

His scent. His warmth. His maddening, fucking presence.

Him.

God, I missed him.

He licks me like it might fix the realm—like every problem, every war, every inch of land touched by the Obscura could be soothed between my thighs.

"God," I whisper, eyes fluttering, fingers weaving through his long hair. "You're so fucking good."

He moans against me like he needs the praise—like it feeds him—and his tongue moves with maddening precision. I stay propped on one elbow, just so I can watch—

watch his mouth working my pussy like it belongs to him, watch the hunger in his eyes when he looks up at me.

"Let me back in."

His eyes hold mine as his tongue flicks over my clit in tiny, teasing strokes that make my toes curl.

"Please, Starling," he murmurs, lips brushing that swollen bundle of nerves like he's kissing something sacred. "I cannot live another second without feeling you under my skin."

And the wall I've held against him—thin and fragile these last few days—crumbles completely.

I release that band around my mind, and the moment I let him in, it's like warmth flooding over winter, melting everything cold I've been clinging to.

The sensation of him rushes down my body, every touch magnified a thousand times—each stroke of his tongue, the way his fingers grip my thighs.

That's it. Let me feel you again. The rich timber of his voice hums through my mind.

I spread my legs wider, scraping my fingers through his soft hair. My hips move in time with his mouth, and I lean my head back, surrendering to sensation.

His voice hums in my head, thick with reverence and heat.

So sweet for me. So fucking wet.

You've missed this mouth, haven't you? Missed the way I talk while I devour you.

Say it, Starling. Say you missed me.

Then—softly, with such tenderness—

I told you I've missed you.

I freeze.

That line. That exact line.

"You—" I pant, breath catching in my throat. "You said that in a dream. Not... not in real life."

He lifts his head, smirking. "Who said I wasn't real?"

Before I can process, his mouth is back on me, lips wrapping around my clit and sucking hard.

"Fuck—Orion—" I cry, thighs twitching.

But I'm not done.

I hook my feet under his arms and twist, using all the momentum I can muster. He lets me flip him onto his back, and I straddle his face, still dripping, still throbbing—but I hold myself just out of reach.

His eyes flash with amusement. He knows I'm feigning irritation.

"The dreams." I arch a brow. "Those were real?"

He growls, leaning up as far as he can, tongue sticking out like he's desperate to taste me again. "Of course they were real," he grits. "You think I dream about *not* eating this pussy?"

A laugh bubbles up in me, but before I can respond, a little zap of lightning—like a spark of static—jumps from the tip of his tongue and crackles right against my clit.

"Ah—fuck!"

I jolt forward, one hand bracing on the mattress, pussy throbbing and slick. If he does that again, I'll come before he's even inside me.

But I don't get the chance to test it—because he moves.

In one lightning-fast surge, he flips me. Faster than I flipped him. I know he let me have my moment; he's far too strong for anything else.

Now I'm beneath him, legs falling open, aching for him.

His hands find mine, fingers lacing together, and he pins them to the pillow above my head.

But he doesn't thrust. Not yet. He's staring at me with a strange look of both wonder and longing.

"Don't shut me out again," he murmurs, voice low and raw, a tenderness in his eyes that aches with every unsaid thing between us.

"Don't lock me up again," I whisper back, barely breathing.

His expression softens, and he leans down, pressing his mouth to mine with painful gentleness. "Never."

Then I open for him—lips parting, legs spreading and wrapping around him—

and he slides into me.

We groan in unison, the stretch of him too perfect, the feel of him too much. My pussy clenches tight, soaking wet and desperate after a month of silence and games.

"Fuck, Starling," he moans, buried to the hilt. "So tight. So fucking wet for me. Were you punishing me or yourself?"

"Both," I gasp.

He doesn't thrust hard. Doesn't slam into me like a brute.

He moves with me—our bodies sliding together like waves crashing and pulling, again and again. Smooth. Deep. Sensual.

One of his arms bands under my back, palm cupping my ass cheek, squeezing it possessively. The other still pins our hands above my head, our fingers laced tight.

"I should've broken sooner," he whispers into my mouth. "Begged sooner."

"You should have," I breathe.

"I'm here now." His hips roll into mine, dragging a moan from deep in my throat. "And I'm not letting go again."

And I believe him.

Because every thrust, every kiss, every whispered word against my skin tells me the same thing—

this isn't just reunion.

It's worship.

Orion thrusts into me with reverence and need tangled into every motion, as though he's trying to carve an apology into my bones. My hand finds his cheek, thumb dragging across the sweat-slick line of his jaw, and his breath shudders.

"I'm sorry," he says, the words strangled and low. "For all of it. For not trusting you. For trying to walk away. I thought if I let you love me... I'd ruin you."

Another thrust. Deeper. Slower. My body clenches around him like it wants to answer before I can.

His forehead presses to mine. "But you never needed my protection. You needed me to stand beside you. And I was too much of a coward to believe I was worthy of that."

"You are," I whisper, lips brushing his as I speak. "Who else could possibly stand next to me?"

His hands brace against the mattress on either side of my head, and the shadows around him flicker like storm-light barely held at bay.

"You were mine the moment I saw you," he murmurs, voice shaking as he moves inside me again. "Not when you came to Avalon. Not when you stood before the courts. Before that—when the Lady showed you to me in the Sanctum. You don't know what that did to me. What it meant."

I gasp when tiny bursts of his lightning power pop

against my clit and nipples as he rolls his hips again, dragging pleasure low and molten through me.

"I waited," he says, burying his face in the crook of my neck. "Age after age, I waited for you. And I'd wait again if I had to. But now you're here. And I won't survive losing you."

I don't realize I'm crying until he kisses the tears from my cheeks.

Then his hand slips between us, finding that aching bundle of nerves, circling slow and sure until I shatter around him—tight and clenching and gasping his name like a prayer.

He holds me through the aftershocks, murmuring things in the old language of the fae that I don't understand,

his shadows curling around us like they know I'm fragile right now.

When I finally open my eyes, he's watching me like I hung the stars.

"Come here," he says roughly, rolling onto his back and taking me with him—his cock still hard between us, his voice hoarse. "Ride me, my queen."

I blink, dazed, but he settles his hands on my hips and urges me up. "Let me see you. Let me give you everything—and take whatever you want in return."

I straddle him, heart still racing, and he talks me through it—guiding me as I sink back down on him, his hands gentle but firm.

"That's it," he says, breath ragged. "Take your time. This is yours, Tana. All of it. All of me."

I move slowly at first, working him in and out of me, savoring every stretch, every flicker of the storm in his eyes.

His hands lift, and I grab them, bracing them over his

head as I ride him harder now—grinding into every thrust until we're both unraveling, until I'm panting above him, the world blurring around the edges.

He watches me like I'm something sacred.

"I love you." I say it without fear this time, without hesitation. "I love you, Orion."

His eyes flare like lightning. His hips buck up—hard and desperate—and I cry out, clenching again.

He groans my name, the sound breaking open and beautiful.

We come together—stars behind my eyes, his shadows crashing like waves around us.

When it's over, I collapse against his chest, still joined, still full of him.

He doesn't pull away. Doesn't move to separate us.

Instead, he wraps his arms around me—one hand splayed over the back of my head, the other pressed flat between my shoulder blades.

And he kisses me—soft, deep, warm enough to melt the frost from every lonely corner inside me.

"I told you," he whispers, lips brushing mine. "I will fight for you until the stars reclaim me."

He kisses me again, so softly it almost hurts. "And I will love you until the last light fades from the realm."

CHAPTER 25

Evenfall stains the windows in soft hues of indigo and pearl, but I don't give a fuck about the time. Not when I've spent every hour since the great hall between her thighs or with her in my arms.

The bed is a wreck. The food Hypnos left hours ago—likely out of pure concern I might starve her—sits near empty by the door. He didn't even knock properly, just tapped once like a ghost afraid to interrupt something holy and left a cart stacked with wine, moonwater, and enough sustenance to feed a small village.

He was right to be afraid.

I'd have let her waste away with me here.

Sated and starving in all the best ways.

There's never been a better day in all my immortal life.

Locked away in this bedchamber with a very large bed and a woman just as ravenous as I am.

My woman. My mate.

The missing piece of my soul that's finally, finally found me.

We lie now in the silence of that knowing—naked, spent, our bodies curved toward one another like gravity itself is conspiring to keep us together. Her thumb traces a lazy path across my jaw. My hand traces the curve of her waist and continues down her hip. Neither of us has spoken in several minutes. We haven't needed to. The language of skin and breath has been more than enough.

But it's not enough now.

There's still too much distance between us—a foot at most, but it may as well be a canyon. I grunt and pull her toward me, one strong arm around her lower back. She laughs, low and warm, and lets her leg curl over my hip right where it belongs.

My hand finds her thigh like it's been magnetized—stroking gently, barely a whisper of touch as I drag my knuckles along her skin. I could worship her for another age and still find something new to love.

Her breasts press against my chest, soft and warm, and her fingers trace circles along my spine, the tips of them dipping into old scars. She's mapping them now, committing them to memory. I wonder if she knows how many were carved in her name—earned before I ever knew her—to defend the throne she is to sit upon.

Her eyes flick up to mine, searching.

Dark and endless and hers.

Then she looks at my mouth.

Leans in.

Her tongue brushes the seam of my lips—just once.

Then her mouth is on mine, slow and unhurried, like we've got another thousand years and she intends to taste every second of it.

We don't rush.

We just... exist.

And gods, how good it feels to just be.

To be hers. To have her be mine.

When we finally pull away, her face is the picture of

peace. A faint smile at the corner of her mouth. Eyes heavy-lidded and soft, the brown of them burnished gold in the dimming light.

"How are your headaches?" I ask quietly.

She blinks, as if coming back into herself. Thinking.

Then surprise flickers across her features. "I've not really noticed, but..." She tilts her head. "Better. I've hardly had one since we arrived."

My hand stills on her thigh. Relief—deep and genuine—breaks open in my chest.

"Good."

I've hated seeing her in pain. Hated the way her shoulders would tense, the way she'd try to hide it behind a mask of iron and will. She's strong enough to bear it, yes—but she shouldn't have to.

"Maybe it's the mountains," she says, voice thoughtful. "Higher altitude. Cleaner air."

I shake my head slowly. "No."

Her brow furrows. "Then what?"

My gaze traces the shape of her face—the slope of her nose, the small scar above her lip, the eyes that could bring kingdoms to heel.

"It's you," I say. "You're opening up to it now. The magic. The power that was always meant to live inside you."

She stills, watching me carefully.

"It's not just Avalon changing you," I continue. "You're accepting it. Letting it root itself in your bones. Letting it bloom."

I brush a strand of hair from her face. "It's a slow returning to something your soul already knows." I can't fight my smirk. "If only my stubborn queen would stop fighting it."

She rolls her eyes—softly this time—and I take her hand in mine, our fingers fitting together like they've always belonged that way. Her skin, dark and warm against my pale, is a contrast that shouldn't make sense but does. It's like looking at the reflection of what we became in that hall —my shadows and her light.

It was beautiful.

It was impossible.

"In the hall..." I murmur, thumb tracing the ridge of her knuckle, "the light."

She nods before I can say more. "I've been thinking about it too."

"My grandmother used to have that power," I say, reverent even now at the memory of her.

Tana's gaze sharpens. "What was it?"

I tilt my head. "What did it feel like to you?"

She hesitates, then whispers, "It felt like moonlight."

"It was." I smile faintly. "A shield made of pure moon-light—one of the purest forms of light that exists. My grandmother could summon it. I've not seen it in ages, Star-ling, and you commanded it as though you've done it your entire life."

Her brow furrows, but I can see the spark of curiosity behind it.

I tighten my hold on her hand and continue, "My mother used to tell me a story—the great war when Avalon dimmed. She said that when Queen Pandora pushed back the Obscura, she did so with a shield of moonlight so powerful it spanned all ten courts. It held the darkness at bay until her death."

Tana raises our joined hands between us, studying them like they hold the key to that story.

"And what about what we did?" she asks softly. "The light and shadow merged. It was beautiful."

I nod, unable to hide the awe in my voice. "I've never seen anything like it. The two forces aren't meant to blend—they balance each other, yes, one necessary for the other. But what we did... it wasn't balance. It was fusion. Something new. Something neither light nor dark could become on its own."

Her lips press together as she thinks, then she says quietly, "Maybe it's because I'm nearly through the trials."

She looks into my eyes now, a gravity not there before suddenly present.

"I completed the Trial of Sword and Chalice. I could feel the realm's approval after the bargain with Granite."

That pulls my attention sharply back to her. I'd suspected, but hearing her confirm it stirs something fierce and protective in my chest.

"Only two remain—I think—the Trial of the Ancients and the Trial of Fate."

I exhale, heavy with the weight of those words as she keeps talking. "Hypnos told me both are largely unknown. Each Queen Rising faces them differently, but these two... their details are always vague. The records were lost or destroyed ages ago."

She grows quiet. Too quiet. Her gaze drifts somewhere beyond me—beyond this room, beyond now. The rhythm of her heart shifts, faster, uneven.

I brush my thumb along her cheek. "Where have your thoughts taken you?"

Her voice, when it comes, is barely above a whisper. "To the Trial of Fate."

A chill crawls up my spine. "And?"

Her eyes meet mine, steady and unflinching. "I think I know what mine will be."

Dread tightens my chest, and I close my eyes. I already know what she's going to say before she says it.

"Tana..."

"I have to die."

The world seems to tilt. For a heartbeat, I forget how to breathe.

Her words hang there between us—terrible, inevitable, true.

No. No, no, no.

But I don't say that aloud. Not yet.

Instead, I reach for her hand again, thread our fingers together like it'll anchor her here in this world with me. Like I can tether her soul with touch alone.

"You don't know that," I murmur, even as something in me already fears the shape of her truth. "The trials are different for everyone. But do not think of it as... death. Maybe it's more of a becoming. A transformation."

Her brow lifts. "Into what?"

I hesitate. My heart stutters.

"An immortal," I whisper. "A fae."

She goes still, and I feel her watching me with that keen, unblinking gaze that always sees more than I want it to.

"Has that ever happened before?" she asks.

I want to say yes. I want to lie for her. For me.

But I can't. Not now.

I swallow hard. "I don't know."

The words taste like ash.

She sees the truth in my face—knows me too well to miss the crack in my voice. Before I can spiral further, she shifts forward and wraps herself around me, her limbs anchoring me to her body. Her warmth. Her breath. Her strength.

I bury my face in her shoulder and hold her tightly.

"The Lady showed me something after you left for the forest. A heart for a heart. A life for a life. A mortal life—" I hesitate, letting the weight of it settle in my mind before I speak it. "A mortal life for an immortal one. A broken heart for one that will never stop beating."

I don't know what the Trial of Fate will demand. But what I do know—what I feel in the depths of my soul—is that the Lady's vision was true. Tana's fate is tied to mine.

"Two hearts. One mortal, one fae. Both failing. Fractured. Suffering not because of some illness or weakness, but because they were meant to beat together."

And right now, they're out of rhythm. Out of time.

"Tana," I whisper. But she's already moving.

She shifts me onto my back, straddling my hips like she's taking back control—not of the realm, not of the trials, but of this. Of us. Of the only thing we have left right now: each other.

Her eyes are fire and moonlight as she takes both my hands, threading her fingers through mine again. Her hips rock forward, grinding slowly against my cock as it hardens between us, pulsing with need and purpose.

She kisses the pad of one finger, then guides my hands

to her breasts—pressing them together, warm and full in my palms. "We're mates, aren't we?"

Heat rushes through me, blood thundering in my veins. She grinds down again, and I nearly lose my grip on the moment.

I sit up, bracing one hand behind me, the other rising to cradle her jaw.

"Yes, Starling," I breathe. "You can feel it?"

She nods, her lower lip caught between her teeth as she rolls her hips in slow, deliberate circles. Her slick heat coats my shaft as she slides along it, her clit catching on the ridges of my cock with every pass.

"Yes," she says, eyes closing as she moans. "I can feel you in my mind. I don't know how to explain it. It's like you're... there. Even when you're not touching me."

"I feel it too, my love." My voice is low, reverent. "In every fiber of my being, you are there. But you are mortal, and I am not. We cannot complete the bond like this. I believe..." My voice falters, then steadies. "I believe that's what the Trial of Fate is. A fated bond—unfinished."

Her hand wraps around me—tight, sure—and she guides me to her entrance, eyes locked to mine.

And then she takes me.

Slides down onto my cock, slow and steady, until I'm buried to the hilt.

Her body tightens around me, pulsing, perfect. Her head falls back, a moan slipping from her lips like a song made only for me.

I kiss her throat, mouth open, letting her pleasure vibrate against my lips.

She looks at me again, one arm wrapping around my

neck, her breast flush to my chest. I grip her ass in both hands, helping her rock against me, helping her ride through the storm building between us.

"I'm scared," she whispers.

I flip her gently, never pulling out, until I'm above her again—my body a shield, my cock still deep inside her, my elbows bracing on either side of her head like I could hold the world in place for her.

"I'm here."

I kiss her, slow and aching.

Then I move.

Every thrust is a vow. Every stroke a promise.

My hand slides between us, palm pressed flat over her heart.

"Right here, Starling," I murmur against her lips. "I'm here. Forever. I'll be with you—whatever fate brings..."

I thrust deeper, harder.

"We'll share it. Together."

CHAPTER 26
tana

The pass to Frosthaven is a total loss.

The scouts came back frostbitten and hollow-eyed, swearing the storm itself had teeth. The other mountain routes are sealed under miles of ice, the kind that won't melt until Avalon spins to a new season.

Granite, at least, is loyal now. His allegiance belongs to me, and he's promised to send his strongest Fae to dig through the pass. But even he admitted it'll take time. Time I don't have.

Every day, the darkness pushes harder against the wards at the Enchanted Forest. The High Fae stationed there have had to double their shifts just to keep the barrier alive. They're drawing on every drop of their wells, working until their hands shake and their eyes bleed silver. If they falter—if the wards fall—the Obscura will pour through.

Mor's words echo in my head: *The Obscura isn't shadow. Not anymore.*

Not the kind of darkness she wields. Not the kind Orion commands. This thing clawing at the edges of Avalon isn't shadow—it's rot. Something that's eaten through the dark itself and made a mockery of it.

But I can't stop thinking about last night—the moment Orion and I stood side by side, his shadows crashing against a shield of moonlight that answered to me. We both meant to shield, to protect, but the magic didn't separate. It *fused*.

Where his darkness met my light, it didn't cancel out—it transformed.

Silver and black braided together, shimmering like oil over water. Alive. Whole.

And maybe that's the answer.

Maybe what can destroy a corrupted darkness isn't pure light... but a different kind entirely.

I'm still turning the thought over when Orion's hand presses briefly to my arm. "We're here."

Evershade.

The Eternal Night Court.

We pass through its wards, and the air itself changes. The magic here is heavy, dense with secrecy, pressing close against my skin like a whisper that doesn't want to be heard. The moment the barrier parts for us, the world grows quieter—not silent, just *listening*.

The sky deepens to ink. Not the soft velvet night of Avalon, but a darkness so rich it feels alive, pulsing faintly under the glow of an oversized moon. The light that touches the ground is thin and silvered, shifting as if uncertain where to fall.

Mist rolls low over the cobblestones, wrapping around our boots as we step down. It smells faintly metallic, like starlight and old lies. A single tower rises from the gloom, carved of obsidian and veined moonstone, the windows dark and gleaming. I can *feel* the eyes behind them, sharp and silent, watching from behind glass.

Even the stars look different here. Smaller. Sharper. The kind that illuminate nothing and promise less.

"Welcome to Evershade," Mor murmurs, her voice laced with a rare thread of caution. "Home of the court that trusts no one."

I believe her.

If Avalon is the realm of night, then Evershade is its secret heart—black, beautiful, and mercilessly still.

As we walk forward, I know one thing for certain:

This is not a place that gives freely.

Not trust.

Not allegiance.

Not even truth.

Our horses' hooves strike against the cobblestone, each sound swallowed almost instantly by the thick, silvery fog curling across the path. Ahead, the world narrows to a single silhouette—an obsidian tower that pierces the sky like a blade. No other structures. No lanterns. Just this lone spire of shadow and moonlight waiting in the hush.

The tower's door opens before we reach it, soundless and deliberate, as though it's been expecting us.

Orion dismounts first, his hand automatically going to the hilt at his hip. "We must request passage first," he says, voice low but certain. "Umbriel's wards won't let anyone past this threshold uninvited."

He looks back at Mor and Hypnos, giving a single nod. "Stay here. Until I call."

Mor turns her horse back toward the barrier of the court. "We will wait outside the wards."

Hypnos decides to remain outside the spire as Mor returns with the others on the other side of Umbriel's wards. I'm almost thinking I would prefer to wait there with them. But I know I can't.

The air shifts as we step through the doorway—dense and humming with layered enchantments. Inside, the light comes from nowhere and everywhere at once, refracting off black stone like the shimmer of deep water. Shadows cling to the curved walls, which rise high enough to make me dizzy when I glance up. The air smells faintly of cold iron and old ink.

A single silver flame burns in a basin at the room's center, its glow too weak to reach the edges. The silence here isn't empty—it's *watching*.

While Orion waits near the flame, his expression carved from stone, I drift closer to the walls. At first, I think they're etched with cracks, but when I move nearer, the markings form into names—branches and symbols looping outward in intricate lines.

A family tree.

The etchings are faint, almost invisible against the black surface. I squint, leaning closer, half tempted to try what I did during the battle. To call the light again.

I lift my hands, turning them over in the pale glow, willing that same warmth to gather beneath my skin. But nothing happens.

Last time had been instinct—desperation. I'm not even sure I *can* do it by choice.

So instead, I shift position, chasing what little light there is until the carvings become clearer.

I find Pandora's name first—the beginning of the line. From her branch, four names extend in graceful arcs: Elaine, Demeter, Hecate and Daphne.

Elaine is Orion's mother.

Demeter is the traitor who murdered her mother and

sister. It is presumed she also killed Daphne, though they do not know.

And Hecate. I know almost nothing about her—only that she resides on Gaea, and that even the Fae speak of her with caution.

My eyes move down the line beneath Elaine's name until I find Orion's—his sigil marked in silver, glowing faintly under the torchlight.

I trace the lines connecting them, following the web of bloodlines until I notice one slashed out completely. A deep gouge carved through both name and mark.

I glance toward Orion. "Will that happen to Demeter's place too? Since she's been condemned for her crimes?"

He looks over, frowning slightly as he approaches. "No," he says after a moment. "The realm may mark her as traitor, but blood remains blood. I've never..." His fingers brush the carved-out line. "I've never seen a name *removed* like this before."

A cool swirl of air dances around my ankles and as it rises up my body, so do whispers. Soft but growing louder. Many voices, like ghosts from the past all telling different stories floats around the dark spire.

If Orion hears it too, he doesn't give anything away, staring at the scratches in the wall.

Before we can wonder whose it was—or who wanted it erased—a new hum ripples through the floor. The air thickens, charged and cold.

A figure steps through the silver flame.

Lord Umbriel.

The Warden of the Eternal Night.

And from the way the shadows bend toward him, I understand why this court never needed guards.

He steps from the dark and at first, I think he's a shadow given shape—until the silver flame catches him and makes him real.

Lord Umbriel is tall. Just as tall as Orion, but where Orion carries his height like a weapon, Umbriel wears his like a warning. There's no muscle to him, no strength in the traditional sense—only long lines and hollow grace, a figure carved from smoke.

He's bald—utterly so. No hair, no brows, just a smooth expanse of gray-toned skin that gleams faintly, like polished stone. His eyes are what stop me. Enormous and entirely black—iris, pupil, everything swallowed by darkness. They reflect nothing, not even the flame, as if light itself refuses him.

His face is mostly flat—no nose, only the faintest ridge where one should be, and a mouth so thin it looks like someone drew it on with a knife. When it moves, it barely disturbs his expression at all.

His ears taper long and elegant, curving back like blades, and his fingers—god, his fingers—are impossibly slender, ending in nails so sharp and black they could cut glass. He holds a tall staff of carved wood in one hand, the top crowned with a rough-edged crystal that hums faintly in the air, as if alive. Threads of shadow swirl lazily inside it, and every few seconds a faint flicker of silver appears—like a thought forming and then dissolving again.

He wears a robe of layered black fabric, thick and heavy, pooling on the floor around his feet. It moves when he does, whispering over stone, but never seems to catch the light.

Those huge, depthless eyes settle on me. For a moment, we simply look at each other—me, the mortal queen trying to pretend I belong here, and him, the creature who embodies every secret this court has ever kept.

I can't read him. But I know he's reading me. Every breath, every twitch, every attempt to mask what I feel. He's already seeing all the ways this conversation could go.

Orion shifts beside me, but Umbriel's gaze doesn't flicker. He doesn't blink at all.

The crystal at the end of his staff pulses once, faintly. Whatever he sees there makes his thin lips press tighter, as if to hide a thought.

Then he speaks, his voice low and measured, smooth in a way that makes it unclear if he's mocking or welcoming.

"Two paths walk into my hall," he says, eyes fixed on mine. "One knows where it leads. The other thinks they do."

I can feel Orion tense at my side, but I keep my chin high.

Because whatever this creature is, whatever power he holds—he's testing me.

And I'll be damned before I let him think I've already lost.

Orion's voice is low beside me, calm but edged like a blade being held too tight. His eyes never leave Umbriel. "Umbriel likes to play games," he murmurs. "You'll come to know this."

The Lord of Evershade gives him only a sidelong glance, the barest flick of those black eyes before his attention slides back to me.

Orion keeps his stance steady. "The price of entering his court," he adds, "is a riddle."

I fold my arms, and my shoulders drop. "We don't have time for riddles. Not when the darkness is clawing at Avalon's borders." I take a step forward before I can stop myself. "I'd like to enter your court, Lord Umbriel, and speak of the strain within the realms. What's coming won't wait for pleasantries."

He doesn't answer right away. His head tilts slightly, expression unreadable. The silence stretches until I'm sure he's doing it on purpose. Finally, his thin lips part, voice smooth and unhurried.

"The Obscura has been here for ages, child of daylight. It is not likely to devour the realm in the next few seconds."

I grit my teeth. "I've heard the whispers from the other courts. If I have, I'm certain you have. You know more than you let on, Lord Umbriel. I would value an ally of your status —someone who hears what others only dare to say in shadows where they think no one is listening."

At that, the faintest curve touches his mouth—something between amusement and warning.

"Not all the shadows that hold secrets belong to me."

I draw a slow breath, steadying my tone. "Then hear reason. I will soon be queen—two trials remain, and there are those who would see me fail. There will come a time to choose a side. When that time comes, I'd like to know if you'll stand with the realm's throne... or with the ones who intend to unmake it."

He lowers his gaze to the crystal on his staff. The black surface flickers faintly, showing shapes I can't make sense of. Whatever he sees there draws the smallest hum from his throat.

"Such confidence," he says at last, "that the trials will be your victory—when you do not even know where you come from, mortal Queen Rising."

Orion's patience snaps like a pulled string. "She pulled the sword from the stone," he says sharply. "You know no other has managed it since the day it fused there. She commanded the same moonlight Pandora once wielded. I've seen the shield with my own eyes. You know as well as I that no mere mortal could be chosen by the realm, much less accomplish those things."

Umbriel looks up slowly, his expression almost indulgent. "I did not say impressive things have not been accomplished," he murmurs. "But it is difficult to imagine a mortal —with such numbered beats of her heart—sitting upon a throne meant for eternity."

Then his gaze slides to Orion, assessing. "The throne would not even warm before her life were extinguished."

The shift in Orion is immediate—palpable. His shadows deepen around him, coiling at his feet, licking up the walls like smoke with a mind of its own. The air thickens, vibrating with tension. Even here, in Umbriel's court, under his wards, it's Orion's power that dominates the space.

Umbriel notices, of course. But instead of answering the challenge, he looks back to me, refusing Orion the argument he clearly wants.

"Let us resolve it, then," Umbriel says, voice low and even. "A question for a passage. Ask what you will of me. The question itself will determine if the gates of Evershade open to you..." He pauses—deliberate, eyes like endless pits threatening to swallow me. "...or not."

Orion starts to speak, but I raise a hand—silencing him before he can.

He stills immediately, though I feel the tension radiating off him like heat from a storm. Those silver eyes stay on Umbriel, never blinking, ready to strike if he thinks I'm in danger.

But this... this I have to do on my own.

I close my eyes for half a breath and reach for that pulse I always feel when he's near—the quiet thrum beneath my ribs that isn't entirely mine. I focus on it, on the electric hum that threads between us.

I need to do this myself, I try to send the thought, the way he's done to me before. I don't know if he hears it until I open my eyes and his gaze flicks to me, a slight nod of his head. Around me I feel the faintest shift in the air—like an answering heartbeat in the dark. *I need to win the courts, not borrow your power to force their loyalty. If I don't, I'll build a kingdom on sand.*

Umbriel is still watching me. Patient. Expectant.

A question. That's the price of passage.

I think for a moment, turning the possibilities over in my mind. Could it be as simple as *May I enter the gates of Evershade?*

No.

It wouldn't be that simple. Nothing in Avalon ever is. Whatever I ask will be dissected, every word twisted for meaning until the truth—or my failure—shows itself.

My gaze drifts to the wall, to the faint etchings of the family line. The gouged-out name catches the light again. I can't stop thinking about the vision I saw in the forest—the woman who looked so much like my mother, the name that echoed through the trees: *Morgause.*

The painting at Cairnvail. The scratched-out figure.

And now, here, a name removed.

They all feel connected, like threads tugging toward the same place. Toward me.

Before I even realize I've spoken, the words are out: "Why is that name scratched out?"

Umbriel's lips pull into something that might be a smile —if it can be called that.

I wish, instantly, that I hadn't seen it.

Rows of long, thin, needle-pointed teeth fill his mouth— black at the base, silver at the tips. The sight sends a ripple of cold down my spine.

"The answer to that question," he says softly, "does not reside within Evershade. Therefore, you may not have passage."

I open my mouth to argue, but he lifts one long-fingered hand, silencing me.

"You pondered," he says, "and chose wrong. The simpler question that lingered in your mind would have granted you entry."

Anger spikes through me, sharp and hot, but I bite it down. He's testing me, just like the rest of them.

"Sometimes," Umbriel continues, his tone almost thoughtful, "the answer lies right there on the surface. At times, hidden within shadow. Other times still, you must look beneath the fresco to see what has been covered. You must learn when to tell the difference."

His gaze flicks to Orion, who tenses his jaw in visible irritation. Still, he inclines his head with the barest nod. Respect, even in frustration.

Umbriel returns it and steps backward—into the waiting dark.

The shadows rise up to meet him, wrapping around his form until the black of his robe and the darkness of the hall are indistinguishable.

And then he's gone.

Not vanished. Not disappeared.

Just absorbed.

As if he were never anything more than a shadow pretending to be a man.

orion

Tana's frustration hums through the air like static. I can feel it—sharp, bright, alive under her skin. Her jaw is tight, her shoulders stiff, and she doesn't even try to hide the anger simmering there. Umbriel's refusal to grant passage, his riddles that looped in circles without giving a single straight answer—it's all carved lines into her patience.

When we step beyond the wards of Evershade, I feel the difference immediately. The air lightens, less pressing, less heavy with his magic. Tana exhales a breath so deep it trembles, like she's been holding it the entire time.

I glance sideways at her as the tension drains from her shoulders.

We rejoin the others waiting beyond the gates. Hypnos is already there, leaning lazily against his horse as if he's been waiting an eternity.

I arch a brow at him. "Figured we weren't gaining passage, so you abandoned your prince and queen?"

He shrugs one shoulder, unbothered. "You did not need me for that outcome. Umbriel is nothing if not predictable."

Tana mutters, "He's an asshole."

That earns a low chuckle from Hephaestus and Merlin's quiet, knowing grin. Above them, the small storm cloud that insists on following Merlin around rumbles with amusement. I swear the lightning inside it brightens when it spots her, and I burn at the sight.

I narrow my eyes at it. Ridiculous.

Jealous of a storm.

I really have lost it.

Tana moves away from the group, toward the edge of the ridge where the land falls away to mist and moonlight. Her back is straight, her chin high—but I know that posture. She's trying to hold it together.

Frosthaven is unreachable.

Evershade has turned us away.

And the whispers will start soon—the mortal queen denied passage, the courts refusing audience. The reasons won't matter. The fae will twist it, chew it, and spit it back as proof she isn't fit to rule.

I can't stand the distance between us another second.

I step up behind her, my hands finding her hips, fingers tracing the line of her waist before I pull her back into me. The wind shifts, carrying her scent—wild and warm and entirely hers. It cuts through the chaos in my chest, settles something that nothing else ever can.

Her hand covers mine, grounding me. She tilts her head back until it rests against my chest, and for a moment we just stand there—watching the silver horizon stretch endlessly ahead.

"There are other courts yet," I murmur against her hair. "Not all will turn us away."

"I know." Her voice is soft, but there's steel beneath it. "But we're running out of time. The fae need to remember who the enemy is. If they keep fighting each other, there won't be a realm left to save."

I press a kiss to the top of her head, my shadows curling faintly around us—protective, instinctive.

"They'll follow you," I whisper, my mouth close enough that the words brush her ear. "I have faith in that. If anyone could bring the entire kingdom to its knees in a single night, it would be you."

She turns her head slightly, just enough that I catch the faint curve of a smile. "Has Avalon ever had a king?"

That pulls a laugh out of me—low, rough, genuine. "No. And the thought is almost comical, isn't it? A male ruling Avalon? Impossible. We're far too emotional for that sort of responsibility."

That earns me the kind of smile that makes every storm in my chest still. Warm. Bright. The kind of smile men would burn kingdoms for.

I can't help myself. I reach for her, pinching her chin gently between two fingers, tilting her face up. The soft press of her lips against mine erases everything else—the cold, the tension, the memory of Umbriel's shadow. I open my mouth, letting my tongue taste what it craves most: her. The sweet, maddening warmth that I know I'll never get enough of.

A sudden clap of thunder cracks overhead.

I pull back just enough to turn my head slowly toward the sound. The storm cloud hangs above us, puffed up and smug, lightning sparking within like laughter.

"Really?" I mutter.

Tana chuckles against my chest. "Leave Rumble alone. He's a harmless little storm."

I stare at her. "You named it?"

She laughs softly. "That was Merlin's doing."

Of course it was.

She lifts her hand, and the cloud—Rumble, apparently —shrinks down obediently to the size of a melon, bobbing toward her palm. It lets out a soft drizzle and a few lazy sparks as it settles there, humming like a content pet.

I blink. "You're keeping it?"

"Why not?" she says with a shrug. "He seems to like me."

I just shake my head. "I'm sure there are other storms he can go play with."

She laughs and rubs her hands up my arms. "Could come in handy to have a storm on your side."

I open my mouth to remind her of the storm she already owns, but before I can say so, her gaze shifts beyond the group. She spots Mor standing off by herself—not unusual —but what is strange is the murder of crows gathered around her, dozens of shadowed birds born of her power.

Every one of them is utterly still, facing the same direction as the dark enchantress.

My chest tightens. I've seen this before.

"A prophecy," I say quietly, my voice dropping to a near growl.

Tana glances up at me. "She can see the future?"

"In a way," I answer. "The future isn't fixed—it's a tapestry of choices, and Mor can see where those threads might lead. She can't see everything, but what she does glimpse... she can influence, if she chooses to act."

Tana's eyes flick toward the horizon where Mor stands motionless, the wind pulling strands of her dark hair like ribbons of ink.

"Umbriel has a version of that sight," I add. "But his only

reaches a few steps ahead—short-term outcomes, immediate turns in the road. Mor's vision reaches far beyond that."

The storm quiets, as if even the clouds are waiting.

"Whatever has her attention," I say, tightening my grip on Tana's waist, "it will matter to us all."

And from the look on Mor's face—calm, remote, and deadly still—I know the next move the realm makes will not be ours to choose.

Then, all at once, she reanimates. The crows flutter, hop, and peck at the ground as though nothing had happened. A few curious ones take flight, wings slicing the air in a scatter of black. Others perch in the trees above, their eyes glinting silver under the moonlight. The boldest of them circle the little storm cloud, testing its sparks.

When Mor turns toward us, the eerie gray mist still clinging to her irises drains away, replaced by the crimson hue of her own eyes. My suspicion is confirmed—the Morrigan has seen a vision.

She approaches, every step measured. Hypnos drifts closer to meet her halfway, his expression grim but unsurprised.

"Starfall will see war on two fronts," Mor says, her voice carrying the quiet certainty of a verdict. "You are making a valiant effort, but no amount of parading or politics will stop it. It is already too far in motion. Every decision you make from this point forward will result in bloodshed at your gates."

Tana's jaw tightens. The muscles in my back go rigid. "Well," I mutter, "just put it bluntly, why don't you?"

Mor tilts her head, unamused. "We were very blunt."

Her tone is matter-of-fact, but her gaze flicks to the others, who have all turned serious—Hephaestus with his arms crossed, Merlin's brow furrowed, Hypnos as still as marble. Every one of them thinking the same thing: war.

"So it's inevitable, then," Tana says quietly.

Mor nods once.

Hypnos exhales through his nose. "Then we need a change of strategy."

Tana looks down, her voice softer now but laced with resolve. "Maybe. But I won't give up hope that it can still be prevented. The future isn't set, right?"

Mor studies her for a long moment. "Some outcomes are."

Tana lifts her chin. "Then maybe there's still time—not to stop it entirely, but to weaken it. To buy Avalon a fighting chance."

"Then we'll use that time," I say. "Mor, send your crows. Deliver word to the courts that might still listen. Some will remain loyal, others will choose neutrality. Astralana will do what Astralana always does."

Tana glances at me. "Neutral?"

"They're the scribes," I remind her. "The recorders. They only intervene if their own islands in the sky are attacked. They'll stay out of it unless the war reaches them."

She nods slowly. "What about Gloamreach? The Twilight Court?" Her gaze flicks toward me, eyes narrowed in teasing suspicion. "I hear its lord calls himself a king."

I can't help the roll of my eyes. "His people took to calling him that. To his credit, he's at least tried to act like he discourages it."

Hypnos smirks faintly. "Lord Eryndor will side with the

queen. He's balanced and fair. He values peace but understands the necessity of conflict."

Tana turns to me. "Then who's within reach now—someone strong enough to sway others if they commit?"

"Umbranor," I answer. "The Shadowed Court. Shade sent his daughter to Starfall to petition an audience about the darkness. They know what's at stake."

Hephaestus steps forward, his heavy boots grinding against the stone. "Then I'll be headin' back to Starfall," he says. "If there's to be a battle, we'll be ready." He gives a quick look around, hands on his hips. "The forge is stocked, but I'll need a few rare bits for the new blades an' such."

He glances at Tana. "Do ye remember the weapon ye gave me when ye first arrived? The gun?"

A slow grin tugs at his mouth. "I've been tinkerin' on improvements," he continues, "but I'll need smolderin' wyrmroot to make the combustibles."

I groan. "Perfect. Of course that's what you need."

Tana frowns. "What's wrong with wyrmroot?"

"It grows exclusively in Eldoria," I tell her.

"Oh, fucking perfect." Her eyes roll toward the heavens. "Liora. My best friend," she says dryly.

Mor's mouth curves faintly. "Your favorite, surely."

"They won't hand it over easily," I mutter. "If at all."

Mor looks between us, her expression settling into something grim. "If war truly is coming on two fronts, you'll need it."

All eyes turn to Tana. The decision is hers.

She tips her head back, gazing up at the endless sky. The moonlight turns her hair to fire, and I can almost see the thoughts racing behind her eyes. When she speaks, her voice carries the weight of command.

"Mor, send crows to Frosthaven, Cairnvail, Gloamreach, and Astralana. Warn our allies, and ask Astralana to share any records they have of the Great War—especially the Valkyries' last stand. Everything changed after that, and I want to know why."

Hypnos nods, offering to go to the floating islands himself to bring back any archives the High Seer will share.

Tana turns to Hephaestus and Merlin next. "We'll go to Eldoria for the wyrmroot. Merlin, once we have it, take it back to Starfall and meet Hephaestus at the forge."

Her gaze finds mine, unwavering. "After that, we go to Umbranor. I want to look Shade in the eye when he gives his answer."

Mor heads toward her duskbane, throwing a look over her shoulder. "Remind your wizard to tread carefully." Her eyes flash gold, as if the Morrigan is just under the surface. "We will begin our fast."

A hush settles over the group. Even the storm above us stills.

"Why are we fasting?" Tana asks, looking around as others find their mounts.

"You will soon see. Come." I wink, which irritates her and makes a smile creep across my face. "Eldoria awaits you, my queen."

tana

The road to Eldoria glows long before we see the city itself.

Where the other courts fade into shadow, this one seems to bleed light. The air grows thinner, tinged with something metallic and sweet—like warm honey poured over stone. The sky above shifts from soft indigo to a pale-gold haze, and the horizon ripples with reflections that have no source.

Everything here shines. Literally. The trees drip silver sap that catches the starlight. The grass is dusted in gold pollen, so every step leaves a glittered print behind. The marble bridges and towers in the distance look like they've been dipped in molten light. It would be breathtaking—if it didn't feel so artificial.

I blink against the brightness, squinting at the skyline. "It's like someone turned up all the lights and forgot to turn them back down." It makes my head pulse, and I hate it after several nocturns free of the headaches that have been plaguing me.

Orion snorts quietly beside me. "It's dreadful."

His shadows are restless, curling around his boots and coiling up his legs like smoke searching for a dark corner to hide in. This much light must be like a poison to him; I can feel it through the tether between us. It thrums with irritation.

"Try not to zap a hole in their floor when we arrive," I whisper.

"No promises," he murmurs back.

A small convoy from Starfall caught up with us. Theren and Aeris join us, and I've never been more grateful to have them. Theren murmurs something about making exceptions to zap Liora, and then he nips at Aeris's neck as she rides in front of him on their shared horse.

Merlin rides just ahead, his tall wizard's hat tilted forward protectively. I hear the faintest rumble beneath it—his storm trying to escape. He clamps one hand on the brim. "Shh now, Sir Rumbleton," he mutters. "None o' that. We're not in polite company."

When we crest the final hill, Eldoria unfurls before us, a city built entirely from light and vanity. Every tower gleams white-gold, wrapped in streams of silk that catch the faintest breeze and shimmer like auroras. The streets are lined with mirrors, polished so flawlessly they reflect the sky instead of the ground. It's beautiful—overwhelmingly so—but it doesn't feel real.

Orion exhales slowly beside me, his expression tight. "A kingdom allergic to shadow," he mutters.

"Maybe they think if it's bright enough, no one will notice what's rotten underneath," I say as we dismount our steeds.

Before he can reply, trumpets blare from the gates behind us—high, melodic, theatrical. The great golden doors swing open, and a parade of fae pours out, draped in silk and dusted in powder that makes them glow faintly under the eternal moonlight.

And at their center, riding on a gilded chariot drawn by four lesser fae: Liora.

She's sprawled across the cushions like an artist's muse come to life, one arm draped over the side, her body barely wrapped in gauzy threads of gold. Her skin is luminous—almost too much to look at directly. Even her hair glints like spun sunlight, cascading over the edges of the chariot as if to bless the ground itself.

The fae around her bow so deeply their foreheads nearly touch the marble.

"By the realm," I murmur. "Does she ever wear clothes?"

"We'd like to see how well that gold shines when mixed with blood," Mor mutters, her tone all knives and disinterest.

"Mor," Orion warns softly.

"We said like, not will." She looks at me like a bored teenager who just got scolded by her father. "He is now the one pooping on parties. Do you not agree?"

It takes me so by surprise I actually snort. I try and fail to hide it with a cough. Orion is totally confused by the comment and leans toward me.

"Why is Mor speaking of fecal matter?"

I just cannot with these two sometimes. Wiping the smile from my face, I get back into serious-queen mode.

The chariot stops before us. Liora stretches lazily, as if waking from a pleasant nap. As if she hadn't orchestrated this entire thing when the courts were informed the Queen Rising would be touring the realm.

She acts almost surprised to see a crowd of adoring fae

gathered around her and puts on an act, gasping, clutching her chest.

The scene earns applause from her court. When she sits up, it's slow and deliberate—a performance for an audience that hangs on her every breath.

Why? I do not fucking know.

"Welcome," she purrs, her voice carrying across the courtyard, melodic and soaked in honey. "What a gift Avalon has delivered to me. The chosen queen herself—and her..." She pauses, eyes dragging over Orion. "...our—most valiant prince."

Orion's entire body tenses.

I have to fight the urge to step in front of him like a guard dog when she shifts from her to our.

Two fae lords rush to her side, offering their hands as she steps delicately down from her chariot. She laughs softly, pretending to be flattered, tilting her head just so— an angle that perfectly catches the light. It's all a show, and everyone watching knows it.

I glance at Orion. His expression doesn't change, but the shadows under his cloak flare slightly, dark as ink.

She stages herself between us before I can object, looping one golden arm through his and the other through mine as if we're old friends. Her skin is warm—too warm— like sunlight left too long on metal.

"Eldoria welcomes its guests," she announces to the crowd, raising her voice theatrically.

From somewhere behind us, a fae shouts, "Long live Queen Liora!"

The title hangs in the air like perfume.

Liora chuckles delicately, pressing her hand to her chest.

"Oh, you flatter me," she says, pretending embarrassment. "You know I prefer lady. Really, there's no need to call me queen."

Her smile says keep calling me queen.

"Eldoria will proudly host Avalon's chosen queen," she adds, placing deliberate emphasis on *chosen*, like it's a curse word.

The crowd cheers again, blind and golden.

I roll my eyes so hard I nearly see my own brain.

When she finally releases our arms, it's only to sweep ahead of us toward the towering golden palace beyond. Her hips sway in an exaggerated rhythm that could only have been rehearsed in front of a mirror. And, of course, she makes sure Orion is in perfect view.

She glances over her shoulder, lashes low, her voice dripping with false modesty. "I am honored you would grace my humble court, Prince Orion. I have long wondered when you would tour the Shimmer Court."

Orion's jaw flexes.

I mutter under my breath, "Humble isn't the word I'd use."

Inside, the air practically hums with vanity. Every surface gleams—walls paneled in mirrored glass, chandeliers dripping with crystal, even the floors so polished that the light from above bounces back up into my eyes. It's like standing inside a jewelry box that's been swallowed by a star.

I've had enough of the spectacle already. "We'd like to speak in your council room right away," I say, cutting through the parade of courtiers and fanfare.

Liora's laugh drips from her throat like honey gone sour.

"Nonsense," she says, running her hands down her breasts, sides, and hips, letting her palms rest on her thigh like she's posing for a portrait. "We must insist you... refresh yourself from your travels."

Her eyes flick over me, slow and deliberate. The corners of her mouth pinch like she's just caught a whiff of something foul.

"And," she continues, her tone rising to reach the gallery of simpering fae above, "we have prepared a special banquet to show the Queen Rising all the splendors of Eldoria."

Her gaze slides to Orion for the last words, voice dropping an octave, languid and suggestive. "A reminder," she purrs, "of just what the Shimmer Court can offer the crown."

The implication is so blatant I nearly choke on it. She might as well have spread her legs and let that glitter cunt air out in Orion's face and called it diplomacy.

"Orion, your suite will be near mine." She gestures down one hall. "Tana, the queen's quarters are here." She gestures down the opposite side.

Before I can retort, Orion steps closer, the movement quiet but deliberate. His arm curves around my waist, pulling me into him. The entire court seems to inhale at once.

"My mate and I," he says evenly, "would prefer to share a room. We will both be seen to the queen's quarters."

The word *mate* hits the room like a thunderclap. Liora's golden mask falters; her face tightens, the color flushing from rose to something dangerously close to purple.

"I—" She gulps like a fish, clearly not expecting that. "Was unaware a mortal and fae could be mates. Are you—"

"And yet it is so." He presses on, unbothered. "And I hear the hot springs of Solis Veil are quite delightful. I'm sure Her Majesty would appreciate the time to wash the road and weariness from herself."

The tone is polite. The look is not.

Liora's lips curve back in something that isn't quite a smile. Her voice sharpens, just enough to cut. "Of course," she says. "We shall see that every comfort is afforded to... both of you."

She snaps her fingers, and two lesser fae appear instantly—slender creatures in translucent robes that ripple with color. "Escort Her Majesty and the Prince to their quarters," she commands, her voice brittle around the edges.

Out of the corner of my eye, Merlin wanders a few steps away from the group, looking around like he's in an art gallery instead of a throne hall. He stops in front of nothing —literally nothing—then pokes curiously as if something is there. I watch him rub his fingers together, bring them to his nose, and inhale deeply.

"Hm," he says to no one in particular, nodding like that confirms something, and then just strolls away as if nothing happened.

I glance at the spot he'd been investigating and find... air. Perfectly empty air. The crazy old man was poking nothing.

Mor grunts behind us, unbothered by the spectacle. "We'll find our own place," she says dryly. "Preferably somewhere with less light."

Liora's smile twitches, her gaze flicking between the dark enchantress and her circling shadows used like a visor against the light. "As you wish," she says, but her tone makes it sound more like *don't touch anything on your way out.*

I catch Orion's eye as we follow the attendants down a blinding corridor, every golden surface reflecting a distorted version of us back.

"Mate, hm?" I murmur, glancing at him as we follow behind my handmaids and the Eldorian escorts.

His eyes flick down to mine, steady and unreadable, before drifting ahead. "She needed to hear it—and so can the rest of the realm," he says, voice low, rough silk. "So there's no mistake about where I stand... or who I stand beside."

The look he gives Liora after that could melt the gold paint from the walls—calm, cold, and final.

He offers me his hand as we start down the hall, all elegance and control, the perfect contrast to the rage simmering in Liora's golden eyes. When I place my hand in his, he lifts it to his lips and presses a slow kiss against my knuckles—deliberate, reverent, and meant for an audience.

He's making a claim even though he doesn't have to. The word alone did it—*mate.*

A claim no amount of starlight or glamour could compete with.

And Liora knows it.

CHAPTER 29
tana

The queen's suite is no less blinding than the rest of Eldoria. Every surface shimmers—glass, gold, polished stone. Light bounces from the chandelier to the walls to the mirrors embedded in the ceiling.

Orion steps in and immediately sends his shadows flooding outward. They slip beneath the furniture, scale the walls, and smother the unnatural brilliance like a tide washing away glitter. They crawl over the gilded sconces and twist the mirrors until they reflect only void.

Theren and Aeris begin pointing where they want our chests placed, working efficiently to unpack what little we brought—despite the fact I'd already told them we wouldn't be staying long. Hopefully.

I exhale sharply when the last shimmer vanishes from the room. The shadows settle over the walls like a thick velvet curtain, turning the suite into something rich and quiet and safe.

I hadn't even realized how tense I'd been until that moment. My shoulders ease. The ache behind my brow disappears. It's like unclenching a fist I didn't know I was making.

Across the room, Orion leans one shoulder against the wall, watching me with smug satisfaction.

"I enjoy seeing you fall in love with Avalon," he says, voice low and pleased.

He pushes off the wall and saunters toward me, unfastening his cloak as he walks. Then his jacket. His corset vest. Each layer peeled away, each motion confident and unhurried. His tunic clings to him like it's desperate to stay, and his pants fit so well it's almost criminal.

When he stops in front of me, he lifts my chin with two fingers, tipping my face up to his. "I enjoy seeing you fall in love with me as well, my stubborn Starling."

I smile—just barely—and before I can say a word, he kisses me.

It's slow. Firm. Possessive.

When he pulls back, his forehead rests against mine. "You're still too tense here in the Court of Bullshit," he murmurs. "We will enjoy the hot springs together."

Theren steps in beside him, quietly helping undo the rest of his vest with careful fingers. Aeris moves to me, undoing the buckles of my riding gear, and I try to focus on her—on the leather slipping off my shoulders, on the feel of air on my skin.

But I can't stop watching Theren.

The way his hands move over Orion's body, how one palm braces his waist while the other slides across his chest, pushing the fabric of his tunic back and off his shoulders.

My gaze flicks up—straight into Orion's.

He's watching me. Every second. His eyes are heated, dark, intent.

Then his voice in my head:

Do you like what you see, Starling?

Heat curls low in my belly. Aeris has already undone the

final strap of my top, and I hadn't even noticed. My breath catches.

I greatly enjoy watching you, Orion murmurs in my mind. The tone of it slides down my spine like a hand.

"Your robe, Your Grace," Aeris says softly, offering the deep gray fabric embroidered with subtle silver stars.

Theren hands Orion his own. Together, we walk to the balcony doors, then descend the marble steps to a sunken pool set into the ground below.

The hot spring is round and wide, framed by a trellis laced with silver ivy that stretches from the castle wall to the earth below. It gives the space privacy—but more importantly, shade. Enough to dull the brilliance of Eldoria's lights, though not completely.

Orion gestures for Theren and Aeris to leave us, and the attendants vanish without a word.

We drop our robes at the same time. Both of us bare. Orion's cock is already half hard, his body carved and perfect in the silver dusk.

He helps me into the pool first, his hands warm against my waist. The water is hot, almost too hot, and I gasp as I sink into it. He follows, lowering himself until we're submerged to our necks.

I groan in delight, letting my head tip back. "This is amazing."

Orion pulls me into his lap, strong hands massaging up my spine, then over my shoulders, his thumbs pressing into the knots I hadn't realized were there.

"Can we get a little more shade?" I murmur.

He smirks and lifts one hand lazily. Shadows bloom above us, blanketing the trellis until the light dims into something cool and soft. A few tendrils hang down like wayward ivy.

I reach up and wrap one around my fingers, then let it slide away.

His mouth finds my breast before I even realize he's moved. Lips brushing over my nipple, tongue swirling, then sucking. I moan, my hands rising to cradle his head as he shifts to the other.

Every motion is unhurried—meant to be felt.

"I want to ask you something," I whisper, my voice rough around the edges.

He lifts his head slowly, eyes narrowing with playful suspicion. "That face," he murmurs. "That's a dangerous-question face."

My cheeks warm. "At Beltane… in the solarium… I was with two women. And you—" I pause, then meet his gaze directly, "—you were enjoying a man on your cock."

His stare doesn't falter. Doesn't flinch.

"We've never talked about it. About what we like. Or… what we're comfortable with."

I run a hand over his chest, slow. "So, tell me, Orion. What do you like?"

His expression doesn't shift at first, but I feel the change in him—the way his muscles go just a little tighter beneath my palms, the way his grip firms at my waist.

He likes the question.

When he speaks, his voice drops—low, deliberate. "Come here."

He pulls me closer until I'm straddling him again, my arms looped around his neck, our mouths nearly touching.

His breath brushes mine, but he keeps that fraction of space between us. Holding it. Stretching it.

"I like passion," he says softly. "Not sex."

I flinch—just barely—but he notices. Of course he does.

Before I can ask, he shifts us through the water with fluid ease, moving until my back presses to the edge of the pool, the warm stone slick behind me, his body still caging mine.

"I like to fuck," he continues, voice velveted heat now. "Long and slow... hard and fast. I like pleasure without limits. No performance. No pretense. Just—" his fingers drift along my side, "—everything raw."

My breath stutters.

"The fae are passionate creatures, Starling. Some take only male lovers. Some only female. Me?" He smiles against my jaw. "I'll take it all."

His hands roam my thighs under the water, dragging me closer until I feel the heavy weight of his cock pressing against my center—hard and hot and deliberate. He doesn't push inside, just slides the thick length along the slick slit of my pussy, the friction delicious and maddening.

"And I know you do too," he murmurs. "I saw the way you took your pleasure. The way you received it. Gods, I could watch you for hours... the way your body moves... the way you melt when someone touches you just right."

He rolls his hips, cock dragging up against my pussy again. I moan, clinging tighter around his shoulders.

"The thought of you watching me?" he says darkly. "Makes my cock fucking throb."

I gasp as he does exactly that—presses the thick head

against my clit for just a moment, sending a shudder through me.

"I know it would make you wet," he breathes. "Wouldn't it? Watching me sink to my knees, take a man's cock in my mouth. Let him fuck into my throat while you watched with those wide, filthy eyes."

I'm panting now, ache pulsing through every nerve.

"Would you like that?" he whispers, words almost reverent. "Watching me fuck a man. Sliding into his tight, perfect ass. Holding him down while he begged for more."

He licks the corner of my mouth—slow and hot.

"Would you like that, Starling?"

"Yes," I gasp before I can stop myself.

That one word wrecks him.

Orion groans low and bites down on my nipple—sharp enough to sting, enough to make my hips buck in the water. My breath punches out of me, pleasure and pain blooming together as his tongue soothes the ache.

He growls against my skin, voice dark and decadent. "You have no idea what it does to me... knowing how filthy you can be."

His mouth trails lower, then up again, kissing the curve of my neck as he speaks between each press of his lips. "I want to see you on your knees, Starling. See you lick a pretty cunt until it's dripping. Watch your thighs shake while someone devours you."

His hands slide down, spreading me wider beneath the water. His voice roughens. "As many mouths on you as you want. As many hands. Let them worship you while you ride my cock." He grinds against me, slow and deliberate. "While

I stretch you open and someone else fills your tight little ass."

A shiver rolls through me.

"Would you like that?" he whispers, his words hot against my ear. "Being so full you can't tell where the pleasure's coming from?"

Before I can answer, his shadows move.

They descend like smoke in water—caressing both our skins. One slick tendril circles his cock, stroking it as it glides against my soaked heat. Another wraps around my clit, cool and teasing, swirling in lazy, torturous spirals.

A third brushes across my nipples, mirroring his touch, pulling soft whimpers from my throat.

And then—deeper. One cool, sinuous thread trailing along the cleft of my ass. Another between his.

"You feel that?" he murmurs, watching me unravel. "That's only the beginning."

His voice drops lower—possessive, reverent, devastating. "Do you want them to fuck you, Starling? Want my shadows to taste you... fill you... own you while I watch and stroke my cock?"

I choke on a moan. "Yes. Gods, yes."

His eyes blaze.

"Do you want it now?" he growls. "Want them inside you —inside us—while I kiss you and feel every inch they take?"

My body answers before I do, arching into him, hips rolling against the shadows and his dick, my fingers clenching in his hair. "Yes—Orion, please."

He crashes his mouth to mine, kissing me hard, shadows coiling tighter around us both. They don't pierce—but they press, filling every space, every ache, every place that craves more.

And in the dark, with his magic wrapped around us like silk and smoke, we fall into something deeper—something wild. Something made not of starlight or shadows—

—but of us.

My head tips back as the shadows writhe against my skin, teasing every nerve, every inch. And then—

His voice.

Low. Wrecked. Drenched in the kind of need that steals breath.

"They're stroking me," Orion rasps, his mouth brushing the shell of my ear. "Tight... slow... dragging along my cock like your heat's already wrapped around me. Fuck, Starling, I can feel them tasting you. I can taste you."

My breath catches. My thighs tremble as the shadow at my clit pulses—slow, lazy circles turning urgent.

He groans, like he feels it too. "They're inside you now, aren't they? Just the edge. Just enough to tease. You're so wet for me. For them. They like it... my darkness likes it."

His hips rock, grinding his cock against the slick glide of my pussy. The pressure of the shadows grows—more daring. One coils, firm and cool, teasing just at my entrance, not quite breaching.

"They want to fuck you," he growls. "To fill you. While I hold you open and kiss your throat. While I watch you come apart from nothing but shadow and power."

"Orion—" I gasp, but my voice is already gone.

"They're wrapping me too," he grits out, thrusting shallowly. "One at the base of my cock. Another down my spine, right where I ache to be inside you. It's maddening—your moans, your scent, your need. They feel it. I feel it."

I whimper, every muscle tightening, every nerve aflame. One shadow slips a little deeper, enough to make my hips buck. Another coils around my breast, tugging at my nipple, pulling a broken cry from my throat.

"Do you feel how close we are?" he murmurs. "One push and we'd both break."

"Then do it," I breathe, eyes locked on his. "Let them. Let us. I want it. I want them everywhere. I want you everywhere."

He shudders, the storm in him trembling loose. "I'll fill you, Starling. With my power. With every dark inch of me. Until your pleasure is mine, and mine is yours."

The shadow plunges inside me—cool, fluid, thick. I scream his name, clenching as my back arches and the coil of pleasure tightens to a blade's edge.

"Good girl," he groans, watching me unravel. "Take it. Take all of it. Let my shadows fuck you the way you fucking love it."

"I'm so—Orion, I'm—"

"I know," he chokes. "Come for me. Let them feel it. Let me feel it."

I detonate.

Pleasure rips through me, brutal and blinding. The shadows pulse inside me, curling tighter as I fall apart, crying out his name. My hips roll, greedy, grinding against the slick tension of power and magic and need.

He follows—head thrown back, hips thrusting against the grip of his own shadows. "Fuck—Tana—"

And when he comes, I feel it.

Not just the twitch of his cock. Not just the groan from his throat.

But everywhere.

Through the shadows. Through the bond. Through the storm inside him now spilling into me.

Darkness. Pleasure. Power.

All of it—ours.

He collapses forward, forehead against mine, our breaths tangled in the dark.

"Again," I whisper.

He laughs—hoarse, wrecked. "Gods, yes."

CHAPTER 30

orion

I wanted to fuck her for hours.

Still do.

But she was hungry, and unfortunately, diplomacy waits for no orgasm.

Especially when the Shimmer Court wants to put on a show.

We need their resources. Their supply chains. Their favor. Which means I have to play nice, and Tana has to smile and curtsy and endure Liora's venom disguised as hospitality. I can stomach it—for a little while. Long enough to get what we came for.

Doesn't mean I like it.

She looks edible.

Dressed in a sheer gold slip Aeris chose—soft and radiant, draping over her curves like molten starlight. Theren braided her hair with gold wire and bright crystal beads, leaving most of it untamed, cascading around her shoulders like a wildfire refusing to be contained.

Just the way I like it.

My preference? Black or silver. Better yet—nothing at all. But this... this makes me want to worship and devour her in equal measure.

"You look divine," I murmur at her side, brushing my fingers down her bare arm, careful not to wrinkle the shimmer of the fabric. "But I look forward to peeling this off and eating your cunt later."

Her lips curve into a chuckle, warm and knowing. "Promising a feast before the first course?"

"I never break a promise, Starling."

She smirks as the double doors to the dining hall swing open.

Unfortunately, dinner is nothing but a stage.

A long marble table, shining with polished glass plates and iridescent goblets. Fae of all kinds seated in carefully chosen places, all arranged to give Liora the illusion of control. And there she is, draped in something so reflective it hurts to look at. Her smile sharp enough to gut a man.

"Tana of Gaea," Liora purrs, standing only long enough to make it look like a greeting. "You look radiant. Tell us, has your... ascension... been kind?"

The laughter is light, false, clinking like hollow bells. Tana smiles, smooth and polite, and answers with the perfect blend of diplomacy and edge.

But Liora keeps going.

"Funny how fast some queens rise, is it not?" she muses, sipping from a glass that hasn't left her hand all night. "Though I suppose being chosen has its advantages. If I recall, those chosen by fae often found themselves... elevated. Overnight, almost. It seems to be taking you quite a bit longer, no?"

I feel it in Tana before she even speaks.

The shift beneath her skin. The pressure behind her temples. The exact note of her irritation, growing louder with every word.

She plays the game better than anyone I've seen. But she doesn't like to be underestimated.

Tana looks around, seeing none of our assembly aside from her pair of handmaids waiting dutifully near the wall.

"Where is Mor?" she asks, her eyes darting from space to space. "I figured she would have a table all to herself with all this food."

I smile. "Mor gets rather grouchy when she does not eat. She would like to fast before the oncoming battle she foresaw."

Tana nods as if thinking it over but doesn't press further. I see her pinch the bridge of her nose—something she does when she has a headache. I signal to Aeris, who brings Tana a thimble of tonic, discreet and unassuming.

When Liora pivots the conversation to some vapid nonsense—court fashion, or perhaps which mountain peak has the best moonlit fog—Tana leans forward, her voice low and commanding, shifting to something more important.

"The realm is fracturing."

Silence.

She doesn't raise her voice. Doesn't need to. Every eye at the table turns to her.

"Obscura is moving. Avalon is bleeding. And Starfall will not hold alone. We'd like to count on Eldoria's support—supplies, aid. Not for charity," she adds, gaze sharp, "but for survival and unity."

Liora stills.

There's something—a slip. A flicker of something behind her mask I can't quite name. Surprise? Guilt? Amusement?

Whatever it is, it vanishes too fast.

She lifts her glass again, lips curling in what she thinks is charm. "Such heavy talk at such a beautiful table. Come now, I've had quite enough of politics."

Another wave of that hollow laughter follows—a symphony of puppets clinging to her cue. I grip the stem of my goblet a little too tightly, imagining how easy it would be to shatter.

Liora stands, arms wide like the stage is hers.

"Let's get on with the party."

The moment Liora claps twice, the lighting shifts— dramatic, intentional. The golden chandeliers dim to a dusky-violet glow, while the walls hum with glamour. Wisps of yellow light dance through the air like fireflies caught in a slow waltz.

And then the performers come.

Lesser fae in little more than beads and silk—sultry dancers moving with hypnotic grace, their bodies glistening under enchantment. Fire-breathers stalk the perimeter, exhaling ribbons of flame to match the beat of the music now thumping through the floor. Above us, long shimmering ribbons descend from the ceiling like vines, and fae begin to ascend, flip, twist—suspended midair in feats of impossible acrobatics.

The room turns into a living fantasy. A deliberate distraction.

But I see when a fae in armor—too rigid, too serious— approaches Liora. Leans close. Whispers something into her ear.

Whatever he says pulls the mask from her face for the briefest flicker.

Her brows knit. Her lips tighten. But then—she smooths it away like it never happened.

"I do hope everyone enjoys themselves," Liora says sweetly, raising her hands. "I'll return shortly. Don't have too much fun without me."

She disappears through a side corridor, her skirts snapping behind her like a curtain falling.

Tana watches her go, fingers tightening slightly on the edge of her plate.

"She's avoiding the real questions," she murmurs. "Dodging. Deflecting."

"She is," I agree. "But patience, Starling. We'll get what we came for."

She exhales slowly, not quite convinced—but she nods.

I speak with Mor in my mind, asking her to keep a secret eye on Liora. I don't trust her. Mor answers, voice more gruff than usual, and it makes me chuckle to myself.

The savory platters disappear, replaced with trays of desserts that look like jewels and temptation—candied fruits dusted in gold sugar, spiced chocolate in delicate shells, whipped creams topped with edible pearls. The bold red wine of dinner is replaced by something else entirely—lighter in color, almost glowing, and faintly iridescent.

I pour her a glass.

But I don't hand it over.

"This is Lunavelle Nectar," I tell her, swirling it once, watching the liquid catch the candlelight. "A very powerful aphrodisiac, harvested from a moon-bloom vine that only flowers during eclipse. One sip, and you'll feel desire burning through your blood for hours."

She lifts a brow.

I lift one back. "Would you like some? To see just how insatiable my queen can be?"

Her nod is slow. Intentional. "Yes. I do."

My blood sparks.

I raise the glass to my lips, take a generous sip—but don't swallow.

Instead, I lean in.

She parts for me before I even reach her, her mouth opening with a sigh as I press mine to hers. Our tongues meet—slick, slow, wanting—and I share the wine with her, letting the sweet burn coat her tongue, letting her taste it from me.

Some of it spills, sliding down her chin.

I chase it with my mouth.

A slow drag of my tongue up her throat, over the soft curve of her jaw, licking away every drop that escaped.

When I pull back, her eyes are darker than they were before.

And mine?

Mine are full of fire.

Several fae begin to drift away—pairing off, slipping behind veils of silk, disappearing into alcoves and curtained lounges. The air thickens with heat and perfume, with moans and laughter and the rustle of hands and bodies. Plates are forgotten, wine glasses abandoned mid-sip. Lust blooms through the room like a spreading fire—subtle at first... then ravenous.

Beside me, Tana shifts in her seat. Writhes, barely.

She bites her lip, her thighs pressing together under that sheer golden slip, the faintest shimmer of sweat at her temples. Her skin flushed. Her pupils blown wide.

I've seen her desperate.

This is something else, and it drives me wild.

I lift her by the waist, effortlessly, and set her on the table in front of me. Plates slide, a goblet tips, and someone gasps.

Tana moans when I push her legs open.

Her cunt already slick through the thin silk. I drag her forward to the edge—uncaring who watches, who moans, who burns with envy.

I bury my face between her thighs.

And inhale.

Fucking gods.

She smells like heaven ruined, like nectar and sin. I press my nose to her cunt, tongue flat against her wet panties just once—just enough to taste her arousal through the slip.

"You're soaked, Starling," I murmur against her. "You want to come with all of them watching?"

"Orion," she breathes, hips rolling toward me, seeking friction.

But I lift my gaze. Steady. Serious.

"Is there anyone here you don't want to stay?"

She hesitates, glancing around the room.

Several of Liora's fae linger nearby—watching too closely, whispering behind jeweled hands. Their smiles too sharp, their hunger too false.

"I don't want her back in here," Tana says at last, her voice low but firm.

I nod once, handing her back the goblet of sweet wine. Peeling down the top of her gown, I expose her perfect breasts to the heat of the room, to my hungry eyes. I twist one nipple between my fingers—dark, taut, begging to be tasted—and she arches into me, lips parting in another desperate moan.

Around us, several of the female fae moan too—aroused by the display, by the sight of me touching my queen like she's sacred and filthy all at once. Two of them begin kissing, hands roaming, as their eyes stay locked on us.

I meet Theren's gaze. Give him a subtle nod.

He steps forward, silent and graceful, leaning down to whisper to the fae closest to Liora's circle. They bristle—but obey. Whatever he says, it works.

One by one, they rise. Gather their things. Leave.

The doors close with a soft, final thud.

And lock.

Now it's just us.

And those loyal enough to know what it means to serve a queen and her chosen.

I turn back to Tana, gaze full of dark promise.

"We're secure now," I say, letting my shadows slither across her skin. "In our den of pleasure."

I grip her thighs and drag her closer again. "And I intend to make sure my queen gets everything she desires tonight."

CHAPTER 31
orion

The bed is massive—round, draped in gossamer sheets and midnight-colored pillows, piled high like a throne of sin pressed against the far wall. Tana's skin glows in the soft violet light as I guide her across the room, the sheer slip fluttering around her ankles with every step.

She doesn't walk.

She glides.

Like royalty. Like temptation wrapped in moonlight.

I sit her on the edge of the bed.

As we pass, several fae pause—captivated. Some meet her gaze, and it's like a tether snaps taut between them. They follow. Silent. Obedient. Entranced.

She commands without speaking.

I kneel before her for a moment, hands trailing up her thighs, reverent even in lust. "What do you want, Starling?" I ask, my voice thick with need, with hunger, with devotion.

She opens her mouth—but before she can answer, Aeris steps onto the bed behind her. Knees parting, crawling gracefully, her hands already at work. The sheer slip slides from Tana's shoulders, fingers brushing over her breasts, thumbs grazing peaked nipples.

Tana gasps—back arching slightly—caught between two kinds of heat.

Theren appears at my side, looking up at me like a supplicant. Wanting. Waiting. Hoping.

He begins to undress me.

Slowly.

As if it's ceremony.

"I want to watch," Tana says, voice low, trembling. "I want to watch you."

My smile is pure sin. "Then you shall."

I take Theren gently by the chin, tilt his head up. His lips are parted, breath warm. "Do you hear that?" I murmur, eyes on him. "Your queen would like to be entertained."

I lick my lips—slow and deliberate. Theren shudders. "Shall we entertain her?"

"Yes," he pants.

I kiss him.

His mouth is soft, desperate, eager—like he's dreamed of this all evening and finally crossed the threshold. He resumes undressing me, loosening my trousers, fingers slipping beneath the waistband until he frees my cock, sliding his hand along the shaft, gripping it firmly. Slowly. Worshipfully.

I moan low in my throat and look to Tana.

She's squirming on the bed, hips shifting, thighs rubbing together in search of touch. Aeris has her naked now, kneeling before her like a dutiful priestess. And another male—bronze-skinned, silver-haired—approaches my other side, drawn like a tide to a moon.

Aeris glances up, lips glistening. "May I service my queen?" she asks, hands already ghosting up Tana's thighs.

Tana lets out a soft, wrecked sound. A nod. Legs parting.

But I lift a hand. "Let's not rush our queen," I say.

Aeris hums, lips brushing the inside of Tana's thigh as she murmurs, "Never, my prince."

And then her mouth is on Tana's cunt—licking slow, savoring, tongue curling deep.

Tana cries out, head tipping back, body arched in offering.

I groan.

Theren's lips press to my chest, kissing, sucking at my nipple, his hand stroking me harder now. The other male presses close, tongue joining Theren's along my skin, a soft moan escaping him as he feels the weight of my cock against his palm.

I let it happen.

Let them both taste.

But my voice stays firm, deep with command, as I slide my hand through Theren's hair.

"On your knees, Theren."

He obeys instantly, dropping before me like a starved devotee.

"Show your prince how hungry you are for his cock."

Theren moans as he takes the tip of my dick into his mouth—lips soft, tongue circling with reverence. I groan, hips twitching forward slightly as he slides deeper, taking more, hand wrapped around the base as he sucks me slow and eager, hungry and practiced.

The other male watches from my side—aroused, silent, mouth parted as his gaze flicks between Theren's mouth and my face.

I turn to him.

"What's your name, handsome?"

He swallows. "Cael."

"Mmm," I murmur, brushing my fingers along his jaw. "A beautiful name for a beautiful male."

I pull him in and kiss him—slow at first, then deeper.

Cael moans into my lips as Theren's head bobs, lips wrapped around my cock, sucking me with a fervent sort of grace that has me curling a hand into his hair and tugging gently.

"Fuck... Theren," I groan between kisses. "You have a very talented mouth."

He hums, the vibration shooting up my spine.

"But I want your ass."

I look beyond them for a moment, gaze caught by the exquisite vision sprawled across the bed.

Tana.

She's falling apart.

Aeris has her spread open, mouth still working between her legs. Another female fae has joined them, her fingers teasing one of Tana's breasts, her mouth sucking at her neck while Tana writhes—utterly overwhelmed. And behind them, at the head of the bed, two other fae are laid out in mirrored bliss, eating each other's cunts in slow, desperate hunger.

It's all heat and hedonism, shadows and silk.

My cock twitches with need.

I take Theren's hand and guide him away from the bed to a chaise lounge draped in midnight velvet. We sit facing one another, knees brushing, legs straddling.

Cael follows—elegant and fluid.

He dips his fingers into a silver bowl resting on a tall stand—viscous lubricant catching the light like liquid starlight. He takes my cock in his hand, smearing it slowly, thoroughly, every stroke indulgent.

I lean back into the cushions, groaning at the sensation. "Fuck, that's good..."

Then I look to Theren, eyes locking. "Lay down for me. Spread yourself for your prince."

Theren doesn't hesitate. He lies back, thighs open, cock already hard, need etched across his face. His hands slide up my chest as I hover over him, my dick thick and glistening in Cael's hand.

I fist myself once, line up with Theren's entrance, and begin to ease inside.

"Just breathe for me, handsome."

Slow.

Measured.

Watching his face for any sign of discomfort. Watching his breath catch and his lashes flutter. I push in deeper—inch by inch—until I'm fully seated inside him.

He gasps, nails digging into my arms.

"You okay?" I ask softly, brushing my nose against his.

"Yes," he whispers. "Gods, yes."

"That's a good boy."

I begin to move.

A slow thrust. Then another. Deep and smooth, our bodies syncing with the rhythm already pulsing through the den.

I lower myself and kiss him—tongues tangling, hips rolling as the tension builds again.

I keep my eyes on Tana.

She cries out—her voice like music turned feral.

She comes on Aeris's tongue, head thrown back, body

arched in bliss. The second female holds her close, whispering something against her skin, fingers still toying with her oversensitive nipple.

Fuck, she is beautiful.

I continue to move inside Theren as I call out, "Aeris—ease her down, but don't stop."

My voice is laced with command.

"She's only getting started."

A soft giggle draws my attention.

Another female fae has joined the growing pile of pleasure around Tana. She leans in close to Aeris, whispering something wicked in her ear—whatever it is makes Aeris laugh, breathless and flushed, her cheeks blooming pink.

Without missing a beat, Aeris shifts back. The new female lies down beneath her, long white hair spilling across a pillow. Aeris straddles her face slowly, reverently—and then sinks down with a gasp, her thighs trembling.

Her moan is swallowed by the mouth now buried between her legs.

But Aeris doesn't stop.

Even as pleasure surges through her, she lowers herself once again between Tana's thighs—tongue returning to her queen's swollen, slick cunt, licking her through her aftershocks with maddening devotion.

Beside them, the female who'd been toying with Tana's breast pulls her into a kiss. I groan at the sight—Tana's mouth open, lips working around the other woman's tongue, their moans melting into each other like warm honey.

Cael slides behind me.

His hands move up my back, across my shoulders, down my chest—and then lower still.

"How can I pleasure my prince?" he whispers, voice silken, breath hot against my neck.

I glance to Tana.

She's laid out like a goddess—glistening, glowing, lost in the haze of ecstasy and opulence. Her breasts heave, lips parted, eyes dark and heavy-lidded, the gold slip now just a memory.

I ask softly, "What would you like, my queen?"

Her gaze sharpens as she looks at me. Or tries to. The lust swimming in her eyes has her drowning in pleasure, her body still twitching from Aeris's tongue.

Her voice is wrecked. Raw.

"I want you to fuck," she gasps. "All three of you. Fuck him."

The words barely make it out—she's so far gone.

But Cael hears them.

And he smiles.

He reaches for the silver bowl again, fingers dipping into the slick. He strokes himself once, then again, coating his thick length in shine. One hand steadies me, the other slides between my cheeks, and then—

Gods.

I moan—loud, unrestrained—as his finger slips inside me, slow and deliberate.

Theren tightens around me at the sound.

"Fucking hell..." I grit out, hips still moving inside Theren even as Cael prepares me. The dual sensation is dizzying—my cock buried in heat and tightness, while slick fingers stretch me open at the same time.

Cael's second finger joins the first, scissoring slowly. I tremble slightly, body clenching around him, loving the burn, the pressure.

And then he pulls his fingers free.

Only for a moment.

He lines himself up.

I lean forward, bracing myself over Theren as Cael presses in behind me. The first stretch is fire—pure and perfect. I moan through gritted teeth, my head dropping to Theren's shoulder as Cael slides in, inch by inch, until he's fully seated inside me.

I'm surrounded.

Tight heat at my front. Throbbing fullness at my back.

Every nerve, alive.

I don't move. Not at first. I just feel it.

And then—I begin to thrust.

All three of us move—Theren rocking up into me, Cael rolling into my hips. Our bodies fall into rhythm, sweat-slick and perfect. Moans echo. Skin slaps. The air grows thick with sex and shadow.

I reach down and wrap a hand around Theren's cock, stroking in time with each thrust, murmuring praise against his jaw.

"Fuck, you take me so well, Theren... squeezing me like you were made for this."

Cael groans behind me. "You feel... gods, Orion..."

"Does he look good inside me, Starling?" I call across the room, not slowing. "Do you like watching your prince get fucked?"

"God, yes."

Tana cries out again, body bucking against Aeris's tongue.

She comes.

Hard.

Her fingers twist in the bedsheets, the female kissing her moans with her. Her thighs tremble, slick and shining under the shifting lights.

And still—Aeris doesn't stop.

Because I was right.

My queen is only getting started.

CHAPTER 32
tana

It's like being drunk on sex.

Drunk on lust. On sensation. On them.

Every inch of me is tingling. Every nerve, every breath, every strand of hair—alive with energy. The kind that blooms from within and melts outward, leaving me slick and glowing and so fucking high on pleasure I can't stop shaking.

I come down from a second orgasm on Aeris's mouth with a cry that isn't even a word. My body quakes, but I want more.

Gods, I need more.

I tug her up, fingers twisted in her hair, and push her back onto the bed.

Aeris gasps in surprise, then grins—eyes shining, lips wet with my slick. I crawl up her body, kissing her mouth fiercely, hungrily, tasting myself on her tongue.

Behind us, I hear Orion moan—low and guttural.

I glance back.

He's sandwiched between Theren and Cael, losing himself in the pleasure of being taken and filled and worshipped—and watching me. His body glistens with sweat and shadows, his head thrown back, mouth parted. He's gone—blissfully, beautifully gone.

The sight makes my pussy throb all over again.

I straddle Aeris's hips, breathing heavy. She moans beneath me when I take one of her legs and throw it over my shoulder, adjusting my angle, lining us up until—

"Oh, fuck—"

Our cunts press together, slick on slick, clits meeting in a kiss of friction and heat. I grind slowly, hips rocking in tight little circles until Aeris matches my rhythm.

We moan in tandem.

Hands grip the sheets, the bed solid beneath us, and our gasps turn into cries as the pleasure builds.

"Tana," Orion calls hoarsely, voice dark and full of reverence. "That's it, Starling. Just like that. Let me hear you both."

I ride her harder, faster, grinding down against her cunt until sparks shoot up my spine. Her thighs tremble beneath mine. Her hands clutch my waist as we chase the high together—panting, writhing.

"That's it, my love. Rub your sweet pussy on hers." Orion's voice wraps around me like a shadowed command. "Come for me. Both of you. Come while I fill them—come while you feel me watching."

We do.

We fall apart—together.

My name and hers tumble from each other's lips, our mouths meeting in a wet, desperate kiss as we fall over the edge.

And just as we come, so do they.

Orion cries out between the two males, his thrusts ragged, Cael moaning against his back, Theren writhing beneath him as all three of them hit their peak together.

The sound. The heat. The power of it.

It nearly makes me come again.

They collapse in a tangle of limbs and sweat and lips. Orion kisses Cael's mouth, then leans down and claims Theren's too.

"Fuck," he pants, breathless. "That was—gods. Amazing."

Their bodies begin to slide apart, muscles trembling from effort. Cael, still flushed, reaches for a shallow silver dish by the lounge and retrieves a warm cloth. Reverent, he kneels and carefully wipes Orion down—between his legs, along the insides of his thighs, across his stomach. Every motion slow. Intentional.

Orion growls low at the tenderness.

Cael meets his eyes.

Still hard.

Still hungry.

"I want you in my mouth, Your Grace," Cael whispers.

And without waiting, he leans in and licks the base of Orion's cock—slow and deliberate, tongue swirling along the shaft, covering every inch. Then he slides down, lips parting, mouth opening wide to take him in.

Orion moans deeply, hips rocking into Cael's mouth as his hand threads into that silver hair.

Behind him, Theren watches—dazed and desperate. One hand stroking himself again.

I'm still straddling Aeris, cunt soaked and throbbing, the slick mess of our orgasms gluing us together. I grind down one more time and she cries out again, nails digging into my thighs.

Aeris lifts her head, panting, grinning like a woman possessed.

"You're insatiable," she says, voice wrecked.

I kiss her again and smile. "So is my prince."

Orion chuckles darkly from across the room. "Then we're well matched."

"I want to watch you feast on her cunt." His voice is thick—reverent. "How well your mouth brings her pleasure."

A flicker of heat ignites low in my belly.

I move without hesitation.

Sliding off Aeris, I lie down opposite her, offering Orion a perfect view as I spread my legs wide, my pussy already swollen, slick, begging for more. Aeris mirrors me, her thighs falling open in invitation.

I crawl closer, tongue already wet, ready to taste her again—when the third female, the one who'd kissed me earlier, slides up beside me. She lowers her mouth to mine, kissing me upside down, her fingers trailing between my breasts, down my stomach, over the mound of my cunt. Two fingers slide easily between my wet lips. I cover her hand with mine, encouraging her inside me and groan when her fingers enter the tight walls of my pussy.

"Is there room for one more?" she purrs. "Another mouth, that is," she asks, working her finger in and out.

"Always," I breathe. Then I nod toward our triangle as she licks me off her soaked fingers. "Aeris, I'm starving for you—lick her."

We settle in a spiral of limbs and want. Aeris lowers her head between the other fae's legs, while I press my mouth to Aeris, licking her cunt slow and deep. The female groans against my pussy—her tongue hot and greedy, flicking my clit before dipping lower, tasting me with soft, wet swirls.

We're a chain of mouths and moans, each of us devouring the other in perfect rhythm.

Orion groans behind me. "That's it… just like that."

His voice is hoarse. Wrecked.

"Make your queen feel good," he tells the fae licking me. "Show her how worthy you are."

From the corner of my eye, I watch him pull Cael's mouth off his cock.

"Turn around," Orion orders, voice rough. "On your knees."

Cael obeys, positioning himself on all fours, looking over his shoulder with parted lips and eager eyes. Orion slicks his cock again, running his hand down the length until it shines with oil.

"Want it hard?" he asks, pushing Cael's chest to the floor as he holds his hip against him.

"Yes," Cael gasps, arching his back, spreading his knees wider for Orion. "Please."

Orion grips him by the hair, jerking his head back. "Filthy fucking fae. You want to be filled by your prince?"

Cael moans, spine arching beautifully. "Yes, gods, yes…"

Orion doesn't wait.

He thrusts in—harder than he did with Theren. Less careful. More primal. He groans deep at the feel of tight, clenching heat. Cael cries out, hands pushing against the floor as Orion begins to fuck him without mercy.

His rhythm never falters, even as he watches me.

My tongue glides across Aeris's clit, hips rocking in time with the fae's mouth on mine. Aeris moans into the woman she's pleasuring, and the room is a chorus of sighs and slaps and the wet sounds of pleasure.

"Theren," Orion growls, his voice cracking with dominance, "bring your cock here."

Theren stumbles forward—still flushed, still hard—and stands in front of Orion. Orion takes him into his mouth without hesitation, lips stretching around the shaft, cheeks hollowing with greed.

Theren groans, his hands tangling in Orion's hair as Orion sucks him deeper—still fucking Cael with relentless thrusts.

The sounds are feral. Beautiful.

Orion moans around Theren's cock, matching every bob of his head with a thrust into Cael's ass until—

"Fuck—Orion—I'm—"

Orion pauses.

And opens his mouth.

Theren releases with a shattered cry, spilling into Orion's open mouth. Orion strokes him through it, his fist pumping every last drop. Some of it drips down his chin—and then, without warning, Orion yanks Cael up by the hair, still buried inside him, and kisses him from behind.

Cum slips between their tongues, just like he'd done with me and the wine.

I moan into Aeris's cunt, nearly coming from the sight alone.

But I want him. Now. I need him to fill me—long and swollen, driving into me until there is nothing left of me.

"Orion," I gasp. "Now. I need you inside me. Please."

He pulls out of Cael slowly, both of them panting. Theren slides in behind Cael, ready to take his place. Orion's body shines with sweat and oil, his cock still rock-hard and coated with release.

He grabs another warm cloth from the silver dish, wipes himself clean, the cleansing oils on the fabric leaving his skin soft and fresh—for me.

The women part around me, moving aside with quiet reverence.

I open for him.

Spread wide.

Waiting.

"I love my queen desperate for my cock."

He comes to me and thrusts inside with one brutal stroke—and it's everything I want.

I scream. My back arches. My vision shatters.

The room erupts again—pleasure blooming like wildfire. Fae moan and gasp and fuck around us, drinking and kissing and falling into each other over and over until they crash, collapsing in tangled heaps of sweat and bliss.

"That's it, Starling," Orion growls against my ear, his thrusts still deep, still ruthless. "Scream for me—let every court hear what a perfect little slut their queen is. So fucking wrecked... and still begging for more."

I lose track of time.

Orion fucks me like he owns every part of me. Like he's been waiting lifetimes. Like I'm the only thing in this realm that matters.

And to him, I am.

I come again. And again. And again—until I can't breathe, can't think, can barely even feel because my body has gone boneless from the weight of too much ecstasy.

When I finally stop shaking, when I finally go still beneath him, I'm drenched in sweat and so full of him I can't tell where I end and he begins.

I try to lift my head, but I can't.

My eyes droop. My limbs are heavy.

And then—I feel him lifting me.

Cradling me.

A kiss pressed to my temple, soft and warm.

"I've got you, Starling," he whispers.

He carries me out of the den of pleasure and into our bedchamber, where the air is cooler—quiet, still humming with the echo of everything we just did.

He sets me gently on the bed and fetches another cloth —warm, damp, laced with oils—and carefully cleans my body. The scent is familiar. Calming. I sigh, too weak to move.

He brings me a glass of moonwater, holding it to my lips, coaxing me to drink.

"Drink, my love," he murmurs. "And the tonic for your headaches—though I've a feeling this time I'm the one to blame instead of the realm."

I give him a weak chuckle. Then he kisses my forehead, slipping a nightdress over the body he's worshipped for hours.

He tucks me under the covers like I'm the most precious thing he's ever touched.

Then he cleans himself. Drinks his own water. And slides in beside me.

We move toward each other instinctively, our bodies pulling together, limbs tangling, chests aligned.

I rest my head on his shoulder and my body melts against his.

His hand finds my waist.

And like that—we fall asleep.

Spent. Wrapped in each other.
And for the first time in what feels like lifetimes—
I dream of nothing.

CHAPTER 33

orion

Liora is behaving oddly. Even for her.

I can feel it in the way the air around her hums wrong—too bright, too sweet. Her court reeks of starlight and honeyed wine, but lately there's something off underneath all that shimmer.

Mor waits in the narrow hall behind the observatory, where light can't reach. The torches along the corridor gutter when I approach. She doesn't bother to turn; her shadows already stretch toward mine—greeting, restless.

"We followed the hag as you asked," Mor says. "Last night. During the festivities."

"So chipper this first shade." I nod once in greeting. I knew she would be right pissy. She's fasting for battle, and when Mor fasts, her patience burns faster than the candles.

"Where did she go?"

"Through the lower streets. Quick, head down, no entourage. She shed the guards halfway through the market." Mor's lips curl, pale in the dark. "Unusual for a creature who likes an audience."

That's one way to put it. Liora likes to be seen—every movement gilded, every breath dusted in gold. Even her skin glitters faintly under moonlight, like she's dipped herself in crushed stars. The Lady of the Shimmer Court, forever trying to outshine the night itself.

"She stopped near the glassmakers' square," Mor continues. "There are new wards. Strong ones. Not ancient work—fresh, deliberate. Woven from her court's light."

I look up sharply. "You couldn't pass through?"

Mor's smile is all teeth. "We could have. But to break them, we'd have had to shatter her signature. The whole court would have felt it. Especially her."

So. She's hiding behind her own magic. Not coincidence, then—intentional.

"How long was she gone?"

"A few hours. Returned before first shade. Looked different. Not tired—emptied."

I drag a hand through my hair, exhaling slowly.

She planned that feast. The low tables. The floor cushions. The wine meant for surrender to passion. Even the desserts were laced with Lunavelle Nectar—crafted to heat the blood and dull the mind. Everything about last night was purposeful, a performance staged to bring me to her. She's been trying to win my hand for ages, convinced a crown can be seduced. No doubt she meant for the evening to end in her bed, to claim a bond she could twist into proof of a mating before the court.

To hurt Tana.

Probably all of the above.

"But she left," Mor says quietly, breaking into my thoughts.

"Yes." My voice hardens. "Whatever pulled her away was more important than her own ambition and scheming."

Mor tilts her head, shadows twitching like the wings of crows. "A lover?"

"Please." I scoff, rolling some lunabloom and lighting

the tip with a spark of lightning. "Liora would have paraded him through the throne room in gold chains and sat her cunt right on his face," I mutter. "No. This was quiet. Hidden. Important."

The thought coils tight in my chest. Who would she risk exposure to meet in secret—and why mask the meeting with wards that hum like her own heartbeat?

Mor's eyes gleam faintly. "We can map the boundaries of the wards. Without breaking them."

"Do it," I say, blowing a puff of lunabloom smoke toward the ceiling.

Mor inclines her head once before dissolving, the shadows folding inward like silk being gathered from the floor. The air hums with the faint tremor of her departure, that electric stillness left in her wake.

I stay a moment longer, leaning against the cold stone, letting the silence stretch.

Liora's court glitters to blind, but darkness is everywhere.

And whatever she's hiding in those wards—

I'll find it.

The scent of fruit and honey drifts through the corridor as I step out into the brighter wing of the palace. Sunlight doesn't exist here, but the Shimmer Court always pretends —walls dusted in gold, illusions of dawn flickering along the marble.

Tana appears ahead, walking with Theren and Aeris, both of them half smiling, half trying not to. There's still that faint glow about them from last night's... celebrations. I can't help the smirk tugging at my mouth.

Theren catches my eye; I give a lazy wink. His cheeks

flush the color of rose quartz. Aeris bumps his shoulder, trying to hide a grin. A tendril of my shadow drifts past them, holding the lunabloom between spectral fingers.

Tana barely has time to turn before I'm there—hands on her waist, lifting her off her feet. She gasps, laughing, the sound cutting clean through the falseness of this golden place. I spin her once, twice, setting her down against the wall.

Her breath catches. Mine does, too.

I lean close, one hand braced over her head. "Liora is scheming," I murmur, low enough that only she hears. "And we need to figure out why."

Before she can answer, a small gathering of Liora's fae pass. I catch Tana's mouth in a kiss—brief but claiming. My lips still against hers as I speak into her mind. *Let's keep this between us. Mor knows. She's hunting.*

Her lashes flutter, but she nods—the smallest movement. When I step back, my shadow offers her the lunabloom. She takes it, fingers brushing the smoke before it disperses.

As we start toward the hall, I notice the faint stiffness in her step. The way her hips shift carefully, as if every movement reminds her of last night.

"You're sore," I murmur, a low grin tugging at my mouth.

"A little," she admits, the corner of her lips curving. "But it's the good kind. The kind that means I had more orgasms than I've ever had."

Pride surges in me—sharp, possessive, dangerous. "Good sore," I echo, dipping my head closer, "but I'll still get something for it from Merlin," I say, fighting a smirk. "He's bound to have a potion or two that will help."

We walk hand in hand through the archway into the breakfast hall.

The spread is obscene—crystal platters stacked with puddings, jellies, pastries shaped like stars. Towers of fruit glisten under glamour. I spot some from the Enchanted Forest—deep-violet citrus that leaks silver juice when bitten. I'll never admit it aloud, but they're a weakness of mine.

Liora rises the moment we enter. Her gown today is a weapon—gold and starlight stitched into arrogance. Her gaze snaps to me before it ever touches Tana.

"Prince Orion," she purrs, voice dripping with false delight. "The Shimmer Court agrees with you, I think."

"And you," I say smoothly—which she takes as the start of a compliment, already angling her body to accept some returned courtesy meant to flatter her, "seem to have forgotten the proper order of greetings in the presence of your queen."

A hush ripples. Liora's smile falters for a breath before she recovers. "Of course. Forgive me, Your Majesty. I did not see you there."

She curtsies to Tana, who offers a polite nod.

This bitch is asking for it. It's a miracle Tana has not antagonized Liora by calling her the wrong name or cut her tongue from her mouth to shut her up.

One of Liora's attendants hurries over with a tray, bowing low. "More wine, Queen Liora?"

A ripple of laughter follows—practiced and false.

Another fae scolds playfully, "She's not queen yet."

Liora only tilts her head toward me, eyes gleaming like liquid gold, a tick of one eyebrow that says, *not yet.*

I slide into the seat beside Tana, making a deliberate show of it. My arm drapes across the back of her chair, shadows curling lazily around her shoulders. There will be no mistaking my allegiance.

I fix her plate first—small pastries, fruit slices gleaming like jewels—before taking my own.

Tana's voice cuts through the chatter. Calm. Regal. "Lady Liora, we need to discuss your wyrmroot harvest. We'd like to see your stores and learn how much you can spare for Starfall."

Liora tuts softly. "Always so dutiful, Your Majesty. You'll make the rest of us look dreadfully lazy. Come—eat, drink. There will be plenty of time for dull trade talk later."

Her court giggles as if on cue.

Liora trails her fingers along her collarbone, voice dropping to a sultry purr. "I'd much rather hear about last night's carnal pleasures."

The gesture is so exaggerated she might as well be trying to seduce the fruit bowl.

The double doors burst open before anyone can reply.

"By the stars, did someone say pleasures?"

Merlin strides in, both arms occupied—two female fae clinging to him, flushed and giggling. His hair is in complete disarray, his coat half buttoned, and his grin far too pleased with itself.

"Morning, my luminous degenerates!" he declares, voice echoing through the hall. "The dawn may never rise in Avalon, but I certainly did!"

Tana's mouth falls open. The two fae peel off from him,

arm in arm, still laughing as they glide toward the side corridor. Their cheeks are stained pink, their hair tangled in a way that leaves little to the imagination.

I glance at Tana. She glances at me. Then at Merlin.

Her expression says everything.

He looks... lighter. Happier. The kind of smug that can only come from a night well spent.

"Don't look at me like that," he says, producing a small velvet satchel from somewhere within his coat. "You'd be in a fine mood too if you'd woken up like I did."

He plops the satchel on the table and rummages through it, muttering until he finds what he wants—a small piece of fruit leather rolled into a perfect sphere. It shimmers faintly, the color of dusk.

"For the soreness," he says to Tana with a wink, placing it in front of her plate.

Tana blinks. "What?"

He just pats her shoulder, utterly unbothered, and moves on.

I take a long drink of wine to keep from laughing.

Tana leans in, her voice a whisper against my ear. "He's a whore." There's brightness in her tone, humor, but also a flicker of genuine disbelief. "The old man's an absolute whore."

Merlin, of course, hears her. He always does, despite looking like he's never paying attention.

"I'll have you know, my dear, I've been the last one standing at more than a few orgies," he announces proudly, pouring himself a drink. "The key to stamina is good hydration."

I choke on the wine.

I could have gone the rest of my immortal life without that image in my head.

He beams, utterly delighted with himself.

Merlin laughs so hard at my distress his ridiculous hat slips sideways and tumbles off his head.

The small stormcloud hiding inside bursts free, zipping toward the ceiling before swelling in size. Thunder rumbles. Light crackles within its churning gray belly, flashing against the gilded walls of the hall.

Merlin scoffs, hands on his hips. "Oh, for the love of starlight, not again. Get back in there, you sulking cumulonimbus!"

The cloud rumbles louder, ignoring him.

Liora shrieks, clutching at her hair as the shadows above dim her precious starlight. "It's ruining my ceiling! Make it stop!"

"I said back inside!" Merlin snaps, waving a finger at the storm like it's an unruly pet.

The cloud growls. Then it rains.

Not a drizzle. A deluge.

Water pours from the air, soaking the entire table in seconds. Pastries dissolve into colorful sludge. Jellies slide off their plates. Fruit rolls across the floor.

Fae scatter in every direction, shrieking as the shimmer paint begins to run from their bodies. Liora lets out a piercing cry, gold streaking down her arms in melted rivulets.

"Get it off me! Get it off!" she wails.

Two attendants sprint to her side, yanking a curtain from the nearest window to fashion a makeshift awning over her head. You'd think she was being dipped in acid the way they carry on.

I'm drenched, dripping, and delighted.

Tana, Merlin, and I are the only ones still seated, enjoying the spectacle.

The rain begins to ease, tapering to a steady drizzle before thinning altogether. The cloud hovers small and grumpy above the wreckage, muttering with the occasional low thunderclap.

I bite back a grin—failing spectacularly. "Remind me to thank your hat later."

Merlin gives me a murderous look, water dripping from his beard. "I warned you about dramatics," he mutters, shoving his hat back onto his head.

Tana doesn't say anything.

She's staring toward the far wall—the one now bare where the curtain was ripped away. Her expression shifts—focused, distant, as if listening for something I can't hear.

"What is it, my love?" I murmur, but she's already rising from her chair.

She crosses the room slowly, water still dripping from her hair, her steps quiet against the marble. She stops before the wall, eyes scanning the surface like she's searching for a crack only she can see.

Then she extends her hand—palm flat—and moves it forward.

Her fingers stop short, pressing against something invisible. The faint shimmer of power ripples across the space like sunlight bending over water.

Her eyes widen. "It's not the wall," she whispers.

My shadows stir.

She turns to Merlin, realization dawning like sunrise across her face. "Is this what you were poking at last night?"

Merlin freezes, caught midwring of his hat.

He blinks once.

Then twice.

"Well," he says faintly, "that depends entirely on whether you mean the barrier or the barmaids."

I ignore the comment.

I'm not letting my mind wander anywhere near the thought of that frail old wizard doing anything that could involve a bedroom.

"Orion," I call, glancing around to make sure the room has emptied. The air still smells of rain and sugar—of wet fruit and burnt pride. "Come look at this."

He strides over, curiosity sharpening the edges of his expression. "What is it?"

"Just look," I tell him, stepping aside.

He leans in, tilting his head. His shadows shift behind him, restless, as if trying to see for themselves. He moves closer, narrowing his eyes, inspecting the wall from different angles.

"What am I looking for?"

I don't answer. I just lift my hand and press my palm toward it again.

The air ripples—thick, viscous—like the surface of firm jelly trembling under my touch. The movement catches the light, distorting it, and for a heartbeat I can feel it pulse against my skin.

Orion inhales sharply. "Fuck me. I see it."

He reaches up, fingers brushing the surface. It shivers beneath his touch, the illusion bending, trying to hold.

"If Hypnos were here, he could help interpret this," Orion mutters, continuing to poke at the barrier.

I turn back to the wall, focusing on that shimmer at the edge of my vision—the ripple I've felt at the periphery, always dismissed as instinct or training.

Back home, when I hunted shifters and vampires, I could sense them before anyone else. See that iridescent shimmer you can never quite focus on.

Now I realize what that was.

What this is.

This faint veil of nothingness—the telltale hum of illusion.

My pulse quickens. "It's a glamour," I breathe.

The others turn toward me.

"The entire castle," I say, stepping back, eyes tracing the walls, the arches, the gleaming chandeliers. "It's all under a glamour."

Orion's shadows still, the air thick with the weight of it.

And for the first time since I arrived in Eldoria, I realize we may not be standing inside a court at all—

but a lie pretending to be one.

We relocate to my suite. Theren and Aeris fall in behind us, all lightheartedness from this morning gone. Merlin takes up residence in the corner, arms crossed and hat dripping. The stormcloud hovers above his head, raining steadily—not enough to soak, just enough to irritate. He smokes his long pipe in defiance, every puff of pale smoke curling up through the drizzle.

The faint patter of it fills the room. Tap. Tap. Tap.

The rebellious little storm didn't appreciate Merlin sticking him back inside his hat.

I run my hand along the wall, fingertips hovering an inch above the surface. There it is again—the same resistance. A shimmer beneath my skin, thick and pliant, like touching the skin of a bubble.

It's everywhere.

The walls. The doors. Even the damn table.

Everything in this place hums with illusion.

"Why in the world would the entire palace be covered in a glamour?" I whisper.

Mor's shadows tighten around her. "The wards surrounding the court are powerful but expected. What's strange," she says, frowning, "is the signature. It doesn't spread evenly. It bleeds strongest from one place."

"Where?" Orion asks. "Where you saw Liora disappear last evenfall?"

Mor nods. "She's using it like a door. The glamour's just the skin of it—what's beyond is being shielded by something stronger. Likely reinforced by the same wards that surround her court."

"Which means," I say, "whatever she's hiding is beyond that door."

Orion and I exchange a glance, and I know we're thinking of the same thing. The darkness.

The Obscura.

There isn't an ounce of me that trusts Liora. Her being capable of selling off all of Avalon to put herself in power is something she would absolutely do if she could.

We need to get behind that fucking door.

"She'll sense if we try to break through," Mor adds. "The wards are tied to her. Any disturbance will reach her immediately."

"So we get her to open it herself?" Theren asks as Aeris sits on his lap, his hands firm on her hips like the mates can't be near without touching.

"She'll never open it," Orion mutters. "We just need to get close enough to it."

I pace to the window, staring out over the glittering courtyard of the Shimmer Court. Everything gleams too bright, too perfect. It looks less like a kingdom and more like a mask stretched over something else.

So bright it hides whatever Liora is keeping secret behind it.

"She's not going to just let us stroll over there," Orion says.

I smile slowly because I already know exactly how this will go.

If Liora is hiding something behind that door, she's not going to show it willingly. But she will react if I push her hard enough. And there's one thing I'm pretty fucking good at—

making that bitch angry enough to show her true colors.

I glance over my shoulder at Orion, a grin tugging at my lips as I reach for Realmbreaker. "I'm going to piss her off."

He groans softly. "Of course you are."

"It's a specialty of mine."

I stride into the hall, fixing my sword at my side, boots echoing on the marble. The golden glow of the Shimmer Court follows us, too bright for comfort.

"Mor," I call without slowing, "send your crows out into the city, but don't let them be seen. The fae here would probably sell their skin before they betray Liora. If they spot shadowbirds in the skies, they'll panic and warn her."

Mor's eyes flash, but she nods. "Understood."

"And I want you to snoop around Liora's bedchambers. See what you can find—letters, wards, trinkets. Anything useful. We'll flush her out."

Orion falls into step beside me, his shadows stretching along the floor like spilled ink. "And how exactly do you plan on flushing her out?"

I smirk. "You'll see."

I glance over my shoulder, catching the little storm's attention.

It peeks out from behind Merlin's shoulder, flashing a faint bolt of light like a guilty child caught mid-mischief. Merlin is far too busy plucking something out of his beard to notice.

I crook a finger. "Come here," I whisper.

The cloud glides over, humming softly as it hovers near my ear. I lower my voice. "Go run amok. Start in Liora's room—just a drizzle, not a downpour. Maybe a lightning flash to hurry her along. Don't soak her, just make her move."

The storm gives an eager rumble, vibrating with delight.

"Quietly," I add. "And make it convincing."

It zips upward, a blur of silver mist and static, vanishing down the corridor.

A few seconds later, Merlin notices the absence above his head. He startles so hard his hat nearly falls off. "Oh, not again!" he cries, spinning in place before tearing off after it, clutching his robes and shouting, "Rumbleton Tempestus Maximus! You disobedient git, we talked about autonomy!"

His voice fades into the distance.

Then comes the sound I've been waiting for—Liora's scream echoing through the marble halls, high and indignant enough to shake the chandeliers.

I exchange a look with Orion.

Moments later, she bursts into view, trailing a cluster of attendants. Her hair is wild, her gown half fastened, and the fae around her are frantically trying to reapply her golden powder with oversized puffs. A faint sparkle of shimmer dust clouds the air behind her like a comet's tail.

Orion exhales a laugh under his breath. "Subtle."

"Effective," I counter, straightening from the wall as the Lady of the Shimmer Court barrels toward us, dripping resentment and half-set curls.

Time to see what else she's hiding.

I put on my sweetest smile. "Ah, London! Just the fae I was hoping to see."

Liora blinks, confusion flickering before she catches herself. She practically trips over her own attendants in her rush to look composed—tossing the last few hair rollers behind her and sweeping her damp curls over one shoulder in an exaggerated pose.

"My Queen," she breathes, arranging her expression into something serene. "That little stormcloud startled me."

"Did it now?" I ask lightly.

She turns to Orion with a simper. "He's so cute. His little lightning bolts."

Orion's mouth twitches. I can't tell if it's amusement or the effort not to smite her.

I don't bother entertaining the charade. "Well," I say brightly, clapping my hands once, "since you're here, Laverne, I'd love a tour of your court. It's so beautiful—I'd hate to leave without seeing all of it."

Her eyes go wide. "Now? Oh—well, I would be delighted, but I have performers arriving soon. Acrobats, actually. From the Vale. I really must—"

I'm already walking toward the open doors. "Perfect. Then let's make it quick—a stroll, a bit of sightseeing—and we'll all be back in time to watch them fall off their ribbons, or whatever it is they do."

Behind me, Orion's low chuckle rumbles like distant thunder.

Liora sputters, caught between panic and protocol. "Your Majesty, it really isn't—"

But the courtyard awaits, bathed in shimmerlight and full of curious eyes.

The moment we step outside, fae begin to pause mid-step, whispering as they bow or curtsy. The Chosen Queen of Avalon—out among them.

Liora sees it too: how the attention shifts, how the light bends toward me rather than her. Her lips twitch into a brittle smile. She can't refuse me now. Not here. Not where the court is watching.

"Of course," she says finally, smoothing her skirts with a shaking hand. "I'd be honored to show you around."

I flash her a grin sharp enough to draw blood. "Wonderful. Lead the way, Lemon."

Orion snorts softly beside me.

And just like that, the Lady of the Shimmer Court—still half damp, hair uneven, pride barely holding together—turns and starts walking ahead, her smile as tight as spun glass.

Exactly where I want her.

CHAPTER 35
orion

Watching Liora trip over herself while Tana runs her to the limits of her patience might be one of my all-time favorite ways to spend the first shade.

The Lady of the Shimmer Court is flushed and frantic, doing her best to appear composed while Tana marches her straight through her own territory. The mortal queen moves with the kind of confidence that makes everyone else look like they're in her way.

We make our way through the city center—winding cobblestone streets that shimmer faintly beneath the ever-present starlight. The air smells of sweet wine and rain-polished stone. Lanterns hang above us in strands of gold and pearl, suspended from the balconies of pale-stone buildings that gleam like they were polished every hour.

Tana doesn't so much follow Liora as she does lead by accident. Each time Liora tries to guide her toward another glittering fountain or sculpture, Tana simply keeps walking, curiosity pulling her in whatever direction she pleases— which, conveniently, keeps angling closer to the southern quarter.

Every few steps, she pauses.

At a silversmith's stall, Tana picks up a delicate pendant shaped like a crescent moon. The metal gleams faintly beneath the shimmerlight, catching the reflection of her fingers.

"This is beautiful," she says, turning it over. "Where is this from?"

Liora's smile sharpens instantly, pride curling her voice. "Of course, everything in the Shimmer Court reflects our own brilliance."

I clear my throat, keeping my tone mild. "That's Gloam-reach work," I tell her. "They forge under twilight storms—see the faint color shift along the edges? It's their mark."

Liora freezes for half a heartbeat before recovering. "Ah. Yes. A gift from our allies in the Twilight Court," she says quickly. "We have the most refined trade relations."

Tana hums softly, pretending not to notice the stumble, and sets the pendant back down.

A few streets later, she pauses beside a florist's display—twisting vines spilling from crystal vases, their blossoms glowing faintly blue. "These are stunning," she says. "I've never seen anything like them."

"They flourish best under our light," Liora says, eager again. "The shimmer here enhances their glow."

"Actually," I say before I can stop myself, "they're Sylvadora vines. They only bloom under the Enchanted Forest's blessing. Imported, most likely."

Liora laughs, brittle around the edges. "Yes, well. We do enjoy sharing beauty across the courts."

Tana looks back at me, eyes dancing. She knows exactly what I'm doing.

We move on. At the next corner, a shop window glitters with glass orbs filled with drifting silver light—like captured stars moving through water.

Tana leans closer, mesmerized. "That's incredible. Like bottled constellations."

"One of our court's specialties," Liora says, voice syrup-smooth again. "The shimmerlight of our skies, suspended for eternity."

I study one of the orbs, tracing a finger along the faint runic pattern around its base. "Astralana craft," I correct gently. "The Celestial Court binds starlight like this. It's their trade."

Liora's jaw works before she finds her smile again. "Naturally," she says tightly, "we inspired the technique."

Tana's lips twitch, amusement flickering across her face. "Of course you did."

I have to glance away to hide my grin. She isn't even trying to cut Liora down, but the woman's composure is unraveling faster than her curls did earlier.

Every turn through the Shimmer Court reveals the same thing: nothing here truly belongs to it. Gloamreach silver. Sylvadora vines. Astralana starlight.

All of it borrowed or bought.

A court built from mirrors reflecting everyone else's glory.

As we move deeper through the streets, I start cataloging the wares in my head. Trinkets from Umbranor. Fabrics dyed in Mirevalis pigment.

But nothing from Eldoria.

Our village at Starfall trades regularly with all the courts —baskets, woven silks, fruit preserves, even the powdered sugar they use for festival pastries. The Shimmer Court used to boast of its connection to Eldoria's artisans, of its devotion to beauty found in creation, not acquisition.

Now it's just imitation.

I stop at a stall lined with sugared confections. The scent is wrong—too floral, too faint. "Do you not make lurefruit tarts anymore?" I ask, feigning idle curiosity.

Liora pauses mid-gesture, that brittle smile flickering. "Oh, they're out of season, I'm afraid."

"Out of season?" I glance toward the sky—if the illusion above us can even be called that. "Strange. It's the perfect moon for their ripening."

Her lashes flutter. "Ah, yes, of course. We... we just shipped the last of our yield to Cairnvail."

"Did you?" I say softly. "Because we were in Cairnvail three nights ago. Not a single lurefruit in sight."

Her posture stiffens, the shimmerlight along her collarbone dimming a fraction.

Through the tether of thought, I reach for Tana. Something more is going on here. The court of vanity has nothing of its own—only trophies from others.

Her response hums through the bond, cool and precise. *Then let's see what else she's hiding.*

Tana's voice slips easily into the air, sweet and deliberate. "Lady Latasha," she says, still refusing to call her by her correct name, "About the wyrmroot export. I'd like to see your stores. You said your court was rich in supply."

Liora's smile freezes. "Oh, yes. The wyrmroot. The lesser fae are still harvesting. It will be some time before the yield is ready."

Tana doesn't blink. "Then I'll see what's been harvested so far."

"It was outlawed, you know," Liora says suddenly, seizing the new path like a drowning woman grabbing driftwood. "After the Battle of Bloodmere. Far too dangerous for civilized beings such as ourselves."

"It was not outlawed," I say evenly.

Her gaze darts to me, challenge sparking. "By Queen Demeter, as a matter of fact."

I smile without warmth. "Good thing we have a new queen. Tana, what say you?"

"Yes," she says lightly, "I decree it's no longer outlawed. Now, let's see it."

Liora falters, words tripping over themselves. She can't refuse outright, not with half the marketplace listening. "Your Majesty is, of course, Queen Rising—but until coronation, the laws remain intact. Perhaps once you're fully crowned, we can revisit the matter."

How neatly she says it—trying to sound respectful while clawing for control.

She gestures toward the main avenue, attempting to guide us back toward the heart of the court. "Now, if you'll allow, the gardens are just ahead—"

But I feel it.

The hum.

That faint, thrumming pulse just beneath the air—a resonance in the stone. A whisper of power the wards can't entirely mask. It's close. Just beyond the next row of archways. A block over.

Tana, I send quietly. Do you feel that?

Her answer slides through my mind, sharp and sure. Yes. I feel it.

Liora keeps smiling, still talking about gardens and fountains and light shows. But the more she tries to draw us away from that invisible wall of power, the tighter her voice gets.

And I know—whatever she's hiding, it's right there.

Behind that hum.

Waiting.

I'm about to interject—another polite correction, another nail in the coffin of Liora's composure—when something catches my eye.

A tether of light.

It snakes through the crowd, faint but unmistakable, connecting a lesser fae to a high fae like a leash to a cart. The lesser trails behind—small, shoulders drawn tight, dressed in simplified clothing that mirrors the cut and color of their master's. Clearly a servant.

But not just that.

Bound.

The sight hits me like lightning to the chest. That practice was outlawed ages ago—abolished when Avalon swore to end the trade of its own people. To see it here, in the Shimmer Court, paraded through the streets as if it were nothing—

My blood turns to thunder.

"Why is that fae in chains?" My voice cuts through the air, low and sharp. Above us, the clouds stir. A rumble rolls across the sky, distant but growing.

Tana gasps softly beside me, her gaze following mine until she sees it too—the tether glinting between them, the faint shimmer of compulsion magic biting into the lesser's wrist.

Liora blinks, caught off guard. "Oh, that?" she says, her

tone flippant. "Who am I to interfere with a private bargain between a high fae and their servant?"

Tana turns to me, frowning. "What does she mean? What bargain?"

"It's an old practice," I tell her quietly, trying to keep my rage in check. "When the lesser courts first formed, lesser fae were traded as wares—sold, bound, compelled to serve. It was barbaric. And forbidden by royal decree."

Liora lifts her chin, eyes glittering. "And yet, as I've reminded you, the throne sits vacant. Without a queen to enforce decrees, some laws... lose their weight."

The air crackles.

"Wait!" Tana steps forward, calling out to the fae.

The bound fae stops dead, eyes wide and terrified, the tether tightening. The high fae they're attached to tugs the line, panic rising. "My lady," he stammers toward Liora. "What—what should I do?"

Tana ignores him. "Why are you bound to this high fae?" she asks the lesser directly, her voice steady but soft.

The lesser's lips tremble. They look everywhere but at her, fear thick in their eyes. The high fae pulls harder on the tether. "Queen Liora—"

"She is not the queen. Answer me," Tana commands, her tone slicing through the air like Realmbreaker's edge. "No harm will come to you."

Liora moves so fast her poise shatters. "I forbid you to answer!" she snaps, voice shrill and uneven.

The lesser flinches, shrinking back. The high fae's hands shake.

Tana turns slowly, her expression pure, cold fury. "Excuse me?"

She draws Realmbreaker. The sound alone makes the street fall silent.

"Something is going on here," she says, voice low, steady. "And I want to know what it is."

She turns slightly, pointing her sword toward the nearest building. The tip grazes the air—and the glamour ripples. The illusion shudders like a disturbed pond, revealing the shimmer of light and ward beneath.

"Why is your entire court covered in a glamour?" she demands.

"I do not have to answer you," Liora bites out, voice shaking now.

"Then I'll find the answer myself."

Tana steps past her. The cobblestones shift beneath us, the hum of power intensifying with every step closer to that sealed block. The air thickens—alive, resisting.

Liora steps back, hands raised, her polished mask fracturing. "Do not take another step over there," she warns, blocking the narrow lane that leads toward the southern block.

Tana's eyes narrow. "What will you do to stop me?"

"You are no longer welcome in the Shimmer Court. Please leave."

"What is that?" she asks, eyes on the shimmering distortion ahead. "What's beyond it?"

Liora darts in front of her, desperation creeping into her voice. "Stop! I said don't move another step!"

Tana's hand drops to her side. She lifts two fingers to her lips and lets out a sharp, piercing whistle.

A beat of silence.

Then the sky splits open.

Merlin's storm answers the call, surging over the castle in a rolling swell of shadow and lightning. The thunder merges with my own, and together they snarl above us, hungry for release.

Liora's confidence fractures completely. For the first time, she looks afraid.

"Take down your wards," Tana orders.

Liora shakes her head, voice trembling. "No."

Tana's gaze hardens. "You should rethink that."

The air vibrates as my sword slides free, steel flashing with stormlight. Liora's eyes flick to it, then back to Tana.

"I won't ask again," Tana says quietly. "Remove your wards—or I'll tear them down myself."

"You can't do that!" Liora cries. "It's against fae law!"

Tana steps forward, Realmbreaker catching the light. "You said it yourself. I'm only Queen Rising. Not yet crowned. Not yet fae."

Her voice drops, dangerous and sure.

"So, the laws don't apply to me."

She adjusts her grip on Realmbreaker, the blade humming with the realm's pulse. "Last chance, Lana. Take them down."

Liora's chin lifts, stubborn defiance flickering in her gold-dusted eyes. "I refuse."

Thunder crashes so hard the air shakes around us.

And in that instant, I know—Tana will not leave until those wards come crashing down.

Tana lifts her chin toward the storm, adjusting her grip on Realmbreaker.

The clouds above churn in response—rolling, restless, aware. I'm anxious to see what her plan is here.

Liora's voice pierces through the rising wind, thin with panic. "You cannot do this! I command you to leave this place!"

Tana doesn't even glance at her. She stares up at the storm, and for a heartbeat, it feels like the sky itself leans closer—like it's listening.

She doesn't need words. Somehow, the storm understands her.

She raises Realmbreaker, moonlight glinting off the blade.

Liora shrieks.

"Now!" Tana's voice rings out—a command that cracks through the storm like lightning itself.

The heavens answer.

A blinding bolt crashes into the sword. The ground trembles. The air ignites with ozone and light. The charge surges through the blade and slams into the wall of wards.

I feel it through my bones—the echo of impact, the web of old magic rippling like ice splintering on a frozen lake. Cracks pulse across the invisible surface before the energy seals over again.

But the wards are old.

Layered upon layer, decade upon decade. Newer weaves knotted over the old ones, tangled so thickly it's impossible to tell where one ends and the next begins. It's not protection—it's containment.

They've been barricading this for generations.

My chest tightens. If she's hiding what I think she's hiding—if she's conspiring with the darkness beyond Avalon—

I summon Mor.

"Come to me," I murmur through the bond of immortality.

She arrives in a plume of shadow, silent and fierce, her eyes burning like twin embers. The Morrigan—ready for war.

The storm above groans, lightning coiling in its belly. Tana lifts her blade again. The blade's glow pulses, faint silver bleeding into bright white.

Liora's voice cracks, shrieking over the thunder. "Guards! Stop her! Stop the mortal!"

I step forward, shadows lashing outward, wrapping Liora in coils of black smoke. She thrashes, but they hold. A final strand snakes across her mouth, silencing her.

"No interruptions," I growl.

The next bolt hits—stronger, sharper.

Then another.

Tana braces, Realmbreaker a conduit between sky and stone. Lightning ripples across her arms, through her shoulders. Her body moves with it, not against it. And I'm mesmerized.

The wards spark and strain under the onslaught, ancient runes flaring in protest. Each layer breaks with a sound like cracking glass, only for another to flare beneath it.

Again. And again.

Mor steps closer, her shadows joining mine, her eyes fixed on the light bleeding from the barrier. "They've buried something," she says under her breath. "The magic runs deep. Very deep."

The next strike comes—and this time, I add my own.

Thunder rolls from my chest like breath; lightning

answers my call, spearing down from the clouds to join the storm's fury. My power meets hers in the air—a roaring collision of storm and shadow.

Moonlight flares from Tana's body, glowing up her arms, threading through the hilt of her sword. The light converges, building inside the blade until it hums like a living thing.

"Again," I command the storm.

It obeys.

Lightning hits the same spot—again and again and again—until the sound is deafening, until my power, the storm's, and Tana's moonlight merge into one blinding strike.

The barriers quake. The air tears.

Layer by layer, they fracture—each older, darker rune peeling apart like ancient bark.

Tana draws in a single sharp breath and lifts Realm-breaker high.

"Hold it this time!" she calls out.

The next bolt hits and stays, suspended in the air, pouring itself into the sword. The steel glows white-hot, singing with lightning, alive with moonlight.

Tana heaves forward, every muscle taut, and swings.

The sword arcs downward in a blaze of power—lightning, moonlight, and storm colliding as she cuts through the final layer.

The impact shakes the entire street.

The wards scream. Then crumble.

A shockwave bursts outward, slamming through the city in a gust of wind that snuffs out every lantern. The glamour collapses in a cascade of dying light.

And as the smoke clears—

the Shimmer Court finally shows us what it's been hiding.

CHAPTER 36
tana

The wards don't shatter all at once.

They groan.

They wail.

The sound is a low, splitting moan that ripples through the air, like the world itself cracking under its own weight.

The first fissure blooms above us in a jagged arc of light, then spreads, spiderwebbing across the invisible dome that's kept the Shimmer Court wrapped in its false perfection.

Another sound follows—the thin, brittle pop of glass breaking under pressure—and the air fills with glittering dust. The shimmer begins to fall.

It's beautiful for half a heartbeat.

Then horrifying.

The golden glow fades from the buildings. The marble turns dull, gray, fractured. The cobblestones lose their luster. What had been gleaming spires just moments ago now look brittle and sunken, their edges warped and uneven.

A gust of cold air hits my face, sharp enough to sting. The scent of rot follows.

I blink, staring up as flakes of shimmerlight drift down like dying snow.

"What..." The word barely escapes me. "What's happening?"

Orion doesn't answer. He's watching, his entire body gone still. His shadows twitch against the ground like they're restless, uncertain.

Then the rest of the glamour falls.

It collapses all around us—the light crumbling in waves, exposing what's been hiding underneath.

The streets are ruined.

Buildings cracked open.

The once-smooth stone of the castle wall reveals deep scorch marks, blackened by fire or time.

Somewhere beyond the courtyard, a scream pierces the air.

Then another.

The fae gathered nearest the palace gates stare upward, transfixed, as the wards peel away in sheets of light. Their shimmer collapses in slow motion, like molten glass dripping from the sky.

The sound builds—more voices joining the panic. Somewhere, a cart overturns. Fruit tumbles across the cobblestones, ripe and glistening one heartbeat and dull, nearly rotten the next. The scent curdles in the air, sour and sweet all at once.

Another scream cuts through the courtyard.

I look up—and meet the eyes of a fae standing near the fountain. His once-perfect face is gray and hollow, shimmerlight fading from his skin. And where his nose should be, there's only an open pit, raw and glistening.

I gasp, stumbling back a step.

He clutches his face with both hands, trembling. "Don't

look at me!" he cries, voice ragged, and bolts, tripping over his own feet as he runs into the panicked crowd.

The chaos ripples outward.

The illusions around them peel away like paint washing off in the rain. The shimmer leaves their skin, the dust sliding down in streaks that stain the cobblestones gold. Gowns become rags. Jewels dissolve into glass beads. Hair once bright as spun metal turns coarse, tangled.

Their eyes—god, their eyes—sink hollow, wide with terror.

Liora stumbles forward, staring at her trembling hands as the last of her golden powder fades into nothing. "No..." she whispers. "No, no, no—look what you've done!"

She whirls on me, face contorted. "Do you see what you've done to us?"

I take a step back, breath catching. "I didn't—"

"You've killed my court!" she screams, her voice cracking. "You've destroyed it!"

Her attendants are sobbing now, clutching one another as if the air itself might rip them apart.

I can't move.

I can't even find words.

Because I don't understand what I'm seeing. It's like watching two worlds bleed into each other—the shimmer of beauty melting away to reveal a skeleton beneath it.

Under my feet, I feel the thrum of the realm—that invisible will that is somehow tethered to me. This was a test. A trial of the queen's coronation. And I passed it. But it doesn't feel like a victory.

I feel the heartbeat of the realm a bit stronger now, like

it's beating in the ground directly under my feet, pulsing up my body and pounding in time with my own.

Orion moves beside me, his expression unreadable. But I feel it through our bond—a ripple of disbelief, then horror, then anger.

"What is this?" I whisper.

He shakes his head once, jaw tight. "By the light of the moon, I can't believe this."

"Orion—"

"They've been draining it," he says quietly, eyes scanning the ruined street. "Feeding on their own shimmer, pulling power from the realm to sustain the illusion."

I look around again—at the hollow-eyed fae, at the broken towers, at the colorless streets—and I feel my stomach turn.

"They did this to themselves?"

He exhales slowly. "Greed always costs something. They built this glamour to hide the truth, and then they kept feeding it—layer after layer, until there was nothing left to give."

Liora sinks to her knees, clawing at the air, weeping. "We only wanted to preserve it," she cries. "We were the brightest—our beauty, our light—it is everything."

Her voice cracks on the last word, and for a moment, she looks less like a villain and more like a broken thing desperate to crawl back into the dream she built.

The fae around her cry harder. Some beg her to fix it; others curse her for the ruin, their voices rising into a chorus of panic and grief.

"Queen Liora, please. You have to do something."

A fragment of the shattered glamour drifts past my face like ash. I reach for it, but it dissolves before I can touch it.

Orion's voice is quiet but firm beside me. "The Shimmer Court is dead."

And though he doesn't say it aloud, I hear the rest of the thought through the bond—

It's been dead for a very long time.

The storm overhead begins to break apart, leaving a heavy silence in its wake.

"Ha! There you are, you ungrateful sack of fog!"

Merlin barrels through the broken archway, chasing the last remnant of his storm. His hat is missing again, his beard full of shimmer dust, and his robes are singed in at least three places.

He stops short when he finally takes in the devastation around us. His hands lower; his grin falters. "Oh," he says softly. "Oh, by the stars..."

I can still smell the shimmer dust on the air—sweet and metallic, like something burning too slowly to notice until it's gone.

And as I look around at what remains, I realize the glamour wasn't just a mask.

It was a tomb.

And I need to see what was buried in it.

The courtyard is chaos—screaming, sobbing, the sound of fae feet skidding on broken stone. Liora's voice cuts through the noise, shrill and trembling. "You've ruined us! You've doomed us all!"

She's still clawing at the air, as if she can piece the glamour back together with her bare hands. I turn away.

Beyond the courtyard, where the wards once stood, the air ripples faintly—like heat over sand.

"I need to see what's behind that door," I say, though my voice barely carries over the storm still grumbling above us.

Mor and Orion fall into step beside me. We move slowly through the courtyard's wreckage, past toppled carts and shattered glass, through the veil of gold dust still drifting down like dead snow. The wards are gone now, leaving behind a wide, gaping corridor of emptiness.

We step through.

And the world opens.

It's not another courtyard.

Not another hall or garden.

It's... nothing.

The land stretches out before us in every direction, vast and colorless. Once, this must have been the rest of the Shimmer Court—the outer districts, the villages, the forests that fed them. Now it's all gone.

Crumbling towers jut like bones from the ground, half-swallowed by dust. The air is still, thick with the taste of metal and decay. Whatever light the realm still had doesn't reach here.

It looks like the aftermath of a war—one fought so long ago no one remembers what it was for.

I can't make sense of it. The silence. The emptiness. The sheer scale of ruin.

Behind us, I glance back toward what remains of the Shimmer Court—the courtyard, the ring of once-golden buildings, the castle at its heart. It's nothing more than a shell, a single bright circle surrounded by endless gray.

"That's all they've been sustaining," Orion murmurs beside me, his voice low, thick with restrained fury. "The heart of the court. The illusion. They've been feeding every ounce of magic into this small center—sacrificing the rest to keep it alive."

I stare out at the dead expanse again, the words sinking in. "They let the rest of it die."

He nods once. "They starved their own land for shimmerlight."

Mor moves a few paces ahead, her shadows sweeping over the cracked ground like searching fingers. "There was life here once," she says quietly. "Forests. Fields. Villages."

I can see the outlines now—faint traces of what used to be. The ghosts of streets. The suggestion of old foundations beneath the dust. A broken well.

And farther off—movement.

Mor turns sharply toward it, one hand raised. I follow her gaze.

A small cluster of lesser fae are bent to the ground, tending a thin patch of dirt. A handful of pale green shoots poke through the soil, withered and brittle.

They move slowly, their faces hollow, hands trembling as they work. And among them—

children.

Tiny figures crouched in the dust, trying to coax life from the dead earth.

My stomach curls. The sight knocks the breath out of me.

"God," I whisper. "They're just trying to survive."

Merlin removes his hat—what's left of it—and holds it to his chest. "A kingdom pretending to shine while its heart starved to death," he murmurs. "I've seen this story before. Never thought I'd see it again."

One of the younglings looks up at us, eyes wide, a smear of stardust on her cheek like ash. She clutches a small wooden bowl—empty except for a single shriveled root.

For a long time, none of us speak. The wind moans faintly across the wasteland.

Behind us, Liora's voice breaks again—pleading, desperate, unhinged. "You don't understand! It's all we had left! We couldn't let it fade—"

But as I look at the barren horizon, I realize she already did.

They all did.

Liora's screams fade into sobs. The sharpness drains out of her voice until she's just a trembling figure in the dust, kneeling beside the ruin she spent centuries pretending wasn't there.

"I was going to fix it," she whispers. "I was going to fix it, I swear."

She says it again.

And again.

Like if she repeats it enough, the land might listen.

I stand there, watching her rock back and forth, hands pressed into the dirt. Her golden paint is gone, streaked away with her tears, and beneath it she looks... ordinary. Small.

And suddenly, I understand.

The theatrics. The endless shimmer. The obsession with being seen—painted, perfect, luminous. It wasn't vanity. Not entirely. It was desperation. She was trying to distract from the truth. To keep the illusion alive long enough to fix what was already broken.

That's why she was so desperate to win Orion. To win the crown.

If she couldn't sustain this place anymore, maybe she meant to move it—bring the Shimmer Court to Starfall, or steal enough power to keep pretending.

I glance toward Orion, but his expression gives nothing away. He's staring out over the desolation, the wind tugging his dark hair across his face. The stormlight still flickers faintly in his eyes, but it's dimmer now. He looks older. Tired.

"Can it be fixed?" I ask.

He doesn't answer right away. Just watches the horizon where the shimmer used to reach, where life used to bloom. When he finally speaks, his voice is low. "I don't know."

"We need to help them," I say.

He nods slowly. "We will. But how? Where do you even start rebuilding a court that's eaten itself alive? They've drained the very soil."

"Then we start somewhere," I say, though I have no idea where that somewhere is.

He exhales, hands sliding to his hips, eyes still scanning the wasteland. "They've probably been doing this for generations. There's no way Liora created a glamour this powerful. Each Lord and Lady must've added to it over the ages, layer after layer—burying the truth until they forgot it was there."

"And the rest of the fae," I murmur, "were too busy bathing in starlight and lies to notice."

Orion's jaw tightens. "As long as they couldn't see the rot on them, they could pretend it didn't exist."

A bitter laugh slips out of me. "Explains why the fae of Eldoria were so far up Liora's ass. God knows it wasn't her personality. She was keeping the fantasy alive—for all of them."

We both fall silent, staring out at what's left of the Shimmer Court. The wasteland stretches on, flat and colorless, the faint sparkle of stardust clinging to the dirt like the memory of something that used to be beautiful.

There's no wyrmroot. No life. Nothing.

I shake my head. "There's no reason to stay. This was a waste of time for our war effort, but—" I look back toward the city's hollow heart, where fae huddle in the dust, their illusions gone. "I'm glad we saw it. God only knows how much longer they'd have kept living like this."

Orion turns toward Mor, who's been silently watching the horizon. "Send your crows. I want seers from Astralana brought here to assess what can be done. If shimmerlight can be restored, they'll know. And send word to Lady Thalassa of Sylvadora—we'll need every High Fae the Enchanted Forest can spare."

Mor inclines her head. "It will be done." Shadows swallow her, gone before the wind finishes her name.

I watch the lesser fae still bent to their hopeless patch of dirt. The younglings cling to each other, eyes wide, faces pale.

"Anyone who wants to leave," I say quietly, "can come to Starfall. We'll make room."

Orion gives a low, tired hum of agreement. "It's getting crowded already."

I look at him, then back at the wasteland that used to be a kingdom. "But where else is there?"

I reach for his hand. The air is cold and heavy, but I hold on anyway.

"Starfall is the stronghold," I say softly. "Even if it's the last star shining in the night sky, it'll be the one that keeps burning."

Orion's mouth curves, but there's no humor in it. "Careful. I'm sure that's what the elder Shimmer fae told themselves when they began all this in the first place."

"Maybe," I admit, meeting his gaze. "But they had too much pride to ever ask for help."

I glance back at the broken city, the fading light, the hollow eyes of the fae who once thought they were untouchable.

"We're not going to make that mistake."

Merlin sniffs, nodding once. "Pride is the easiest thing to bury and the hardest thing to dig back up."

The wind shifts, carrying the scent of dust and starlight, and for a moment the world feels unbearably quiet—like Avalon itself is listening.

I take one last look at the ruin behind us, then turn toward the road home.

"Let's go," I whisper. "We've got a war to prepare for."

CHAPTER 37
orion

The storm has finally quieted.

For the first time since Tana tore down the glamour of the Shimmer Court, the air doesn't hum with false light—it feels clean. Real. Heavy.

The revelations of just how bad things were keep coming, and each one shocks us more than the last. The hardest for me to understand was the siphoning. The High Fae were binding themselves to Lessers, drinking what little power they had like leeches. That is why the Lesser Fae were bound by chains to the Higher.

Truly terrible.

We haven't seen Liora since the night the veil fell. She refused to return to the castle, clawing at the ruined courtyard as if she could piece her illusion back together with her bare hands. When we left, she was kneeling in the ashes of what used to be her court—cradling them, whispering to the shimmerlight to come back.

It never did.

Now, under the pale glow of the nocturn sky, we're ready to move on.

Tana and Mor finish packing their duskbanes, the sleek black steeds pawing at the damp stones. I run a brush through Omen's long, inky mane. She tosses her head, half in pride, half in annoyance, while Merlin sits cross-legged nearby, blowing smoke rings of lunabloom into the small stormcloud hovering at his shoulder.

They've reached a sort of truce, it seems—Merlin will no longer try to stuff the cloud into his hat, and the cloud has agreed to stop zapping him in the ass every time he does.

Progress.

I find I'm starting to enjoy the little storm. The thing hums like a petulant child, following Merlin everywhere, sparking when it gets bored.

Tana's voice cuts through my thoughts. "I still think we should try to reason with Thorn."

I glance over. She's strapping a satchel to her saddle, her jaw set but her eyes soft—always trying to find the humanity buried in monsters.

"Thorn would rather cut off his own arm," I tell her, "then chew it off again each time it grew back, than stand down. Once an idea has woven into that mind of his like an invasive vine, there's nothing to do but rip it out by the root."

Mor adjusts her gloves, expression grim. "All roads lead to war, Queen Rising. The question is only which one you want to die on."

Tana stills. For a long moment, she looks out across the valley—the people of Eldoria moving like ghosts through what remains of their market square. Dull. Gray. Half-starved. Her shoulders square.

I step closer, lowering my voice. "You're not ready to go back to the castle yet. I know. And I'll follow you wherever you choose. But Thorn won't bend. So where will your time mean something, if war is coming to Starfall's gates?"

Her fingers trail along Omen's reins as she thinks. "You really believe Shade could be an ally?"

"I do." I nod. "He's neutral by nature—has been for centuries. Mostly because if he and his brother ever share a border again, they'll destroy half the realm in the process."

Her brows lift. "His brother?"

"Umbriel," I say. "Same father, different mothers. Umbriel was meant to rule Umbranor. Shade was destined for Evershade. Then something happened—an inheritance twisted by politics or prophecy, depending on who you ask —and Shade took Umbranor instead. The larger court. The stronger one."

Mor snorts softly. "Umbriel's never forgiven him. They've avoided each other's realms ever since. Best for everyone, really. If those two ever join a side—either side— there won't be enough left of Avalon to rebuild."

Tana hums, thoughtful. "Umbriel wasn't exactly fond of me."

"No one is when you take their prophecies and smash them to dust," I say with a faint grin. "Shade might side with you purely out of spite for his brother."

She gives me a look—half warning, half hope. "Then that's a start."

I step closer, lowering my tone again. "Most of the lords and ladies will conspire for their own gain first. Don't mistake opportunity for loyalty."

"I won't," she says. Then, softer, "But we have to try. We've only secured the Stone Court, and that won't be enough if the Obscura pushes through the passes. I'd rather face war knowing someone else will stand beside us."

I study her for a moment—the way the wind catches in

her hair, the quiet steel behind her resolve. She's still mortal, still human. And yet she speaks like a queen who's beginning to believe the realm might actually listen when she commands.

Finally, I nod. "Then to the shadowed court."

Merlin claps his hands, startling the cloud into a crackle of lightning. "Excellent! I've always fancied a visit to Umbranor. Terrible cuisine but delightful death traps."

I turn toward him, amused. "Not this time, old man. You should go with the caravan back to Starfall. They'll need a guide, and a powerful wizard might come in handy if trouble finds them on the road."

Merlin gasps in genuine offense, clutching his beard as if it were a string of pearls around his neck. "Are you implying I'm more useful as a babysitter than a war asset? I'll have you know I once held back the Obscura with nothing but a single gust of wind!"

I glance at Tana, who's trying very hard not to smile. "I'm sure you did, old friend," I say dryly. "And I'm sure it was a very dramatic breeze."

He squints at me, muttering something about ungrateful shadow princes, but he doesn't argue further. Instead, he waves his staff, gathering the lesser fae and the few remaining soldiers of the Shimmer Court. The little stormcloud hovers above his shoulder, sparking irritably, as if it knows the journey is about to begin.

Theren and Aeria are already mounted, escorting a small group of refugees from the fallen court. Most are lesser fae—their wings dulled, eyes hollow but grateful.

I never understood why many of Eldoria's winged fae stopped flying and made peace with having their feet on the ground in a permanent agreement. Now I understand, seeing the holes and tears that mar their wings.

The High Fae, though—those gilded and proud—remain in the ruins, kneeling in the ash around their shattered court, unwilling to leave the remnants of their illusion.

As Merlin leads the convoy out of Eldoria, the cloud trails after him reluctantly, flickering once before floating on. It keeps glancing back—if clouds can do such a thing—looking at Tana like a sad puppy being led away from its master.

We set off soon after, the air cool and damp with the memory of the storm. The path to Umbranor cuts through the Ebon Hollow, but Thorn's wards lace the borders. Any misstep and we'd be trespassing—a declaration of war before the first word is even spoken.

Tana studies the map spread across her saddle. "If we go around the wards, it'll add at least three nocturns to the journey. We don't have that kind of time."

Mor tilts her head, eyes following the crow that's approaching from the east. "No. We don't."

The bird dives suddenly, a blur of black feathers and shadow, landing on her shoulder. Its beak parts, releasing a low whisper that only Mor can hear. She listens, expression unreadable, then nods once and strokes the crow's sleek feathers before it dissolves into mist.

Tana straightens. "What is it?"

"Hypnos," Mor replies. "He's traveling with High Seer Astrael to Starfall. He says he found something in Astralana you'll want to see. He'll have it prepared in the castle archives for your return."

Tana exhales, relieved to hear Hypnos's name. "Did he send word of what it is?"

Mor nods. "No. It is not safe to. Many shadows have ears, and where they report their observations to can be quite unknown." She pauses, her expression darkening slightly. "There's more. We found something in Liora's chambers before we left. We've kept it in our darkness—it's too fragile to expose. Even a breath could destroy it."

Tana's brow furrows. "What is it?"

"A sketch," Mor answers softly. "Of the mural at Starfall. The Valkyries' Last Stand."

I glance over at Tana, watching as shock flickers across her face. The giant mural is the very one I showed her, hoping it would convince her of her connection here.

The nickname she shares with Avalon's strongest warriors—Valkyrie.

Their last stand—their defeat—was probably the darkest day Avalon has ever seen.

"Why would Liora have that?" she asks, voice quiet.

Mor's shadows stir faintly around her shoulders. "It seems to be the artist's sketch."

The wind picks up, carrying the scent of rain and the whisper of distance between worlds. Ahead, the road bends toward the horizon—a long, dark ribbon leading into the unknown.

Tana closes the map, and I fix it back to my saddlebag. "Send word to Shade," I tell Mor. "Tell him we're coming. If he'll meet us halfway, maybe we can avoid Thorn's borders entirely."

The sterling moon hangs fat above us, a lantern too bright for this quiet stretch of road. It makes the world look sharper—silver-edged trees, ink-dark sky, the faint shimmer of Tana's hair as it catches the light.

Aeria packed satchels for the journey, and we eat as we ride. The duskbanes don't require much rest—creatures of twilight and shadow, tireless so long as the night stretches before them—but we keep our pace steady. The thunder of their hooves could be heard for leagues if we ran them hard through the open courts. We can't risk that kind of attention, not now.

By the time we stop, the moon has drifted low and the night air smells like rain. A stream cuts through a cluster of trees, the water murmuring softly as it winds around smooth stones. Mor settles herself near the edge of camp, blade across her knees, shadows weaving around her like a second cloak. She doesn't sleep. I know better than to offer food—she's still fasting, and I've seen what happens when someone disturbs the Morrigan before she's ready to break it.

Tana joins me by the stream, crouching beside me as I watch the slow flash of movement beneath the surface. I spot a fat fish—two, actually—and smile faintly. With a flick of my wrist, shadows curl up my arm, shaping into the arc of a bow. The air hums as I draw the string back, the arrow formed from a single thread of night.

I hold my breath. Release.

The arrow cuts the surface, spearing both fish clean through. Ripples break across the water as a tendril of shadow pulls them up, dangling them in the air like a trophy.

Tana's eyes widen, amusement softening her face. "Nice shot."

I grin, the sound of her approval doing far more for my ego than it should. "My grandfather, Galahad, taught me to fish."

She sits beside me as I start to clean them, my knife glinting faintly in the moonlight. "Was he a good teacher?"

I snort. "No. He was terrible. Never caught a single fish."

She laughs quietly, and I find myself wanting to keep her laughing. The sound is soft—human—and somehow it tames the wild in me.

I begin to clean the fish, blade gliding along the slick skin. "He went mad after Pandora died. They say it was grief, but I think there was more to it, knowing the truth of Demeter. Perhaps he knew what Demeter had done—how she'd killed her own mother, her sister. I believe she hollowed him out and left him alive as torment."

"That's terrible," she whispers.

The knife stills for a moment. The memory sits uneasily, like a ghost pressing cold fingers to my chest.

"He spent his last years by the Misting Lake," I go on, forcing my hands to move again. "The sprites called him the Fisher King. He'd sit for hours, casting a line into the water over and over, waiting for something that never came. I used to sit beside him, just to keep him company."

Tana tilts her head. "But there are no fish in the Misting Lake."

I glance at her, a smile tugging slow at my mouth. "I know."

She snorts a sad laugh and piles bits of wood for a fire. For a moment, the world feels still—no looming war, no ghosts of gods or dying realms. Just her beside me, the moon above, and the quiet rippling of a stream that doesn't care who we are.

CHAPTER 38

orion

"So, was it your father that actually taught you to fish?" Tana asks, voice soft in the hush of the trees.

I pause, glancing over at her. "No," I say. "My mother did."

She looks at me, curious. I finish tying off the fish, letting them roast over the crackling fire before I add, "Fathers don't leave much behind. It's the women who leave the legacies."

Tana tilts her head. "I like that."

She grows quiet, eyes following the path of the moonlight cutting through the canopy. "In Gaea…"

She's stopped saying "Earth." I've noticed. She's stopped saying "my planet." Stopped pretending she belongs somewhere else.

"There, it's different," she continues. "The men run everything. They write the laws, hold the power. We're taught to shrink. To smile. To be polite when we're threatened. Grateful when we're not. When a man shows restraint, we're expected to call it kindness."

A slow, dangerous burn lights in my chest. "They should be slain to death."

That startles a laugh out of her—a real one. Not bitter. Not pained. Full and bright. "I agree."

The sound wraps around me like a balm. Gods, I'd set fire to her whole realm just to keep that laugh alive.

Mor doesn't return to camp. I know she won't. She never sleeps and will keep watch all night from the shadows. That's just who she is.

Tana and I unroll our blankets from the saddlebags. My shadows weave upward, winding through the long-hanging vines and mossy branches, forming a soft enclosure. A place of privacy. Protection. Maybe even peace.

She stands at the edge of it, moonlight kissing her skin, and begins to undress.

Slowly.

Deliberately.

I strip my tunic and boots, my silver eyes locked on hers. Each button she opens, each tie she loosens, my cock hardens. She knows exactly what she's doing to me—and I love her asserting what she wants.

Especially when it's me.

When we're both bare, we don't rush. We close the space between us with unhurried steps, reverent and full of ache.

My fingers thread into her curls, and I tilt her mouth up to mine. I kiss her like it's a promise, like it's the last thing I'll ever taste. Her lips are soft but hungry, her hands sliding down my waist, over the sharp lines of my hips, until she palms the curve of my ass with a low, appreciative hum.

I pull her tighter. She fits against me like she was carved from me.

Gods, I want to devour her.

"I want to taste you. Worship you. Sink to my knees and

drown in your pleasure until you forget every realm but this one."

But then her mouth brushes mine and she whispers, "What if I want to get on my knees… for my prince?"

We smile against each other's lips, both of us dropping slowly to our blankets. My hard length rubs against her belly, her nipples brushing against my chest—peaked, perfect. She shivers, not from cold but from the tension thrumming between us.

I murmur, "Looks like there's only one way to solve this."

We shift, lying on our sides, heads at opposite ends, knees bent inward.

I wrap my arms around the swell of her ass, tugging her forward until my face is buried between her thighs. I inhale deeply, moaning into her heat. She's already slick, already throbbing.

My queen is so ready for me.

She lowers to me in kind, fisting my cock at the base and running a long, deliberate lick up the length of me—slow, wet, devastating.

I groan against her. She gasps against me.

And together, we begin to worship.

She tastes like dew and moonlight, the kind of sweetness that punishes.

Every sound she makes pulls deeper from me—each breath, each tremor. When her climax breaks, it's easy and beautiful.

Her thighs tremble around my head, that final cry breaking in my mouth as I suck every last wave from her— slow, deep strokes of my tongue drawing out every moan, every twitch. I lap up her release like the offering it is, licking her clean until her hips jolt and her fingers twist around my dick.

"Orion—" she gasps, breath hitching on the edge of a sob. "I can't..."

"Yes, you can." I kiss the inside of her thigh, sharp and possessive. "I know your hungry cunt is starving for more."

She's still shaking when I roll her over, guiding her limbs like a rag doll, until her knees are planted on either side of my head.

"Up here, little Starling. Ride my mouth like you're meant to."

She moans, sinking down, her slick heat meeting my tongue again. My name is a breath on her lips—just before she wraps her mouth back around my cock.

Gods.

Her hips roll instinctively against my face, chasing the friction, the pleasure. Her moans vibrate down the length of me, muffled around my dick as she sucks harder. She's so wet, dripping from the corners of my mouth as I tongue-fuck her, letting her grind, letting her take what she needs.

"That's it," I groan against her. "So desperate to come again you'll ride your prince's mouth while choking on his cock? Filthy little thing."

She moans around me as I speak into her mind, a high sound that shoots straight through my spine.

After her second orgasm, my shadows twitch at the edge of the room, restless. Hungry.

"On your side," I murmur when her thighs start to quiver. I lift her off me gently, even as she whines at the loss. "Now. Lie down, my queen."

She obeys without question.

I slide in behind her, nudging one leg up until I can hook it over the crook of my arm, baring her entirely to the open night—and to my shadows.

"You're so fucking beautiful like this," I whisper against her shoulder, guiding the thick head of my cock into her with a slow, perfect thrust. "Can you feel how tight you are around me?"

She gasps, arching back as I bury myself deeper.

"Yes," she whimpers. "Fuck, Orion—"

"I love the way you take me. Every inch."

A tendril of shadow snakes down her belly—thin, sharp, and precise. It flicks against her clit with laser focus, a serpent's tongue lashing her little bud.

"Oh—god—" she cries out, spasming around me.

"That's it," I growl, holding her steady as I thrust harder. "Take it. Take me."

Her leg trembles in my grasp, the wet slap of our bodies echoing in the night.

"You want to scream, don't you?" I grit out, the pressure building fast. "But you'll wake the whole damn realm."

I let my shadows bloom and clamp across her mouth— gentle but unrelenting. Muffled cries spill out as her orgasm crashes through her, rippling around my cock like she was made to milk it.

I thrust harder, faster, using the grip of her body and my hold around her leg to chase my own release.

"Fuck—fuck—" I snap my hips forward, spilling into her with a deep, groaned curse.

The shadows twitch violently, wrapping around her thighs, her hips, her throat.

And still, I'm not done.

As I slide out of her, still hard, still aching, I lean over and murmur in her ear:

"Don't you dare think we're finished."

She whimpers again, her face flushed, her body slick with sweat and drunk with need.

"I don't want finished," she breathes. "I want more."

I smirk as she climbs on top of me in a straddle. Our mouths meet, our tongues dance as she fists my soaked cock, stroking me, rubbing my head along the lips of her pussy until I'm growling into her mouth.

She puts me out of my misery and sinks down onto me, sitting up and resting her hands on my chest as she begins to roll her hips.

"My shadows want to fuck your tight little ass while you ride my cock again. You'll let them, won't you?"

She shudders above me, my cum dripping from her cunt and running down my balls. "Yes."

"You'll spread those thighs wide and let the darkness devour that sweet hole of yours."

"Yes, Orion—god, yes."

"Because you're desperate," I whisper, licking a strip up her neck, "to be filled. By me. By my shadows. Every inch of you claimed."

"Please," she begs, voice trembling. "Please take me again. All of me. I want it."

She turns around, looking behind her at the darkness there. She reaches around and grabs her own ass cheek, opening herself to the waiting shadows. "Come fuck me."

I grin, the shadows answering her before I do—tightening around her throat like a lover's grip, possessive and inescapable.

"Oh, yes."

"That's my queen."

The obscurity of my power swells behind her like another body, another heat. It spills out from me in waves—ink-black and sentient, dripping down her spine, coiling around her thighs. The air hums with it. Hums with us.

"Ride me," I growl, gripping her hips as she bounces on my length. "Let me see how desperate you really are."

She sinks down slowly, and her tits bounce with each pulse. She moans my name like a prayer.

"Fuck—Orion—"

Her pussy swallows me greedily, clenching already. But it's not just me she's giving herself to.

My shadows curl behind her, black tendrils weaving into shape—dense enough to form hands, wrists, muscle. The moment she finds a rhythm, grinding down, fucking herself on me, they move too.

One thick, invisible hand grips her hips. Another cups her ass. A third slides down her back. As many limbs as she needs to fulfill her pleasures.

"Oh god, you feel so good," she cries, arching violently.

They stretch her open from behind, sliding into her ass with perfect, punishing pressure—my darkness filling her everywhere at once.

She shudders and keens, the sound raw and ruined.

"That's it," I pant, thrusting up to meet her. "Stuffed full of cock and shadow. Is that what you wanted, my queen?"

"Yes—fuck—yes, Orion, more—don't stop—"

My power groans with hunger. Shadows twist tighter

around her nipples, pinching, rolling the dark buds until her head falls back and her cries tear free.

"You like it when I watch you get ruined?" I taunt as my darkness tugs her hair hard enough to pull a gasp from her throat. "Look at you. Bouncing on my cock while the void fucks your ass. My perfect little whore of the night."

She whimpers, riding harder. Chasing her next high like it's life or death.

"I love it," she breathes. "I love how you fuck me. How your shadows own me. I want all of it—Orion, please—please make me come again—"

"Beg for it," I snarl, gripping her hips hard enough to bruise. "Tell me whose you are."

"I'm yours," she cries. "Yours, Orion. Your shadows." She cries out, and I feel her pussy tighten around me. "But you're mine too, baby. Aren't you?"

"Gods, yes, Starling."

"Mine to fuck. To own. My throne to sit on any time I want pleasure, and you'll give it to me."

I lose it. "Fucking always."

I snap my hips up into her as my shadows slam into her from behind, her entire body jerking with each thrust. One tendril wraps tight around her throat again—another slips between her thighs and circles her clit in fast, relentless flicks.

Her moans hit a fever pitch.

"I'm going to—fuck—I'm—"

"I want to feel you come around me," I growl, dragging her down until her chest is pressed to mine, her mouth by my ear. "I want to feel your pussy milk my cock while my shadows fill your tight little ass. So come for me, love. Now."

I give her the last of my command just as the walls of her cunt suffocate my dick.

She screams, body locking up as the climax rips through her—pussy spasming, ass tightening around the shadows, her whole body shaking in my arms. She comes hard and messy, tears slipping down her cheeks as I hold her down and fuck up into the aftershocks.

"Good girl," I rasp, losing myself as her walls clench and flutter. "Such a good fucking girl—so tight—so mine—"

I come with a snarl, spilling inside her just as my shadows pulse one final thrust into her from behind. Her body goes limp—boneless and beautiful—wrapped in my arms and still trembling as my darkness slowly uncoils.

We collapse in a tangle, sweat-slick and breathless. Her body still wrapped around me. My shadows still stroking her thighs, possessive, unwilling to let go.

Not yet.

And fuck, neither am I.

We'll never let her go.

CHAPTER 39
tana

When I wake, the world is soft and dim.

The tent Orion built for us still hums faintly—woven vines and shadow stitched together in lazy curls overhead. Dew gathers along the edges, glinting in the early light like a thousand tiny stars. He's gone, but not really.

A single tendril of shadow slides along my bare hip, tracing lazy shapes across my thigh. It lingers for a breath before brushing my cheek in a quick, mischievous kiss— then dissolves back into nothing.

I can't help the smile that tugs at my mouth.

Even when he isn't here, his power stays close. Protective. Possessive. Comforting in a way it shouldn't be.

I gather my clothes and small satchel and step out into the morning. The air smells like wet earth and pine. A thin river glitters a few yards away, winding through moss and stone, steam curling off its surface in the chill.

I strip the rest of the way and wade in.

The water bites at first—crisp and cold—but it's the kind of cold that wakes you up, that makes every nerve sing. I sink deeper until it laps at my chest, tilt my head back, and let the current pull the last of the sleep from me.

Being in the special forces means I've spent more nights under the open sky than in beds with sheets. Dirt under my nails, frost in my lungs—none of it's new. But the fae make roughing it almost... luxurious.

I reach into my satchel and pull out one of the small beads I've been hoarding. The moment it bursts in my palm, it blooms into a thick, silken lather that smells like honey and wild mint. I work it through my curls, feeling it melt the tangles with an ease no Earth-made conditioner ever managed. The foam catches moonlight like spun gold.

For a few precious minutes, it's just me, the water, and the quiet.

No courts.

No bargains.

No looming war.

Just peace—and the faint echo of shadow still clinging to my skin like a promise.

A twig snaps behind me.

I freeze, water dripping from my hair, heart hammering. The forest is still for half a breath—then a breeze stirs the branches.

"Orion?" I call quietly, but there's no answer.

Instinct kicks in. I turn slowly, scanning the brush. Every sound sharpens—the low murmur of the river, the rustle of leaves overhead, the faint creak of bark. Something's here. Watching.

I take a cautious step toward the bank, peering into the dark pockets between ferns and hanging moss. For a moment, there's nothing—just the sway of green and shadow. Then I see it.

Two burning eyes.

The massive, malformed head of a Cŵn Annwn pushes through the undergrowth, drool and darkness dripping from its jagged maw. A creature of the Obscura—twisted, starving, wrong.

It snarls once before lunging, a blur of bone and teeth and rot—

—and then darkness hits from both sides.

A thick column of black crashes across the river, wrapping the beast midair. One strand coils around its neck, another around its ribs, dragging it backward with a guttural shriek. A second wave of shadow answers from behind me, sharp and cutting. The two collide—Mor's and Orion's—tearing the creature clean in half. The halves vanish into mist before they hit the ground.

I stand there panting, every nerve still electric.

Mor steps from the opposite bank, calm as ever, a faint smirk curving her mouth. "We get to claim that one," she says blandly. "We got to it first."

"I'd call it a tie," Orion answers, appearing behind me with his own darkness receding into his skin.

"Aw, you mad she stole your thunder?" I tease, wiping my face.

"My what?" He blinks. "She could never steal it from me."

"We could if we tried," Mor calls from the other bank.

"Relax, Rambo—it's an expression. It just means someone outshined you," I say, grinning. "No need to get your lightning bolts bent out of shape about it."

"I happen to take my element very seriously."

"I can see that."

"Clearly."

He tilts his head, eyes glinting with that steady, unnerving calm. "Just remember, Starling," he murmurs, "no one can steal your thunder... if you become the storm."

For a heartbeat, the air between us crackles—too charged for the moment. Then I huff a laugh, breaking the spell. "Okay, Storm God, maybe dial it down a notch."

He offers me a small towel, the corner of his mouth lifting as I take it. "You all right?"

I nod, still catching my breath. "Yeah. Just... it got intense for a second there."

"You two are sickening." Mor's smirk deepens. "We will check the perimeter one more time. That should have been the last of them." She vanishes into the trees, her shadow moving with her.

Orion's gaze lingers on me as I dry off. When I reach for my tunic, he steps closer and presses a slow kiss to my lips.

"I wanted to be back before you woke," he murmurs against my mouth, "so I could wake you with my tongue."

The laugh that slips out of me is breathless. "I could always go back to sleep. I'd hate to deny you that."

He grins, low and wicked, but the moment breaks when a sharp whinny splits the air.

Omen—Orion's shadowmare—tosses her head as she trots through the trees, hooves striking sparks on the stone. Beside her, Havoc barrels forward, feathers of shadow rippling from his mane. Both mounts are restless, uneasy.

"They're anxious to get moving," Orion says, eyes narrowing toward the dark line of forest beyond. "Mor found several more of those things last night while we slept. They're straying farther from the Wastelands."

A chill slips down my spine. "That means the darkness in the Enchanted Forest is spreading."

He meets my gaze, grim. "Yes. They can move outside their territories now."

The air feels heavier suddenly—thick with the scent of moss and distant thunder. Whatever peace the morning had offered is gone.

We pack in quick order after that. The forest is still quiet, but the stillness feels wrong now—too heavy, like the woods are holding their breath.

Havoc is restless, pawing at the ground and flicking his tail hard enough to sting. He keeps throwing looks at Orion like he's offended by something only horses or duskbanes understand.

Orion just huffs out a laugh and walks to Omen. He lays both hands along her sleek, shadow-dark mane, the silver veins of his magic flickering faintly where he touches her. His palms trail down to her midsection, lingering there as if he's listening.

Then he smiles. Broad, bright, real.

He looks to Havoc, who tosses his head and snorts, and Orion chuckles.

"You old dog. Congratulations."

He turns to me next, eyes soft. "Omen is with foal."

My mouth falls open. "Seriously?"

He nods, still rubbing her mane, and Omen presses her head into his chest with a low rumble of contentment.

I glance between the two mounts. "And how do you know Havoc's the sire?"

"They're a mated pair," he says, his tone almost reverent as his fingers comb through Omen's mane. The mare's eyes —pure black, with tiny stars flickering inside—reflect the light of first shade. "It's written in their bond."

He looks up at me then, that faint grin returning. "I'll take it as a good omen. New life in such times of despair."

I can't help smiling back as I step closer and wrap my arms around his neck. "I kind of like that our horses are mated," I murmur. "Feels... fitting."

He bends, wrapping his arms low around my hips and lifting me easily off the ground. I brace my hands on his shoulders, laughing as he tilts his head back to look up at me.

"Everything in this realm is drawing me to you," he says softly, his voice a low rumble against my chest. "The stars. The storm. Even the earth beneath our feet. I could fight it for a lifetime and still lose."

My heart stumbles in my chest. "You could never fight me," I whisper.

His mouth just brushes mine when a dry voice cuts through the clearing.

"Oh, our poor eyeballs." Mor steps out from the trees, unimpressed as ever. "If your horrendous mating ritual is over, we have a message from Shade."

Above her, a shadow-crow circles once before diving down, landing neatly on her shoulder. Its feathers ripple like ink in water. She lifts a finger, and it croaks out a sound halfway between a caw and a whisper.

Mor tilts her head, listening as the sound shapes itself into words. Her expression hardens, jaw tightening.

"Thorn is calling the High Lords and Ladies to assemble with the Clave."

My stomach dips. "Why?"

Mor's eyes flick toward me, her tone flat. "You. Of course. What else?"

It hangs in the air like a stone dropped into deep water.

Orion swears under his breath, low and dark. "Fucking asshole."

"What does he want?" I ask, though the answer is already twisting in my gut. He wants me off the throne.

"He's called an emergency session to discuss 'the mortal threat to Avalon's balance.'" Her mouth curls into something like a sneer. "Fae and their ridiculous formalities."

I exhale slowly, the sound shaky. "So can we get an invitation to this party?"

"We won't need one." Orion steps closer, shadows flickering faintly at his feet. "The wards around Thornspire will be open to receive the traveling lords and ladies. It would be the only time Thorn would drop them this low."

He looks between Mor and me as I nod along with the plan he's forming.

"We sneak in while the gates are open. He'll be too busy making his case to the Clave to notice the shadows listening in."

"Eavesdrop on his meeting," Mor murmurs. "We agree this is a good idea."

I'm quiet for a moment, the weight of it settling in. "If we're caught—"

"We won't be," Orion cuts in. His hand brushes mine, grounding. "Thorn's arrogance is our cover. He'll be too consumed with his performance to notice the shadows in the rafters."

I look at him, searching his face. "And Shade? You think he'll actually help us?"

"He'll help himself." Orion's mouth tightens.

"If Shade took the time to send the message, that means

he is planning to go. What if he's planning to side with Thorn?"

"What if he's planning on going against Thorn?" Orion fixes one boot in Omen's stirrup and pulls himself onto his horse. She shakes and ruffles her black wings. "If I were trying to form an alliance with a partner who cannot trust me, I would do the same. A public declaration."

I hoist myself onto my own horse and take his reins.

"As you said, he took the time to send the message. He could have kept it to himself." Mor uses a tendril of shadow to help her up the tall back of the duskbane before throwing a leg over the saddle. "That has to count for something."

Mor tucks the crow onto her shoulder, its feathers rippling with faint darkness. "Then we move fast. The gathering starts at evenfall. If we ride hard, we can reach the outer wards before they rise again."

I glance between them—the fae prince and the night-born shadow. My unlikely allies. My impossible family.

"Then let's ride," I say, squaring my shoulders. "If Thorn wants to make me the villain of his story, I'd rather be there to hear how it ends."

Orion's grin is sharp and dangerous. "There's my queen."

He whistles low, and Omen and Havoc move to us at once, their eyes gleaming like twin constellations. As I swing into the saddle, the faint hum of wards awakening in the distance curls through the trees—a reminder that the game is already in motion.

And this time, I don't plan on playing fair.

CHAPTER 40
orion

Omen's wings slice through the mist, each beat a deep, soundless pulse above the storm. The clouds stretch wide beneath us—thin veils of gray and silver that shroud Thornspire from view. The storm is a blessing. A gift from the realm or fate, I can't tell which.

Lightning flashes in the distance, painting the sky in veins of white. The thunder follows a breath later, low and steady, enough to drown out the whisper of the duskbanes galloping toward the castle. Below me, rain falls in fine sheets, a steady drizzle that slicks the thorns of the forest and soaks the fae below.

Good. Let them be miserable.

Reaching forward, I brush the wet strands of Omen's mane as she banks lower. We're both keeping an eye on Tana and Mor as they ride hard below us. A single tendril of my power wraps around her bodice like a harness, a thread of me anchored to her so I can feel every jolt of her ride. Every heartbeat.

The duskbanes are fast. Too fast, sometimes. Their hooves can cover leagues in minutes, but the thunder they summon as they run would be a dead giveaway—an echo of Starfall's cavalry approaching.

That's why I keep the storm moving with us. My thunder, my lightning—it's just enough to hide them in the chaos of the sky. A whisper of disguise as they race across the court to reach Thornspire in time for the assembly.

Below, the kingdom sprawls out like a wound in the land. Dark forests claw at the horizon, their canopies dense with thorned vines that glint like steel in the rain. The city itself sits at the heart of it—spires of black iron and red stone jutting upward like broken blades.

The fae here are as wild as the thorns they live among—fierce, brutal, unpredictable. The kind that wear cruelty like a crown.

The streets are alive tonight. Lanterns flicker in the rain, casting warped gold across the slick cobblestones. Even from above, I can see the flow of bodies—fae pouring into the square, cloaks and antlers glistening under the downpour.

Too many.

My stomach knots.

If the city is this alive, it means Thorn's call has already gone out. He isn't just gathering the Clave—he's gathering his army.

Lightning flares again, and for an instant I catch sight of Thornspire's central tower—the great black spire that pierces the clouds. The top burns faintly red, as if the heart of the forest itself is bleeding.

I don't like it.

I don't like any of it.

This isn't diplomacy. It's a rally. A declaration.

And the pit growing in my stomach tells me Thorn has already made his choice to go to war. He's just been waiting for the moment he can declare it.

And I think we may have given him the excuse he needed.

The duskbanes are the only land creatures that could have crossed Thorn's court in time. I can feel their pace slowing through the thread of shadow I left looped around Tana's bodice—her pulse, her breath, the rhythmic stretch of muscle beneath her as Havoc comes to a halt.

I angle Omen downward, slipping through the cloud cover until the forest swallows us whole. The canopy here is thick enough to blot out the moon entirely. Perfect.

We land in silence, only the rustle of wet leaves betraying us. Omen lowers her head, ears flicking as she scents the air. She doesn't need me to lead her; she already knows where her mate is.

Within minutes, I catch the telltale glow of Havoc's eyes burning through the dark. The pair moves toward each other through the trees—Omen's soft rumble answered by Havoc's low, fiery snort. Their reunion is quiet, powerful in its own way.

Tana and Mor emerge through the underbrush, cloaks slick with rain. I nod to them. "The castle's surrounded. Crowds already filling the streets. Thorn's preparing his stage."

Tana frowns. "So, it's begun."

"Looks that way."

We guide the horses into a dense pocket of brush where the roots of three massive oaks have intertwined to form a sort of hollow. I coax the shadows outward, stretching them like a curtain until the darkness thickens and hides the entrance completely.

"They'll rest," I murmur, running a hand down Omen's flank. "They know to stay put until we return."

Mor wipes rain from her cheek with the back of her hand. "Good. Now how do you plan to get us through an entire city of Thorn's soldiers without being noticed?"

I glance at her, then at Tana, and let a small smile play across my lips. "Like this."

A pulse of power flickers through me, and shadows ripple outward, curling around them both.

Tana gasps softly as the glamour settles over Mor first— her hair shifting from near-black to a tangled shade of rose-briar red, her skin darkening to the earthy hue of the forest folk. Her features sharpen, eyes turning a luminous green. She's still recognizably Mor... just not our Mor.

"Briar-born lesser fae," I explain. "Common enough in Thornspire. No one will think twice."

Tana's eyes widen, and she lets out a soft laugh. "You even made her taller."

Mor's new eyes narrow, unimpressed. "We do not appreciate comments about our stature."

That earns her a grin from me. It's strange seeing her nearly eye level with Tana instead of a foot shorter.

Tana shakes her head, still marveling. "It's incredible, Orion. I can feel the magic, but I can't see through it."

I give her a look that's equal parts pride and warning. "Then don't stare too hard at anyone else's. The High Fae tend to notice when you look too long."

She sobers at that, and I reach for her next. The glamour slides over her like silk, twisting her human brightness into something quieter, softer—a dusky fae girl with pale, moss-colored skin and deep brown eyes. Her light still hums beneath it, but muted enough to pass.

When I finish, I catch her reflection in a slick patch of stone. Even she doesn't recognize herself.

"Stay close," I tell her, brushing my thumb against her chin to tilt it up. "The High Fae always greet each other with power—flaring, measuring, comparing. But the lesser fae?"

"They fade into the background," Mor finishes dryly.

"Exactly," I say. "And tonight, that's where we need to be."

Tana's jaw tenses, and I can't help the swell in my heart at her disapproval of the way the lesser fae are treated. I know when the crown sits upon that beautiful head of hers, she will do something to change it.

I sweep the glamour over myself last, tucking my own power deep beneath the skin until even my shadows still.

Tana looks between us, lips twitching faintly. "I can't believe we're doing this."

Mor smirks. "Welcome to fae politics. No one wins without a little treachery."

I extend my hand toward Tana, palm up, and the corner of my mouth lifts. "Ready, my love?"

She slides her hand into mine, fingers cold but steady. "Let's go crash a meeting."

The walls of Thornspire rise like a crown of thorns around the city—black stone laced with living briar, its vines pulsing faintly with the same crimson hue that stains the tower above. We pass beneath the outer gate with the rest of the lesser fae, heads bowed against the drizzle. No one spares us a second glance.

The air smells of wet iron and smoke. The streets inside the wall are narrow and slick, every surface glinting with rain. Lanterns flicker under carved awnings, casting light across carts loaded with wine barrels and crates of produce.

Tilt your chin down, I murmur across the thread between our minds. *Lesser fae don't look like they're seeing the world for the first time.*

Tana startles slightly and then lowers her gaze. *Sorry. It's just—everything's so alive. Even the walls are breathing.*

They bite, too, if you get too close, I warn, the image of the thorned vines flashing through her thoughts so she knows I'm serious. Her soft laugh echoes back along the link, warming something tight in my chest despite the chill.

Ahead of us, a cluster of lesser fae unload crates from a wagon. Mor and I each take one without a word. Tana grabs a woven basket overflowing with damp vegetables, the glamour making her arms look leaner, fae-touched. We fall into the line of servants heading toward the inner gates, the rhythm of labor disguising our purpose.

No one even glances at us.

The gates open onto the castle proper—walled again, this time in briar that gleams like wet obsidian. Fae guards stand at each archway, their armor grown from living metal. They don't bother looking at the workers; lesser fae are invisible here.

A snatch of conversation drifts on the rain.

"King Thorn's feast tonight," one mutters.

"A celebration after the assembly, they say."

"Feasting while he plots war—typical."

Another voice—older, sharper:

"He'll deal with that mortal girl soon enough. Pretending to be queen. Pretending to be anything but food."

My jaw tightens, shadows twitching at my feet. I force them still.

Don't, Mor says in my head, her voice cool and immediate. *They'd notice if the air started bleeding darkness.*

I'm fine, I lie.

Tana's thought brushes mine, gentle as a fingertip. *Let it go. We'll prove them wrong later.*

You are already proving them wrong, Starling. I inhale through my nose and keep walking.

She spots him first—a Clave envoy in emerald robes, the silver crest of Thorn's court glinting at his throat. He strides quickly through the crowd, and we adjust our pace to follow, keeping to the outer ring of workers. The envoy disappears through a side archway flanked by guards. None of them look at the stream of servants passing nearby.

Down the corridor, another cart is being unloaded— sacks of grain, barrels of mead. We merge with the group, set our burdens down beside theirs, and move on. No challenge. No second glance.

Inside, the air shifts. Warmer. The scent of roasted meat and spice thickens the hallway, guiding us toward the kitchens.

It's chaos in there—dozens of briar-sprites darting between steaming pots, lesser fae shouting orders and stirring cauldrons. Firelight flickers off copper pans and slick tile. The noise is perfect cover.

"Through there. Up the servants' stair; two floors down

is the council chamber." A thorny briar fae barks an order to another carrying a tray of goblets and mead.

Mor shoulders past a whirl of sprites carrying a tray of pheasants and nods toward the back passage.

I nod once, eyes sweeping the room. Tana's gaze lingers on a sprite no taller than her finger who's shouting at a fae my size. The corners of Tana's mouth twitch despite herself.

Don't get distracted, I murmur through the link, a smile ghosting across my own lips.

You're one to talk, she fires back. *I know you were thinking about clearing out the entire courtyard because someone called me "food."*

Fair.

I am the only one allowed to feast on the queen and the delicacy that is her pussy. To prove my point, a thin splinter of shadow slides from her body harness and sweeps through the warm lips of her cunt. I hold back my groan at the taste of her. *Me—and the lovers who keep your healthy appetite well satisfied.*

She gasps and missteps as she climbs the servants' stairs, looking back at me with a glare that could set the entire briar to go up in flames. *Can't you behave?*

Where is the fun in that when you are so delicious? I smirk back at her.

We slip deeper into the heat and noise, shadows closing around our edges until we vanish into the rhythm of the castle itself—three ghosts walking straight into the dragon's den.

CHAPTER 41
tana

We trail the fae servant carrying the drinks, matching his pace so naturally it almost feels choreographed. The door ahead of us—the one carved with vines that twist into a crest of thorns—opens at his touch. Warm light spills into the corridor, the hum of voices slipping out for just a breath before the door shuts again.

Orion doesn't slow. He brushes my arm lightly as he passes and speaks through the thread between our minds. *Keep moving. There'll be servant passages somewhere along the outer wall.*

We round a curve in the corridor, and there it is—a narrow stair spiraling up between the stone, so tight it looks like it was meant for ghosts instead of people.

Mor glances back once before leading the way. Orion follows after me. The air grows cooler as we climb—thinner. I can hear the muffled cadence of the meeting through the walls: soft, deliberate voices with too much power behind them.

At the landing, Orion nods toward Mor. She doesn't hesitate. Darkness pours from her hands—heavy and slow-moving—coating the walls and the floor and us.

It's thick, almost viscous.

I shudder as it touches my skin. The sensation is...

wrong. *It feels like walking through slime,* I whisper in my head, grimacing and glancing down at my arms as if I'll see something crawling there.

Mor's soft chuckle ripples through the dark. *Better slimed than seen, Your Grace.*

The hallway above is narrow, wrapping in a semicircle around the council chamber. The walls are laced with small windows—no larger than a pair of hands pressed together—just enough to look through, not enough to crawl through.

We find our place and peer inside.

The council room is larger than I expected. A long oak table dominates the center, surrounded by a dozen carved chairs. Two remain empty at the head—one, I'm sure, for Thorn. The other... I can't tell. Maybe a consort. Maybe someone worse.

The Clave is here and seated—a member from every court, regardless of whether their lord or lady is also present.

Across the table, one more seat is unclaimed, its nameplate etched in silver. Whoever it's meant for hasn't arrived yet.

The rest are occupied.

Self-appointed king, Eryndor of Gloamreach, sits to Thorn's left—his skin kissed by twilight, that strange shimmer of the day's end and the night's beginning blending in the lines of his face. Even from here, he looks composed, hands folded neatly on the table. His eyes—violet and amber—flicker like the sky caught between sunset and dawn.

Beside him, the Swamp Court. Duchess Morwen of

Mirevalis leans back in her chair, half shadowed. Her skin looks translucent, faintly green beneath the torchlight, as though she's carved from river glass. Strands of moss hang from her damp sleeves, trailing across the stone floor. Her gaze moves like a serpent's—slow, unblinking, measuring.

And then there's Umbriel.

Even seated, he's unmistakable—that flat, expression-less face, as if someone sculpted him from clay and forgot to breathe life into the features. His presence drags at the air— quiet but wrong, like gravity bending around him.

I swallow hard, forcing my breathing to stay even.

The sound of chairs scraping draws my attention back to the table. The air crackles faintly as fae magic stirs— someone powerful is about to enter.

Behind me, Orion's mind brushes mine again, calm but alert. *Stay quiet, Starling. Whatever Thorn's planning, this is where we'll hear it first.*

I nod faintly, pressing closer to the small window. The storm outside growls against the glass, thunder rolling like a heartbeat.

The energy pressing against my skin isn't coming from one fae. It's two.

Their combined magic is a tide all its own—heavy, magnetic, impossible to ignore.

Arrogance and trickery. That's what it feels like. The air in the hall beyond the door twists with it, flooding through the gaps before they even step inside.

Thorn is first through the door.

He fills the threshold like a storm given flesh. His hair is a snarl of living briars, each strand catching the light and glinting like wet thorns. Vines coil around his armor, shifting and tightening with each movement as though the forest itself breathes with him.

His eyes—emerald green, wild, burning—find Umbriel across the table and never waver. The room seems to shrink beneath the weight of it.

Then the second presence enters.

The temperature drops, the shadows stretching to greet their master. Shade doesn't walk so much as glide, his form constantly shifting, the edges dissolving like smoke. His eyes are twin voids, devouring the light around them.

The tension between him and Umbriel is instant—electric. Predatory recognition. Mortal enemies forced into proximity.

Thorn turns, closing the door behind them. The sound echoes like a thunderclap.

Wards hum to life, sealing the chamber so tightly it feels like all the air has been sucked out. I have to resist the instinct to gasp.

"You have sworn a truce until first shade," Thorn says, his voice a growl that fills the entire chamber, "while within the boundary of the Briar."

His gaze cuts to Shade and Umbriel in turn—sharp, warning, promising violence if he's crossed. "Break that truce on my land, and I will tear the both of you from your shadows."

Umbriel raises his hands, pale and still, in silent acknowledgment. Shade merely inclines his head. Then his shape flickers and reforms on the far side of the table, never once walking—simply appearing.

To our left, something shifts in the darkness of the passage hiding us—a soft, deliberate scuff against stone.

All three of us—Mor, Orion, and I—turn at once.

Standing half in shadow, half in the dim torchlight of the servant's corridor, is a creature I've never seen before. No taller than my knee, with long, pointed ears and enormous eyes that glimmer like spilled ink.

We freeze.

It freezes.

A silent standoff.

What is that? I think, my pulse spiking.

It's a brownie, Orion answers in my mind, his tone oddly calm.

A what?

A hobgoblin. They keep the castle clean. Have you never noticed them at Starfall?

I shake my head. Definitely not.

Orion greets the little thing with a quick nod of his head, fishing in his pocket until he finds a hard candy. He crouches slowly, extending it toward the creature.

The brownie stares, then scuttles forward, snatching the sweet with both hands.

Orion lowers his voice. "You never saw us here." He presses a finger to his lips.

The little creature nods solemnly, clutching the candy to its chest, and tiptoes away the same way it came.

I exhale a shaky breath, relief bubbling into a faint, incredulous laugh.

All I can think is *Dobby has been given a sock.*

Orion glances at me sideways, the faintest smirk tugging his mouth. "It never hurts to befriend a brownie. They can be very handy."

I bite back another laugh and turn my gaze back to the window.

Inside the chamber, Thorn takes his seat at the head of the table, vines crawling higher across his shoulders as if crowning him anew. The hum of power in the room sharpens, aligning like drawn blades. His voice cuts through the silence, deep and commanding.

"The Clave is now in session."

The storm outside answers him with a growl of thunder.

Thorn doesn't waste time with pleasantries.

The moment the Clave settles, his voice rolls through the chamber like a wave of thunder. "Let us speak plainly," he says. "A mortal on the throne of the fae is an offense to every law written since Avalon first breathed. And her actions"—he slams a hand against the table, vines tightening around his wrist as if echoing his fury—"are an even greater one."

The room hums with agreement. I can feel it in my teeth.

Across the table, Duchess Morwen is the first to nod, her damp fingers curling around the edge of the table. "She brings ruin with her," she says, her voice carrying the rasp of deep water. "The darkness grows stronger every day since her arrival. That cannot be coincidence."

King Eryndor says nothing, his expression unreadable—stoic, thoughtful, watching every player on the board. He neither agrees nor disagrees—just weighs.

Shade, however, remains utterly still. No voice. No face. Just those two fathomless voids of eyes fixed on the table before him, absorbing everything.

Umbriel, though—Umbriel looks up. Directly at me.

For a heartbeat, the world narrows to his eyes—flat,

dark, bottomless. My scalp prickles; the air feels thin. A pulse of dread works its way down my spine.

He can't see us through Mor's darkness, Orion's voice murmurs through my mind, steady and grounding. *He's only looking at the shadows.*

Are you sure about that? I think back, unable to look away.

Umbriel holds the stare a second longer than he should—too deliberate, too knowing—before he turns back to Thorn. I'm not convinced he's ignorant of us being here.

Thorn's fist hits the table again, snapping my attention back, having missed whatever comment was just made. "You call her chosen?" His tone drips with derision. "You would have me believe the realm itself reached across time to crown a mortal girl? Tell me, then—how can you be certain?"

The council stirs. Eryndor shifts, voice calm but firm. "We have seen signs. The grove reborn at Demeter's end. The seed of moonlight that came from her hands. Life where there was only death."

Murmurs ripple through the room.

Morwen leans forward, her eyes glistening like swamp water. "Parlor tricks. There are other magics that can mimic the realm's will."

Thorn's smile is a baring of teeth. "Exactly." He pivots toward the others, pacing along the table's edge. "Who else was there that day? Hypnos, the Dreamkeeper—a master of illusion. And let us not forget His Royal Highness"—his tone turns mocking as he glances toward the empty seat that would bear Orion's sigil—"our noble prince of Starfall. Do we not think he might have found a way to... influence the outcome?"

My chest burns. I can feel Orion tense beside me, though he stays silent.

"You cannot deny she pulled the sword from the stone. She carries it at her side for all to see." Umbriel's voice cuts through the tension—low, deliberate. "You forget, Thorn, that many have tried and failed to draw the sword. Including you."

That lands like a blade.

"I was there," Umbriel continues, his tone maddeningly flat. That makes me suck in a breath. I hadn't seen him there —though I was furious with a particular prince at the time and maybe not paying close enough attention. "I watched the moonlight shine upon the blade. Watched her pull Realmbreaker free. Tell me, how would she do that if she were not chosen—if the realm did not answer her hand?"

The room stills.

Though Umbriel didn't let me pass into his court, he sure seems to be defending me now. There may be an ally within him yet.

Thorn's head turns slowly, his eyes burning brighter, vines tightening across his armor with a sound like grinding glass. For a moment, I think he might launch himself across the table.

Then he smiles—slow, feral. "Perhaps she is chosen," he says. "But not by the realm."

The silence that follows is heavy enough to crush.

"The Obscura," Thorn growls, leaning forward, both hands braced on the table. "You all saw what Demeter carried to execution—darkness bound to her soul, power drawn from something far older and far more dangerous. I say the mortal made a bargain with the dark itself—just as the traitor did long ago with that same cursed sword."

Gasps ripple through the chamber.

Beside me, Mor's shadows stir in agitation. Orion's mental voice brushes mine again, quiet and hard-edged. *He's laying the groundwork for war.*

I can only nod, staring down at the scene below, where my fate—and maybe the realm's—is being rewritten by men who've already decided what they want to believe.

And Thorn? He's smiling.

Like a man who's already won.

CHAPTER 42
orion

The conversation spins itself in circles—new words, same venom. Every point rephrased until the sharp point goes dull.

They debate my queen like she's an idea instead of flesh, heart, and will.

While they talk, I catalog.

Everything I saw from the sky.

Everything I smelled in the rain.

Everything I felt in the pulse of the court.

Thornspire isn't just crowded with fae—it's crowded with soldiers. Rows of armor laid out to be mended and oiled. Weapons stacked in neat formations under the awnings. Rations packed and sealed for travel.

Even the air tastes of iron and anticipation.

And everywhere, those looks.

Fae lovers clinging to each other in the shadows, knowing the next time they meet might be across a battlefield.

Thorn doesn't want discussion. He wants justification.

He'll start a war before this Clave is over, and Starfall will be the first place to burn.

Shade's voice breaks through the hum of argument—if it can be called a voice.

It's not sound so much as movement in the air, the soft distortion of reality folding inward.

When he speaks, it feels like standing too close to a storm's eye, like every whisper you've ever tried to forget suddenly turning toward you.

"It is a grave accusation," the shadows say, overlapping, deep and hollow and endless. "To accuse the Queen Rising of such betrayal without proof. Tell me, Lord Thorn—are you truly willing to risk your end on a theory?"

The air wavers as he finishes, the sound fading like smoke through the rafters.

"It is King Thorn in the Briar." Thorn's lips twist into something that might be a smile, though there's no humor in it. "And it is not a theory if it can be proven."

And somehow, I know what's coming before he says it.

"We can do just that."

The words land like a death knell.

Every head turns when the hidden door opens—a section of the wall melting away into shadow. The chamber holds its breath. Even Eryndor stiffens, his usual calm fractured by disbelief.

Through the opening steps a figure, half shadowed and familiar.

I know her silhouette before she ever meets the light.

Liora.

Tana tenses beside me, the air between us snapping tight. I can feel her pulse racing through the thread that links us, feel the sick realization blooming like frost in her chest.

Liora looks nothing like the exuberant fae performing for all to see.

Her skin dull, her eyes sunken. The gilded paint she always wore has been washed away, leaving her bare, colorless. Her once-perfect hair hangs limp and tangled.

No foxlike smirk. No teasing sway.

She looks like someone half-dead, dressed in mourning black that turns her gray skin nearly translucent.

Thorn doesn't rise as she approaches. He just extends his hand, palm up—a silent command.

In my head, the words come unbidden. *That son of a bitch.*

A marriage alliance.

She takes his hand. Their fingers lace. Their chins lift in unison. Shoulders square.

The pact between Thornspire and the Shimmer Court is sealed for every watching eye.

Umbriel is the first to break the silence, his tone flat and dry.

"Well," he says, the corner of his mouth twitching just enough to count as a smirk, "it seems congratulations are in order."

Thorn turns toward Liora, who gives a single, delicate nod.

But she doesn't speak.

He does.

"The mortal queen has made her parade," Thorn begins, his voice rich and heavy with inflated seriousness, "and in her path she leaves nothing but destruction."

He starts to pace, every step measured, vines shifting and curling along his armor as though the forest itself is feeding his rage.

"She destroyed the eastern pass to Frosthaven, trapping

the ice fae in their own prison of winter. Even the giants of Mont Saint-Michel were seen fleeing her wreckage."

I can feel Tana's shock through the bond—sharp, disbelieving.

He's twisting everything, she thinks.

He's building a narrative, I answer. *That's what tyrants do.*

Thorn goes on, his voice smooth as venom.

"She tricked Lord Granite into servitude. His entire court now bound to her will."

Eryndor lifts a hand, breaking the rhythm of Thorn's performance. "Granite entered into that alliance of his own making," he says, his tone even, calm. "He was outbargained. The mortal outsmarted him, nothing more. That is no evidence of dark magic—merely Granite's own stupidity."

A murmur ripples through the room—agreement from some, irritation from others.

Thorn's gaze snaps to Eryndor, but he only smiles, patient as a man who has rehearsed every retort. "Cunning?" he repeats softly. "Or whispering? Do we truly believe a mortal can outbargain an ancient fae lord without aid? Without dark alliance whispering instruction into her ear?"

He lets the question hang, then softens his expression, turning toward Liora with feigned tenderness.

She bows her head just enough for a single tear to slide down her cheek, perfectly timed.

"The savage mortal annihilated the Shimmer Court," Thorn continues, lowering his voice to something mournful. "All but ruin now—save the city center and the palace. The land itself lies dead." He gestures toward Liora with the drama of a stage actor. "And yet this brave lady protected her people, gathering what she could in the heart of the court to save them from the mortal's wrath."

He pauses, the room holding its breath. "You can see the toll the battle took on her."

Every eye turns toward Liora. Her skin looks gray in the torchlight, her former glow extinguished. It's convincing. Too convincing.

Eryndor's jaw tightens, but he says nothing.

Umbriel shifts, turning his hollow gaze toward the Clave member seated at the far end—the Enchanted Forest's representative of Lady Thalassa. Thalassa, whom I'd called away to Eldoria myself to examine the destruction the Shimmer fae inflicted upon their own court.

"My shadows tell me," Umbriel says, voice cold and clinical, "that the lands of Shimmer have been dead long before this mortal queen ever set foot in Avalon. Tell me, is that true?"

The Clave member bows their head, careful. "Yes, Lord Umbriel. Lady Thalassa was ordered to dispatch to aid Eldoria. She went herself with many high fae to see what can be done. The decay there predates the Queen Rising's arrival by many ages."

The silence that follows is thin as glass.

Thorn's hand slams the table. "So, the Clave of Sylvadora calls Lady Liora a deceiver?" His voice booms like a struck bell. "An accusation punishable by death in my court." He straightens, his vines bristling like quills. "And I, of course, am prepared to defend the honor of my betrothed."

The word lands like a curse.

Tana's breath catches beside me, fury flaring through our link. *Looks like Liora found someone else to sell herself to.*

I nod in agreement.

The Clave member pales and drops their gaze. "I meant no disrespect."

Eryndor intervenes before Thorn can press the threat. His voice cuts clean through the rising tension.

"Perhaps it is unwise to make accusations when not all courts are represented," he says, his tone calm but edged with warning. "If their honorable Clave members cannot answer without the threat of death, they merely answered the question posed by Lord Umbriel. There was no charge of false testimony against the Lady of the Shimmer Court."

For the first time, Thorn falters. Just slightly. The smallest twitch of irritation creases the corner of his mouth before he smooths it away.

But it's enough for me to see it.

He's losing control of the narrative, and he knows it.

And around us, I feel the faint stir of my own shadows—restless, hungry, waiting for my command.

Mor's voice brushes against my thoughts like smoke.

Control yourself.

Her warning slides through the link, sharp and cold. *Your shadows are bleeding through. Shade will notice. So will Umbriel. And we cannot be certain either is ally or enemy.*

She's right. The air around us is vibrating with my anger, the faintest tremor of shadow crawling up the stone. I pull it back, force it to still.

Barely.

Mor thickens the darkness around us, and Tana buckles slightly under the force of it, her hand reaching out to brace against the stone wall.

Shade's head turns ever so slightly as Thorn's voice

slices through the room. "The time for discussion is over. The realm needs action."

He sweeps his gaze around the table, eyes alight with a predator's satisfaction. "So—who will stand with the Briar?"

For a moment, no one moves. Then the soft scrape of a chair breaks the silence.

Eryndor rises.

My heart hammers erratically in my chest. I had hoped his army would ally with Starfall. Against Thornspire, Eryndor's forces are equal in measure.

Thorn's smirk turns feral, his expression flickering with something dark and triumphant—until Eryndor begins to speak.

"Avalon is suffering," Eryndor says, voice even and solemn. "What it needs is unity, not war. We cannot turn our blades upon one another while the Obscura grows hungrier by the hour."

He paces slowly, meeting the gaze of each lord and lady in turn. "Every day, the darkness creeps farther from the Wastelands. The hounds of the Obscura have been seen beyond the Enchanted Forest—at the very walls of Starfall. The Cŵn Annwn roam freely because the shadow is spreading freely. That is our enemy. Not each other. And not the mortal chosen to wear Avalon's crown."

His words land like flint on stone.

Across from him, Thorn's expression hardens, that brief satisfaction curdling into contempt.

Eryndor takes his goblet, flicks the last of his mead to the stone floor. Then he turns the cup upside down, the rim striking the oak table with a clean, final sound—stem up.

"I reject your petition for war," he says.

The silence that follows is absolute.

Eryndor lifts his chin, addressing the room at large. "Should soldiers march on the wards of Starfall and demand blood... should Starfall call for aid... should the Queen Rising herself call for the swords of Gloamreach—we will answer. And we will stand with the heart of Avalon's throne."

Pride surges through Tana beside me, bright and fierce.

I squeeze her hand, a quiet promise between us.

She gives me a small, tight smile in return—eyes shining in the dark.

Eryndor moves toward the door. At the threshold, he looks back at Thorn.

"I fear the next time we meet, our swords will be crossing on the battlefield, old friend," he says softly. "Though I pray to the moon I am wrong."

Then he's gone, the heavy door closing behind him with a deep thud. The wards shudder as they reseal, the weight of them sinking like lead.

After him, Duchess Morwen lifts her cup and drinks what remains. When she slams it down, the rim faces upward. "Mirevalis will stand with the Briar," she says, voice low but resolute.

Thorn inclines his head slightly, pleased.

Umbriel's gaze drifts to Shade. No words pass between them, but when he finally speaks, his voice is quiet, certain. "The position of Evershade will not sway from one alliance to another. We give our devotion only to the night."

He leaves his cup untouched—neither rim down nor up. Neutral.

One by one, the remaining members of the Clave make

their declarations. Most follow Umbriel's path—neutrality. Caution. Fear.

Then the delegate from Cairnvail rises, placing their goblet rim down with deliberate defiance. "Cairnvail stands with the Queen Rising," they say.

Two courts.

Too many passive.

It's not enough to stop the derision, but it's enough to make my heart stir with something dangerously close to hope.

Thorn wanted more.

The crack in his composure shows when he slams his chair back and stands, vines writhing along his armor.

"Cowards," he snarls. "Every one of you. You speak of unity while this false queen toys with the dark that devours your borders."

He sweeps his gaze across the chamber, voice rising to a roar. "I have the strength to act when others will not. And if I must stand alone against the corrupted mortal on Avalon's throne, so be it."

The air crackles, thick with the scent of iron and bramble.

"War will come to the mortal queen's gates," Thorn declares, raising his arm. "And it will be Thornspire that rings the bell."

He extends his hand to Liora.

She takes it without hesitation, their palms clasping—a union of deceit and ambition sealed in front of the entire Clave.

They turn, leaving through the same hidden door that had first revealed her.

Mor's shadows shift restlessly beside me.

The silence after Thorn leaves is deafening. Even the storm outside hesitates, waiting.

Tana looks at me—no fear, no doubt, only the fire that refuses to die. My queen is already a warrior, battle-proven on her own realm.

I lace my fingers with hers, and for a moment the world steadies.

If war has come, it will have to pass through us both.

And they will find it a much more difficult endeavor than they believe.

CHAPTER 43
tana

We file out of the narrow stairwell one by one, careful not to draw attention. The shadows still cling to us, heavy and damp, though Mor's obscurity is starting to thin.

The council chamber below is dissolving into nothing—chairs scraping, guards standing watch. Some of the Clave have already left. Shade was one of the first, slipping away like smoke. Others followed, their courts retreating to plot behind closed doors.

Umbriel stayed behind. He sat in silence, fingers steepled, the darkness around him so thick it pulsed. Watching. Waiting. I didn't need Orion's thoughts to know the idea of him lingering made us both uneasy.

By the time we wind our way back through the kitchens, the noise from the chamber has dulled to a low rumble. Servants are still working, oblivious, and no one looks twice as we pass through the steam and into the alley.

Once the door shuts behind us, Mor stops and turns. Her expression is unreadable, her white hair plastered to her temples from the drizzle.

"A betrayal will occur on the battlefield of Starfall," she says quietly. "One from tonight's table will shift their alliance."

Orion's jaw tightens. "Can you tell who?"

Mor shakes her head. "No. Nor whether the betrayal will favor us or destroy us. We'll only know when the blood starts to fall."

"Well," I mutter as we start walking again, "that's reassuring. Nothing like a little ominous prophecy to really set the mood for war."

Mor doesn't respond. Seems my little friend with a bottomless stomach is getting a tad hangry in her pre-battle fast. I wonder what the ritual is behind it. Some custom from her realm. Maybe a superstition.

Our glamour still holds as we move through the dim corridor, boots echoing softly against the stone. We pass beneath a high archway, a narrow bridge overhead casting long shadows that crawl down the walls.

That's when I feel it.

A pulse of presence—like gravity shifting.

Before I even think, my blade is out, drawn from the sheath strapped to my thigh. I turn and thrust upward, the tip poised against the hollow of a throat—if shadows can even have throats.

Shade.

Orion and Mor react a heartbeat later, but Shade just stands there, still wrapped in darkness, both hands raised in mock surrender.

And then, to my surprise, the shadows peel away.

A man emerges where the shadow stood—skin the color of ash, long black hair falling shaggy around his face. He wears a trench coat that nearly sweeps the ground, a simple black tunic, worn leather pants.

I keep my blade where it is. "Hello, Shade."

He inclines his head. "Queen Rising."

His voice is low, soft, with a strange echo that seems to hum in the bones.

"You've passed my test," he says after a moment. "You noticed me when the powerful prince and the dark enchantress did not."

"Lucky me." I don't lower my weapon, and he smiles at it, eyes glinting with amusement. "What do you want?"

"I would like to form a truce with Starfall."

Orion's tone sharpens. "Why? You and your brother have always stayed neutral."

Several guards pass by the mouth of the alley. One turns his head, looking at our small assembly, but they keep going.

Shade flicks his head toward the narrow alcove ahead. "Walk with me."

We follow, keeping to the shadows until we reach an empty stretch of wall beneath an arch. The rain murmurs above, steady and quiet.

"My brother is making a play for my court," Shade says, glancing up toward the castle towers. "And what better strategy than to remain neutral while the courts around Umbranor pledge themselves to opposite sides?"

"You think he'll enter the fight?" Orion asks.

Shade nods once. "I do. A third front. An unexpected strike while the others bleed each other dry. Then—when the dust settles—he will call in his repayment. The victors will help him seize Umbranor."

The realization chills me to the bone.

It fits perfectly with Mor's earlier words. A battle on two fronts. A betrayal on the field.

Shade folds his arms, his voice carrying the weight of

centuries. "Umbriel has long coveted the court our father betrothed to me. He claims the child of Father's favored mate was placed above the eldest. A decision I had no part in making, but one I will honor—because it was his will."

The rain patters against the stones around us, soft but relentless. The air feels colder now, as if the mention of Umbriel himself invites the shadows to listen.

"What are your terms?" I ask.

"Simple." His gaze settles on me. "I will fight on the battlefield of Starfall. In return, should the courts along my borders turn their blades toward Umbranor, Starfall will lend its swords in my defense."

I glance at Orion. He's already looking at me, weighing the offer with the same quiet precision I am.

Outside, the clouds shift, and a seam of moonlight breaks through the storm. It paints the wet stones of the Briar castle in silver, revealing the faint etching of words carved into the arch above us. The script glimmers faintly before the light fades again. I squint, trying to read it, but the letters blur before I can make them out.

When I blink and look back, Shade and the others are waiting.

"Before I answer," I say, "how did you know we were watching from the council chamber?"

Shade's grin is all shadow and teeth. "A little brownie you bribed to keep your secret."

Orion stiffens slightly.

"The creature would not tell me what it found," Shade continues. "But it left empty-handed and returned one piece of candy richer. Your token earned its favor... but also gave you away."

I turn to Orion, arching a brow. He just shrugs, looking far too pleased with himself.

"Still kept his mouth shut, didn't he?" he murmurs.

Shade chuckles low. "For a sweet tooth, perhaps. But secrecy is currency, and that one is now paid twice over."

Mor exhales sharply. "We should get out of sight before the patrols return."

I barely hear her. My thoughts are still spinning around Shade's offer. A third front. A neutral court tipping the scale. The choice shouldn't be this easy—but war never leaves room for comfort.

There's something about Umbriel that sits wrong in my bones. Even through Mor's darkness, when his eyes met mine, it felt like standing on thin ice—like he could see too much.

And I trust that feeling.

Whatever side Umbriel stands on, I'll keep my eyes on him.

Finally, I nod once toward Shade. "We'll accept your terms."

He inclines his head, a shadow of satisfaction crossing his face. "Then I will meet you at Starfall, Your Grace."

His form dissolves back into darkness, fading into the night until there's nothing left but rain and the faint shimmer of moonlight on the wet stones.

I sheathe my blade, feeling the weight of what I've just agreed to settle heavy in my chest.

One alliance sealed in secrecy.

One betrayal yet to come.

Mor and Orion speak in low tones next to me, their words half swallowed by the rain.

"Thorn's never been one for patience," Mor says. "He's called for war—he'll march within the nocturn."

"We'll need to prepare the castle quickly," Orion murmurs. "He'll want the glory of striking first."

Their voices fade as my attention drifts upward. The arch above us gleams faintly, wet stone catching the moonlight just enough to reveal what I'd only half noticed before.

Etchings.

Lines of script carved into the curve of the stone—aged, almost lost to weather. I recognize a few of the courts from Hypnos's lessons since I arrived in Avalon. Etched in a fae tongue I can't read.

"What does it say?" I ask, pointing.

Orion steps closer, brushing rain from his lashes as he studies the worn letters. "Nocturna."

As soon as the last syllable rolls off his tongue, a swirl of cold wind rushes around my feet, up my legs. With it, I hear the whispers of a thousand voices speaking at once—the same sensation I felt in Evershade when I looked at the family tree and the name they'd scratched out.

I look to Orion, silver eyes still fixed on the etchings like he didn't just feel that or hear it. Then to Mor—she, too, felt and heard nothing.

Swallowing down the unease clawing at the back of my neck, I ask, "What does it mean?"

"Of the night," he says. His tone is distant, thoughtful. "Most things around here are."

"Does it mean anything to you?"

He hesitates, gaze still on the carving. "A gift my grandmother gave to a powerful goddess once—a wedding present. A shadowmare named Nocturna. The first foal of Omen and Havoc."

I glance up sharply.

"But it seems odd, doesn't it? To list the name of a horse among the courts."

I trace the edge of the inscription with my eyes. "Maybe it's part of a phrase. Something like 'These are the courts of the night.' The beginning's missing."

"Maybe," he says quietly. But something in his expression tells me he isn't convinced.

Before I can press, movement ripples across the wall— an ink-black shape unfolding from the stone itself. The shadowed silhouette of a horse walks toward us, its mane fluttering like liquid darkness.

There's no sound, no body—just the image.

And then, softly, I hear a faint huff—the exhale of a living creature.

"Orion..."

He's already looking. "Omen is telling us it's time to return."

I lift my hand, reaching toward the shadow. My fingers meet cold stone. Nothing more.

"Shadowmares are powerful creatures," he says, his voice low. "They can jump through shadows not only across distance but through the veil of reality itself."

"I'm going to need that translated into human," I mutter.

He glances at me, a small smile flickering. "She's where we left her—with Havoc. But she's sent her shadow to the other side of the veil to warn us."

He goes still, head tilting as though listening to a sound I can't hear. Then Omen's shadow rears, wings unfurling in a sweep of darkness that ripples up the wall.

Orion's face tightens. "Briar fae," he says. "They've found the bramble where we hid them. They're looking for the horses."

Mor steps forward, her eyes already darkening to pools of black. "We can portal there."

"It'll trigger Thorn's wards," she warns after a beat. "He'll know we're in his court."

"He's already declared war," I say, gripping the hilt of my blade. "What more can he do?"

Orion nods. "She's right."

Mor ticks an eyebrow. "Very well."

The shadows around her thicken, rising like ink through water, swallowing the walls, the rain, the cold light of the moon.

A single heartbeat—and the world collapses.

The castle, the courtyard, the flickering torches—all of it vanishes in an instant as the darkness rushes through us like a wave.

When the shadows peel away, we're back in the thick brush where we hid the horses. The air is damp and heavy, smelling of moss and rain. The glamour that hid us melts away, and for one suspended breath, everything is still—until it isn't.

The vines surrounding us jump to life.

The whole thicket comes alive, swaying like snakes, a sound rising—high and shrill, like a kettle's furious whistle.

Two Briar fae stand barely a few yards away, torches raised, blades drawn. They were hunting. They knew something was hidden here.

Orion's darkness erupts outward before either of them can take a breath to speak. It shoots out, devouring moonlight and sound as it crashes into them.

The shock on their faces lasts only a second. Then the shadows lash out—long, sharp whips that snap through the air and wrap around them. One quick pull, and I hear the wet, awful rip as their limbs are torn from their bodies.

Their screams cut through the night. The torches hit the ground, snuffed out in an instant by the dark.

I can't dwell on it—because the forest itself turns on us.

The vines writhe, striking, snarling, their thorns flashing like teeth. Thorn's wards—alive now, awakened by Mor's portal.

Mor flicks her hand lazily, and a blade of shadow slices through the nearest tangle, severing it mid-swing. "Annoying," she mutters.

I draw Realmbreaker. The blade sings in my hand, cutting through the brush concealing our mounts. Omen and Havoc are already on their feet, nostrils flaring.

A vine snaps toward me from the right—fast. I barely have time to raise my sword before something cold and bright rushes through me.

Silver light bursts around me in a wave. Moonlight.

The vine hits the light and disintegrates, burning to ash before it even touches my skin.

I did it again—summoned moonlight without meaning to.

My triumph lasts half a breath before the forest answers with another screech that rattles my teeth. The vines convulse, their cries joining in a rising chorus—the wards screaming the alarm.

Mor looks toward the maimed fae still alive on the ground, writhing and sobbing amid the tangle of their own blood. "Thorn will be quite displeased," she says, smiling faintly. She sounds delighted.

"Stop your screaming." Orion casts an annoyed look at the fae writhing on the ground. "Your limbs will grow back." His shadows lash out again, this time covering their mouths, muffling their cries of pain.

"Since we are already in the game of offending the Lord of the Briar, there is no sense tiring the horses—can you portal us from here?"

Mor arches a brow. "His wards make it difficult." She glances toward Omen. "But we can manage it quickly with Omen."

"Then do it," he says.

Mor summons her power, climbing onto her massive duskbane's back. The creature's size dwarfs her completely. I swing up onto Havoc, his muscles rippling beneath me. Orion mounts Omen, and the storm hums to life around them both.

I can feel the change in Mor before she even opens her mouth—the moment she shifts from Mor into the Morrigan. The air itself trembles, charged with the pulse of her darkness.

Omen bows her head, great wings unfolding. She flaps once—twice—not to fly, but to stir the air, to shape it. The space before us begins to twist, a vortex of shadow and light coiling into form.

The ground shakes. The pressure builds until my ears pop, the sound replaced by a deep hum that rattles through my chest. Havoc stamps and snorts, impatient.

Then—an explosion.

The world detonates in darkness. I duck, clutching Havoc's mane as the power crashes over us like thunder breaking the earth in half.

When I open my eyes, the storm is gone. The air is cold and wet again—but it smells different.

I look up, and my chest tightens, the knot there dissolving before I realize it was even there.

Starfall.

Its towers gleam against the night, torchlight flickering in the windows. The waves crash against the dark cliffs below, the scent of mist and rain washing over me like a benediction.

I grin, exhaling. *Home.*

Orion chuckles beside me, shaking water from his hair. "Are you making it a habit to destroy the wards of every court we visit?"

Mor smirks. "We are enjoying the pastime. Besides, as you said—he's already declared war. What more can he do?"

She urges her duskbane forward, the hooves thudding against the slick stone path.

Orion takes my hand, placing a kiss on my knuckles, and together our horses walk forward, following Mor's lead. "It will give us extra time. Thorn won't leave his court unguarded, and it will take him a few nocturns to weave his wards again."

I adjust my grip in Orion's hand, glancing toward the looming towers ahead. "We'll take it. A few more days to prepare for war is as good a chance as we're ever going to get."

CHAPTER 44

Two nocturns have passed since Thornspire.

The castle hasn't slept since.

Every night, the wards are reinforced—each sigil redrawn in moonlight and shadow, every barrier reanchored against the creeping dark pressing at the edges of the Enchanted Woods. Hestia works herself raw, her fingers blistered from tracing runes that crackle and spark. Even Mor hasn't complained, which says enough about how dire things have become.

Hephaestus took the news of the wyrmroot badly. The forge's fire dimmed the moment I told him. Without it, his new weapons will never hold aetherlight. The forest where wyrmroot once grew—the one once belonging to the Shimmer Court—is gone, devoured by the very fae who called it home.

Messengers were sent to Cairnvail and Gloamreach the same night we returned. None have come back. Whether that means their courts are mustering aid or simply ignoring our calls, I can't tell. The silence feels heavier each hour.

The villages surrounding the castle have emptied. Refugees crowd the halls now—fae from the borderlands, lesser kin from the outer woods, all seeking sanctuary from the darkness spreading through the realm. The latest group arrived only hours ago. Barely alive.

The Cŵn Annwn tore through their caravan, and though some escaped the hounds' fangs, the Obscura's touch marked them. Their eyes clouded black within hours. Not dead. Not alive. Turned.

Merlin stayed with Hestia through the night tending the wounded, his ridiculous little storm cloud floating over his shoulder, crackling each time someone shouted. He's been quieter lately. The sort of quiet that means even he doesn't know how this ends.

It's first shade now—the faint silver before the moon reaches its height.

Tana stands on the balcony of my bedchamber, her hair lifted by the night breeze. She's begun to favor my bedchamber instead of her own. I don't ask why. I think she feels the same pull I do—neither of us finding rest unless the other is near.

I move to stand behind her, my hands finding her hips, my mouth pressing against her neck. Below, the lake mirrors the sky, denim-blue glass shimmering with thin trails of starlight. The wards hum faintly in the air—a vibration felt more than heard.

"What's on your mind?" I ask.

She huffs a soft laugh, the kind that isn't really one. "Everything. The war, the refugees, the darkness spreading faster than we can fight it. Take your pick."

I place my hand over hers, tracing my thumb over her knuckles. "We'll find a way through it."

Her gaze softens. "You sound so sure."

"I have faith in my queen."

She hums and rests her head on my chest. For a moment, the noise of the realm fades—the distant clang of the forge, the murmurs of those sheltering below. It's only us and the hum of power in the air, the pull of something coming.

Then a sharp knock breaks through. Aeris's voice, muffled but urgent.

"My Queen—my Prince. Hypnos has returned with High Seer Astrael from the Celestial Court. They request your presence immediately."

Tana's eyes meet mine, a flicker of eagerness sparking in their depths.

I nod once, squeezing her hand before letting go. "Then let's hear what they've found."

Together, we turn from the balcony's edge, walking into the shadow of what comes next.

The council chamber hums with quiet energy, the air thick with moonlight and anticipation. The great round table dominates the center of the room—its wooden surface veined with silver, carved with the sigils of every court that still remains. I've always thought it looked like the night sky turned to stone. Tonight, it feels like the universe itself is holding its breath.

Hypnos stands opposite us, tall and still as a statue. His eyes are the same milky white as moonstone, his scalp smooth and gleaming in the low light. Blind, yet somehow seeing more than anyone else. He doesn't look toward us, but I can feel his awareness shift as we enter—the faint tilt of his head, the way the air ripples when he senses Tana's presence.

Beside him stands a figure draped in robes that shimmer

like constellations come to life: the High Seer of the Celestial Court. They rise as we approach. Their hair moves like a living thing—flowing strands of stardust caught in a celestial current, shimmering between silver, violet, and deep blue. Their eyes are filled with galaxies, as though they gaze not at us but through us, seeing constellations we cannot fathom. Crowned with a faint halo of light, they are both breathtaking and terrifying.

When they bow, their wings unfurl—vast, translucent, refracting the light in iridescent colors that ripple like oil on water.

"Your Majesty," Astrael says, voice calm but resonant, like sound carried on starlight. "Queen Rising."

Tana nods, composed even in the face of something this otherworldly. "High Seer Astrael. It's an honor."

Astrael's expression doesn't change, though I feel a flicker of warmth in the room. Respect, perhaps. Or recognition.

On the table between them rests a single object—a leather-bound book, thick and heavy, its cover a deep midnight blue streaked with faint veins of light. A sigil is pressed into its center, a spiral of stars interlocked with runic lines I've never seen before. It feels old. Older than Avalon itself.

Hypnos gestures to it with care. "We found this in the sealed archives of Astralana while searching for records on the Obscura," he says, his voice carrying that unearthly calm that always precedes a storm.

Astrael continues where he leaves off, their tone both distant and deliberate. "It was not written by one of the Celestial Court. How it came into our possession, we do not know. It has remained locked for millennia—its wards unbroken by any hand."

Tana steps closer, her gaze fixed on the sigil. "Locked?"

Hypnos inclines his head. "Bound so it could never be read."

Her fingers brush the cover. The faintest light stirs beneath her touch, the silver veins pulsing once—like something beneath the surface just took a breath.

"What does it mean?" she asks quietly.

The High Seer's starlit gaze turns to her, then Hypnos. Their voice drops to a reverent murmur, as if speaking the name itself carries weight.

"It is the mark of the Court of Dreams."

The words ripple through the chamber, sinking into the air like thunder waiting to break.

The Court of Dreams.

The name feels strange in my mouth, like something too old to belong to language. I turn it over in my mind, the weight of it heavier than it should be.

Tana looks at me, confusion written across her face. I can practically see her running through the courts in her mind—the Twilight Court, the Briar Court, the Winter Court. Counting them as she always does, the way she did that first night in the archives when the idea first took root. Ten sigils. Ten rulers. Ten realms. But everything screamed at her, saying twelve was the balance of the realm.

My gaze drops to the round table between us. The surface gleams beneath the dim starlight, etched with the crests of the known courts. Ten carvings in perfect symmetry, each filled with silver light. And between them—two empty spaces. Places where symbols could have been. Should have been.

At the center, the crest of Avalon burns faintly, its ring of sigils encircling it like planets around a dying sun.

I reach out and trace the smooth edge of one of the empty spaces with my fingertips. The air around it hums faintly, as though the table remembers something the rest of us have forgotten.

"So, there was another court," I say, looking to Hypnos.

His sightless eyes lift toward me, and he inclines his head once. "It seems our Queen Rising had it right all along. Avalon was once home to twelve courts."

Tana releases a slow breath, like she's been holding it since the moment we entered the room.

Hypnos places his hand on the book and pushes it across the table toward us. "And both are named in this account. The Court of Dreams—"

Astrael finishes softly, "and the Court of Nightmares."

The words seem to echo off the stone walls. For a heartbeat, no one moves. Then Tana and I exchange a look—one of disbelief, and something else. Fear, maybe. Or the dawning sense that everything we thought we understood about this realm is about to unravel.

"Nocturna?" She whispers it as she pulls out a chair and lowers herself into it. I do the same beside her. The book sits between us like a heartbeat—alive, ancient, waiting.

"Yes." Hypnos nods. "The Court of Nightmares."

Tana sets her eyes on me, the weight of generations suddenly showing in their brown depths.

She slides the book closer, her fingertips tracing the bindings, the faint warmth of the crest beneath her hand.

I glance to Hypnos. "And what is this an account of?"

"The realm's trials," he says quietly. "Of Queen Pandora."

The name lands like a bomb. Everything stills. Even the wards that hum faintly through the walls seem to fall silent, as if the realm itself holds its breath.

Tana's gaze flickers to Hypnos. For a moment she says nothing—just studies him, searching for something in his pale, sightless eyes. He gives a single, solemn nod.

She opens the book.

The scent of old magic spills into the air—starlight and parchment, faint traces of moondust and ink. The pages are thin, almost translucent, covered in writing so delicate it could have been painted with a whisper.

"She wrote it herself," Tana murmurs, leaning in.

I shift closer, reading the slanted script over her shoulder. The ink gleams faintly in the low light—ancient, but unaged. It looks as though it was written yesterday.

Her fingers trail lightly over the page, tracing the graceful strokes. "How is it still so..." She pauses, searching for the word. "Alive."

Hypnos's voice is low, almost reverent. "We believe she sealed it after the last passage."

Astrael inclines their head. "And a seer brought it to Astralana for safekeeping. It has remained untouched since that day."

Tana glances up. "So how did you manage to open it now?"

Astrael looks toward Hypnos. The faintest trace of something—grief, perhaps—crosses their expression.

Hypnos takes a slow breath. "It would appear Queen

Pandora was to be High Lady of the Court of Dreams when she was chosen by the realm to be queen. She sealed the book with a sigil that would only open for another fae of the same court."

The meaning hits me instantly. My mind races through the possibilities, each one collapsing into the same inevitable truth.

God of dreams. Master of illusion.

"Hypnos..." My voice trails off before I can finish the thought.

He nods once, confirming what neither of us wants to say aloud.

"It would appear," he says quietly, "that I am the only living fae from the Court of Dreams."

tana

Around me, Orion paces. The low echo of his boots against the stone floor keeps time with the wild rhythm of my thoughts. Across the table, Hypnos and Astrael murmur softly to one another, their voices like overlapping threads—dream and starlight weaving through the air.

I try to focus on the book. On her book.

The script flows across the page in long, elegant lines—beautiful but unreadable. It's written in the ancient fae tongue. I trace the ink with my fingertips, desperate to understand. To see what Pandora endured. What her trials demanded.

I turn a page and stop, looking at the hand-drawn map.

The ink is so precise. The lines of Avalon stretch across it in perfect symmetry—mountains, forests, rivers—each court marked with care.

And there, in the farthest reaches, where nothing but the Wastelands lie now, two names are written in graceful script:

Nocturna.

Aetherwild.

The Court of Nightmares.

The Court of Dreams.

I stare until my pulse drowns out everything else.

My fingers hover over the word *Nocturna*—the same name carved into the stone walls of Thornspire. Probably something the realm has forgotten was even there.

"This wasn't lost," I whisper. "It was erased."

Orion stops pacing. Hypnos tilts his head slightly, though it's Astrael who speaks.

"History has a way of protecting its wounds," they say softly. "What cannot be healed is buried."

I shake my head. "Not everything was buried."

They look at me, waiting.

"The fresco in Cairnvail," I say. "A figure was carved out of it. You can still see the outline. Someone was there once."

Astrael's eyes gleam faintly, galaxies shifting within them. "A deliberate omission."

"Exactly." I glance between them all, my pulse quickening. "Pieces of—of a story—still exist. We just don't know what we were looking at."

I flip through another page, looking to Hypnos. "Have you read the whole thing?"

He nods, and I swallow down the question I think I already know the answer to.

"Does Pandora name anyone called Morgause?"

Hypnos and Astrael exchange a long look, as if communicating something silently—perhaps trying to determine how to answer.

It's Astrael who steps forward. "She does indeed, Queen Rising." They bow their head, as though summoning strength from the moon. "Morgause is the cousin of Pandora."

They pause, and I know there's more.

"And—"

"And," Hypnos's chest swells like he's fortifying himself for the revelation, "Morgause was also selected by the realm to participate in the trials of the queen."

Holy shit.

Two.

Two queens selected. Two champions competing for the same throne.

Liora had threatened as much during Beltane, when she was flashing her annoying glitter cunt all over Starfall. I wonder if she knew two queens had once reached for the throne.

Then I remember—

Mor went through Liora's room and found something.

"Mor," I blurt out, looking quickly at Orion.

The air around us stirs before Orion even calls her name through their minds.

A ripple of darkness forms in the corner of the room, spreading like spilled ink until it takes shape. Mor steps through her own shadows—eyes glowing bright red, skin paler than I've ever seen it. The air around her hums with hunger. She's still fasting, and by the looks of it... starving.

"What is it?" she asks, her voice low, frayed at the edges.

"The artifact," Orion says. "The one you took from Liora's room."

For a moment, her expression flickers in confusion—then faint recognition. "We almost forgot about that."

The shadows around her swirl and coil. When they clear, something floats down onto the table, gentle as a feather. The darkness evaporates, leaving behind a single sheet of parchment, yellowed and brittle with age.

We all lean closer.

It's a sketch—a rough rendering of the great mural inside the Valkyrie's cavern, the one carved into the stone wall where the winged warriors are painted in perfect detail.

Only this one is... different.

The castle's giant mural shows the Valkyrie—war-ready, wings drawn, armor gleaming. In the center, their queen and commander, Pandora. The other side of the mural shows the aftermath—the loss of the Valkyrie after their final stand.

The artist's sketch before us is notably different.

Pandora is not in the center but stationed behind her army—a general ready to give her orders of war. The Valkyrie are the same in this old sketch as they are depicted on the wall.

But on the other side—where I remembered only a barren field of bones and shadow—there's something else entirely.

A second army.

An army cloaked in darkness, their armor jagged and black as obsidian. And behind them stands their general.

A woman.

Her hair flows down her back like a river of ink.

I feel the breath catch in my throat. My heart thuds in my chest, and I know Orion feels the change in me.

"What is it?" he asks, hushed, worry lacing every syllable.

"I've seen her before."

All eyes turn to me.

"When we met with the woodland fae," I say slowly, "Oryn told us about the darkness. About the missing courts. He knew more than he admitted. And afterward..." I swallow hard. "I saw her. In the forest. I thought it was a ghost. She was just standing there—watching me."

The parchment's ink seems to shift in the torchlight, and for a heartbeat, I swear the woman in the drawing moves. Her hair stirs, caught in an unseen wind. Her eyes lift toward me.

It feels like she could step out of the page and into the room.

I can almost see her standing there, facing Pandora across a battlefield—their legions of light and dark ready to collide.

Something stirs inside me. Not sudden, not loud—just a slow unraveling. A pulse that starts somewhere deep in my chest and spreads outward until I can feel it humming beneath my skin.

All at once, the scattered pieces start to fit.

The whispers I've heard in empty corridors. The shadows that seem to watch me when no one else is near. The half-erased murals. The symbols carved into stone. The way certain places feel like they remember me, even when I've never been there before.

A history pieced together from what should have been forgotten—what someone wanted buried.

And then the image flashes behind my eyes: the woman in the sketch, her hair black as ink, her gaze steady and knowing—the same face that haunted me in the forest.

It plays in my mind in slow motion: her turning toward me through the trees, the faint lift of her chin, the way the shadows bent to her like living things.

The air in the room thickens. Every sound fades. Only

that one word echoes, bouncing through my skull like an echo across a canyon.

I lift my head, my voice low but clear as I look around the table—at Orion, at Hypnos, at Astrael's starlit gaze.

"Morgause."

The name leaves my mouth like a spell breaking, and for the briefest moment, I swear the air itself listens.

"If Pandora was the radiant moonlight of Avalon, Morgause is its darkness." I hold Orion's stare, his eyes wide with everything unfolding tonight. "And I don't think it was a ghost I saw in the forest that day."

My fingers run over the thin piece of parchment, its rough surface holding something so much more monumental than the old paper can support.

"The Obscura isn't just darkness. It's the High Lady of the Court of Nightmares." Locking eyes with each person around the table, we all know it to be true. "She's still here. And she still wants her throne."

Silence stretches heavily around the room. Then —movement.

The shadows in the chamber shudder as if startled, then rip away, streaking toward the windows like smoke drawn into a vacuum. The glass trembles in their wake, the torches guttering out one by one until only the faint silver light of the moon remains.

Except... the moon isn't silver anymore.

Above the castle, Avalon's great moon hangs dimmed— shrouded by a moving veil of darkness, a cloud so thick it devours the light. The Obscura.

A low, distant boom rolls through the air, rattling the

glass and lead of the stained windows. The walls seem to breathe with it.

Thunder.

It comes again, closer this time. Then again.

I look at Orion. "Is that you?"

He's already scanning the ceiling, shadows rippling faintly across his hands. "No."

Something in his voice makes my stomach twist.

"Mor," he says, his tone sharp as steel, "take us to the ramparts."

Her shadows unfurl like living smoke, swirling around us in an instant. The world folds, bends, and then darkness swallows everything.

When it spits us out again, I stumble forward onto cold stone, shivering. I don't think I'll ever get used to that sensation—the feeling of falling and standing still at once.

The night wind cuts across the ramparts, cold and electric. I lift my gaze to the horizon—and freeze.

At the edge of Starfall's boundary, far beyond the shimmering curve of the wards, a burst of light blooms in the darkness. It's blinding for a heartbeat before fading, leaving only the echo of its brilliance burned behind my eyes.

A moment later, the boom follows—deeper, sharper, reverberating through the stone beneath our feet.

Mor smiles, and in the silver wash of the dim moonlight, she looks almost inhuman—her beauty sharpened to something sinuous, dangerous.

Orion and Hypnos stand silent beside her, faces carved in shadow. Astrael steps back, bowing low, their wings catching the light like fractured glass.

"I will retrieve the others," the High Seer says softly.

"And return to Astralana. Whatever has begun here—it is beyond my reach."

When they vanish in a whisper of starlight, I finally understand what I'm seeing.

It isn't a storm.

It isn't lightning in the clouds or thunder rolling across the hills.

It's magic—violent, focused, and striking the wards of Starfall like hammer blows.

Lord Thorne has come with his Briar army.

His high fae are attacking.

I turn to Orion. Our eyes meet, the realization sinking between us like a heartbeat.

He takes my hand, bringing it to his lips. His mouth is warm against my knuckles, his breath steady even as the night splits open with light and sound.

The storm gray in his eyes glows brighter, alive with something fierce and unyielding.

When he speaks, his voice carries the quiet gravity of prophecy.

"So it begins, Starling.

The war has finally found us."

CHAPTER 46

Half a nocturn.

That's how long they've been at it.

Twelve hours of attacks and fire, of spell and counterspell—and they still haven't broken through the first of Starfall's wards.

For now.

The wards hum around me, vast and alive, stretching across the valley like the skin of a living creature. Omen's wings cut through the thin upper air, each beat steady and strong as we circle high above the castle. I test the boundaries every few passes, letting my power brush against the outermost veil, listening for weakness.

There isn't any. Not yet.

But it won't hold forever.

Thorne will find a way. The wards of Starfall are among the strongest in Avalon—but even the strongest wall needs a queen behind it, and Tana hasn't ascended yet. Without the power of a crown reinforcing the barriers, they can be broken.

It's only a matter of time.

On the other side of the wards, the Briar army sprawls across the plains like spilled ink. Rows upon rows of tents, small fires flickering between them. Warriors resting, eating, sharpening blades that will drink from both sides before this is over. Some lie on the cyan grass, their armor still on, sleeping in shallow bursts before the next assault begins.

I guide Omen into a low bank, the wind hissing past us. Thorne's command tent glints faintly in the distance—banners of twisted thorn and blood-red silk snapping in the breeze.

He stands outside, surrounded by his generals, a scowl evident on his face even under the shadow of the storm. He's studying the wards, and I know he's angry he hasn't made more progress by now—especially after how easily Mor destroyed his own wards.

Thorne tilts his head up, seeing our shadow along the ground. Not that I'm trying to hide. On the contrary—I'm flying openly so he can see Avalon's prince is ready for him.

I smirk, lift one hand from the reins, and raise my middle finger.

A gesture I learned from my fierce little Starling. She used to give it to me every time she said she hated me—and every time, I knew she didn't mean it. I'm pretty sure.

Thorne doesn't quite understand the meaning behind it, but he knows enough to be offended.

I laugh at him in mockery and give Omen a gentle nudge with my knees. She banks away, wings cutting through the thinning clouds as we head back toward the castle.

Omen lands in the courtyard with a low whinny, her hooves striking sparks against the stone before she folds her wings.

"Good girl," I murmur, sliding from the saddle.

Across the field, Havoc lifts his head. His midnight coat

ripples with faint light, embers burning in his dark eyes. He smells her before he sees her, and by the time she trots toward him, he's already moving.

They meet in the pasture, necks brushing, a soft nicker passing between them. Mates—bound by the same strange magic that seems to run through every corner of Avalon.

Havoc nuzzles her once, then lowers his head to graze. Omen follows suit, content now that he's near.

I watch them a moment longer, something tight in my chest easing at the simple sight.

Then I slide my hands into my pockets and turn toward the castle.

If the realm is going to end today, I'd rather face it with the only thing in it worth fighting for.

My lover.

My queen.

My Starling.

I find her in the throne room.

Scrolls are spread across the long stone table—maps and ledgers and battle accounts inked in the spidery script of hands long dead. Among them sits the leather-bound book—my grandmother's journal—open to a page where the ink still glows faintly with starlight, like it remembers being written.

Tana stands over them, her jaw tight, her shoulders drawn like a bow that's been strung too long. All of Starfall feels it—the tension in the air, the way every breath seems borrowed. But none of us carry the weight like she does.

She hasn't just inherited a kingdom. She's inherited its ghosts.

I wish I could take the burden from her. Just for a

moment. Just long enough for her to remember she's not alone.

She looks up as I cross the chamber. The second she sees me, her shoulders ease—just slightly—and she sets the scroll down.

"How was your patrol?"

She's in a dress.

And fuck, she's beautiful.

It's not the riding leathers she's favored while trudging through courts and skirting pompous high fae.

The dress clings in all the right places. Fitted at the waist, dipping at the neckline—dark, soft fabric gathered in folds that sway when she shifts. It leaves her arms bare, the skin kissed with silver from the stained glass overhead.

My mouth goes dry.

"Thorne is still there, intent on sacking us."

She stretches, back arching, neck shifting, and I watch the tension ripple out of her piece by piece.

Then, while my eyes are locked on her like a starving man, she brings her hands down slowly—reaching for the laces at the front of her dress.

The first knot comes loose.

Then another.

Then another.

She doesn't fully undress—just enough to let the sweetheart sleeves slide slightly off her shoulders. The tops of her breasts curve into view, soft and perfect and so fucking tempting I have to clench my fists to keep from dropping to my knees right then.

"You know..." she murmurs, turning to face me as she

backs a step toward the dais, "I was just about to get something to eat."

"Mmm, I could certainly go for something." I tilt my head. "What do you recommend?"

She hums thoughtfully. "Roasted vegetables?"

"No." I take a slow step forward, unfastening the first buttons of my vest.

"Spiced lamb?"

"Try again." Another step. The vest hits the floor, and I start rolling my sleeves, watching her with heat simmering behind my gaze.

She bites her lip, backing another step. "Stewed apples?"

My smirk sharpens. "Closer."

She lets her dress slip just a little lower on one shoulder. I follow, each step drawing her back toward the throne like gravity itself wants her seated there.

When her knees brush the edge of the seat, I stop. She does, too.

Our eyes lock. The tension tightens like a blade between us.

I move close, one hand braced beside her hip on the carved stone. "You want to know what I want to eat?" I murmur, low and filthy.

She nods once.

I drag my mouth to her ear. "Your cunt."

She exhales sharply, her whole body blooming with heat as I run my tongue up the column of her neck.

Then—slowly, gracefully—she lifts the hem of her dress and gathers it in her hands, revealing the bare skin of her thighs. She sinks into her throne like the goddess she is, legs spread just wide enough for me to kneel between.

I nod toward her, eyes fixed between her legs. "Wider, my queen. You know one of my favorite views in all of Avalon is your pussy absolutely dripping for me."

"Is that so, my prince," she says, voice steady and sinful. Those two words out of her mouth make my cock ache for her. "Show me how the master of lightning and shadow worships his sovereign."

I drop to my knees without hesitation.

"Gladly."

Her scent hits me first—ripe and sweet, already slick with anticipation. My hands grip her thighs as I drag my mouth to her heat, my tongue tasting her like I've gone too long without.

"Gods, I missed this pussy," I groan against her, licking a slow stripe up her center. "So fucking sweet. So fucking perfect."

She exhales a sharp moan. "Don't tease. Earn it."

I grin against her wet lips, sucking her clit into my mouth and flicking it with the tip of my tongue until her hips twitch against me.

She gasps, one hand threading into my hair as it spills across her thighs. "Yes. Just like that. Fu-u-ck, you're so good."

I slide two fingers into her—curling them just right—and groan at the way she clenches around me.

"Greedy cunt," I mutter, thrusting them again. "Takes everything I give her. She knows who she belongs to, doesn't she?"

Her breath stutters. "Yours."

"Tell me how you are mine."

"All yours, Orion," she moans, her head tipping back,

hips rolling as she works her pussy against my mouth. "Your queen. Your whore. Your everything."

I growl, dragging my tongue faster now, sucking and matching the rhythm of my fingers as her thighs tremble around my head.

"Oh, my God. You're going to make me come soon."

"That's fucking right, Starling," I snarl, teeth grazing just enough to make her shudder. "You're going to come all over my fucking mouth and let me drink it like the gift it is."

I massage her clit between my tongue and teeth. She cries out—and I know her orgasm is hard.

Her voice is high and wild, and I feel her breaking apart—grinding against my face, hips rolling, her hand fisted hard in my hair as she falls over the edge.

"Fuck, don't stop, baby. Fuck." She's squinting her eyes shut, still fucking my mouth. "Oh, yes."

Her orgasm pulses against my tongue—hot and wet. I stay there, licking every drop, every shake, until she collapses back into the throne, panting, flushed, radiant.

When I finally look up, her eyes are half-lidded and wicked. Her voice—breathless and commanding—wraps around me like a leash.

"Get up here," she says, voice still rough from moaning, "so I can sit on my other throne."

I fucking grin.

We rise together, mouths fused, her tongue licking the taste of herself off my lips like she's reclaiming it. My hands find her waist as hers drag down my chest, tugging at the laces of my tunic. We work in tandem—my tunic pulled over my head, her dress sliding down her hips and pooling at our feet in a whisper of silk and heat.

Her fingers find my cock—already hard, already aching.

She wraps her hand around it and squeezes—slow, possessive strokes that make my head fall back and my hips twitch into her fist.

"Fuck, look at you," she purrs. "Hard already and I haven't even sat on you yet."

"I've been hard since I saw you in that dress," I growl as she pushes me back by my chest, eyes daring me to try and survive this.

I sit. She straddles me.

And when she sinks down onto my cock, we both groan like we've found salvation.

"Fuck—Tana." My fingers grip her hips, grounding myself. "You're so fucking tight."

She arches, grinding down deeper, her breath stuttering out in a broken moan. "You're huge, Orion—fuck, you're so deep—"

I thrust up into her and she gasps, nails digging into my shoulders.

"Feel that?" I grit out. "That's your cunt taking every inch like it was made for me."

"It was," she hisses through clenched teeth, riding me harder now, her thighs flexing, sweat slicking her skin. "God, I need you."

I catch one of her nipples in my mouth, sucking hard while she bounces in my lap—her rhythm desperate, powerful. She's riding me like she's trying to erase every shadow of war.

And fuck if I won't let her.

"Orion—fuck—fuck—don't stop—"

"I'm not stopping until this throne drips with you," I

snarl, driving up into her, one hand gripping the base of her neck, the other squeezing her tight ass cheek, hard. "I want to feel you come around my dick, Starling. Let this realm hear who you belong to."

Her climax hits fast—tightening around me as she moans my name, forehead falling against mine.

I let her catch her breath for all of three seconds.

Then I stand—and flip her around.

She braces her knees on the seat of the throne, her ass lifted. I slam back into her from behind with a sharp smack to her ass, grabbing her hair and yanking her head back so she's moaning into the vaulted chamber.

"This," I growl, "is how you fuck a queen."

"Then do it," she pants, voice wrecked and perfect.

I fuck her hard—hips slamming into ass, our skin clapping with every thrust, the throne creaking beneath us. Her cunt is soaking, gripping me like it doesn't want to let go.

"You feel that?" I grunt, slamming deeper. "That's my cock ruining you—stretching this perfect little hole until all you can think about is how full you are."

"Yes—fuck, yes—Orion—God, you feel so good—"

"You're taking me like you want to break."

"I do."

I spit on my finger and reach around, rubbing her clit—fast and rough, just how she likes it. "Then break for me."

We come together—her sobbing through her orgasm, me roaring her name as I spill inside her, hips grinding, bodies shaking, shadows curling around us like they never want to let go.

When it's over, she slumps into the throne, and I fold

over her back—both of us breathless, bodies tangled, claimed.

There is a war coming.

But right now, all that matters... is this.

Her.

Us.

Everything we'll destroy to protect it.

CHAPTER 47

leep doesn't come.

Not even for a minute.

Orion's breathing is slow and steady beside me, his hand still draped across my hip. He's warm, even in sleep. Grounding. But the weight on my chest won't lift—not with Thorne's army outside our gates and the sound of cracking wards echoing through my skull.

Carefully, I slide out from beneath the sheets. I press a kiss to his shoulder before pulling my silk robe tighter around me and easing the door shut behind me.

The hall is quiet, dimly lit by moonstone sconces. The silence feels brittle, like the castle is holding its breath.

I find my way to the study.

A fire burns low in the massive hearth, and for a moment I just stand in the doorway, watching it. The flames cast long shadows across the room—gold and flickering.

Mor sits in a high-backed chair facing the fire, posture perfect, gaze fixed on the low table in front of her. Across from her, Merlin is slumped forward in sleep, head tilted awkwardly to the side, one hand still hovering over a carved game piece.

Some fae game I don't know the name of—like chess, but older. More brutal, judging by the shapes of the figurines.

Mor hasn't moved a muscle. It looks like she's been sitting there in absolute stillness, simply waiting for him to wake up so she can annihilate him.

His moonhorn sleeps at the foot of the hearth, curled like an enormous cat. Even sprawled out, he barely blocks the heat of the flames.

At the table to the side, Hypnos is bent over Pandora's journal, fingers trailing the edges of a worn page. He looks up as I enter.

Without a word, he gestures to the chair beside him.

I cross the room and sit.

"Did you know I was coming?" I ask, trying for levity. It falls flat—my voice tight, my hands cold even next to the fire.

Outside, the wards still hum with tension. The second of them is under siege now. The first fell hours ago.

He doesn't smile, but there's a flicker of something close. "I assumed you would have a fitful sleep and come in search of something to pass the time."

"Fair assumption." I exhale slowly. "Would you tell me more of the accounts? Not all of them—just the ones that differ from what we already have in the Starfall archives."

He nods once, turning a few more pages. "There are some entries unique to this version. Records of experiences during her trials that were never transcribed anywhere else."

I lean forward, elbows on the table. "When I tore down the Shimmer Court's illusion, I felt something... shift. Like the realm responded. Like it was watching."

Hypnos flips to a section marked with a silver thread.

His fingers pause on the header of a page. "The Trial of the Veil," he murmurs, tapping the script.

I've never heard of that one.

"Not in any of our records," I say.

"No," he agrees. "Perhaps it was added for her. Perhaps... it's being rewritten now. For you."

I chew my bottom lip, hesitant. But the question won't leave me alone.

"The trial of fate," I say. "That's the final one, isn't it?"

He looks up. There's a gentleness in his expression— something rare. "Yes."

He doesn't need to say it aloud. I know he can feel the tangle of emotions bleeding off me. Worry. Dread. A thousand unspoken fears.

He rests a hand lightly atop mine, cool but steady.

"Queen Pandora was already fae. Already immortal. I cannot know if the realm intends to make you so. And I cannot pretend to know what it would require."

"Have any of the other queens been... turned?"

"I do not know," he answers honestly. "But I know it is possible."

He glances past me.

To Mor.

Once-mortal, now something entirely other. Her shadows move even in her stillness, flickering like smoke around her feet.

"It is possible," Hypnos says again, voice lower. "But the trial of fate is rarely about the outcome. It's less a question of destiny... and more a test of whether you believe in it. Whether you trust it enough to step forward without knowing where your foot will land."

I try to breathe around that.

Before I can ask more—before I can press for any hidden truth Pandora may have left behind—

A great boom shakes the walls.

We all freeze.

Wind howls outside the study windows, shadows streaking past like smoke caught in a storm. The fire gutters low, then flares as the pressure builds.

Mor rises from her seat. Merlin startles awake. The moonhorn growls.

And then—

The horns blare.

The bells of Starfall ring.

The battle... has begun.

T he bells don't just ring.

They scream.

All around us, the castle erupts into motion.

Lesser fae rush through the halls—some carrying children, others guiding elders or the injured. Guards shout orders over the sound of boots on stone, directing them toward the tunnels that lead beneath the castle or to the warded village tucked just beyond the outer walls.

Everywhere, panic simmers just beneath the surface.

Orion grabs my hand, and we move fast, shadows and wind racing alongside us as we make our way to the lower armory.

Hephaestus is already there, sleeves rolled up, sweat gleaming on his brow despite the chill seeping in through the mountain stone.

He looks up as we enter, his massive arms crossed over his chest. "About bloody time," he says in that deep Highland brogue of his. "Ye come ringin' the bells like the world's on fire, and I've got yer armor waitin' right here."

We stop short.

Because the armor isn't what we expected.

It's not the heavy, ceremonial plating that's all show and no movement. This is different—lighter, stronger. Still elegant but made for war.

"After Her Highness complained—loudly, I might add—about not bein' able to bloody lift her arms above her head," Hephaestus grunts, "I went back to the forge and made somethin' useful. Try not to die in it, aye?"

I run my hand over the curve of the chest plate. It's sleek but reinforced. Flexible. Like it was meant for me.

Orion's already halfway into his. He rolls his shoulders, draws his shadow-bow into existence with a flick of his hand—darkness coalescing into an obsidian arc of power. Then he dispels it and draws his sword instead, taking a few smooth practice swings.

"Maker's flame," he mutters, impressed. "It moves like it's part of me."

"That's because it is, lad," Hephaestus says, slapping the chest plate with one meaty hand. "Crafted for yer magic. Just don't get cocky."

"I'm always cocky," Orion says with a grin, then nods toward me. "She likes me that way."

I roll my eyes and buckle my vambraces. "Focus, prince."

The door behind us opens, and Hypnos enters, trailed by Mor.

She looks like a storm given shape—eyes burning

brighter than ever, her skin paler than bone, shadows pulsing just under her skin like something alive.

"You doing okay there, hangry?" I tease, anticipation of the oncoming battle turning butterflies in my stomach.

She surveys the armory, then looks at me and shrugs. "We've been fasting quite a long time."

Then she smiles. "Dinner is here."

My blood runs cold.

"Wait—" I glance at Orion, voice low. "She's not going to eat them, is she?"

He just winks. "Define 'eat.'"

Oh my God.

Hypnos clears his throat and gives half a bow, and I notice he also has new armor. Mor is wearing none. "There is still no sign of our allies from Cairnvail or Gloamreach."

"None of them? Shade?"

He shakes his head once.

"Do you think they betrayed us?" I ask, the words burning in my throat.

Orion frowns, shaking his head. "Granite would likely die from breaking his bargain with you. He would not risk it."

"Maybe he's stuck behind a mountain that froze shut. The frost courts aren't known for their agreeable weather," Mor says lightly, examining a dagger.

"So it's just us," I say quietly.

Hypnos meets my gaze. "It would seem so, Your Grace."

I look down at the armor on my hands, at the trembling breath in my chest, and turn to Orion.

"Then we make do. And we hold Starfall."

His storm-gray eyes are alight with the lightning that powers the blood in his veins.

We march out together—not in formation, not as soldiers or strangers, but as something else. A group of friends, of chosen family, walking shoulder to shoulder toward whatever waits for us in the dark.

The castle is lined with lesser fae as we pass.

Mothers clutching children. Elders standing tall, with fear burning in their eyes but refusing to turn away. Small hands clutch skirts and weapons too big for them. All of them still, watching, listening to the horns of war echo from the hills like a curse.

Hestia stands at the center of the main hall, her arms wrapped around the youngest of their brood. The rest are gathered tight, pressed close against her sides.

Hephaestus stops, just for a second. He leans in and presses his forehead to hers.

Neither of them says goodbye. But it's in the silence between them that the word lives.

Her voice is steady as she whispers, "I expect you back in one piece. No new limbs lost."

He gives a gruff chuckle and touches her cheek. "I'll be back, love."

I can't look for long. It's too much.

We move on.

Me. Orion. Mor. Hypnos.

Hephaestus walks behind us, his massive hammer slung across his shoulder. His steps are slow but unshakable, the weight of his promise heavier than the weapon in his hands.

We cross the drawbridge together, the thick iron chains

groaning with each step. The wind has picked up. The night hums with pressure.

Just as we step onto the other side, Hephaestus halts.

He turns back one last time.

Hestia stands just inside the gate, shadows painting her silhouette in warm light. The children are gathered around her like a shield. She lifts her chin.

He nods.

Then, without a word, she steps back into the castle. The heavy doors shut behind her with a thunderous clang.

Hephaestus raises his hammer.

With a swing that shakes the stone beneath us, he slams it into the giant bolt fixed into the drawbridge mechanism.

The chains scream as they pull tight, groaning and creaking as the massive bridge begins to lift. Inch by inch, the path back to the castle disappears behind us.

When it locks into place, he steps into the center of the path, wide-legged and braced, the castle sealed behind him.

"I'll hold the gates," he mutters, gripping his hammer. "Won't be no Briar fae gettin' past me to my family."

Orion steps forward and clasps his wrist. "We'll try not to be too long."

Hephaestus just grunts, and the two release each other.

I shake my head, exhaling, and we walk.

The path opens into the wide, rolling glen that stretches from the foot of Starfall's mountain to the far ridge where the horizon burns red with campfires.

And beyond them—

Thorne.

The Briar army.

Their fae hammering at the final ward, still pulsing in

the air like glass about to break. The last wall before they march into the heart of Avalon.

Straight for me.

The mortal woman the realm chose to wear the crown.

I square my shoulders, and we walk toward war.

The glen stretches before us, wind curling through the grass like it's bracing, too. The line of Starfall's warriors waits just ahead, armor gleaming, blades drawn, breath held.

But before we reach them, Mor speaks.

"I believe," she says casually, "our queen has a ritual of battle."

I blink, turning to her.

She's not looking at me—just straight ahead, her hands swinging at her sides, her steps graceful and lethal as ever.

But there's a knowing smile curving her lips.

I laugh under my breath, surprised. "You weren't supposed to know about that."

"Oh, but we do," Hypnos murmurs, a trace of amusement in his voice.

Even Orion glances sideways at me, a slow grin creeping across his face.

Mor lifts one brow. "So then. Who dies today… Valkyrie?"

I smirk, letting the tension burn off in the fire of what I know deep in my bones.

"Not us."

CHAPTER 48
tana

We wait.

The ward still holds—for now.

The final shimmer of magic wavers in the distance, visible only to those who can feel its pulse in the bones of this realm. And we do. Every one of us.

We talked about this last night, in the dark.

He sat on the floor between my legs, both of us facing the fire as I braided his long white hair back, readying him for war. The sides freshly shaved. He wanted a lock of my own hair braided in with his—for luck, he said.

Orion knows he can't keep me from the battlefield.

And I know the risks.

I could die.

But I didn't come here to be a hero.

I came to stand with the fae who are willing to bleed for the realm I'm meant to rule. For the throne I'm meant to sit on.

For the crown I'm supposed to wear.

The moment holds—stretching thin, a breath not yet exhaled.

Orion whistles—one sharp, piercing note that slices through the waiting.

A beat later, Omen circles above us. Her dark wings catch the light of the oversized moon.

She lands beside him with a thud of power, hooves churning the earth.

Orion puts out his hand, and she lowers her massive head, nuzzling his palm like the realm isn't about to bleed.

He presses his forehead to hers, eyes shut. "Stay with the queen," he whispers.

She exhales like she understands, then he looks at me.

And I look at him.

He pulls me in by the waist and kisses me.

No words.

No promises.

Just him. Just me.

Then he lets go.

He and Hypnos move to the front of the army—two shadows cutting across the glen, the wind hissing in their wake.

Mor stays behind with me.

Omen stomps the ground once, twice, three times—impatient or nervous, I can't tell.

The army of Starfall waits between us. Tension builds like a storm behind the ribs.

Then Merlin approaches, riding bareback on the broad back of his massive moonhorn, robes fluttering, staff across his lap. His little storm cloud bobs above him, crackling with what sounds suspiciously like glee.

He comes to a halt beside us, perfectly balanced, gaze scanning the horizon. Stoic. Regal. Unexpectedly imposing.

Mor lifts an eyebrow. "Aren't you a little old for the battlefield, wizard?"

He doesn't even blink. "I'll have you know I was quite the looker in my day. Hair like a god. A jaw that could cut glass. Don't let the old-man façade fool you—I still have all my original bones."

He rattles on, something about moonroot tonics and a trio of redheads, but I don't hear him.

Because I'm watching Orion.

He glances back at me, just once—over his shoulder, that stormborn gaze meeting mine.

And then—

The final ward breaks.

It doesn't shatter. It bellows.

Magic rips through the glen like the sky itself has been torn. Light fractures. The air distorts. The ground shakes.

And then comes the sound—

The thundering roar of the Briar army.

A tide of boots. Armor. War cries.

They're coming.

And they're coming for me.

War is chaos.

Even when you know it's coming.

Even when the horns sound and the sky breaks open and your soul is braced for the scream of steel and shattering bone—

It's still chaos.

The Briar army crashes into our lines like a wave against rock.

High fae and lesser fae clash in bursts of brutal, glittering violence. Blades drawn. Magic erupting. Roots tear up from the ground, curling around ankles, while gusts of wind slam into bodies, flinging them back. Spells sizzle. Shields flare. Someone screams.

And at the rear of the oncoming army—crowned in twisted briars and gold—

Thorne.

Wearing a crown like it was forged for him.

Wearing a king's crown on his traitor's head like he's already claimed the realm.

It gleams in the firelight, a mockery of what should be mine.

I stay back for now, standing in the shadow of the rise just behind the line, waiting for the moment they break through. Because someone will.

They always do.

I have my sword.

My armor.

My rage.

But my focus...

It's all on him.

Orion moves through the battlefield like he was born for it.

Shadow dances across his armor, curling off his shoulders like smoke. His sword is a thing of darkness and lightning, slicing through Briar fae with devastating precision. Every strike is calculated. Every movement—graceful, deadly, inevitable.

His bow manifests in a ripple of night, and the arrows he looses are forged of pure shadow. They pierce through enchanted shields like paper, and when they hit—they devour.

He disappears into a swirl of fog and smoke, only to reappear behind a target and end them before they can even scream.

God.

I've seen him spar. Seen him protect.

But I've never seen him unleashed.

And I can't look away.

Beside me, Merlin lobs something over his shoulder—a small, crystalline orb that explodes in a puff of purple smoke and glittering shards.

The moonhorn beside him lets out a huff of steam and continues watching with bored disdain.

"Honestly," Merlin mutters, his little storm cloud crackling like it approves, "these Briar brutes could use a lesson in flair. Where's the drama? The entrance? That one just walked into the fight like it's a bar brawl."

Mor hasn't moved.

Her eyes are on the ridge behind us.

She stands like a statue, like a blade left in the earth—still but not at rest.

She hasn't drawn her shadows.

She hasn't glanced at the battlefield.

Because she's waiting.

Starfall will see war on two fronts.

And now she's watching for the second.

"Something stirs," she murmurs, too low for anyone but me to hear. "I can feel it in the breath between spells."

I grip my sword tighter.

Another burst of wind tears through the lines, and I look back just in time to see Orion drive his blade through a high fae cloaked in briar magic, shadows coiling around his body like armor, like vengeance.

A pulse of energy hits the ground and cracks the earth beneath his boots.

He looks up—

And finds me.

Through the chaos, the magic, the storm of bodies and blades—

His eyes find mine.

I nod once. A signal. A promise.

I'm okay.

Don't worry about me, Orion. I press the thought into the bond between us. Go be the storm. I've got this front.

I feel his response like a rush of heat through my chest— no words, just power. Then, with a wink, he's gone again, swallowed by smoke and steel.

The battlefield shifts.

A high fae from Thorne's line breaks through a weak point in the left flank. Two more follow, faster than the rest, sharp spells already forming in their palms—

And they're heading right toward me.

My blade sings as I draw it.

The first one comes fast. Briar vines wrap around his arms like armor, thorns glistening with poison. I duck beneath his swing and drive my sword up through his ribs, twisting once before yanking it free.

He collapses.

The second launches a streak of violet flame—

I roll sideways and slam the hilt of my sword into her jaw. She stumbles, dazed, just long enough for me to run her through.

The third draws a blade wreathed in something darker. Something—

A crack of thunder splits the air beside me.

The fae convulses mid-step, then crumples to the ground, twitching.

I blink, looking over my shoulder, confused.

Sir Rumbleton Tempestus Maximus.

The little storm cloud hovers beside me, arcs of lightning dancing along its edges like it's proud of itself.

"Good Rumble," I murmur, chest heaving. "Keep watch."

It zips into place just over my shoulder, spinning in a tight, angry circle like a bodyguard ready to fry anyone who gets too close.

To my left, the galloping thump of large hooves booms toward me.

"MAKE WAY!"

I glance just in time to see the old wizard come barreling through the smoke.

He's standing barefoot on the broad shoulder of his massive moonhorn, robes flying behind him like a cloak, long white beard trailing like a scarf. One hand clutches the beast's antler; the other swings his staff in a wide arc, cracking it against the face of a Briar fae who goes flying.

I shudder at the sound the staff makes against skull.

Merlin hoots like a drunk bard on festival night, whooping and hollering as he hangs on, striking enemies like a wild man possessed.

"Ah, nothing like the scent of war to wake the bones!" he bellows, nearly falling off as he swings his staff with alarming precision. "Who needs tea when you've got carnage at first shade?"

His moonhorn barely seems bothered, steam curling from its nostrils as it barrels through the fray.

I ready myself again. Another fae surges toward me, snarling, blade raised—

I parry, twist, and bring my knee up hard into his gut.

He crumples—but more are coming.

I stand tall.

Blood on my blade. Lightning at my side.

Just behind me—still, silent, unmoving—

Mor stands with her eyes fixed on the ridge behind us.

One hand hangs loose at her side, while the shadows at her feet twitch, like they smell something coming.

A low growl curls from her throat, dark and feral. A shiver runs down my spine at the sheer power rippling off her.

"Well, well, well." She draws each word out like a death knell. "We were right. Again."

She looks over her shoulder at me—red eyes shifting to burning yellow.

Her teeth turn slate gray as black ooze drips down them. Tar clings to her hair, and her skin yellows as the transformation takes root.

The Morrigan has finally joined the battlefield.

And that can only mean one thing.

"We have a traitor in our midst."

The battlefield is chaos.

Steel clashes. Fae magic lights the sky. The scent of blood and burned bark fills my lungs.

And I'm right where I need to be—carving through Thorne's bastard line of briar-spawn like a blade through silk.

I slam my sword into one fae's side, twist, and pull. He goes down with a choked scream, already forgotten as the next takes his place. They're relentless—more weed than warrior. But for every one I cut down, two more seem to bloom.

"Fucking coward," I growl, scanning the ridge.

Thorne still hasn't entered the field.

He stands atop a rise behind the chaos, cloaked in thorns and draped in the illusion of power—a crown he's not fit to wear gleaming on his brow, as if he rules anything more than the rot that spawned him.

The sight of him stokes something primal inside me—a storm gathering just behind my ribs.

He started this.

He should bleed for it.

A fae lunges at me, teeth bared, vines whipping from his wrists like whips. I duck, twist, and drive my blade straight up through his gut. His body crumples against my chest as I shove him off and whirl toward the next.

I catch the flicker of movement in the distance—Tana.

She's holding her ground, eyes blazing, shadows at her back. She's already bloodied her blade.

My queen.

Lightning cracks just behind her, striking a fae dead mid-leap.

The little storm cloud above her head practically hums with delight, zipping around like it wants to fight ten more. I'd scoff if I wasn't so damn grateful the thing's taken to her. Guess it's not so useless after all.

"Eyes front," Hypnos says smoothly, appearing at my side like a ghost. A blur of silver sweeps through the air as his curved blade slices across a fae's throat. "She's holding her own."

"I know." I duck another blow, drive my dagger into a stomach, and rip upward. "Doesn't mean I like it."

"She wouldn't be your queen if you did."

My old friend has a point.

I glance at him—stoic, elegant, lethal. The perfect second. The perfect contrast to the war humming in my veins.

A fresh wave hits us. These are stronger, magic-enhanced. One hurls thorns that explode midair like shrapnel; another grows a shield of bark from his arms. Hypnos dances through them with fluid grace. I use brute force. Shadow whips crack from my hands, slicing through flesh and bark alike.

They fall, one by one, until I have a moment to breathe.

A haze of blue robes and a flash of white beard dart through the battle.

"Fucking hells, Merlin," I mutter.

He's riding the damn moonhorn bareback—hanging off the beast's side, flinging a crackling orb of light into a cluster of fae like it's a party favor. The blast sends them flying.

He whoops. "Make way for greatness, lads!"

The moonhorn bellows, charging straight through the ranks.

"Insane old bastard," Hypnos grumbles, but there's no venom in it. "The fool wears no garments under his robes—and at battle?"

Amid the blood and death, it rips a laugh from me.

Omen rears and whinnies, shadows billowing from her wings as she flaps them. My faithful steed stays with my mate, replicating herself into a half-dozen more shadow-mares, forming a barrier between Tana and an advancing line of briar warriors, her eyes glowing like stars, daring anyone to come closer.

Tana doesn't flinch, advancing on the fae she is battling. She doesn't need to. She's power wrapped in mortal skin.

I let myself watch her for one breath.

Just one.

Then the air shifts. The temperature plummets—sharp and sudden.

The weight of it hits me like gravity thickening around my limbs. Every sense on alert.

Mor, still as death. Shadows twitching at her heels like living serpents. Her head tilted slightly, the way a predator does just before it strikes.

She shifts into the dark being that manifests when the power of three souls possesses her body at once. Tar streaks down her skin like veins made of rot. Her voice curls out of the silence like smoke from a funeral pyre.

"We have a traitor in our midst."

A ripple of pressure rolls across the glen—different from the wild chaos of the briar onslaught. This one is colder. Deeper.

And from the ridge behind us, darkness begins to rise.

Figures step out of that darkness. Hundreds.

Silent and lethal.

The assassins of Umbranor.

Their movements are smooth, predatory—so precise they almost look rehearsed. They don't charge like the briar horde. They glide. Unseen, until they want to be seen.

And at their center, his cloak barely fluttering in the stillness...

Shade.

Lord of the Shadowed Court.

That son of a bitch.

Our eyes lock across the field, and the bond between us crackles with silent fury.

Liar, I send through the thread between us.

His lip curves just slightly. A smirk without kindness.

I promised to fight, Shade murmurs into my mind. *I never said who for.*

I take one step forward. Shadows pulse at my fingertips. *You come for our queen—I'll make your death last for days.*

He has no interest in seeing your queen dead. Only kneeling. In chains.

A low, primal growl builds in my throat. *Thorne.*

It is the Morrigan who answers. *You try to touch her—and we will make you bleed shadow for the rest of your cursed days.*

Shade's smile is quiet. Cold. *She wouldn't be harmed. Just claimed.*

That single word—*claimed*—snaps something in my chest.

Behind me, the clamor of battle keeps raging. Steel against steel. Screams. Magic. Death.

But the fury in my blood is singular.

He won't kill her. He'll break her. And that... that's worse.

And still—no sign of the courts who claimed alliance.

The Stone Fae. The Twilight Court. Even the Swamp Court, who pledged themselves to Thorne, have yet to arrive.

Maybe they wait to see who bleeds first.

Maybe they hope to wear us down.

I don't know how long we can hold.

We fight to defend Starfall. To protect our queen. But if the courts truly unite against us...

I won't stop until I've torn their lands down to the roots.

Before I can take a step toward him—before I can leap into the shadows myself and drag him into his own court and gut him from the inside out—the air shifts.

The battlefield drops ten degrees in an instant. My breath fogs. The ground seems to hum with something ancient.

Not Umbranor's shadows.

Not even mine.

Something else entirely. This is thicker. Older. Like ink leaking from the cracks in the world. Something ravenous.

The Morrigan is no longer still, no longer waiting.

She steps forward slowly, her face splitting with a grin that doesn't belong to any court.

I refocus on the front line. Shade and his slippery bastards may try to flank us. But I won't worry with them.

Let the goddess eat.

And gods help Umbranor—

because she has been fasting.

And the depth of her hunger knows no bottom.

CHAPTER 50
tana

She doesn't run.

She doesn't scream.

She doesn't even blink.

The Morrigan walks forward at a slow, measured pace—each step deliberate, each breath a silent promise.

Her glowing yellow eyes stay locked on Shade. Not his army. Not the flanking warriors. Just him.

Like the only reason she's here is to reach him. To unmake him.

He doesn't budge—perhaps believing his forces will overwhelm her in numbers alone.

It's his assassins who charge.

Silent. Fast. Made of shadow and bone and nothingness.

But she...

She doesn't change her pace.

She doesn't lift a weapon.

She doesn't need to.

The shadows around her feet writhe as if alive—tangled and twitching, feeding on the dread rising from the earth.

With each step, the ground splits open beneath her, veins of black cracking outward like a sickness spreading under skin.

A deep tremor rolls across the field—the kind you feel in your bones.

I stagger and nearly fall, catching myself on Omen's side as the ground groans beneath us.

Even she lowers her head, nostrils flaring—like whatever this is, it's older than war. Older than gods.

A column of pure black erupts from the dirt at her feet—so fast it's just a blur.

It shoots into the sky like a spear of night, climbing so high the moon flinches behind a cloud.

Then it shatters.

Only then do I see them—what the darkness is.

Not smoke.

Not magic.

Crows.

Thousands of them.

They explode into the air like a second storm, wings beating with such force they drown out the battle behind us.

Their caws are discordant. Too loud. Too wrong. Like they echo through the mind instead of the air.

Still, the assassins press on—undaunted, like they've been trained to resist fear.

To fight without sound. Without soul.

Without mercy.

But not without minds.

And the crows find their way in.

It starts small—a stumble, a turn of the head. One assassin falters. Another slows.

Then it spreads.

Screams echo from their ranks—but not the kind born of pain. The kind born of confusion. Terror.

Each fae hears something different.

The one closest to me jerks violently and drops his dagger.

"No," he breathes. "No, no, Talis, don't—don't make me do this—"

Another spins around, slashing at the air.

"You lie! He wouldn't say that! You're not him! You're not him!"

The crows dive in.

They pluck out eyes.

They tear at faces.

And through it all, they scream.

But it's not just screaming. It's... voices.

To one assassin, it's the pleading of a dead lover.

To another, it's the voice of their commander ordering retreat.

To another still, it's the sound of betrayal—of brothers turning blades, of lovers whispering heartbreak.

They hear their worst fears. Their deepest guilt. Their darkest memories.

Not shared. Not uniform.

It's personal.

A crow lands on the shoulder of a fae and caws into the cavity where an eye used to be.

The fae claws at their own face, screaming, trying to rip it out—but it's not really there.

There's nothing to touch.

Because it's not a bird.

Not truly.

It's shadow. Shadow that is different from their own—shadow that doesn't recognize them or their power.

It's a living hallucination conjured by something far more ancient than nightmares.

The battlefield is a madhouse now—black feathers whirling in the air, blood spattering the grass, screams slicing through the storm of wings.

The assassins turn on each other, unable to tell friend from foe, sight from sound, memory from present.

And all the while—

The Morrigan never stops walking.

Her arms are at her sides, fingers slightly curled. Her black hair streams behind her, streaked with tar. Her teeth gray. Her skin waxen.

She is not rushing.

She is approaching.

Like hunger with feet.

The blood and shadows and fog and madness fall away from the battlefield and curl toward her—wafting like smoke, drawn to her body, to the writhing dark mist that coils around her ankles.

It absorbs into her.

The destruction she causes—the fear, the pain, the rot— feeds the thing inside her.

It doesn't stain her.

It nourishes her.

This isn't magic.

This isn't war.

This is consumption.

And she—

She has been fasting.

The Morrigan walks through the chaos like it's a garden she's tending.

With each step, the earth splits again—dark vines creeping outward from her shadowed path like veins spidering beneath skin.

They slither through blood and grass, sprouting massive lotus-like buds in her wake.

The flowers sway.

They're looking.

Searching.

Then they bloom.

One by one, petals peel open with a wet, unnatural unfurling—and strike.

Long, sharp barbs shoot out from the center of each blossom with a sound like bone cracking. They cut through the air and find their marks in the skulls, chests, and spines of the fae still screaming, still staggering, still bleeding from the crows' assault.

Where they strike, the assassins collapse—not dead.

Worse.

Paralyzed.

Eyes wide. Minds intact.

Trapped inside their own screaming bodies.

And then comes the slime.

It seeps from the vines in thick pools—clear at first but tinged with an oily darkness that makes it shimmer like it's alive.

One assassin, crying blood, runs blind from a swarm of crows—

He steps straight into it.

The moment his foot breaks the surface, it begins to smoke.

His scream tears from his throat as his boot dissolves—flesh sloughing off in curls of steam and red.

He crumples. A barb shoots into his neck, locking his muscles in place, his mouth frozen open.

But I can see it.

The eye the crows left behind strains. Veins bulge. Blood vessels pop.

He feels everything.

Feels the slime crawl up his body.

Feels it devour his soft tissue.

Feels it eat his tongue before it can scream.

And still—

The Morrigan ascends.

Her gaze doesn't stray. Her feet don't hurry. Her power doesn't falter.

She keeps walking—directly toward Shade.

He has the good sense to look scared now.

Not angry. Not cocky.

Afraid.

It's too late.

His remaining assassins start to flee, breaking rank and sprinting past him, desperate for the tree line—

But the low-hanging darkness that clings like fog shifts. Moves.

Reveals something worse.

Hands.

Rotten ones.

Fingers blackened and split at the seams. Bone jutting out where skin has long since given up.

Corpses.

Half-rotted things crawl from the ground like they were waiting—waiting for the scent of fear.

They don't stand.

They pull and drag.

They grab at legs and ankles, clawing and yanking.

Where their decayed flesh touches living bodies, the transformation is instant.

Skin yellows.

Veins turn black.

Boils rise and burst, pus spilling in bubbling streams as the rot spreads like wildfire through muscle and marrow.

Fae scream.

They try to claw away from themselves, their own limbs becoming foreign.

They fall, twitching. Melting.

Some are dragged below the surface—down into the grave they tried to outrun.

And around it all are the crows, still circling.

A vortex now, swirling around the edges of this horror she has summoned.

A perimeter.

A prison.

A storm of wings and madness making sure nothing escapes her wrath.

I've seen death.

I've seen war.

I've killed gods with my bare hands.

Faced vampires with illusion and speed and claws like razors.

Slain gargoyles. Shifters who turned into wolves midfight, midlunge.

But this—

This is something else entirely.

This isn't battle.

It isn't magic or power.

It's divinity.

It's judgment.

It's hunger.

The Morrigan doesn't wield her power—she *is* power.

Every step she takes is a prayer answered in blood.

Every breath she draws is a curse made manifest.

And still she walks.

And the darkness—eats.

The sound that pulls me away from the southern flank isn't the clash of swords or the low roar of thunder—it's a scream. Sharp. Panicked. Human in a way that cuts through the war cries around me.

It forces my gaze to turn. Forces me to tear my eyes from the chaos the Morrigan is unleashing.

And when I do, I see it.

Not the battle. Not the briar horde still pouring from the plains. But what lies beyond. Below.

The village.

Smoke curls up from its edge like warning signals too late to matter. Tiny homes—smaller even from here—dot the base of the cliffs. Meant for lesser fae and those without allegiance to a court. Too fragile to withstand siege. Too far from the gates to find safety in time.

And now... they're being hunted.

Swamp fae are emerging from the misting lake, their scaled armor slick with algae and water, their movements slow and assured—like they already know no one will stop them.

They move in formation, blades drawn, feet churning the ground like a tide marching straight for the village.

The lesser fae are running. I can see them—familiars clutching younglings, elders stumbling toward the makeshift shelters already crumbling under wind and ash.

And even as they flee, the air begins to shimmer. Sprites— tiny points of living light—rise from the grass and drift toward the village, forming a wavering curtain between the oncoming swamp fae and the terrified families. Their glow is soft, pulsing in rhythm with the realm itself, weaving together like threads of starlight until they become a thin, trembling wall.

It's beautiful in the way a candle is beautiful before it's blown out—delicate, doomed. The shield won't hold; it can't. But still they try.

They won't make it, and neither will I.

There's no time. No path that doesn't end in failure.

And no one else can go.

If the Morrigan leaves the assassins, Orion and the forces of Starfall will be surrounded. If anyone diverts their troops from the main field, we lose everything.

My heart thunders in my chest. But beneath it—woven into it—there's something else. A deeper beat. Older. Not mine.

It's Avalon.

Realmbreaker hums in my hand—not buzzing, but vibrating. Pulsing. Alive. Each beat shoots up my arm like a jolt, sharp and rhythmic, like it's trying to sync itself to my heartbeat. Trying to remind me I'm not alone.

I look down.

The ground beneath my boots glows faintly, the cyan-colored grass lit from underneath. Then I see a vein of light winding like a root just beneath the surface, a line of magic pulsing in time with the rhythm in my chest.

It's like the blue glow of the rock in Merlin's tower—the one that thrust me into a vision the moment I touched it. A vision of war like this one, but different.

I kneel. Press my hand to it.

And I feel it.

Magic. Raw and wild and ancient. So strong it shudders beneath my fingertips. It calls to something in me—and I know what that something is.

Realmbreaker.

The sword is buzzing, singing, resonating with the line of magic beneath the soil. Every time I've bent the moonlight, every time I've called power I shouldn't have—this sword was in my hand.

It's not just a blade.

It's a key.

A conduit.

A relic that channels the will of Avalon itself.

And it listens to me.

I stare at it now, silver catching the flicker of lightning overhead. I think of the woman in the vision—the one who looked like my mother. The one they said betrayed her sisters, brought darkness to Avalon. But I think they were wrong.

I don't think she unleashed the dark.

This sword isn't corruption.

It's moonlight.

It's salvation.

And I have to use it.

The village is seconds from falling. The swamp fae are nearly at their doors. And still no reinforcements. No one is coming.

Except me.

I scan the battlefield one last time. Orion—still standing, though bleeding. Hypnos—deadly and precise, his calm the eye of every storm around him. Merlin—still mounted, still launching glittering chaos into the Briar like a child with a bag of fireworks and no supervision.

Too many are falling. Too many still coming.

And overhead... the storm. Merlin's little menace. Flickering now. Smaller. Nervous.

It sees me.

I whistle—sharp, commanding. And the moment I do, it answers. I feel it recognize me—as if some piece of it has always known I would call.

"Gather the clouds," I shout, lifting my hand to the sky. "Take in the mist—we need a storm. A big one."

And gods, it listens.

The sky shifts on a dime. Wind changes course. The temperature drops. Clouds churn and stack and swirl, thickening into something volatile. Something massive.

Raindrops fall like they're testing the ground—and then it all comes at once. A downpour so dense the battlefield blurs. Lightning slashes the sky like cracks in the world itself. Thunder roars.

That's it. That's what I need.

I look toward the village one last time.

They are out of time—and so am I.

I raise the sword.

"One strike," I whisper. "Just one. Right on the hilt."

I grip Realmbreaker tighter than I ever have. Feel it pulse in my hands.

I count.

One...

Two...

Three.

I bring it down.

Not gently. Not with grace. I slam it into the glowing root vein beneath my feet with every ounce of power and desperation I have.

The storm answers instantly.

Lightning arcs through the clouds and crashes into the blade.

It hits me like judgment—white-hot, cosmic, infinite.

It tears through my arms, my chest, my spine. I can't breathe. Can't think. Can't let go.

But I don't.

I scream as the power burns through me, a sound torn straight from my soul. I drive the blade deeper until magic explodes.

It's light—blinding, brilliant, and celestial.

It pulses from the impact like a shockwave, bursting through me and out in every direction.

I'm thrown backward. My vision goes white. My heart is silent, and my ears are ringing with nothing but light.

Everything vanishes.

The screams fade.

And time—stops.

CHAPTER 51
tana

My skull is splitting.

Not just a headache. Not like the ones I've had every day since the bond snapped—not like the dull throb I've learned to function through. This is something else. Blinding, pulsing, sharp behind my eyes.

I'm on my hands and knees before I even realize I've fallen, forehead nearly pressed to the ground, palms buried in cool, damp grass. I suck in air, shallow and ragged, ears ringing so loud I can't hear anything else.

The battlefield is gone.

Or maybe I'm still there. Maybe I've been knocked out.

Maybe I'm dying.

I squeeze my eyes shut and force them open again. Once. Twice. Blink until the blur fades enough to make sense of the ground beneath me.

Cyan-colored grass.

Not stained red with blood, not churned by boots and hooves and clawed limbs—just gently glowing blades of blue, swaying under a sky that looks wrong.

No smoke. No mist. No shadow-choked wind screaming across the valley.

I flex my fingers between the blades, feeling for the hilt of Realmbreaker, but it's gone. Maybe I dropped it. Shaking my head, I feel around, but I can't find it.

Where am I?

No.

That's not quite right.

Where *was* I?

The ringing in my ears warps—fading in and out like sound underwater. I try to sit back on my heels, but the dizziness tilts the horizon. Shadows shift across the field, long and elegant, sweeping over me one after another like ripples in a lake.

I've seen shadows like these before. When I had the vision of a battlefield and everyone I love fighting around me, these same shadows crossed over the ground.

I brace both hands behind me and lift my head.

It must be Omen. Maybe a herd of shadowmares, finally arriving to help.

But when I look up—

The breath in my lungs stills.

Wings.

Massive. White. Not feathered like birds but something stronger, denser—made for war. They glide overhead in formation, banking hard as they descend. A dozen of them. Two dozen.

Each wingbeat throws moonlight across the field, flashes of silver and blue cutting the air like blades.

My gaze follows them. I twist around, still half seated in the glowing grass, and watch as the winged figures soar lower, circling the stretch of land behind me.

This isn't Starfall.

This isn't even *now*.

The salt-stung wind is gone. The iron scent of blood, the screams of fae torn apart—none of it's here.

Instead, there are rows upon rows of white tents stretched across rolling hills. Their flaps ripple in the breeze, campfires flickering between them. The kind of structures you throw up quick—and tear down even quicker.

I push myself to stand, legs trembling, vision clearing just enough to take in the full view.

They're everywhere.

The warriors.

They walk the camp in twos and threes, sharpening blades, tending to gear, laughing around fires, pouring water over their wings, and checking the braces that anchor them to silver armor. Sapphire cloaks trail behind their shoulders like banners.

Hundreds of them.

Some are young, no older than me. Others wear age and fury like crests of honor.

All of them are lethal.

And unmistakable.

The legion of the Valkyrie.

Living myths. Warriors of the gods. The ones who chose death—and were reborn in its image.

I turn in place, slow and deliberate, surrounded on all sides. I'm not just seeing history—I'm in it.

This is their camp.

The center of it, by the look of things.

And I'm no longer wondering *where* I am.

Only *when.*

My breath catches.

Not because of the army.

But because of the woman standing just a few feet ahead of me—her back straight, her posture effortless in its command. Her hair is woven with silver thread and pulled into a braid that falls between her shoulder blades like a war banner. The crown nestled in her hair gleams faintly in the moonlight.

And with the faint glow of power around her, there's no mistaking her.

Queen Pandora.

I've memorized every detail of her portrait. I've stood before it in the throne room, tracing the lines of her armor with my eyes, wondering how she wore it—what kind of strength it took to lead an entire realm.

But nothing prepared me for this.

Not the weight of her presence.

Not the reality of her form.

And gods—not the moment when she turns and her sapphire-blue gaze lands on mine as if she was always meant to see me. As if she's been waiting for me.

And as my heart stutters in my chest, I know—

This is no ordinary dream.

This is a memory.

Pandora lowers her gaze to the flower in her hand—its petals the color of moonlight, its stem thin and brittle like spun glass. She turns it slowly between her fingers, careful, reverent. A bloom so small it looks like it might vanish in the breeze.

In her other hand, she holds a leather-bound book.

My breath catches as my heart leaps forward a beat.

It's the same one I opened only yesterday—the account of her trials. Her hand, her ink, her truth.

She lifts her chin, drawing a slow breath. "Starling."

The name hits me like a blade in my gut.

That's what Orion calls me—has called me from the beginning. And hearing it now, from her lips, makes the air around me hum.

But Pandora's not looking at me. She's looking at the flower.

"Pardon, Your Majesty?" another voice asks gently behind me.

I turn, stepping aside.

The woman who speaks has clear, translucent wings trailing behind her robes—robes I recognize. A high seer. But not Astrael.

Pandora offers a small smile, still watching the flower in her fingers. "The bloom," she says softly. "It's a starling."

She opens the leather cover and places the delicate thing just under the front flap, pressing it flat and sealing it away.

"It's the last one," she murmurs, brushing her fingers across the cover like she can still see the flower through the leather. "The Court of Dreams is all but dead."

There's something in her voice that makes my chest ache. Not just loss—but longing.

The seer steps forward, hands outstretched, and Pandora hands her the book without hesitation.

"Why tonight, Your Majesty?"

Pandora lets out a quiet chuckle, but there's no joy in it. "The Lady doesn't take time to explain the visions she shows me," she says. "I only know tonight is the night she's shown me a hundred times. This night matters."

She casts a look across the camp—warriors sharpening blades, wings being strapped into place, flames dancing in small rings. Her gaze passes over me without pause, without focus.

And I freeze.

She didn't see me. Not truly.

It felt like it earlier. But now I know better.

I'm not here—not really. I'm just a shadow in someone else's memory.

Pandora nods once to the seer. "Take my accord to Astralana. It will open again when the time is right. Tell no one."

The seer bows deeply, cradling the book like something sacred, and glides off between the tents, disappearing into the camp's belly.

I check the grass around me, feel the empty scabbard at my hip. Realmbreaker is not here. I suppose it wouldn't be, since this is only a dream.

Pandora turns away and walks to a barrel beside one of the tents, lifts a wooden ladle from its perch, and scoops water to her lips.

I take a step closer and peer over the edge, sucking in a deep breath when I see my own silhouette standing next to Pandora's—reflected in the dark pool of water.

Her hand lowers for a second dip—and freezes midmotion as she stares into the trough.

She can see me there.

Pandora turns her head—slow, deliberate—and her gaze lands right where I'm standing.

I don't breathe.

Her eyes don't settle on me. They sweep around, searching.

"Hello?" My voice bounces around in a whispered echo—like it's too far away to reach this memory.

She reaches out, her fingers trembling as she extends her

hand toward me and passes through like smoke. Pandora inhales sharply, drawing her hand back to her chest. She looks down at the figure standing with her in the water.

"I don't know who you are," she whispers. "But the Lady never showed me anything after this moment."

She glances down again, lips parting like she's seeing not just a figure—but meaning. A puzzle piece she never knew was missing.

And then, softer:

"I hope you find what you're looking for."

From a few tents down, a sudden cheer splits the air.

"A celebration indeed," a Valkyrie calls, snatching two wooden mugs from a platter as she spins. Her voice is low and rich, full of mischief. "Not every nocturn sees mates united under Avalon's moon in the middle of war."

Laughter and toasts follow, mugs raised high, bodies swaying. Two Valkyrie kiss in the middle of the path, arms tight around each other, and the camp erupts in more cheers. Pipes and drums strike up from somewhere unseen, the beat infectious, wild.

Pandora smiles but doesn't stop. Her steps don't falter, don't aim. She just walks like she's always trusted fate to know the way.

I keep close, the dream pressing warm against my skin, too clear to feel imagined.

Two Valkyrie pass with towering platters—roasted skewers and glitter-dusted sweets. Pandora plucks a cube of golden cake from the edge and pops it into her mouth.

"Your Majesty." The servers bow.

She nods and brushes crumbs from her fingers as she walks.

Then the air shifts.

The celebration fades a little behind us, and I hear something else—soft, steady, unmistakable. I glance sideways. A tent flap hangs loose, and inside, a beautiful scene is unfolding.

I shouldn't look—but I absolutely do.

Inside, a blonde Valkyrie is on her knees, breathless, swaying, one hand twisting her own nipple while the other works between the thighs of the woman beneath her—dark-haired, stretched flat, mouth buried in the blonde's cunt, devouring her like she's starving for it.

The blonde moans, grinding down, eyes fluttering open—and she sees Pandora.

"My queen," she breathes, not missing a beat.

Fuck.

Pandora just nods and keeps walking. Not shocked. Not disturbed. Just... familiar.

I linger a second longer, because of course I do—just in time to see the dark-haired Valkyrie smack the blonde's ass and pull her tighter onto her mouth.

A groan splits the air like silk tearing.

God. This is their life. Not all war and carnage. Just... living.

As I move to catch up, I notice Pandora has veered slightly off the main path, drawn toward a small pen nestled between two wide tents. Inside, a shadowmare the color of deepest night lies stretched along the ground, her flanks still heaving. Her mane is like smoke given shape, and her coat shimmers faintly—darkness woven into flesh. At her side, a newborn foal stands on legs too long for her body, trembling and wet with birth. She sways once, then steadies.

Pandora pauses at the edge of the pen, hands folded in front of her. She says nothing at first—just watches, quiet, reverent.

Then, to the stablekeeper who stands nearby, she murmurs, "What a happy omen she is."

The fae nods, brushing straw from his tunic. "Indeed. Such beautiful life in such dark times."

Pandora touches the top of the pen, her expression unreadable for a moment before she turns and continues on.

I linger, stunned. It's nearly the exact thing Orion said when he discovered Omen was with foal.

Omen? Could that actually be her? Orion's shadowmare —his familiar, his terror on wings?

But she's just a foal.

Or... maybe not *just* anything at all.

I shake the thought and jog to catch up, heart still echoing with that one word.

Another tent flaps open ahead, and a man steps out.

And I stop walking.

He's tall. Broad. Shirtless, with brown trousers slung low on his hips and thick leather suspenders hugging his shoulders. His skin is dusted with sweat. His chest is lean and muscular, ink running in clean lines down his arms. There's a tuft of dark hair on his chest, a trail leading down.

He lifts a wooden mug and drinks deep, throat flexing.

My mouth is... open. Fully open.

Who the actual fuck is that?

Then he glances up—right as Pandora approaches.

"Anything from your spies?" she asks.

He lowers the mug, wiping his mouth with the back of

his hand. "They're still watching. No movement yet," he says, voice a low scrape. "But you'll be the first to know."

Giggles spill from the tent behind him. A teasing voice sings, "Merliiiin?"

Wait. What?

My brain short-circuits.

No.

No, absolutely not.

That is not Merlin.

That's not the old man with a beard like a fleece blanket and eyebrows that twitch whenever he's about to say something insane. That's not the barefoot swamp cryptid who collects shiny rocks and sometimes forgets pants.

This man? This absolute sin-stained god of a man? Is Merlin?

Holy motherfucking shit.

A redheaded Valkyrie struts into the tent opening—completely naked. Curved, glowing, hair gleaming like firelight. "Merlin," she purrs, back arched. "You're not finished with us yet, are you?"

Another redhead joins her—her twin. She cups her sister's breast and sucks her nipple into her mouth like it's the only thing worth tasting.

A third waits behind them, lounging in the shadows.

Triplets.

I swallow. Hard. Oh my god. The redhead triplets. They were real.

Merlin doesn't blink. Just nods to Pandora, already backing toward the tent. "Duty calls," he murmurs.

But then—his eyes cut to me.

And they hold.

About three seconds too long as he takes one step back toward the tent, then another.

I freeze. It's not coincidence. He saw me. He *fucking* saw me.

He turns, dragging his eyes away from me, and returns to his guests. "Now, who has been a bad girl?" His voice is deep with dark promise, and giggles erupt.

I nearly choke on my spit as Pandora keeps walking. I follow, pulse still hammering from the unexpected visual trauma.

We walk on a moment when I feel a tremor. Faint. A whisper under my feet. I almost think I imagined it—until Pandora stops.

She turns her head slightly, the way someone does when they're trying to catch a sound that's not meant to be heard.

I go still.

Another tremor. Stronger this time—and real.

Pandora's gaze lifts. Her whole body shifts—subtle tension, the way a storm senses itself before it breaks.

Then she turns. Sharp. Intent.

And walks down a new row of tents.

I don't even hesitate. Whatever it is... she felt it too.

And I think we're about to find out what the fuck it means.

CHAPTER 52
tana

Another tremor ripples underfoot. This one stronger than the last.

Pandora's pace shifts—no longer a stroll. It's a purpose-driven march. I scramble to keep up, breath catching as the narrow rows of tents begin to thin, giving way to larger ones spaced farther apart. Command tents, I realize. Perimeter dwellings. The kind where leaders sleep. Or the wounded lie waiting for the gods to make a decision.

Two Valkyrie stand rigid outside one of them, eyes flicking sharply toward Pandora as she approaches. Tension pulls at their shoulders. One straightens as if to intercept her.

"Your Majesty—"

Pandora doesn't even glance at her.

The second Valkyrie, stationed closer to the flap, shifts a foot into her path.

"Please, Your Grace—"

"Stand aside," Pandora orders.

The weight in her voice stops time.

The Valkyrie hesitates, clearly torn, but finally steps back. Her eyes flick to her sister-in-arms, a silent exchange that says everything they don't dare speak aloud.

Pandora pushes through the flap.

I follow without thinking.

The air inside is heavy. Still. Too still.

A handful of Valkyrie crowd the tent, silent but tense, their faces drawn tight with unease. Several stand gathered near a bed, forming a barrier with their bodies—until Pandora parts them like water.

"Your Majesty, we can explain—" one begins, voice high and cracking.

Pandora raises a single hand. The Valkyrie silences instantly.

She moves forward.

I follow her path, but it isn't until I shift to the side, squeezing through the lantern-lit shadows, that I see what she sees.

And the breath is ripped from my lungs.

It's her.

The woman from the vision. The one with the dark hair, the tilted chin, the familiar wildness in her features. The one who looks so achingly close to my mother that my throat closes.

She lies in the bed, pale and sweating, curls stuck to her forehead. Her nightdress clings to her chest and shoulders, soaked through. Her arms cradle something small and still.

A baby.

No more than minutes old.

The woman's eyes are shut, her lips parted in shallow, fevered breaths. Her fingers twitch protectively over the infant's back.

I take a step closer, and my knees nearly give out.

Because it isn't just resemblance anymore. It isn't just shared features.

This woman is blood.

And I'm staring at the past like it never truly left.

Or maybe like it's been waiting for me all along.

The woman stirs. Her lips part. Her voice is a rasp.

"Please, Pandora," she croaks. "Please... don't."

Pandora approaches with slow, deliberate steps—like she's easing toward a frightened animal, one wrong move from flight. The Valkyrie part for her instinctively, their formation breaking as their queen passes.

The woman's arms tighten around the infant.

"It just... happened," she says again, but her voice cracks. Her eyes glisten, and the tears that swell there make Pandora soften—not visibly, but something in her posture eases.

Pandora speaks gently. "Eira." The name lands soft as a vow. "You have broken no law of Avalon. Only the creed of your sisters-in-arms."

Eira sobs.

Pandora kneels at the bedside, her gaze pinned not to the woman—but to the child she's holding.

Then she reaches out, laying her palm against the baby's tiny head.

And that's when I understand.

The tent lights shift. No—the air itself does.

That soft moonlight glow that always radiates from Pandora—Avalon's blessing made flesh—now emanates from the child too. It glows from her skin where Pandora touches her. Faint. Ethereal. Undeniable.

Gasps ripple around the tent.

"It's true," one Valkyrie breathes.

Another lowers her head and murmurs a quiet prayer to the moon.

Eira clutches the infant tighter. "Please... don't harm her," she whispers. "Please."

Pandora's hand moves, now resting gently on the woman's head. "Do you think so little of your queen?" she asks, and this time, when she smiles, it's real. Wide and warm and devastating.

"It is already written in the stars," Pandora says softly. She settles herself on the edge of the bed, voice a hush shared only between mother and monarch. "When the stars reclaim me, my crown will turn to ash with me. The realm will choose a new queen."

She looks down at the baby again, a bittersweet smile tugging at her lips.

"It seems it already has."

Her hand strokes gently across the baby's head. The glow appears again—brighter this time—but only where Pandora's fingers touch her skin. It pulses faintly, then settles.

But something changes.

Pandora's expression darkens.

The soft lines of awe on her face harden into concern. Her breathing shifts—shallow, tight. Worry creeps into the set of her jaw, the tremble of her lashes. Something's wrong.

She lifts her gaze to Eira, and her voice is a whisper laced with urgency. "You must run."

Eira blinks. "What?"

"You must go." Pandora is breathing faster now. "Take her and leave the realm. My cousin cannot know she exists."

Shock fractures through the tent. The baby stirs, sensing the tension.

Pandora keeps speaking, each word landing like a blow.

"Morgause will stop at nothing to wear the crown. If she knows you carry the line of the queen—if she knows this child is touched by Avalon—she will kill you. Kill your baby. You must leave. Now."

"Where?" a Valkyrie demands, panic rising. "The portals are sealed!"

"There's no way out," another argues. "The crossing has collapsed—how can they leave?"

Pandora rises without a word, her face unreadable.

She crosses the tent to a chair tucked in the corner— where a long sword leans. A sword I now know well.

Realmbreaker.

She lifts it like it weighs nothing.

"The lake did not gift you a sword of legend for nothing," Pandora says, her voice steel and stars. "This is your destiny." She looks down at the child. "It is her fate."

Then a violent crack splits the sky. Wind roars into the tent like a living thing. Flames gutter. Shadows stretch long and violent. The baby wails. Eira curls around her child. Pandora throws herself over them both.

The gust fades as quickly as it came, and silence returns.

Then Pandora looks toward the tent's entrance, spine going rigid. Her lips part.

"She knows," she whispers.

Terror blooms in her eyes.

"And she's coming."

The camp explodes into movement.

Pandora steps from the tent like a storm given skin— calm, poised, deadly. Her hair is plaited back in sharp lines. Fae rush to her with each piece of her armor, fastening burnished plates to her arms, her chest, her shoulders, while she issues orders without raising her voice. The steel crown that arcs across her brow casts shadow down her face, making her look half moon, half war.

Inside, the tent becomes a battlefield of its own. The mother—Eira—tightens the buckles of her leathers with the help of her sisters. Her nightdress lies in a puddle on the floor, forgotten. The baby stays wrapped to her chest, bound by a deep-green sash, tucked close beneath a fitted chestplate.

"You're sure you can ride?" one of the Valkyrie asks.

Eira grips the hilt of her sword. Her jaw is set with purpose. "For her?" She glances down. "To the ends of the realm."

Outside, the world readies for war.

Valkyrie take to the skies in streaks of silver and shadow. Others mount duskbanes, their vast, downy wings tucked tight as hooves pound the dry earth in rhythm with the thunder rolling overhead. The ground itself seems to tense, as if Avalon is holding its breath.

Time fractures. Everything is happening too fast—and not fast enough.

I walk quickly behind Pandora, trying to take it all in. Trying to find the thread of this vision the realm meant me to follow. Maybe it's not one thing. Maybe it's everything.

Overhead, the sky darkens. A vortex of black clouds coils and builds like a living creature—ominous and slow and endless. Lightning veins through it, a spiderweb of warning. A night of ruin. Of reckoning.

"She is nearly here," Pandora says without looking back. Her voice is even. Certain.

They don't ride far—only to the edge of the field beyond

the camp. An open stretch of scorched, cracked plain. No barriers. No walls. Just fate, waiting.

Rows of Valkyrie stand ready—wings tight, blades out. The front line of Avalon's fury.

Pandora takes her place behind them, flanked by four. Two I recognize as the tent guards. The third was with Eira at her bedside. Her generals.

And then Merlin steps forward.

Gone is the strange old man who talks to weather and forgets his boots. He's younger now—barely—but the power around him thrums like a storm trapped beneath skin. His robes are sapphire, shot through with silver, and he walks like he's carved from prophecy. His staff is the same— tall, twisted, tipped with a glowing orb that swirls like a storm in miniature.

"She brings her entire dark army," Merlin says.

Pandora doesn't flinch. "I know."

He looks at the baby in Eira's arms—and something shifts in his expression. Awe. Wonder.

"Amazing," he whispers. "You are doing the right thing."

Eira's hands tremble as she adjusts the sash at her chest.

"Your daughter's daughter's daughter will one day return," Merlin says softly. "The realm's chosen queen of Avalon. Worry not, mother. I can see it is foretold."

"But how?" Eira asks, voice cracking. "How will she know to come back?"

Pandora answers, eyes fixed on the storm.

"When the time is right, a door will open. And she will walk through it. The realm will provide a way."

The wind howls. The ground groans like it's in pain.

They all turn toward the storm on the horizon. Closer now. Closer by the second.

"You must go. Swiftly. To Starfall."

The generals nod. No fear. Just resolve.

They help Eira mount her duskbane, the baby tucked tight to her chest. The three generals do the same—each atop war-horses with ember eyes and oil-slick manes.

Pandora steps forward, her sword in hand.

"I fear this will be the last flight of the Valkyrie," she says. Her voice cuts cleanly through the wind. "And should we fall, you are the last line. The fate of Avalon is depending on you."

The women bow their heads. Then they ride.

A crack splits the sky above.

Merlin lifts his staff. Inside the orb, the storm coils in sync with the one overhead—feeding it. Calling it.

Some Valkyrie leap into the sky, wings flaring wide before they vanish into the dark.

And all I can do is stand there, heart in my throat, watching the end of a legend begin.

CHAPTER 53
tana

Eira rides into legend.

The thundering hooves of her duskbane—and those of the three generals at her side—fade into the rising wind. A line drawn in the dirt. A promise carried toward the last hope of Starfall.

I don't follow. I can't.

Something is happening here, and I have no way to follow.

The storm that churns above us growls low and guttural, like a throat clearing before a scream. The black clouds on the horizon ripple—shimmering like oil over water—and the battlefield holds its breath. Every sword glints. Every wing twitches.

Then comes the sound.

Not thunder. Not wind.

A growl. Deep. Inhuman. Hungry.

It rolls across the scorched plain in a wave that makes the bones beneath my skin rattle. The hairs on my arms stand. Even the duskbanes shift uneasily, snorting and stomping as if they, too, know something unnatural approaches.

The wall of darkness ahead begins to lift.

Not like mist—but like a curtain.

And there, walking from it like she's arriving late to her own coronation, is the ghost from the forest.

The specter who whispered promises into my sleep.

The thing that should have been myth.

Morgause.

Her body is flesh now, but it might as well be shadow. She's draped in a gown the color of a bleeding eclipse, fabric trailing behind her like smoke. Her long hair floats in the air as if gravity is too afraid to touch her.

Eyes like eclipses and a smile that doesn't reach them. Her skin the color of bleached bone, stretched over sharp, knowing angles. A face made for worship or ruin—maybe both.

As if the realm carved her from shadow and sorrow and crowned her with a hunger that never ends.

Pandora takes a step forward. No hesitation. No fear.

The wind tosses her braids behind her like flags. Her sword is already in hand.

"Cousin," Pandora calls. "You look well for a corpse."

Morgause stops and smiles like a snake shedding skin.

"You always were the pretty one," she says. Her voice is smoke and broken glass. "But look at you now—brave little queen, playing martyr on a pyre no one asked you to build."

Pandora doesn't flinch. "Turn back. Return to your court of nightmares and you'll be spared."

Morgause tilts her head and laughs. "Oh, darling. That was your mistake. You thought I left. But I've been here all along. Whispering. Waiting. And now?"

Her smile widens, splitting her face with something that doesn't belong to mortals or monsters.

"Now I've come to collect what's mine."

Pandora takes one step forward, raising her sword to the sky.

"Then you'll have to take it."

"Oh, sweet cousin." Her voice drips with promise. "I intend to."

The air shudders with war cries and wind.

Morgause lifts a single, pale hand. Her forces surge forward like a black tide—silent at first, then roaring as they run. A wave of bodies. Fangs. Steel. Shadows with shape and eyes that burn.

The Valkyrie hold.

Not a single blade drawn yet.

Only the archers move—

Moonlight bows drawn tight, their arrows humming with magic. The first volley whistles high, a silver arc that slices the storm-heavy sky.

When they land, Moonfire erupts in lines, veins of silver flame carving across the earth. The front ranks of Morgause's army scream—bone-chilling even beneath the thunder—as they burn from the inside out, bodies buckling, twisting, collapsing to ash.

But they keep coming.

They climb over the burning. They eat pain like candy.

A second line of Valkyrie archers steps forward.

A hundred more arrows soar. Then another. And another.

Each volley punches through the flames, the arrowheads igniting midair and hammering the front lines—striking like warhammers more than projectiles. I watch in disbelief as soldiers are flung backward, limbs rag-dolling from the force of the impact.

God. These weren't arrows.

They were declarations.

And still—still—the dark army comes.

Behind the front, Merlin lifts his staff.

His lips never stop moving, mouth full of old power.

He draws a circle in the air, then another—faster now. His staff swirls above him like a pendulum with fury, whipping the air into shrieking winds.

Lightning crawls across the clouds like veins bursting under skin. The sky howls. The ground shakes.

And then—

The storm breaks.

A vortex drops from the clouds like a god's fist, punching into the earth with a deafening crack. The impact knocks enemies off their feet—some trampled, some swallowed by the opening ground.

And from the storm above—they fall.

The Valkyrie.

Those who had vanished into the clouds before the charge.

They drop from the black like avenging stars—dozens of them, wings folded, bodies tight. And as they descend, each one births a tornado, wind screaming outward in furious spirals.

Funnel after funnel rips across the battlefield, devouring Morgause's army in toothless mouths of sheer force.

I can barely breathe.

The storm. The fire. The earth screaming.

The death. The beauty of it.

Then a horn sounds.

A single call. Deep. Final.

Pandora's charge begins.

She holds a curved horn toward the sky and blows, its deep bellow commanding her warriors into the fray.

And the Valkyrie obey her call. Hundreds of them—silver and bone, winged and armored, weapons raised.

This is it.

The last flight of the Valkyrie.

They run to die.

To protect one baby. One bloodline.

One last hope.

I can only watch—heart racing, eyes wide—as I search for clues, commit everything to memory, knowing something that happens tonight is important for the war I'm going to return to.

The air is thick with smoke and shadow. Screams echo across the plain. Magic crackles in every breath.

Behind me, the scorched trail of the duskbanes still glows—embers and ash marking the path Eira and her three protectors cut through the night. Part of me wants to follow. To see if they make it. How they make it. But something in me knows I can't—not yet. This isn't done.

War surrounds me now.

Silver-winged Valkyrie clash midair with monsters made of rot and bone. Their blades spark with moonlight. Their cries are defiant, but their numbers are thinning. The darkness keeps coming, and worse—it keeps regrowing.

Merlin stands at the edge of the battle, still channeling the storm—holding back more than half of Morgause's forces with nothing but his will. Pandora is too deep in her own fight to see what I do—what's creeping around the edge of the storm.

Morgause.

Not a general. Not a queen. A force.

Her eyes are fixed on him now, her mouth a hard line of fury.

She doesn't waste time.

As Merlin whips his staff into another arc, summoning a second cyclone from the heavens, Morgause lifts her arms. No chant. No incantation. Just will. The clouds above her turn wrong—blacker than night, thick and churning with something oily. Something alive.

It isn't just darkness.

It's tainted.

It's the Obscura.

Her. Not Eira. Not the sister who fled. It was never her. The door wasn't opened; it was already here. Morgause is the door. And it obeys her.

She stares at Merlin like he's already dead.

He sees her now—but too late.

He gathers both storms—two raging tornadoes. Lightning flashes from the tips like wild fangs.

With a wordless cry, he releases them.

They charge at her like beasts let loose.

But her darkness reaches him first.

It hits like a tidal wave, a swarm of black smoke and teeth. I scream—he doesn't hear it.

The cloud surges into his mouth, his eyes, his ears—every orifice, every crack.

He falls.

Convulsing. Eyes rolled back. Fingers curling like claws.

He's being eaten from the inside out.

And everything breaks.

The Valkyrie start falling—sliced from the sky, dragged to the ground. The storm tries to fight back—cyclones smash into Morgause—but the dark around her folds in like armor. It shields her. Feeds her.

Pandora's scream rips through the fight just before a blinding ray of moonlight slams into the battlefield, searing the dark like acid. It washes over Merlin's body—burning the Obscura away, burning through it. The storm's roar becomes a wail, as if it's mourning the wizard who manifested it.

Pandora is on her knees, cradling him.

"Merlin?" Her voice cracks. "Please."

He doesn't answer.

She looks up, and I see the truth in her eyes. This battle is lost. Her forces—her sisters—are dying around her. She's out of time.

But she doesn't look at the battlefield. She looks back.

Past it.

I don't know if she can see Eira and the three generals galloping for the horizon. But maybe she doesn't need to see. Maybe she can feel them.

Pandora always knew this was a losing play.

And she played it anyway.

Lose the battle. Win the war.

And she'll never know if it worked.

She looks down at Merlin—eyes closed, his breath faint—and something in her breaks.

"Go, Starling," she whispers.

The words punch the air from my lungs.

I gasp. My heart stutters.

Her eyes turn, just slightly, toward where I stand—

toward my shadow cast across the mud and blood of the field.

A silhouette beside her, tall and still.

Me.

"You need to see," Pandora says. "To watch. There is nothing more for you here."

She's speaking to me—my soul, my shadow. The part of me tethered here, stuck in this dream, or this memory, or this prophecy.

Merlin stirs.

His eyes flutter open, cloudy and unfocused. "Who are you?" he asks, voice distant.

Pandora sobs. "Merlin…"

He smiles faintly. "Hello, Merlin."

"No…" she weeps. "You are Merlin."

His smile deepens, dazed. "No, old friend. You are Merlin."

His lids flutter. His head lolls. He fades.

And so does the storm.

Pandora turns back to the battlefield as her world collapses. Her warriors are being slaughtered—Valkyrie torn from the sky, spears through wings, screams lost in the wind.

"Go," she says again. "It's almost time."

And suddenly, I know what she means—the moment I'm meant to see.

My shadow moves. Stretches. Widens.

There is a ripple, a shift, and then—wings.

Dark wings unfurl from the dirt like smoke solidifying into bone. A mane appears next—long and black, fluttering as if underwater.

Then she rises.

Omen.

A horse of shadow climbs out of the ground.

"Omen?!" I choke.

She nickers low and nudges me hard with her nose. Her wings flap once, stirring my hair. Her eyes flash silver as she stomps the earth.

And I remember.

I remember when Omen crossed the veil at Thornspire and cast her shadow onto the wall to warn us—and when Orion told her, "Stay with the queen."

It seems she listened and followed me here.

"You're such a good fucking horse," I whisper.

I swing onto her back. The shadow-forged reins form in my hands.

"Let's go." I barely breathe the words out, and Omen obeys.

With one powerful leap and two slamming beats of her wings, we are airborne.

The ground falls away beneath us—battle, fire, screams. My body slams down into her back from the force of our climb, stomach lurching as we tear through the smoke and storm—

racing toward the sky.

Toward whatever waits when we reach the ground again.

I look back just once and watch Pandora rising.

Her crown has fallen, her armor is cracked, and her body is streaked in blood, both silver and black. But her spine is straight. Her chin is high.

The only one left standing on the battlefield.

All around her, the Valkyrie she commanded lie still—bodies strewn across the charred plain like fallen stars. Avalon's mightiest warriors. Her army, all gone.

And still, she lifts her sword.

Moonlight bursts from her like a star being born—blinding, furious, final.

It slams into the earth, rising high into a gleaming wall between her and the monsters coming for her.

On the other side, Morgause's legions scream and roar and surge. They'll break through—of course they will—but not before she makes them bleed for every inch.

Pandora will hold the line alone.

And I know she survives this night. She lives on, marries, and has four daughters. One of them births a son—

a prince who will grow to be my mate.

Who will one day kneel before me and call me queen.

Who is ready to die for me.

Just as she is.

I should turn back and watch her sacrifice—how she fights, how she holds the line. I want to.

But I fly on.

The duskbanes carry the legacy she hopes to protect—four horses charging through stormlight toward Starfall. Eira rides at the center, her cloak whipping in the wind, her face set like stone. One Valkyrie rides at her flank, two more at her sides, and they do not slow. They do not falter.

They ride like the end is chasing them.

Because it is.

Behind me, I feel it before I see it—the moment the wall of moonlight finally breaks.

It shatters with a sound like stars screaming.

And the dark comes.

A wave of endless night surges over the hills, devouring light, life—everything. It's too fast.

Omen screams beneath me, wings flaring wide to gain more height, and I clutch the reins tighter. Ahead of me, the castle rises higher with every beat of her wings—Starfall looming in the distance like a beacon of hope carved in stone and memory.

But the darkness is catching up.

And the Valkyrie feel it too. The two riding at Eira's side turn, their horses' hooves digging into the dirt, sparking against the scorched earth as they wrench them around, racing back toward the tide of shadows that threatens to consume us all.

They call out, spurring their horses faster, long hair and cloaks billowing behind them.

They don't hesitate. Don't even look to each other.

They simply move, as if the choice were never in question.

With seamless grace, they rise from their saddles, balancing atop the broad backs of their duskbanes like warriors sculpted from moonlight and fury. For a single breath, they stand silhouetted against the storm, wings unfurling with a flash of silver that catches the last shards of starlight.

And then—they leap.

Arcing high, they climb into the air, spears gripped in hand, their wings slicing upward as they split apart—just enough to draw something between them. At first, it's only a glimmer—a thread of light, tenuous and thin.

But it stretches. Grows.

A chain of radiant energy forms between their outstretched hands, pulsing brighter with every beat of their wings. It glows so fiercely now that it casts the battlefield in eerie twilight.

Then it begins to shift.

The light bends, twists, takes shape—no longer just magic but memory.

Ghostly figures emerge from the chain—Valkyrie long fallen, sisters from a thousand battles past. They rise in silence, called forth by the courage of the living, drawn into the world once more by duty, by love, by sacrifice.

The spectral host expands, spiraling behind the two warriors in a helix of luminous power. Together, they dive—spinning faster and tighter, a single stream of vengeance wrapped in moonfire and mourning.

The darkness surges forward to meet them, hungry and endless.

But so are they.

The spear of starlight cuts through the tide like a blade through flesh, parting the Obscura with searing heat. A path opens in the wake of their fury—just long enough to glimpse the shattered field beyond, the dying sky, and the castle still standing.

They don't falter.

They aim for the heart of it.

For Morgause.

The sorceress raises her head too late, shadows writhing around her like serpents.

The twin spears strike her chest with impossible force, and the moment of impact is blinding. A shockwave erupts, starlight exploding outward in a ring of pure energy that blasts back the dark and rattles the earth beneath us.

Omen's wings shudder from the force, and I clutch her tighter, my vision white at the edges.

When I blink the brightness away—there's only smoke.

No Valkyrie. No ghostly chain.

Only ash curling in the wind.

But Morgause is no longer untouched.

She staggers to her knees, clutching at her chest, the fabric of her robes burned away in places, her skin smoking. Her magic flickers erratically, like a candle fighting against a storm.

She's hurt.

For the first time, I see it with my own eyes—Morgause, the nightmare, the whisper in my mind—is not invincible. She can be wounded.

But the moment doesn't last.

Rage floods her face. Her mouth opens in a scream, sharp and guttural and full of fury so raw it sends a tremor through the air.

And the shadows respond.

A new torrent of Obscura tears itself from the ground, from her outstretched hands, from the sky itself. It surges forward like a tidal wave of teeth and rot and unholy sound, bearing down on the final riders fleeing toward Starfall's gates.

They gave everything.

And still, all they could buy their sister was a moment of time.

Omen banks low overhead, her wings casting great sweeping shadows across the battlefield, racing now just above the three remaining duskbanes below. The wind screams past us as we ride the currents higher, closer.

Below, the final guard at Eira's side glances back—and sees it.

The wave.

The darkness swelling again, hungrier than before, flooding toward them like a plague-tide that cannot be outpaced.

Her expression doesn't waver. She turns back toward her sister-in-arms. The two lock eyes, still thundering forward, duskbanes foaming at the bit.

"I will meet you again in the stars," she says, her voice carried by the wind, just loud enough to reach Eira. "And if the goddess wills it—on the battlefield once more."

It isn't panic. It's a vow.

She pulls the reins hard, letting her horse fall back by several strides, and then she moves—flipping off her saddle in one fluid motion. Her boots slam into the ground with a force that cracks the earth, her wings catching behind her to slow the impact. She skids in the dirt, digging deep trenches in her wake.

I turn in the saddle, twisting around to watch.

She doesn't hesitate.

Reaching behind her, she grabs something—nothing visible at first—and then her arms tense. Her back curves. Muscles strain. Her boots slip for half a second, but she finds her stance again and pulls.

At first, I don't understand what she's doing. There's no weapon in her hands. No visible magic.

And then I see it.

Moonlight.

Strands of it, thick and shimmering like molten silver, begin to rise from the ground around her feet. Not conjured—but claimed. As if it had been resting here for centuries, waiting for someone worthy to wield it.

She swings the first strand wide, and the movement forces the others to follow. The light moves like rope—heavy ropes, impossible ropes—and she spins them over her head with brutal momentum until they transform into whips.

Twin arcs of silver fire that crack against the air with the sound of thunder.

She turns, lashes them toward the darkness. They strike with a sizzle that lights the sky, the force behind them carving deep into the shadows, sending bursts of lightning scattering like shrapnel through the ranks of Obscura.

She doesn't stop.

She dances—flicking, twisting, her body a perfect conduit of wrath and grace. Her wings flare wide, and with a single violent snap, she sends half a dozen feathers slicing into the dark like throwing knives, each one honed and lethal.

And with each strike, she begins to glow.

Not with magic.

With power.

Pure, ancient, terrifying power.

The glow builds in her skin, her eyes, her hair—until she looks less like a Valkyrie and more like a star plummeting toward the earth. A living nova. Her body no longer a vessel of flesh and bone but a fuse, lit and nearing detonation.

And I know. I feel it deep in my gut.

She's going to burn herself alive to stop what's coming.

I can't look away.

The heat reaches me even from above. My throat tightens. My fingers clutch Omen's reins harder, the hair on my arms rising as her light intensifies to an unbearable white.

She lets out one final cry—not of pain, but of victory.

And then—

She releases it.

A pulse of brilliance tears through the battlefield, surging forward in a wide, devastating arc. It cuts into Morgause's forces like a scythe, vaporizing everything in its path. The shockwave rocks Omen in the air, forcing her to flap hard to steady us.

Below, the Valkyrie is gone.

Only a scorch mark remains where she stood.

But Morgause stumbles.

The sorceress reels back, struck hard by the blast. Her hood is half-torn, her lips bloodied, her magic flickering like a dying flame. She clutches her side, where the burst hit hardest, and for a moment—just one moment—she falters.

Behind me, Eira looks back.

She's seen it. Felt it.

And she knows what it cost.

Her mouth hardens. She leans low over her duskbane's neck, heels digging in deep. The beast roars, its legs pumping harder, lungs flaring, finding a final surge of strength born from grief and rage and purpose.

They ride.

And I fly above them, heart pounding, knowing this isn't the end.

It's only the beginning of the last stand.

Eira rides hard—goddess, she rides like the fury of the realm is at her heels, and maybe it is.

Behind her, Morgause's wrath sharpens. Her screams fracture the sky. Darkness hurtles through the air in jagged bursts—streaks of pure Obscura that crackle and smoke, hammering down across the fields like cursed cannon fire.

But Eira keeps moving. Dodging. Weaving. Each dodge a fraction slower than the last. She clutches the baby to her chest, every ounce of her strength bent toward keeping that tiny life out of the dark.

For a heartbeat, I think she's heading toward the caves —toward Pandora's ruins, where the broken portal lies dormant and waiting, where old magic still lingers, desperate to be called.

But no. That's not it. I know where she's going.

I've seen it.

That pile of rocks. That vacant stretch of grass where the temple hasn't yet been built. The sword isn't in the cave.

It's here.

The sword she will drive into the earth. The sword I will one day pull free.

Omen senses it too. She banks low and lands without being asked. I slide off her back, legs shaking from the ride, the air thick with grit and power. My boots barely hold steady on the grass, but I force myself upright. I have to see this.

Eira's duskbane finally slows. She swings her leg over and drops to the ground, cradling her child tighter against her chest, never missing a beat. Her wings stretch once behind her, trembling—not from weakness but with purpose, with knowing.

This is where she will make her stand.

Not in glory.

But in defiance.

She runs—runs, just hours after giving birth, sweat pouring down her face, her steps unsteady but unrelenting —toward the rocks, toward the place where legend will root itself into stone.

There's no altar. No monument. Just earth.

Just history waiting to be made.

She stops at the center. Her sword is already drawn. She plants it into the dirt beside her like a claim of intent. Her free hand reaches to her thigh, pulling a dagger I know too well.

The same one strapped to me now.

Orion's gift. The one I thought Hephaestus forged for me. But no—he forged it for her. And fate carried it forward.

Eira slices her palm clean and fast. Blood wells, thick and red and holy. She drops the dagger into the dirt like an offering and grips her sword instead—Realmbreaker.

My sword.

Above us, Morgause howls. She sees the defiance. She sees the risk.

And she understands too late.

Obscura floods the field like a rising tide, ravenous and vengeful, reaching for mother and daughter alike.

But Eira doesn't flinch.

She holds the baby close, her voice calm as the storm builds behind her. She begins to speak—words I don't recognize, but I feel them, carved in bone, etched in blood. A promise made beneath moonlight to the goddess who watches and waits.

"I give what I was given. Immortality born of starlight. Power pulled from the tide. Let it feed the blade. Let it shape the way."

The baby stirs. Eira cups her cheek with one trembling hand, her expression softening even as the sky screams above her. She looks up, eyes hardening as she locks gazes with Morgause.

"My line will not end here," she promises. "Fate will reopen this door, and through it... war will come for you."

Her wings begin to burn.

Not with fire—but with light. The edges fray like paper kissed by flame, curling and blackening, disintegrating into stardust as the energy pulls from her body into the blade. Her soul. Her eternity.

She grips Realmbreaker with both hands. Blood races down her wrists, trailing the hilt, tracing the runes that haven't yet been carved.

She screams—not in fear.

In fury.

And drives the sword down.

It's the moment I saw when I fell into the dark river. The slow-motion moment. The silent scream, the rage behind the thrust of her sword that seems to take minutes as I watch it inch closer and closer to the stone.

The darkness curls in—thick, coiling, sentient. It rises around her like smoke, hungrily reaching for her baby, for the blade, for the last breath of resistance in Avalon.

But Eira doesn't waver.

She holds fast, her hands locked around the hilt, blood still running down the blade as the last of her strength burns into the metal. I watch as her wings fall away—ashen ribbons disintegrating into stardust. Her power sears through the sword like oil over flame, and the rock beneath it begins to glow, ready to accept it.

The image of Eira flickers and changes.

One by one, they appear—mother and daughter, life after life. Each pair a link in a chain, bound by blood and sacrifice and fate. Hand in hand, passing something down—until the final two stand before me.

My mother.

And me.

Small. Innocent. Unaware of what waits for me in the dark.

The shadows crowd closer. Eira's hands remain firm around the hilt.

And just as the tip pierces the stone, I see one final image—

Me.

Alone.

Facing the dark.

And then a flood—a final promise that sears into my chest, burning me like my heart is on fire.

Everything dissolves into nothing as radiant white moonlight explodes around me, endless and blinding.

CHAPTER 54
tana

The moment the blade pierces the glowing root, the world snaps back into place.

Moonlight ignites—erupts—from the sword in my hands, not just pouring out but surging, alive and divine, exploding in every direction like a star breaking through the earth.

I don't see it so much as feel it. The force tears through me, through the ground beneath me, racing across the battlefield in waves of silver fire. It hits the swamp fae at the lake's edge just before they reach the line of sprite warriors —brave, foolish, glowing with magic and fear—and throws the enemy back like dolls caught in a gale.

The Morrigan stops feeding on Shade the moment the moonlight rips away from me. She pauses, still holding the Lord of Shadow in the air, her darkness having drained the last of his soul, devouring it.

She drops him like a sack of soiled food. His body decomposes in an instant, rotting before turning to ash and blowing across the battlefield where so many of his assassins are gone.

Those who haven't been devoured by the Morrigan are slammed down and pinned beneath the light. Held. Crushed. Purified.

Everything stops.

The Starfall warriors, the surviving Briar Court soldiers, even the fae locked in bloodied duels—every one of them turns. Every head tilts toward the center of the battlefield where I now stand, surrounded by a pulsing dome of silver radiance.

Not because of who I am, but because they can no longer deny what I am.

Chosen. Anointed.

And still—the moonlight keeps pushing outward. Reaching. Searching.

I feel it brush against something distant. A barrier cloaked in shadow, far beyond the battlefield.

A shield.

A prison.

And behind it—I feel them.

Our allies. The ones who came to fulfill their oaths and are trapped.

Gloamreach, and the Lord of Twilight who was so adamant in his declaration against Thorne. The Stone Fae of Cairnvail bound by bargain. Held back, not by failure, but by treachery.

Shade.

He not only sent assassins to slaughter me under cover of alliance—he sealed the gates, locking our strongest behind a wall of shadow to keep them from reaching me. From reaching us.

The fury rises like a second heartbeat.

And the moonlight answers it.

The next pulse of power races across the realm, faster than breath, faster than sound—and shatters the shield of shadow as if it were nothing more than smoke.

The air clears. The path opens. Their swords can rise again.

The power still sings through the sword, static dancing across the blade, whispering with the voice of every mother who came before me since Eira.

I walk forward, each step deliberate, crushing moss beneath my boots as I cross the ruined lawn toward the traitor.

Toward the would-be king who marched to my gates with an army.

Who threatened my people and came to take me, wanting to make me bow to him.

Not tonight.

Not ever.

Thorne is on his back, thrown there by the initial blast of light. His face is streaked with ash and blood, one hand raised as if to ward off more. But it won't save him now.

I stop above him, raise the sword, and point it directly at his throat.

The tip sizzles with power, a bead of blood welling at his skin where the blade kisses it.

He glares up at me, still defiant, still wearing the thing he calls a crown—twisted briar and thorn woven into a grotesque mockery of something sacred.

"There are no kings in Avalon," I say, voice low. Steady. Final.

Behind me, I feel Orion approach. Not touching. Not interrupting. Just there. A wall of shadow at my back.

"Only queens rule here."

Thorne's lip curls, but he doesn't move. Doesn't speak.

"Remove your crown."

He hesitates a beat. Not because he doesn't understand, because he does. He just doesn't fucking like it. That he was wrong. Made a fool of after all his grandstanding.

He sees the truth now: the moonlight in my hands, the sword burning with magic no mortal should be able to wield.

Slowly, he lifts his hand and removes the crown. He drops it in the dirt with an unsatisfying thud.

"Now…" I say, blade unwavering. "Kneel."

His jaw clenches. He looks at me like he'd rather die.

But I press the sword harder to his throat, and he feels it then—the heat, the light, the weight of Avalon itself behind me. "I have no problem spreading the ash of your remains across this battlefield, Thorne."

His fight drains out of him like smoke, and finally he lowers his eyes.

And kneels.

The realm holds its breath, but I don't, because now I know.

I know what's consuming Avalon, and I know exactly where it is.

Moonlight radiates from me; my sword continues to pulse around the realm, and it's as if I can see every rise and divot of the land. I'm being pulled toward the area where I know this plague is lurking, waiting. The Wastelands.

Rot fills my mouth as the moonlight shield races toward it, and already I know what I'll find before I get there: a wall of dark power. Warded. A massive glamour that I can feel vibrating all the way from where my boots are planted on the battlefield.

Without having ever seen it, it's as if I know what's waiting behind the veil.

And why the realm has suffered so long in silence.

It wasn't weakness.

It wasn't failure.

It was the cost of waiting—of keeping that door sealed until the bloodline returned, until the sword remembered its name and called to the ancestor destined to wield it. Until I stood here.

And no man will have the power to stop what is going to come. Especially the sad little man kneeling in front of me.

"Fate will reopen this door," Eira had said, "and through it... war will come for you."

I hold Thorne's stare for a beat too long—long enough for him to shift, just slightly, just enough, like he suddenly realizes how close I am to driving that blade through his heart anyway.

But then I turn and sheath the sword, walking toward Starfall.

Not to rest. Not to rebuild. But to prepare.

Because the door is open now.

And war is here.

The dungeons of Starfall are full—the belly of the castle groaning with traitors to the crown. The air down there is thick with damp and iron, the moans of the condemned echoing through the corridors like a dying song.

Thorne is held in the blackened cell that once confined Demeter—the traitor queen who traded her soul for a bargain with darkness. He keeps as far as he can from the corner where the blight still stains the stone, where the moonlight refused to reach during her final hours.

The fae ignore her name and refuse to speak it. Not since the day she died and the castle walls began to hum with her curse. But I can feel it—the faint pull of it beneath my skin. The echo of a queen who once believed she could have Avalon by destroying it.

Now, another queen bears the weight of what's left.

I lie on my side, the sheets tangled around my legs. Orion sleeps beside me, his breathing slow and steady, the shadows at the edges of the room quiet and still. I watch him—watch the scar that splits his eyebrow, the three gashes that mar his scalp. I never even asked how he got them. Figured it was a story he'd tell when he was ready.

Now I wish I had.

I didn't tell him what happened during the blast of moonlight. That I was sent into the memory of the realm's darkest nocturn. That I walked with his grandmother and saw her call the realm's mightiest legions to lay down their lives for one thing. One little baby wrapped in a swaddling.

The fate of Avalon.

I couldn't tell him I watched them all die and the monster that came to claim them. That the realm wanted me to see it. See the history they tried to hide.

But now I understand why they did. If no one knew the baby existed, no one would look for her. No one would hunt her and give the darkness a way to claim her before her bloodline's fate could come to pass.

So they called her mother a traitor. Removed her from

murals. Never spoke of the baby who escaped only because of the realm's greatest sacrifice.

Orion said Pandora used to sit at the sword and speak to it as it rested within the stones. He believed she could hear the dark whispers of the realm, but maybe that's not it at all. Maybe she sat waiting, hoping to see the return of the realm's savior. Or maybe she laid out her regret there and prayed for forgiveness. Maybe she questioned her choices and feared that she made a mistake.

That she sent the Valkyrie to the Void for nothing. That the Obscura devoured Merlin's sanity in vain. That she was fated to watch the realm she loved so much fall into nothingness.

But the very truth is exactly what I needed for my last challenge—the test I've been fearing. The Trial of Fate.

It means I must do something he would try to talk me out of—would definitely try to stop me. And I can't allow that. The realm will see it come to pass, and if it's going to end this way, it's going to be on my terms.

He shifts slightly. His hand, still warm and possessive on my hip, tightens a fraction. A deep hum escapes him before he settles, and it stabs at my gut.

I lean forward and press a soft kiss to his lips. "Forgive me," I whisper.

The words barely exist, but they lodge like a blade in my chest.

I rise carefully, padding across the cold stone floor to the open balcony windows. The breeze is so gentle compared with the violence the battlefield just saw over the ridge.

Closing my eyes, I feel for that moonlight. I search across it until I reach the wall of darkness and open my eyes as if

I'm standing right there in front of it. In my mind, I press a hand to it, knowing a monster waits on the other side.

Morgause has been building her army all this time. The forces she had all those ages ago were powerful enough to devour the strongest warriors the realm has ever known. And I know they are only stronger now.

If we thought the battle against the darkness was going to be hard, it feels nearly impossible now.

But all I've ever known is how to beat the odds. How to look gods in the eye and drive my blade through them without blinking. And if Morgause thinks she'll be taking this realm without the biggest fight of her life, then she's fucking wrong.

A ray of moonlight follows my will and presses upon the wall. I can feel her there. Eira.

Her power. Her sacrifice.

It's what's holding the Obscura back from complete ruin. She is what gave the realm time to wait, but the Obscura is leaking through forming cracks—through weak spots in the wall of power containing the realm's greatest threat.

And I know that what happens next will bring this wall down. Will unleash the darkness and free Morgause to step into the courts of Avalon once more. To claim the crown she wanted so long ago and to end the bloodline destined to bring her down.

Well, let's get this show on the road, shall we?

Three thumps against the wall bang with each beat of my heart, sure and steady despite everything racing within me.

Knock, knock, bitch.

I send my message to the wall, hoping it travels on the moonlight and filters through the barrier of the Wastelands, then I turn and leave.

The bedchamber door groans as I ease it open, the sound dragging through my nerves. I flinch when it shuts behind me, too loud in the stillness.

I was purposeful tonight—I left my sword in my chambers so I couldn't change my mind. Couldn't wake him by accident or by weakness.

I look back once. Just once. The door, the quiet, the man inside it—all of it feels like the kind of ache that won't heal cleanly.

A single tear escapes before I can stop it. I press my hand to the door, breath shaking, and seal it with moonlight. The spell takes shape in my palm—soft, glowing, final. The barrier hums once and fades from sight.

He won't be able to follow me. Not until it's too late.

The halls of Starfall are heavy with the quiet aftermath of war. Mor has been in the kitchens since the battle ended, and the lesser fae gossip in whispers about the mountain of food Ylsa keeps cooking for her. Platters, bowls, breads— Mor devours it all. Hunger has always been her truest form of prayer. And it seems she did not worship enough on tonight's battlefield.

I move past them silently, my boots echoing on the marble as I reach the main hall.

Hypnos waits there, and I'm not surprised to see him. In fact, I think part of me suspected it.

He doesn't speak at first—only watches me, his expression unreadable. I feel the weight of his gaze, how it sees too much, how it knows.

"I have to," I say, my voice low, because we both know what I'm talking about. Neither of us needs to admit it.

He holds my stare a moment. "I know."

He's holding the *Account of Pandora* in his hands. I look at it differently now—remember how Pandora herself touched it, the way she rubbed the leather binding as though comforting an old wound.

I cross the space between us and take the book. I open it carefully, peeling back the cover. The fragile little flower is still there—pressed between the pages, its white petals veined with silver light.

Hypnos's mouth parts in surprise, though he masks it quickly.

"It's the Starling flower," I murmur, twirling it gently between my fingers. "From the Court of Dreams."

I hand it to him. He takes it reverently, his thumb brushing the stem.

"It was the Trial of the Ancients, wasn't it?" he asks.

I nod. "How did you know?"

"I am a lord of dreams. I can recognize them." Hypnos smirks. "What did you see?"

I hesitate, feeling the echo of that vision, the weight of what it revealed—and what it took. "What I needed to."

Hypnos studies me for a heartbeat, then steps aside. He bows, deep and solemn. "He will wake soon. Best not to linger."

I nod once.

And without another word, I descend the spiral staircase into the belly of Starfall—the place where queens fall or rise and the dark remembers every choice they make.

The iron stench of the dungeon clings to my skin as I

reach Thorne's cell. The torches here burn low, their light swallowed by the damp. He's sitting on the floor, back against the wall, wrists chained to the stone. His eyes lift when I stop before him, a mix of defiance and exhaustion.

I pull the key from my belt and hold it through the bars. "Go to the lakeshore," I tell him. "Near the caves of Pandora. Wait for me there."

He stares at the key, then at me, suspicion flickering across his face. "Why?"

"Because I said so."

He doesn't move. Doesn't speak. I can see the doubt warring behind his eyes, the thought that this could be a trap. But I don't repeat myself. I simply extend my hand a little farther until he finally reaches out and takes it.

I turn before he can ask anything more, my footsteps echoing as I leave him behind. He won't use the key until I'm gone, testing whether freedom is real or a trick.

The air grows colder the deeper I descend. The torchlight dances on the walls, and a low wind coils through the tunnels like breath from something ancient. It leads me down the same twisting halls Orion once led me through, when I'd demanded answers from the shadowed prince who'd stolen me from my world.

The tunnel opens into the cavern—vast, silent, its gaping mouth staring out across the realm. Mist rises from the lake below, the water rippling with the reflection of the full moon. I walk to the edge, the stones slick beneath my boots, and turn toward the mural carved into the far wall.

The Valkyries' Last Flight.

Once, it looked like legend—painted heroism, frozen

glory. But now I see the truth beneath the gilded wings and shining blades. It's not triumph. It's sacrifice. Every streak of crimson across the battlefield is blood I've smelled before. Blood I stood beside and watched spill.

Pandora stands at the mural's center, her head bowed, crown held in trembling hands. Around it, I notice tiny etched blossoms—Starling flowers, scattered like starlight.

Every choice, every death, every shattered crown—it all led here. To me. The queen Avalon chose to finish what Pandora began.

To complete the Trial of Fate.

A heart for a heart. A life for a life.

Orion told me what the Lady showed him. He tried to believe there was another way, but deep down we both know there isn't.

I must give up my mortal heart—the one that beats too fast, too fragile for this realm. I must trade it for one born of the stars, so that I can stand against what's coming.

And I know exactly how I have to do it.

I draw the sword from its scabbard. Moonlight runs down the steel like liquid silver, brighter than it's ever been. The blade hums in my hands, alive, hungry, knowing what comes next.

I look up at the moon—at Avalon's eternal witness—and feel its light pour over me.

"I take back what was given," I whisper, the words trembling through me like a prayer and a curse all at once. "Immortality born of starlight. Power pulled from the tide. Let me feed from the blade. Let it shape the way."

The cavern holds its breath as I repeat the prayer that

left my ancestor's mouth only hours ago for me. Words spoken ages ago.

I close my eyes.

Then, with every ounce of strength left in me, I drive the sword through my chest.

The impact steals the world. My breath catches, my vision shatters. The blade burns like moonfire as it pierces my heart, and the sound that leaves me is barely a gasp.

The lake roars below, the realm tips on its axis, and for one impossible moment, I feel the stars themselves lean closer to watch.

Then—everything in me goes cold.

My hands go slack around the hilt, fingers losing strength, and the weightlessness hits all at once. My body feels distant—wrong—like I've stepped outside it. Every limb drags me downward, heavy and uncooperative, while the rest of me floats somewhere far away.

I tip.

There's nothing more I can do except fall—slowly, endlessly—through air that tastes like iron and starlight.

The wind catches my hair, cool against the fever burning through me. The blade still pierces my chest, the metal searing even as my skin goes numb. My heart beats weakly against it, defiant but failing, like it hasn't realized the war is already lost.

The lake rushes up to meet me, black and shimmering. The sword slips free a breath before I strike, tumbling beside me, a streak of silver spiraling down.

The impact is brutal—like hitting stone. It knocks the air from my lungs, rips a soundless cry from my throat. Needles of cold pierce every inch of me as the water swallows me whole.

Then silence.

I sink, and the pain blurs into something softer. The lake folds around me like a satin sheet drawn over overheated skin—cool, smooth, almost kind. My limbs move with the sway of the water. My eyes stay open, unblinking, staring at the distant shimmer of the surface above.

My body spasms once, sharp, then again—an involuntary jolt. Bubbles escape my lips, tiny pearls rising toward the light. Some buried instinct claws at me to breathe, to fight, to live.

But I can't.

I'm too tired.

The water grows darker the deeper I fall. The sword passes before me, its tip pointed down, sinking faster than I ever could. I reach for it—too slow, too weak to actually catch it. It vanishes into the black.

My vision dims. Shapes blur.

Something moves beyond the edge of sight—a ripple of silver through the murk, graceful and vast. A warm hand takes mine, and I'm glad I don't have to be alone as I die.

It could be Orion, rushing to the lake to try to save me, and I want to comfort him. Tell him not to be sad. We both know we are fated to die. I'm just putting my hope into a different fate and praying I'm right about this.

But just in case, I let my last thoughts be of him.

His touch. His kiss. His infuriating resolve. And I hope that if I truly die and this is the end, I leave him with this final thought.

I love you.

I send it across the realm—or at least think I do—and know I can't wait for him to answer. But then a voice—melodic, kind, resonant as the tide—wraps around me, not spoken but felt, the sound vibrating through the water and into my bones.

"Valkyrie."

CHAPTER 55

orion

The cold wakes me.

Not the pleasant kind—the draft through open windows or the chill of night air seeping past the curtains—but the unnatural kind that settles bone-deep, the kind that means something's wrong.

My hand drifts to her side of the bed. The satin is cool beneath my palm. Not warm. Not even fading. Cold.

I'm on my feet before the thought finishes forming. The sheet falls to the floor. My clothes are on in a heartbeat. My sword follows, the familiar weight sliding into my grip as I reach for the door—

And stop.

Her magic hums against my skin before I touch the handle. A pulse of moonlight, faint but unmistakable. My shadows recoil from it, hissing, curling back into my spine.

She locked me in.

Tana.

My heart gives one violent kick in my chest, like it's trying to tear itself free.

"Fuck." The word rips from my throat, low and raw.

For a moment I can't breathe—can't think. All I can do is feel her power pressed into the wood, sealing me in with that soft, silvery calm she wears when she's already decided something I won't like.

Anger hits first—sharp, blinding. Then panic floods in right behind it, cold and fast.

"Damn it, Starling." My fist slams against the door. The moonlight ripples across the surface, solid as steel. "What have you done?"

My shadows surge, clawing at the barrier, shredding themselves against it. The smell of crackling energy fills the air. I press both palms flat to the door, let darkness pour through me, let the lightning crack and coil and rage.

For a second the shield holds—my Starling always did love to test me—but it trembles under the weight of mine, and I think, if she were immortal, this shield would have held me.

If she were immortal.

The panic that grips my throat is overwhelming, and my power flares in an instant.

The moonlight fractures like glass. With a final push, it shatters, the burst echoing through the room like thunder.

I don't waste a second.

I'm already moving, boots pounding down the corridor, shadows sweeping ahead of me like a living tide. I call for her—*Tana, answer me*—but the bond stays silent, the wall between us high and merciless.

She's shut me out.

That alone is enough to send my heart into a sick rhythm, skipping beats, tripping over itself. I grab the first fae I see by the shoulder. "Have you seen the queen?"

They stammer something useless—*no, my lord, not since*—and I'm gone again, running harder, faster.

Every corner I turn feels too empty. Every second stretches into something unbearable.

By the time I reach Starfall's main hall, my lungs burn. The wide double doors swing open before me, moonlight spilling in, and standing in its center is Hypnos.

He doesn't move. Doesn't speak. Just looks at me with that damned expression—the one that says he knows more than he wants to admit.

"Where is she?" My voice comes out low, feral.

"You cannot stop this, Orion."

The words hit harder than a blade. My nostrils flare. My pulse breaks into chaos.

In two strides, I have him by the collar. "Where. The fuck. Is she?"

For a moment, he just stares at me—calm, infuriatingly calm—and I almost throw him through the nearest wall.

Finally, he exhales. "The lakeshore," he says quietly. "By Pandora's caves."

The world narrows to a single point of sound—my heartbeat hammering too hard, too fast, too wrong.

I don't remember moving. One moment I'm staring at Hypnos; the next I'm gone, shadows exploding from my back and flinging me down the hall like a storm unchained. The castle blurs around me—arches, torches, terrified faces. Someone calls my name; I don't hear it. My magic tears through the corridors ahead of me, searching for her, desperate to feel her.

Nothing.

No warmth, no tether, no pulse in the bond that should hum between us. Just silence.

When I burst through the gates of Starfall, the night nearly splits open from the force of my power. The courtyard is chaos—fae gathered, murmuring, confused. Thorne stands among them.

Thorne. Out of his fucking cell.

Granite's beside him, Eryndor, Astrael—every one of them looking toward the same thing.

Me, rushing across the courtyard like a berserker without a mind.

My eyes sweep the lakeshore—empty. My shadows rip outward, a black tide crawling over every rock and blade of grass, searching for her signature, that flicker of moonlight she always leaves behind.

Nothing.

I'm already running toward the caves before anyone can stop me. The ground trembles beneath each step, the lake hissing against the shore as if recoiling from me. I dive into the mouth of Pandora's cave, shadows spiraling ahead, my lungs burning from a breath I can't release.

The air inside hums with old power. The portal at the far end glows faintly, like the heartbeat of the realm itself, the sound vibrating through the stone. But she isn't here.

Not even the faintest trace.

It's like she's been gone for many moonrises, though I know it's been minutes at most. The bond between us— dead quiet.

My sword slams into the cave wall, the sound deafening, sparks raining down. "Tana!" My voice breaks against the rock, swallowed by the echo. "Starling!"

No answer.

I turn, fury clawing up my throat. My magic lashes out, snapping at the walls until chunks of stone collapse into the pool at the portal's base. I can't think. Can't breathe. There's only that void where she should be.

By the time I storm back out to the lakeshore, I'm shaking. Thorne turns toward me, eyes wide, and before I even realize it, my blade is at his throat.

"What did you do?" I snarl. My grip tightens. "Where is she?"

He holds up both hands, palms trembling. "She told me to wait! To—"

"To what?"

But the rest of his words vanish—because I see her.

High above us, on the lake's opposite shore, framed by the moon and mist, she stands at the cliff's edge. The same cliffs where the Valkyries once took flight.

For a second, I can't move. My mind can't catch up. She looks small from here—fragile against the vast, burning light of the moon.

"Tana..." I breathe her name like a prayer. My shadows surge upward, instinctively trying to reach her, but they can't—not from this distance.

Then she moves.

One heartbeat she's still. The next—

She drives the blade straight through her chest.

The sound that leaves me isn't human. It's the cracking of worlds, the breaking of every star in the sky.

And before the scream can tear free, she's already falling.

The scream tears through me, but it isn't sound—it's sensation.

A raw, electric agony bursts through my chest and rakes every nerve as if the sword that impaled her has struck me too.

My breath catches.

One heartbeat.

Then another.

Both of them—mine and hers—struggling in the same fractured rhythm.

The bond seizes open like a wound ripped wide, and her pain floods through me. The cold. The suffocating dark. The water pouring into her lungs.

"Tana—"

I can feel it all.

The weight of the lake pressing her down. The sting of iron in her blood. Her chest rising once, twice—then stuttering.

My knees hit the ground. The impact barely registers over the firestorm of pain spreading through my ribs. My fingers dig into the earth, clawing at the dirt as if I can find her heartbeat there.

"Don't," I choke out. *Don't you fucking do this.*

The next pulse hits me like lightning.

Her heart fights. It fights—weak, wild, terrified. I feel it hammer against the blade, every beat a cry, every shudder a plea.

Then slower.

Slower.

Slower.

The water floods her veins, her pulse fading like the last flicker of a candle in a storm. I can't breathe—her lungs are burning, mine with them. My throat convulses as if I'm the one drowning, salt and air and grief tangling together until I taste blood.

I press a hand to my chest, as if I could hold her there. As if I could force her heart to keep beating.

"Come back," I whisper, voice breaking. "Please—come back to me."

But she's slipping.

The bond frays—thin, trembling—like a string stretched to breaking. My vision swims. The world tilts. My magic surges, shadows bursting upward, spiraling into the storm above as lightning cracks through the sky.

Her heartbeat falters again—one weak thump, like a bird's wing against glass. Then another.

Then...

Nothing.

The silence hits harder than the pain. It's deafening.

My body arches, a choked sound ripping from me as the last of her warmth dies inside my chest. The shadows recoil, screaming through the air, lightning exploding outward in blinding, uncontrolled bursts. The ground trembles, the lake surges against its banks, and the sky splits open with my grief.

My heart won't settle. It can't. The rhythm's gone—hers was the rhythm. The steady anchor.

Now it beats wrong, stuttering, desperate, hollow.

I collapse forward, gasping, trembling, the air thick with ozone and shadow. My fingers tear into the earth.

Ages. I waited ages for her.

Lifetimes spent in silence, searching for the soul that could bring mine back to life.

And now—after all of it—

I'm here on my knees, choking on her death.

The stars burn cold above me, and the only sound left in the world is the echo of what used to be her heartbeat—fading, fading, gone.

Her voice, so soft and distant in my mind as I hear her goodbye.

I love you.

The silence stretches so long it stops being silence at all—becomes a presence, a living thing pressing down on every soul gathered at the lakeshore. The wind has gone still. Even the water seems to hold its breath.

I can't move.

Can't breathe.

My body's locked between worlds—the one that had her, and the one that doesn't.

And then it hits.

A force—raw, electric—slams through me. My lungs seize, my muscles go rigid. Fire rips through every vein, and I arch backward, a strangled sound tearing through gritted teeth. It burns so savagely I can't even scream. My shadows twist around me like living agony, flaying the air.

My heart surges. Too fast. Too hard.

It's not beating—it's thrashing.

I press a hand to my chest, but it's useless. The rhythm gallops out of control—each beat sharper, louder, more desperate—until I'm sure it's going to burst through my ribs.

I can taste blood. Feel it pulsing in my throat. The edges of the world start to dissolve.

I can't breathe.

I can't feel her.

"She's gone," I rasp, voice breaking against the words. "She's gone—"

A heart for a heart.

A life for a life.

She gave hers for the realm, and I—

I am nothing without her.

The pain crests—unbearable, infinite—and just as I know this is it, that I'm about to follow her into the dark—

The realm moves.

A single pulse rolls through the ground beneath my hand.

Then another.

And another.

Each one stronger. Deeper. A heartbeat not my own.

The lake trembles.

At first, it's only ripples—small, delicate rings spreading across the surface. Then light—silver and white and impossibly bright—seeps up from the center, winding through the mist. The water glows as though the moon itself has sunk beneath it, and the sound—gods, the sound—is like thunder wrapped in song.

More fae have gathered and stand frozen, breathless, their eyes wide with terror and awe. The light swells until it blinds us all.

And then the water parts.

Something rises from its depths, slow and deliberate, and with it I feel my heart returning.

Her head breaks the surface first, droplets sliding down dark skin. Then her shoulders emerge, clad in silver armor; her torso—stronger, radiant—and her hands. One of them grips the hilt of *Realmbreaker*, the blade gleaming as it rises with her, dripping light instead of water. A billowing cape—dark blue like the waters of the lake she is emerging from—dances on a wind that blows only for her.

I can't move. My chest is still aching, but my heart—my heart—beats again. Not wild, not fractured, but steady. Syncing with the rhythm rising from the lake.

She opens her eyes.

And I swear the world tilts to look at her.

They're brighter than I've ever seen—like someone took the moon and shattered it behind her irises. The same eyes that burned with fury and loved me now carry the weight of eternity.

Gasps ripple through the crowd, more fae arriving each moment as word spreads through Starfall.

Not at her beauty—though it's enough to unmake gods.

Not at the crown.

Not even at the way her ears taper now to fine, elegant points, betraying what she's become.

But at the wings.

They unfurl behind her in a slow, shattering bloom of white—vast, endless, radiant—each feather tipped with silver light. The air fills with the sound of them, the deep whisper of something both holy and terrifying.

Avalon itself bends around her presence. The stars reflect in the water, the sky crackling with new constellations.

And I—on my knees in the mud, blood on my lips, chest heaving—can only stare.

My mate. My queen. My heart returned to me.

She rises from the lake like vengeance and salvation entwined, and every fae on the shore falls silent before her.

Tana—

no longer mortal, not merely queen—

but Valkyrie reborn.

CHAPTER 56
tana

I remember dying.

The cold. The silence. The way my heartbeat slowed—one echo, then another—until there was nothing left but stillness and the pull of the lake around me.

Then light finds me. Not above but inside. It builds until I can't hold it, until everything that was human in me breaks open. The pain is endless, and the peace beneath it even greater. My bones knit themselves from starlight. My lungs drag in water and breathe it like air.

The realm answers.

Threads of power slip through my skin, stitching me to every drop, every leaf, every whisper of shadow. The pulse of Avalon and mine beat the same rhythm, slow and immense.

A voice moves through the current—ancient, patient.

You will not die this day, Valkyrie.

The Lady's tone is both lullaby and command. *Rise, Tana. Queen of Avalon.*

When I gasp, the air cuts differently—metal and moonlight. Colors fracture into shades I never knew existed. The night hums; I can feel it waiting. Then the pain returns, molten and deliberate, running down my spine until my body arches.

My back splits open.

The sound is wet, holy.

Wings burst free, drenched in light, heavy as memory. The air catches under them, and the ache turns to awe. They move because I think it, because they are me. For the first time since the world began, a Valkyrie breathes again.

I stand within the circle of the lake, water sliding from me like it knows who its queen is. The moon bows low.

And beyond the shimmer of its reflection—him.

Orion kneels at the edge, head bowed, shadows coiling wild and uncertain around his body. He looks wrecked, emptied, like a man who hasn't yet decided whether he's still alive.

The moment our eyes meet, everything else disappears. The bond that's haunted us since the first night finally snaps taut, the pull sudden and absolute.

He rises. I move.

The water parts between us.

When he reaches me, he doesn't speak. His hand finds mine—warm, trembling, real—and the world steadies. His fingers trace the wet light on my skin, like proof, before he drags me against him.

The kiss isn't frantic; it's a return. The first breath after drowning. He tastes of salt and shadows and something unbearably human. I feel the bond ignite, a surge of heat through every vein until I can't tell where my power ends and his begins.

For a moment, there are no gods, no crowns, no wars—only this. His heartbeat against my chest. My wings curling around us like shelter. The realm hums its approval, distant and infinite, while I hold the only thing in it that feels like home.

The world comes back one breath at a time.

The lake stills around us, mirror-smooth except for the ripples spreading from our bodies. The bond hums beneath my skin, soft as a vow. When I lift my head, I realize we are not alone.

They line the shore—the High Lords, the High Seer, the warriors who bled for this realm, the lesser fae who fled the dying villages. Hypnos stands among them, and Mor beside him. Hundreds more spill down the slope, silent and wide-eyed, faces turned toward the water and the woman who walked out of death.

The moon lowers, its reflection bending into a crown of light around my head. It flares, and I feel the weight of metal settle against my brow. It isn't ceremony. It's recognition—power itself shaping to a truth that can't be denied.

Queen.

For a heartbeat, no one moves.

Then, one by one, they fall to their knees.

The High Lords. The High Seer. The warriors who bled for Avalon. Fae, high and lesser alike.

Hypnos is the first to break the silence. His voice carries, calm and sure.

"I always had faith in you, Your Highness."

He bows—slow, deliberate—a gesture so reverent it stills even the wind.

Mor sits cross-legged on a fallen log, tearing into what looks like half a loaf of bread. She eyes my wings, expression unreadable.

"Huh." A bite. "I thought they'd be bigger."

Gasps ripple through the crowd.

She shrugs, chewing. "Still shiny, though."

The tension fractures—cracked glass letting in a little light.

Then Merlin, bless his chaos, wades knee-deep into the shallows, hitching his robes high to keep them dry.

"Has anyone seen my snail?" he mutters, peering into the water as the storm cloud crackles over his shoulder. He glances up mid-search, blinking owlishly at the sight of hundreds kneeling.

"Oh. Is this the coronation, then?"

The storm zaps him.

He yelps. "I take it that's a yes." Then finally turns and finds me. "Have you done something different with your hair?"

Laughter spills through the crowd—uncertain at first, then genuine. For the first time in several nocturns, Avalon takes a steadying breath.

The sound fades slowly. The air cools. Moonlight sharpens.

I sweep my gaze across the gathered fae, their devotion laid bare. All but one.

Thorne stands at the front of the crowd, armor scorched, his once-gold crown dented from battle. His sword hangs loose at his side, point buried shallow in the dirt. The defiance in his eyes is colder than steel.

He doesn't bow.

He just looks at me—as if daring me to make him.

I hold his gaze, and the silence between us feels older than the realm itself. Then I speak.

"You haven't seen what I have," I begin, my voice carrying across the lake. "You couldn't. The truth was buried

—sealed beneath the blood of those who died to keep it hidden."

A ripple moves through the crowd, unease chasing the silence. I keep my eyes on Thorne.

"I saw the night the realm broke. I saw the Valkyrie fall, not as legend tells it, but as it happened. The darkness you've all feared wasn't born from a Valkyrie traitor—it came from within you."

I pause long enough for the words to land. "From one of your own High Fae."

The wind stirs, restless, as if the realm itself listens.

"She has a name. Morgause. Cousin to Queen Pandora. The second chosen of the realm—the one who believed she could wield the night itself and rule creation through it. The Valkyrie didn't destroy Avalon. They sacrificed themselves to seal her away."

Murmurs rise—fear, disbelief, the beginnings of denial.

I let them speak, then cut through it with calm.

"That seal is breaking. I felt it. The same shield that kept her locked beyond the Wastelands is cracking. And when it falls, the war that ended the last age will begin again."

My gaze sweeps the shoreline, but my words belong to him.

"We can stand together or fall alone. But make no mistake—when she rises, she won't care who called himself king."

The silence that follows is deep and absolute. Even the moonlight flickers, uncertain.

Silence holds.

Even the lake forgets to move.

The air thickens with moonlight, stretched so thin it

hums. I can feel Avalon listening—its pulse shivering through water and root and bone—as if the realm itself waits for the next breath.

Then the light falters.

A single heartbeat.

The moon dims, its silver draining to gray.

The ground trembles. Cracks web across the shore, bleeding shadow instead of dust. The air warps, bending inward on itself until the stars distort and the sound becomes unbearable—a low, pulsing roar that lives beneath the skin. The fae stagger. Wings flare. Power shatters like glass.

And from that fracture, she steps through.

Her hair moves like smoke, long and black and endless. Skin pale as moonlight, untouched by time. A gown of blood-dark silk that drinks in every glimmer around her. Her eyes—void and gleaming—find me first. The faintest smile curves her mouth, cruel and patient.

Morgause.

The shadow that outlived the gods.

The reason the Valkyrie fell.

Around me, the air recoils. The High Seer gasps; the High Lords sink lower to the ground. Only Thorne remains standing. His sword lowers—not in surrender but in salute. The dented crown tips as he inclines his head toward her, the faintest mark of respect from one darkness to another. When Morgause's gaze finds him, his lips curve—not fear, not awe. Recognition.

"Well," Morgause purrs, voice a blade wrapped in silk. "Avalon does love its pretty queens."

Her gaze slides to me, slow and deliberate. "But I'm afraid you're sitting on my throne."

The moon gutters out, and darkness swallows the lake.

More Works By

Rebekah Sinclair

The Forgotten Goddess

A completed Series available on Kindle Unlimited

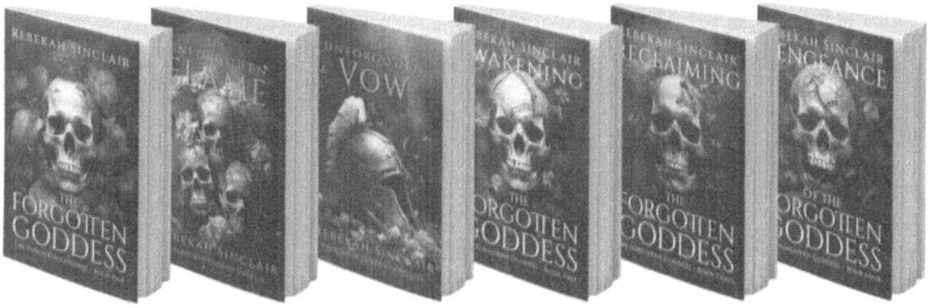

Greek Mythology

Urban Fantasy

Fated Mates

Star-Crossed Lovers

She is the goddess time forgot

He is the god that never stopped looking for her

Welcome to
The Black Ledger

Where every desire has a price...
and every contract is final.

A new dark romance series
coming Summer 2025

The Black Ledger
Billionaires

Check Out www.RebekahSinclairWrites.com for more!